MASTERS OF DECEPTION

A LEGENDS OF TIVARA STORY

JC KANG

This is a work of fiction. Names, places, characters, and events are either fictitious or are used fictitiously. Any resemblance to actual events, locations, organizations, or persons, alive or dead, is entirely coincidental and unintended.

Copyright © 2018 by Dragonstone Press, LLC
http://www.jckang.info
DragonstonePressRVA@gmail.com

All rights reserved, including the right to reproduce this work or portions thereof in any way whatsoever, as provided by law. For permission, questions, or contact information, see www.jckang.info.

Cover Layout and Maps by Laura Kang

Logos by Emily Jose Burlingame

Cover Art by Amalia Chitulescu:
http://www.amaliach.com/

To my wife Yuki, for putting up with me.

MAPS

Tivaralan

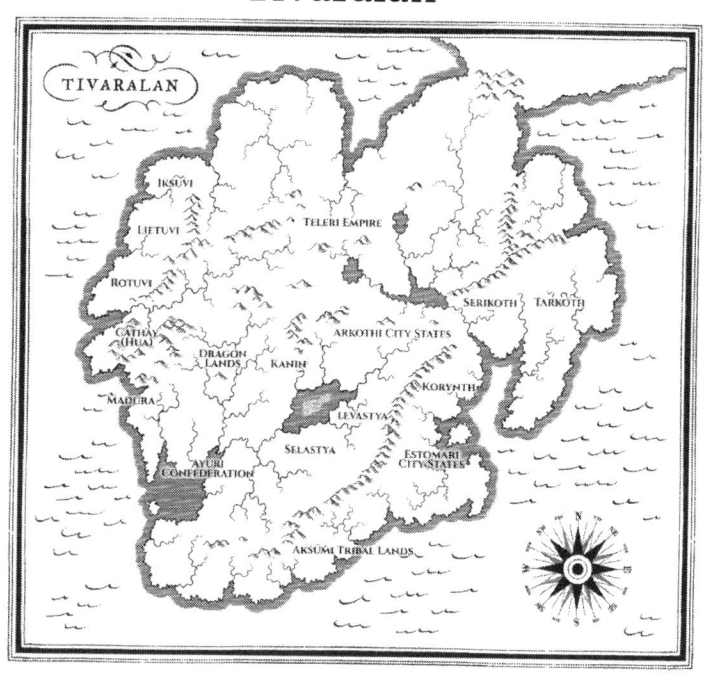

Map of the Estomar

Map of Tokahia

1. Mafia Territory
2. Entertainment Dist
3. Megalith Circle
4. Iron Avatar
5. Pyramid
6. Cassius' Mansion
7. De Lucca's Office
8. Seafarer Inn
9. Bovyan Compound
10. De Lucca's Home
11. Orchid Fountain
12. Colliseum

MASTERS OF DECEPTION

PROLOGUE:

A Thousand Years Before

The whip seared across Tatiana's back, just as she'd seen in her visions.

"Kneel." Priest Krzz snarled the word, exposing the full length of his tusks.

Tatiana dropped to her knees, the moist ground warm in the afternoon sun.

The other villagers pointed and muttered. She knew the next words from her vision.

"Daydreaming again," one whispered.

"No, just crazy," said another.

Before bowing her head, she snuck a glance to see if the crystalline Dragonstone atop the pyramid had gone dim.

As she'd foreseen, its blue light flickered and blinked out. The Whispers of the True Gods went silent. Which meant...

She covered her ears, even though the others stared at her as if she were stupid.

An ear-splitting squeal pierced the air. Around her, everyone dropped their shovels and hoes, threw themselves to the ground, and covered their heads. Only Priest Krzz remained standing, his turquoise skin glinting in the afternoon sun.

The surrounding farmland darkened in an instant, lit only by the flaming chariot that appeared overhead. The ground shook, vibrating through her.

The priest's jaw wiggled, sending his tusks shifting back and forth. His gaze raked across all the workers. "On your knees! Show obeisance!"

The chariot of the gods passed above. Its crackling flames tortured the souls who bore it through the skies.

It was so loud, Tatiana's ears still hurt through her hands. Her chest squeezed around her racing heart, choking out her breath.

Then it passed, revealing the sun. The Dragonstone at the pyramid's summit flickered and lit. The True Gods' Whispers resumed, though she only understood a few words. She blew out a breath.

Priest Krzz harrumphed. "On your feet. Back to work. Laziness in life means—"

"Eternal labor in the afterlife," the villagers all finished in unison.

He bobbed his head. "Yes. The laziest of you will pull Tivar's chariot for all eternity."

So they'd been taught for time immemorial.

Tatiana knew otherwise. Once she deciphered the Whispers of the True Gods, mankind would overthrow the Tivari.

CHAPTER 1:

Dueling Fates

Cassius Larusso consulted an astrological chart, knowing damn well he could answer the merchant's question without it. Still, the longer he made a show of diagramming constellation positions, the larger the crowd would grow around his megalith circle, and the further his fame would spread.

The merchant, standing on the other side of the central altar, first adjusted his orange hat, then his sleeveless purple longcoat about his rotund belly. "Well?"

Cassius held up a hand. "The future is a volatile thing. You paid for the best. The best cannot be rushed."

Around the circle, the crowds clapped and laughed, the bright colors of their longcoats, frilly dresses, and stockings threatening to give Cassius a headache. The merchant pursed his lips, making his pig face look more like a duck's.

Satisfied, Cassius peered west through a dwarf-made scope, past the flickering Dragonstone at the pyramid's summit, to the Iridescent Moon. Never moving from its reliable spot in the heavens, it now waned toward new—indicating an auspicious birth hour for expectant mothers, but more importantly that it was close to lunchtime. Of course, his rumbling stomach proved more reliable than the dance of stars in this regard. It was time to end the charade.

He turned some of the gears on his star disk. Placing it over the map on the stone altar, he spun it.

Eyes expectant, the merchant tapped his toe. "I need to get a consignment of glassware to Cathay before my rivals."

It was too easy to make money off these money-grubbers. Cassius raised a hand. The spectators went silent. He steepled his fingers under his chin, and then beckoned the merchant closer so that the jostling crowds could not hear. "Then you must contract Expedient Shipping. Their ship, *Ocean's Breath*, departs for Korynth in three days."

"Expedient Shipping?" The merchant slapped a hand over his deposit. The rings on his fingers clinked on the coins. "They lost a barge to the Pirate Queen last month."

"*Ocean's Breath* will make it safely to Korynth…" …if only because Expedient Shipping had paid Cassius to find an auspicious day for travel. Of course, Cassius had later made arrangements with the Pirate Queen to leave the *Ocean's Breath* alone.

The merchant's hand pulled back from the deposit. "And then?"

"The *Ocean's Breath* will arrive in time to unload and transfer your precious cargo to the Tarkothi Royal Ship *Indomitable*." Something Cassius knew from bribing a clerk at the Tarkothi trade office. "It will take your goods to Ayudra, where you should contract Victorious Trading's *Wild Orchid*."

Muttering curses under his breath, the merchant furiously scribbled notes in some coded language. He sighed. "All these damn shipping companies, siphoning a bit off our bottom line."

Cassius shrugged. "That's the price of doing business. Just be happy you live in prosperous times, when there is a market for your glassware, and that trade agreements between Cathay and Tarkoth keep shipping lanes open. As per our contract, your cargo is guaranteed to arrive safely."

The merchant snapped his fingers at his two guards. With a flourishing bow, he stomped off through the crowds with his men and heavy cologne in tow.

Stashing his scope and measure into his longcoat's inner pocket, Cassius adjusted his hat and beckoned to his own guards. "I'm off to lunch."

Hands on their rapier hilts, they helped push through the throng, shoving away anyone who tried to touch him. The only assaults they couldn't fend off were the peoples' puffy, garish clothes burning his eyes, and the cloying perfumes clogging his nose.

As always, the barrage of questions began.

"When is a good date to get married?"

"Which gladiator will win the summer tourney?"

"Where is the best place to bury my father?"

A run-of-the-mill astrologer could answer these questions. Cassius snorted. Being a thirty-seventh generation descendant of Tatiana, the lover of the Elf Angel Aralas who helped win the War of Ancient Gods, came with the benefit of high-paying clients. It also came with the hassle of fortune-seeking freeloaders.

"Signore Larusso! Cassius!" A stunning blonde waved as she jostled to the fore and batted her eyelashes.

Her! The money-grubber. What was her name again? Ella? She was the latest in a long list of women who'd proclaimed their love for him, when in fact they only loved his money. His chest tightened at the thought of the first one, when he'd been young and naïve. He hurried on, but not before glancing at Ella's cleavage, which peeked out from the low neckline of the frilly red dress he'd bought and stripped off of her one too many times.

Once he'd cleared the crowd, he ducked into an alley between the daub-and-wattle row houses. Two of his guards held back to keep anyone from following him on the path to his favorite noodle shop, while the other two trailed after him.

No matter how many twists and turns he took, Tatiana's Eye atop the pyramid sparkled above the shingled rooftops. The Dragonstone magnified the Gods' Whispers, fueling the Divining power he rarely deigned to use.

A few blocks into his stroll, the hairs on the back of his neck stood on end. He searched the heavens. Unseen in the noon sky, the constellation of the Hunter was rising to face the red star of the Conqueror, usually indicating safe travels for him; yet something—a shooting star, perhaps—had just passed between them.

An ill omen; unavoidable, but ameliorable.

Sometimes, real magic was worth the cost. He took a deep breath and drew in the Whispers of the Gods. His shoulders slumped for a split second as the Whispers coursed through him. Reaching into his vest pocket, he withdrew a single card from his tarot deck and looked down.

Death.

His heart lurched into his throat. Given his birthdate and the position of the stars right now, it meant his own demise. Still, there were likely ways to avoid it. With the Whispers fading in his core, he drew another card.

The Knight.

Brave. Solitary. This was a problem he'd have to face by himself, or make the situation worse. He held up a hand to his guards. "Stay here."

They all bowed. Like all good help, they knew not to question him.

He continued without them—all the better, since he wouldn't have to feel bad about eating while they looked on, hungry. Up ahead, a heavy-set man with a pointed beard and a long mustache was leaning against a building. A rapier jutted from his black longcoat. Dark eyes peered out from under his hat.

He stepped into the alley, blocking the way. The sword swept out of its sheath, tip pointed at Cassius' throat. "Signore, you are a fool to walk alone."

"I've been told I'm a fool for love." Cassius shrugged out the listlessness in his limbs and squared his shoulders. The interloper was no common ruffian. No, everything about him screamed *Mafia*. However, for one to appear in this part of town violated the unspoken agreement between the Signores and the crime families. Cassius tipped his hat. "To what do I owe this visit?"

"To inform you, we know how to find all the signores unguarded like this. Call off your secret attacks in our territory, or else our cold war will get quite hot."

Secret attacks? What was this goon talking about? Weren't the crime families engrossed in their own turf war? No matter, he was now standing between Cassius and lunch. He harrumphed. "Whatever you say."

"I'm sorry," the man said, with a grin that suggested he was anything but. "I'm supposed to leave a message. A cut on your cheek will do. If you resist, the message will be much stronger."

Cassius covered his cheek with a hand. No one would scar him, Mafia enforcer or not. "If you wish to mark my cheek, you will have to kiss here." He patted his ass.

"I'm glad you said that." The man's grin broadened as he lunged with a stab.

It hadn't taken magic to predict the move. Cassius had already reached across his waist, and now whipped out his dagger and rapier. His sword deflected the incoming attack. The mobster parried Cassius' riposte. Metal rasped on metal in a cacophony of clinks and clangs. After three exchanges, the man proved to be talented, perhaps even more skilled than Cassius insofar as swordplay was concerned.

The risk of injury was too great, enough to risk the fatigue of Divining, even if changing the future would raise the ire of Heaven's Accountant. Disengaging, Cassius took three steps back, rooted his feet to the ground, and took a deep breath. Again, energy fled his arms and legs, longer this time than the first; but in that moment, the Gods' Whispers revealed the man's next six moves.

A normal duelist might've fallen for the two feints, but armed with foreknowledge, Cassius sidestepped the real attack. In a different future, the stab would've caught him in the gut and very likely led to his death. Instead, he drove his rapier into the man's chest. The blade slipped between two ribs and penetrated his lung.

Sinking to his knees, eyes wide, the thug clawed at the wound with his free hand.

Cassius took two steps forward and slashed the assailant's sword-arm with the dagger. The rapier clattered to the ground. Cassius kicked it out of reach. He stepped back, slipping his own sword out from between the man's scarlet-slickened fingers.

Somewhere in the Beyond, Heaven's Accountant no doubt frowned as he adjusted his holy scales and tore pages from his Divine ledger. There would be an accounting; perhaps in this life, but most likely the next.

For now, though, Cassius wiped the blood from his rapier on the man's sleeve. "Go back to your don, and let him know how you met my blade. Though with that punctured lung, your only message will be the wounds on your body." Not like anyone would believe the renowned Cassius Larusso had done it.

Each shortened breath heaved in the man's chest, and his eyes bulged like a goldfish out of water.

Bile rose in Cassius' throat. Fortuna's quim, he'd just dealt a mortal wound. The man wasn't going to make it.

He'd deserved it, right? He was a criminal, with ill intentions. There was no choice, right?

Cassius turned on his heel and continued on his way. As long as he didn't see the man take his last labored breath, who knew what would happen? Maybe the wound wasn't that severe. Maybe a True Akolyte would pass by and heal the man with the holy magic of foreign gods. With each step, the guilt lightened. Of course the man would survive.

As he worked his way through the side streets, Cassius' energy trickled back. By the time he pushed open the door to the dimly lit tavern, his stomach was growling again.

As always, it was near-empty, even at noon. No matter how delicious its food was, the building occupied an inauspicious location...for now.

"Signore Larusso." The owner's pretty young wife curtseyed in her plain grey felt dress. It lacked the puffy sleeves and blinding colors that were now all the rage. Her faint honeysuckle perfume was muted compared to the popular musks and perfumes. A true classic beauty. She extended an open hand to a chair right by the window. "I have your favorite seat ready for you."

Cassius nodded. Sitting would be good right about now. "Thank you, Misha."

She offered him a friendly smile as he took his seat in a chair worn to his butt cheeks' shape, at a weathered table. "Business is so slow. We're just scraping by. Perhaps you'll tell your clients about us?"

"As I have said, no amount of promotion in the world will help you in the near future. Don't worry, you'll make it." In three years' time, after the Godseye Conjunction, the owner's fortune would change for the better...as long as the world didn't come to an end. In the meantime, Cassius would enjoy his favorite meal in peace and quiet.

Misha poured a glass of cheap wine from a metal pitcher and curtseyed again. "I'll be back with your chicken sauce over noodles and sautéed spinach."

"You always know what I want. Maybe you should be the Diviner." Cassius flashed his admittedly devilish grin, the one which had women flocking to his bed. Of course, wealth and charm helped as well.

"You always order the same thing." She winked back and left.

He watched the sashay of her hips, daydreaming about what could never be. No wealth, no charm in the world could overcome Ayara's Eye looking over this woman, nor Solaris' light shining on her husband. The couple's undying love, like that of the two gods, would persist over several deaths and rebirths. He wiped the wistful expression off his face. How silly, to cling to such silly ideas as undying love.

The flourish of a black cape brushed by him with a whisk of air, blocking the magnificent view of Misha's ass. A large man with an olive complexion and dark hair lumbered into the seat beside him. A prominent chin emphasized his chiseled features, though a jagged scar marred his forehead.

Cassius' stomach leapt into his throat. Fortuna's quim! Nothing in the star charts spoke of meeting strangers today, and yet this was the second in half an hour. That one shooting star had ruined his well-planned day. He kept his face impassive. "Excuse me, sir, that seat is taken."

"By me." The man's Northern accent, as well as his sheer size, could only belong to a Bovyan warrior of the Teleri Empire.

There'd been an influx of the brutes in the last half-year, as several of the crime families had recruited them as muscle; and to keep up, many signores had hired them out as caravan escorts and bodyguards. They'd yet to approach him... until now. Was he here to send another message on behalf of the Mafia? Or to market his services? Too much uncertainty hung over this interaction, where a stranger held the upper hand. Curse that shooting star.

Cassius sucked in a breath, ignoring the aroma of roasting potatoes, and drew on the Gods' Whispers for the third time in a day. He'd be so drained, he'd have to call off his afternoon appointments. With an innocuous brush of his hand, he knocked his glass. Some wine sloshed out before he caught the handle. He peered at the splash pattern on the wood.

Fatigue crept into his limbs, yet it was worth it. The wine splatter resembled Death and Fortuna embracing. Wealth, at the risk of death. He grinned. "You are here to extend an offer. Tell me."

The man's eyes looked like the Blue Moon at its widest opposition, though not nearly as beautiful. "Your legend precedes you, Signore Larusso. Very well. I am Phobos Bovyanthas—"

"Purveyor of ancient art," Cassius said. The name was well known among the Signores, who paid exorbitant amounts for artifacts from the Sundered Empire. All but him turned a blind eye to the fact the Teleri acquired them through plunder and conquest.

"Your reputation for Divining proceeds you." Phobos thumped his chest and bowed his head. "I am honored to make your acquaintance. I need to know exactly when the *Intimidator* comes into port. I will pay a thousand drakas."

Stroking his beard to its tip, Cassius feigned disinterest, even if the generous offer was ten times his normal fee—enough to buy noodles every meal for the rest of his life. Still, it hardly constituted a fortune, let alone worth the risk of death. Unless there was more to the story, something worth coaxing out. "You can find this information out from the Serikothi trade office. Their birds might not fly as fast as the Gods' Whispers, but the information comes much cheaper." Both in money and the cost on Cassius' soul for gleaning Divine secrets.

Phobos shrugged. "Our mutual friend tells us the *Intimidator* will carry an Aksumi Mystic and an apprentice, and my country wishes to reach them first."

By mutual friend, he undoubtedly meant the Pirate Queen. "What do Bovyans need with Mystics? Your people hate magic."

The Bovyan's face flushed like one of the orc gods' fabled flaming chariots. "And yet I am here, meeting with you. The new First Consul is unorthodox in his ways, and his strategies are bearing fruit."

"Very well, a thousand drakas." Cassius withdrew a brocade pouch from his belt. Taking a deep breath, he drew on the Gods' Whispers, reached into the pouch, and cast fine white sand onto the table. His limbs grew heavy and his vision faded, longer this time. True Divining once a day was taxing enough. Twice, in the span of a few minutes, and an unprecedented four times in a day...

Phobos' face scrunched up as if he'd sucked Fortuna's tits and found her luck sour.

The grains of sand would look like a scattered mess to the Bovyan, but to Cassius, the picture was clear. The Hunter pursued Ocean under the Sun. Cassius took out his dwarf scope and measured the distance between shapes.

"The *Intimidator* will make it here tomorrow, just before the Iridescent Moon's fourth waning crescent."

Phobos whistled. "That is fast."

Cassius shrugged. "Two great naval powers are racing. The *Intimidator* is being pursued by the *Indomitable*."

Misha appeared at the table, plate in hand. Her mouth rounded like the sun.

"I'm sorry about the mess." Cassius grinned. "My guest will pay for any trouble."

Her eyes fell on the Bovyan. Lips trembling, she set the bowl down and took a step back.

Of course. The warlike Bovyan were feared, especially by women, who were treated like breeding stock in the Teleri homeland. So disgusting! Cassius made a show of tipping a hat, an apology. "My guest was just leaving."

Misha dipped into a quick curtsey and fled back to the kitchens.

"I don't think I will be welcome back here if you extend your stay." Cassius motioned to the door.

Frowning, Phobos stood and set a very heavy bag of coins beside the dish. "Signore Larusso. Thank you for your information." With both hands on the table, he leaned over, a monumental task given his height. He lowered his voice. "I know the Great Cassius Larusso hears the Gods' Whispers, but in my humble line of work, I often glean important news from idle chatter. I know of something that might be concerning to you."

Cassius favored the art dealer with an arched eyebrow. All information came at a cost, and no doubt this Phobos wanted something in return. Of course, it wasn't part of his soul, as the gods demanded from those who eavesdropped on their muted murmurs. He feigned nonchalance, as if anything Phobos would say was already known.

The brute leaned in further. "The crime families are uniting, and plan to take over the city."

Cassius supported a snort. That was hard to believe. The crime families couldn't agree on a time to meet for tea, let alone coordinate an attack on the Signores' interests. Not to mention, such hostilities would be bad for business. Cassius' eyes shifted to the scattered sand and splattered water patterns on the table.

Nothing implied that the—wait, there it was, the Betrayer hiding in the corner, watching over the pyramid. Blood drained from Cassius' head. He looked up. "They want the pyramid."

"You live up to your reputation." Phobos bowed his head. "I hear they plan to steal its Dragonstone, and sell it to the Orc King."

Cassius kept himself from sucking in a sharp breath. Supposedly, only the orc gods or a dragon could dislodge a Dragonstone from any of the nine pyramids around the world. His own ancestor had helped vanquish the former from the world a millennium before, and the only surviving dragon seemed content with the one he'd stolen from another pyramid thirty-odd years ago. "They can't be so foolish as to bring doom on all of us."

"Why take a chance?" Phobos shrugged. "I understand it is your family's Divine mandate to protect the pyramid. What is the legend? Something about the return of the orc gods on their flaming chariots?"

The flippant tone made Cassius' skin crawl. The Bovyan race hadn't even existed when the orcs enslaved humanity, so this lout wouldn't understand. "Go on."

"I'd like to propose an exchange of favors. Our mutual friend tells us that you have skills besides Divining, and those have made you quite wealthy. It is those that we need."

Curse the Pirate Queen for revealing too much. Phobos had known all along. Still, Cassius kept his face impassive. "Tell me, then."

"When the *Intimidator* docks, I will send the Aksumi to you. They seek the location of a missing master from their Order of Mystics. We need you to convince the Aksumi woman to stay here for three days. We will retrieve her from your villa then."

It was almost too easy, besides the expense and boredom of having to host some wizened old matron for a few days. Still, it was always best to drive the most advantageous deal possible. "That would be an exceedingly difficult task, what with the Aksumi's xenophobia."

"In return, my country will eradicate the Mafia presence in your fine city within three days. And give you credit, of course."

Fortuna's quim! For an unparalleled Diviner, there sure were a lot of surprises for one day. His carefully-crafted mask of nonchalance must've slipped, given that his mouth was hanging wide enough for the entire noodle dish to fit.

Thoughts zipped through his mind like a shower of shooting stars as he balanced out costs and benefits. Costs were a trifle, really; but was the purported benefit even possible? The Signores had tried to defeat the Mafia for decades before giving up and tolerating their presence. With no crime families, the Signores would rule unquestioned. And, of course, the pyramid would be safe, keeping the orc gods at bay.

Where was the wealth, at the risk of death, that the earlier Divination suggested? For once in his life, he couldn't find words.

"It looks like even the famous Cassius Larusso can be surprised." If the Bovyan's smile could get any wider, it might stretch across the Shallowsea. "Please consider our generous offer. If your Divination is correct, the Aksumi will be arriving tomorrow." Pounding his fist against his chest, Phobos turned and left.

Cassius started to brush the sand back into his pouch, when the outline of the spilled wine changed as it seeped into the wood. Now, Love dueled with Fortune.

He chuckled. There was nothing more useless than love. More than useless. A weakness, which a conniving woman could exploit to suck a man's bank account and soul dry. That had to be the risk the earlier Divination foretold.

CHAPTER 2:

Failure's Reward

Flames danced in Brehane's hand, but their heat wasn't what made her palm glisten with sweat. She swallowed hard. This was her last chance to pass. Her last chance to restore the honor of her father's shamed tribe.

Outside the crystal powder encircling the Pyromancer's dueling ring, her classmates whispered among themselves.

"Traitorous Biomancer."

"We'll finally be rid of her."

Not today, they wouldn't. In the tests for the other schools of magic, she'd already outwitted, outlasted, or overpowered the best candidates they could throw at her. With her free hand, Brehane clasped the crystal hanging from her neck. Cool and reassuring, the hard edges dug into her fingers. Breathe, breathe. She locked her gaze on her opponent.

Of course the testing committee would choose Brehane's own maternal cousin, heir apparent to the Pyromancy clan, for the final trial. Makeda stood at the other end of the ring, her frumpy training suit making her look like a hippo. It belied her deadly skill, and only a fool would mistake her nonchalant stance for laziness.

Brehane took a deep breath, sensing the Resonance of the Universe. This was the chance to validate the choice she'd made long ago. Every nerve ending tingled. Each second stretched into eternity, each heartbeat a slow thrum in her ears. Any moment now...

The Pyromancer matriarch brought her hand down in a sharp cutting motion.

Brehane hurled the flames at Makeda.

Barking out guttural words of magic, Makeda waved her hand. The air crackled as bright flakes of fire dispersed around her fireshield. Her curling lip bared her teeth. She pointed and grunted.

A fire bolt sped toward Brehane.

She spat out the syllables, coaxing the Resonance. The hissing flames froze inches from her chest. With a sharp exhale, she repelled it. The vitality in her limbs guttered. She locked her knees against their desire to fold, and focused past the blurring edges of her vision.

Growling out more sounds, Makeda swept a blazing hand into the path of the dart, absorbing it. She ran forward and extended her flaming palm.

An illegal spell for a candidate challenge! The Resonance buzzed loudly in Brehane's core. Makeda was drawing on power far beyond the parameters of the test. Brehane choked out a fireshield, which hissed around her. It wouldn't be enough, not against the amount of power Makeda was channeling.

Grunting more sounds, Brehane invoked a Hydromancy spell to fortify her fireshield. Humidity condensed and froze in a thin layer on her training suit, just before the flaming hand pressed into her shoulder. Steam rose, hissing from where the heat seared through the ice layer, the fire ward, and the bulky, flame-resistant cloth.

Shoulder burning, Brehane stumbled back two steps, her knee sinking to the hard-packed dirt.

Along the edge of the arena floor, fellow candidates applauded.

The master swept a black flag at her. "Brehane is disqualified for tainting her Pyromancy with Hydromancy."

Hunching over, fighting for breath, Brehane looked up to the master and pointed at Makeda. "She used a spell forbidden in tests, and drew on too much energy."

"Dirty Biomancer," Makeda hissed. She rolled her eyes, even as she straightened from the strain of magic use. The heavy practice robes made her look pudgy, like the pig she was. "Always blaming other people or your own failings. I had to use more power because I knew you were going to steal my energy for the spell."

As if such Biomancy still existed, beyond theoretical descriptions in texts. That ugly *assama* always played tricks like this, trying to sabotage Brehane's chances. She stiffened. "Master—"

"Enough." The Pyromancer matriarch slammed her palm down on the stone podium. "Candidate Brehane: you never know when an opponent will try to trick you."

Of course the master would side with her niece, even when she cheated. Brehane's shoulders slumped. She'd never had a chance. There was no way the university would accept a candidate from the Biomancers, even three centuries after the ban.

Makeda leaned in and whispered, "If only you'd chosen our clan—the clan of your mother, foolish though she was—over a pack of traitors. Go back to infusing light baubles."

Perhaps keeping city streets lit was all Brehane could do, now that her dreams of restoring the Biomancers were dead. Struggling to her feet, she clasped her crystal.

Makeda's eyes locked on the heirloom, passed down from the First Mystic. Her lips pursed. Even though the mother Brehane had never met had once been heir apparent to the Pyromancers, the stain of her forbidden love ran through her veins.

The master waved her hand. "Candidate Brehane, the High Conclave convenes at noon. You will present yourself before us."

Brehane looked northwest toward the Iridescent Moon, never moving from its spot in the heavens. It waned past its fourth crescent, indicating less than two hours until noon. Her heart sank. She'd been so close. Against all odds, she'd mastered the basics of the other eleven schools. Despite the obstacles they'd put in her way and the talented candidates she'd faced, she'd passed all the tests.

Save for this one.

It was all for naught. She hung her head.

No promotion to Initiate. She'd never restore her tribe's honor. She snuck a glance at Makeda.

Their gazes met. Her cousin's smile transformed into an ugly curl of her lip. *Assama*, she mouthed.

Ugly pig, indeed. Brehane snorted. They both looked the part, with sweat matting their hair. She'd feel less so once she changed out of the bulky Pyromancy training robe, even if that wouldn't strip away the weight of failure. She bowed her head to the master and pushed her way through the chattering candidates, who now crowded around her cousin.

Past the arena's stone columns, Geomanced to look like pillars of flame, Brehane trudged along the inner ring road. It circled around the vaulting bundle of hexagonal basalt columns of the university's central pyramid, and passed through each school's district. The Biomancy section stood at almost the opposite end, delaying the inevitable breaking of bad news.

No, this wouldn't be the end. Maybe there was still a chance to plead her case. The clan deserved it.

Pulse thumping, Brehane hastened her stride. No walls demarcated the boundaries between districts. The only way to tell was the change in architecture as she crossed avenues, which radiated from the pyramid like wheel spokes: the myriad shapes, colors, and materials of the Transmutation School. The circular stone and blocky steel domes of the Divination School. The brown rock and earth formations of the Geomancy school. The crystalline blocks of the Artificer School.

These, along with the classrooms and dormitories of the university's other schools in the opposite direction, had all been created by the First Mystic's magic. At last, Brehane reached the Biomancy district. The First Mystic had used Biomancy to create the buildings, fusing together bones from the orcs who'd enslaved humanity in ancient times. Now, the district was almost completely abandoned. Besides her house, only the classroom had any use—once a year, the clan matriarch would teach a single, basic cantrip, and then lecture the candidates on how Biomancy was once practiced—before the Great Betrayal and purging of all the spellbooks.

Brehane sighed. One day, she'd become clan matriarch. If she failed to convince the Conclave to pass her, she'd only be allowed to return to the university once a year to teach history and that simple spell. Her grander dreams, of restoring their honor and reinvigorating the district, would be dead.

Outside her home, she bowed in turn to the two people sweeping the road. The first, an old warrior from her clan, wore a loincloth on this hot spring day. He wiped sweat from the dark skin of his brow, and acknowledged her by placing fingers over his heart, then his lips.

"I...I failed," she said.

He flashed a toothy smile. "You tried your best, Mistress Brehane."

The second person, silent as always, bowed. Build hidden by a bulky, roughspun robe, Kirala could've been male or female. Nobody knew, but the students, teachers, and elders politely referred to her as *she*. Only the pointed ears, protruding from behind an expressionless metal mask, and the large violet eyes revealed her elf heritage. That, and the rumors that she had worked at the university for hundreds of years—an advanced age for even an elf, yet she had lustrous golden hair tied back into a ponytail.

As always, Brehane studied Kirala. Why she didn't live among her reclusive kinswomen in their secluded mountain realms was the subject of wild speculation. Some guessed she'd been exiled for some crime, while others assumed she must be so ugly, she was ashamed to live among the rest of her beautiful people.

As was often the case when Kirala was around, the Resonance shifted. She withdrew a small, black leather-bound book from a pocket that should've been too narrow to hold it, and proffered it in two hands.

Brehane flashed a smile. "Another?"

With a nod, Kirala grunted. Brehane received the tome and pressed it to her forehead in thanks. She looked down and read the title, emblazoned in gold Aksumi script. *Dragonstones.* One of her fascinations. She flipped through the pages. All blank, like every other book Kirala had given her. Despite the eccentricity of the gift, no other student had received attention from the enigmatic elf, so perhaps it was an honor of sorts.

Kirala pointed at the book, which vibrated in Brehane's hands.

Affording her a polite nod, Brehane opened the door to her house and trudged in. She peeled off the bulky fire suit and tossed it on her pallet. *Dragonstones*, she added to her small library of arcane knowledge, wedging it between several of the other blank books Kirala had given her over the years. *Martial Magic of Paladins. Artistic Magic of Cathay. Estomari Divining. Arkothi Demon Draining.* All hinted at an aspect of magic distantly related to her own people's Mysticism. Brehane had once hoped to rediscover Biomancy through them, only to find them all blank. She might soon have to pack them up and move back home.

She trudged over to the basin of water. It was tempting to use Hydromancy to blast away the sweat and dirt. But, needing to conserve her vitality for the Conclave in the highly unlikely event they gave her a second chance to prove her magic, she grabbed a washcloth and scrubbed like a regular person. Once clean, she donned her ceremonial white Biomancy robe, put on bone and shell bangles, and rested.

When the moondial window showed the Iridescent Moon waning halfway past its fifth crescent, she rose. No sooner did she step out than chants erupted from the tribal warriors lining the streets. The old warrior must've brought them. Their dark faces were painted in the shape of white skulls. Wearing ceremonial bone armor, they snapped to attention as she passed. Despite the tribe's fighting prowess, the other clans disdained them for their historic treason, and their lack of higher magic. Brehane had been their hope, their first Mystic candidate since the Hellstorm.

Brehane's spirit soared. Yes, there was still a chance. Had to be.

Kirala shouldered through the crowd. With another grunt, she held up *Dragonstones* and then tucked it into the fold of Brehane's dress and patted it.

Gawking, Brehane looked back toward her house, where she'd left the book. The tome buzzed at her breast again, sending a surprised jolt up her spine. She reached for the fold in her dress.

With a shake of her head, Kirala stayed Brehane's hand.

Recovering her wits, she smiled and waved as she strode toward the pyramid, towering high at the university's center. Once a monument to the orcs' foul gods, it now represented the pinnacle of human magic. From this district, fused orc bones formed the Biomancy steps to the pyramid's summit. It served as a warning to any orc who thought to steal the Dragonstone and summon their vile gods' flaming chariots.

It didn't deter Brehane. Near the apex, she faced the bone door to the high conclave chamber. She clasped the crystal hanging from her neck, which had given her the standing to study at the university when other members of her father's tribe were banned.

"Brehane, daughter of Gadise," a sonorous voice announced. "You may enter."

Her lips tightened. Her mother, Gadise, had fallen in love with the wrong man and had been disowned by her tribe. Still, the Conclave recognized her Pyromancer heritage, which Brehane herself had renounced in favor of a loving father's tribe.

A tribe whose members no longer had the magic to open the bone doors. With Biomancy studies limited to a simple cantrip, Brehane had to use her hands.

Inside, the room sparkled light blue from Makeda's Tear. The multifaceted Dragonstone hung high in the air of its own accord, above the font where the Resonance coalesced and fueled magic. Its subtle vibrations echoed in Brehane's core. Her hand strayed to the crystal at her neck again. Here were two Dragonstones, two more than in Kirala's blank book.

Which buzzed again.

Ignoring it as hostile gazes fell on her, Brehane entered the ring of twelve seats, each made from a unique material, each occupied by a bejeweled matriarch, bedecked in the colors and jewelry of their respective clans—save for the bone chair of Biomancy, where no one had sat in three hundred years. She'd once hoped to claim it for the tribe that had raised her, and maybe even recover the dragonskull headdress of the Biomancers.

Underneath Makeda's Tear, a tall man turned and faced her. Teacher Dawit, her former instructor in Neuromancy, favored her with a frown. The students all whispered about how handsome he'd been as a youth. Now, even black pearl powder couldn't smooth his rough skin, nor could dyes fully hide the grey peppering in his tight curls of black hair. His ceremonial grey loincloth, embroidered with black and white stitches and sparkling with clear gemstones, exposed too much of his sagging torso; and the matching armbands exaggerated the flaccidity of his arms. His silver jewelry did little to distract from the physical toll of age. Still, he was one of the most powerful Neuromancers, and might've been promoted to Master had he been a woman.

Brehane's heart sank. Perhaps he'd lodged a complaint about her advances, giving the Conclave one more reason to expel her. Men were such funny creatures. So demure and proper.

"Makeda, daughter of Kidist," the page called.

If Brehane's heart could sink any further, she'd have to pick it up from the base of the pyramid. The ugly *assama* was no doubt here to testify. Expulsion seemed imminent. She turned to look at the Pyromancer door of flames—the entrance she would have used herself had she not stubbornly refused to adhere to matrilineal customs.

The fire blazed brighter, then parted. Outside, Makeda hunched over her knees, not because the rose-gold tiara and earrings weighed down her head, but rather from the strain of magic. Lifting her chin, she strutted in like a pigeon savoring a victory. Her gold bracelets and necklaces glinted and jangled as she marched to the center, her red and orange silken robes swishing like fire made solid.

Such a beautiful robe, which only the wealthiest could afford. Brehane shuffled on her feet. The rough cotton of her own white robes seemed to chafe even more in this moment.

Makeda bowed. When she rose, her lip curled into a sneer as her eyes met Brehane's. Again, her gaze shifted to the crystal around Brehane's neck. Brehane's hand strayed there. Money and influence could buy silken robes from Cathay, but not a contested heirloom.

The Head of the Conclave, the old Summoning matriarch who disliked Brehane only a little less than the Pyromancers did, cleared her throat. It did little to make her voice less gravelly. "Candidates Makeda and Brehane. You have been assigned to accompany Teacher Dawit on his mission."

Brehane's heart, just at the bottom of the pyramid, might've leaped into her throat. Apparently, this wasn't an expulsion hearing. They were still referring to her as *candidate*. She turned to find Makeda's narrowed eyes fixed on her. Burying the first question that came to mind, Brehane looked back to the head. "Why are candidates accompanying an adept?"

The Illusionist matriarch, adorned in iridescent robes and metal jewelry of multicolored gemstones, held up a colorful cotton cloth and opened it. Five glass baubles clacked together.

Makeda scoffed. "Do you wish for Brehane to infuse them with light? She might be up for the task one day."

Such disrespect! For Brehane, and the Illusion tribe. Sure, their clan had never recovered from the Biomancer betrayal and was limited to mass-producing light baubles, but that was no reason to mock them. And unlike the Biomancers, their matriarch was still allowed to wear a ceremonial headdress. Brehane shuffled on her feet again.

The Illusionist glared at Makeda. "These belonged to Adept Melas. He has gone missing."

Brehane sucked in a sharp breath. Melas was the most talented Illusionist in three centuries—a kindred spirit who'd researched and experimented to revive a neutered school of magic. With such promise, he'd been one of the few males ever allowed to leave the safety of Aksumi lands, for research only he could do. Last anyone heard, he'd been in Vyara City, searching for Illusion texts that had been stolen by the Ayuri Empire just before the Hellstorm.

She and Makeda met each other's gaze again. It was becoming clearer why they'd been given to this most unusual task. Many students had tried to sleep with Melas, in hopes of absorbing some of his skill. Like most males, his virtue didn't come easily, and it was well known that only she and Makeda had succeeded.

The Illusionist matriarch picked up one of the baubles from the cloth. As soon as her bare hand touched the glass, her form shifted from a middle-aged woman with dark skin and coarse black hair, to a young woman with olive skin and flowing fair hair. Her colorful clothes, jewelry, and headdress remained the same, however.

The hairs on Brehane's neck stood on end. Creating such a detailed illusion was beyond the skill of all but the most talented of that tribe. To capture and sustain it in a glass bauble was inconceivable. Melas—a man, no less—had progressed far in the art of illusions. She extended a hand. "May I, Matriarch?"

Predictably, Makeda interposed herself and plucked one of the beads. Her form shifted, too, this time to a skinny but pretty young Cathayi girl, with silky black tresses and a yellowish skin tone. Still, she spoke with Makeda's grating voice as she grunted words of magic and spun her finger in a circle. Her shoulders slumped as the patch of air she'd demarcated took on a mirrored surface. When she looked at her new reflection, she chuckled.

The Illusionist matriarch offered a bauble to Brehane. From what she could tell, craning over Makeda's shoulder and looking at the mirror, her image had transformed into the same olive-skinned Estomari as the matriarch had.

The Head of the Conclave cleared her throat. "Melas has progressed far beyond what any other Illusionist can do, so it especially concerns us that he has lost contact. Teacher Dawit has been searching for him.

He bought these from an Estomari merchant in Vyara City, who claimed to have acquired them from Melas in Tokahia."

Brehane shuffled on her feet again. Dawit served the Conclave, using his unique Neuromancy skills to track down fugitive males—two who'd slipped their chaperones in Tokahia while on a sanctioned visit to the old pyramid still remained at large. A minor Pyromancer and mildly talented Transmuter. "Why us?" Besides their carnal knowledge of Melas?

Exchanging glances, which sent their jewels dancing in sparkles, the matriarchs shifted uneasily in their seats. They were hiding something.

Teacher Dawit turned to Brehane and nodded. "I requested you, the last female descendant of the First Mystic."

The Pyromancy matriarch shook her head, an amazing feat given the weight of her rose-gold headdress. "Not the last descendant. That is why the Conclave insists that Makeda joins in as well. She has excelled at all the schools, especially enchantment, I am told. Teacher Dawit might need help as he tracks down his friend."

Friend. Brehane's eyes widened. That was it. Despite his proven loyalty and service, they didn't fully trust Dawit. She had been chosen not just to help, but to keep an eye on Teacher Dawit. And Makeda had been chosen to keep an eye on her. Despite all the pretty words, the truth was, it wasn't worth risking an adept when a candidate from the shamed Biomancy tribe would suffice. She started to speak.

The Head held up a hand. "You must be careful. The Divining magic of the Estomari is different from ours—not just the ability to see the future, but perhaps even alter it. If Dawit has somehow learned any of it..."

The hairs on Brehane's neck stood on end again. All magic was fascinating, and she theorized that they all had similarities. After all, Paladins could supposedly see the future in combat, which sounded a whole lot like Estomari Divining. And wasn't it the elves who'd taught humans magic before the War of Ancient Gods? It was amusing how Kirala's blank books had sparked the hypothesis, which would border on blasphemy if the teachers and masters didn't just dismiss Brehane as the crazy Biomancer candidate. Perhaps experiencing it firsthand would allow her to challenge the sacrosanct fundamentals of magic, and also piece together the lost magic of her tribe.

The head pointed toward the harbor. "The Conclave has booked passage for you on the Serikothi ship *Intimidator*. It will depart this evening. Prepare for your journey. If you succeed, you will have earned the right to study higher levels of magic. If you fail, Candidate Brehane..."

Brehane gave a stiff nod as the head master trailed off. If she failed, it meant expulsion. It didn't matter, because here was the opportunity of a lifetime, to visit another pyramid, and perhaps experience Estomari Divining.

After dismissal, Brehane hurried back to her house. Her pulse fluttered.

Two hands on her shoulders stopped her in her tracks. So absorbed she'd been in thought, she hadn't noticed Kirala standing there. The elf pulled *Dragonstones* from Brehane's robe and opened it.

Brehane sucked in a sharp breath again.

Completely blank before, the book now had two new entries: Makeda's Tear, illustrated in vibrant color; and Aralas' Heart—the clear gemstone looked exactly like the heirloom hanging from her neck.

Brehane looked up to meet Kirala's gaze.

The elf grasped the necklace and drew it close to the book. With a nod, she pointed at Brehane, and then to the harbor. A black-hulled ship, likely the *Intimidator*, was coming into the docks.

CHAPTER 3:

Smoke and Mirrors

Standing by the aft bulwark on the *Indomitable*, Yan Jie was about to let personal affection get in the way of a mission for the first time in her life. With effort, she tore her gaze away from the handsome foreign prince giving orders from the quarterdeck, and looked across the stone quay to the black-hulled, five-masted behemoth she was supposed to infiltrate.

The *Intimidator* might've been the *Indomitable*'s twin. Its crew had already withdrawn the gangplank and were busy casting off the moorings. Meanwhile, she fidgeted on the *Indomitable* as it finished docking procedures. There was no time to cross the wharf and board the other ship, which she suspected harbored the assassin who'd murdered two lords back home.

But if anyone could do it, it would be her, an orphan half-elf raised in the Black Lotus Clan.

She looked at Aryn one last time, his refined features a vestige of his people's traces of elf blood. He was so handsome, and charming, and amazing between the sheets. And above the sheets, or with the sheets twisted into bindings. He'd been a fun diversion, to keep her mind off a certain clan brother back home, who never saw her as anything more than a little sister.

He turned, a smile blooming on his face. Oh, that handsome face! There was no time for a long, passionate farewell kiss—their fling had been a secret to his crew, anyway.

Fixing her expression to vapid girl in love with a prince, she waved back, all the while gauging the distance from deck to dock. At about forty feet, it was much too far to jump without leaving a bloody splatter of half-elf on the grey stone. However, the dockworkers had already moored the ship, and the calm harbor kept the lines taut. Even in the cute pink dress, she'd be able to tightrope-walk down one of them, while giving the sailors and dockworkers a view of the lacey undergarments Aryn had given her. Then again, a display of acrobatics would compromise her identity as a simple translator sent from Cathay.

Or maybe she could hedge her bets, just in case there really wasn't enough time to get down, grab a pole, dash up the dock, and pole-vault to the Serikothi ship's stern gallery.

Aryn turned his head to one of the deck officers. No one was looking.

Gathering her skirts in the crook of her elbow, she turned and dove over the gunwale. She hooked her elbow over the line. The dress' smooth satin slipped down the rope—

—A little too easily.

The dock rushed up to meet her. Her billowing skirts must've put her flat body on display for the likely undiscriminating sailors and dockworkers who might happen to look up. In seconds, she'd become the aforementioned bloody splatter of half-elf.

She pulled herself up and wrapped her legs around the line. The fibers, while fine, first warmed, then seared into her thighs and calves. Nevertheless, rope burn was far preferable to death, and her descent slowed to a manageable speed. At the last second, she tucked and rolled several times over the dock's seamless stone, bowling over a couple of laborers along the way.

Despite preventing a concussion, her head swam from the spins. The dock was cold beneath her back...and smooth. Dwarf-carved, perhaps? Seagulls cawed above, either mocking her, or in disappointment of being denied half-elf splatter for dinner.

Shouts erupted. Burly dockworkers in baggy pantaloons and white shirts joined other men with black armbands in rushing over and crowding around her. The stench of man sweat and stagnant salt air did little to clear her head.

"Are you all right?"

"Anything broken?"

"Stay still."

She'd saved time by sliding instead of tightrope walking down, but now hands held her down. Feigning disorientation—or perhaps not feigning it—she peeked out from the throng at the Serikothi ship. It was free of its moorings, and a tug was pulling it clear of the dock. There was still a chance, when the *Intimidator* set oars to guide it out of the harbor and into open seas. Maybe she could swim out, climb up an oar, and squeeze through the oarlock before the sails took over.

Right. Getting off one ship had required the skills of an actor and an acrobat—maybe a career change to opera singer would be safer—but getting onto the other ship with that harebrained scheme would need talents beyond even her wide-reaching abilities. In retrospect, not even the clan's three legendary-but-long-dead young masters could've accomplished the feat, given the exceedingly slim window of opportunity.

With a sigh, she brought her focus back to the center of the commotion and splayed out on the dock. Another opportunity to get aboard the Serikothi ship would present itself at the next port. Perhaps that would be her last chance to root out the conspirators. In the meantime, she could spend a little more time with—

Prince Aryn and his marines pushed the gawking bystanders aside. He waved his hands back, then knelt beside her. "Stand back. Give her space."

Men grumbled, but otherwise complied.

His eyes roved over her in a more professional way than she was accustomed to. When he spoke, his Arkothi accent mangled her name in the most sensual way. "Jyeh, are you all right?"

Her insides twisted in delightful ways. She propped herself up on one elbow while covering her forehead with the back of the other wrist. "I...I think I'm okay. I tripped over the gunwale. Only my butt hurts. And I seem to have some rope burns."

Aryn blew out a breath. "You are so clumsy. That could've been a nasty fall onto concrete. You're lucky you managed to catch the dock line."

If only he knew. At least for now, she hadn't betrayed her cover. "Concrete?"

"Yes. Quite ingenious." He stamped on the ground. "It's used throughout the North, since the Arkothi Era."

She gingerly staggered to her feet. Aryn shot out an arm to support her.

Lightning jolted up and down her spine, perhaps from an unseen injury, but more likely from his touch. "Thank you, Your Highness."

"Are you sure you're all right? Come along now, let us see if we can find you a doctor." He gestured toward his marines. "Men, go find a healer."

Behind him, his aide-de-camp, the enormous Peris, snorted. "She looks fine to me."

"She fell over twelve meters!" With a growl, Aryn pointed back to the *Indomitable*.

She looked from one to the other. Driving a wedge between the lifelong friends had been as inadvertent as ending up in Aryn's bed, but only the pesky emotions attached to the latter had sparked a modicum of guilt.

"I'm all right. Nothing seems broken. Let's just walk." She waved toward the storefronts, but stopped as the pyramid of Tokahia came into view. When they'd been well out to sea—six kilometers according to Aryn's standard of distance—the crystal at the pyramid's pinnacle twinkled like a night star.

Up close, with the sun setting behind it, the massive structure cast a shadow over the one and two-story daub-and-wattle buildings along the waterfront. The shade didn't dim the garish storefronts, nor the equally flamboyant clothes of people gesticulating in large enough motions to kick up the wind. The thick wooden soles of their platform shoes clopped on the cobblestones. Hawkers pawned all kinds of colorful wares of varying practical use. Delicate glassware. Intricate jewelry. Detailed oil paintings. So far, the Estomari were living up to their reputation as artists and merchants.

"I'm fine," she repeated. "Let's just go for a stroll." Why not, when they had one, maybe two days while the *Indomitable* re-provisioned? She pointed to where the stone-paved street curved north along the harbor. Elegant white plaster buildings with actual glass windows and brown-and-red tile roofs lined the streets. They stood in stark contrast to the gaudy stores at the other end. Neither architectural style resembled the wooden structures back home.

Aryn shook his head. "Not that way, Miss Jyeh. That's Mafia territory." He pointed in the opposite direction. "It's safer this way."

Following his finger, Jie took in the cityscape. It looked no different from the supposed *Mafia territory*—in itself a novel idea, since in her homeland, the emperor held absolute power. "How do the Signores tolerate a challenge to their authority?"

Peris scoffed, looking at her as if she were an imbecile. "In the Estomar, authority only reaches as far as the tips of the Signores' swords."

Aryn gave her a tug in the direction of a market. "There's an unspoken understanding: as long as the crime families don't meddle with the Signores' affairs, the Signores won't move against them."

Following along, Jie nodded. It wasn't that much different from the entertainment district in her homeland's capital. As long as they paid taxes, they were free to govern their territory with their own conventions, and the emperor left well enough alone.

"The status quo might be changing," Peris said in a low voice. "Our informants say the crime families are organizing and plan on making a move to seize the city."

"In any case, everything we could possibly need is this way." Aryn continued past several stalls selling jewelry and other trinkets, without any sign of concern about political upheaval

Jie followed along, but wondered. If she were in Aryn's boots, instead of his pants, she'd be more concerned about the implications. Still, control of a faraway city had little to do with her own mission. She looked back to Peris.

Instead of chastising Aryn for his lack of interest, Peris kept flicking his eyes to a large man with a jagged scar on his forehead, who stood in the doorway of an antique shop at the far end of the docks. A man who seemed to be looking at them.

She careened into Aryn's back.

Turning around, he grinned and slid a bracelet on her wrist. "Here, a reminder of home."

Jie looked back to the large man, only to find him gone. With a sigh, she examined the gift while Aryn paid the vendor. The bangle was made of cheap nephrite, called *fake jade* back home. Still, a talented craftsman had carved it into an impressive coiled dragon, complete with the five claws reserved for the emperor. If anyone outside of the imperial family was caught wearing it, they might lose a hand.

"Oh, look!" Aryn pointed, jerking Jie's attention away. In the direction he indicated, a crowd gathered around a street vendor of some sort. "A fortune teller."

Seriously? She met Aryn's gaze and raised an eyebrow. "Do you really believe this?" After all, fortune tellers back home tended to find fortunes in the pockets of the gullible.

"Don't you know? Estomari can predict the future, with magic. Come on!" Aryn's face lit up like Black Lotus Clan children when they received their first throwing star. With the marines clearing the way, he tugged her along through the masses of bodies to the vendor.

Jie followed, rolling her eyes. While everyone on Tivaralan knew the tales of Tatiana, the first Diviner, it took a special kind of naïveté to believe her predictions had helped humans overthrow their orc masters a millennium ago...or that the magic of the pyramid's Dragonstone now prevented the orc gods from returning on their flaming chariots.

Still, with the mission on hold until they could catch up with the Serikothi ship, Jie might as well humor the prince. Let him believe in fate and destiny; no prophecies hung over her.

At the front of the crowds, a brown-haired young man shuffled cards in his hands, flipping them in and out of his fingers with mesmerizing dexterity. The brilliantly painted cards matched his flashy orange longcoat, puffy red shirt, and purple hosiery. "Come, learn your future from me, Roberto Romero, the best Diviner in Tokahia! No, the best in all the Estomar! I predicted the rise of the Pirate Queen and the election of Haros Bovyanthas to First Consul of the Teleri Empire. My results are guaranteed!"

Aryn flicked a gold draka into the air. "A reading for this pretty young woman."

Roberto swiped the coin out of the air. The smile which started to materialize on his face slipped as his eyes met Jie's and widened. Blanching, he shook his head. "I'm sure your future hasn't changed since the last time you came. No refunds."

Jie cocked her head. "What?"

The fortune teller tucked away his cards and started folding up his table. He scowled at her. "If you haven't succeeded in killing your father, that's not my fault."

Aryn gawked at her, while somewhere behind them, Peris chuckled.

Heat flared to the tips of her ears. The crowd gasped and stared as she shook her head incredulously. As satisfying as it would be to find the dastard who'd abandoned her as a baby and stick a knife between his ribs, no one had ever told her her future. At least, not beyond the occasional—no, alarmingly frequent—prediction, *Prepare to die*. That particular fortune had yet to come true.

"Come on, let's forget about this." Jie turned to Aryn, when a ghost from her past strode by.

Her jaw dropped. Princess Kaiya, the daughter of Cathay's emperor, took uncharacteristically long steps and swung her arms in the most unladylike fashion. White silken robes with bright embroidery on the hems fluttered behind her. It looked nothing like a court gown, and instead of imperial guards, she was accompanied by a tall, middle-aged man and an attractive young woman, both with dark skin, coarse black hair, and similar but cheaper robes that marked them as Aksumi Mystics. Both the princess and the woman gesticulated with broad motions, while dismissing the man whenever he tried to speak.

No, it was impossible. Even though the emperor had given the princess more leeway after she put down a rebellion with the budding magic of her music, he'd never let her come this far from home. Certainly not without an army of imperial guards. Not to mention, she'd been in Cathay's capital when Jie had departed. There was no way she could reach Tokahia first. Jie took a longer, more careful look.

While the young woman resembled Princess Kaiya, she was too pretty, too filled out, too... Jie sucked on her lower lip. The face and curvy figure were less like the actual princess, and more similar to the illusion from the magic bauble which the aforementioned rebel leader had used in plotting an assassination of the Imperial Family. Which meant these Mystics might be tied to the conspirator aboard the Serikothi ship, and the clan traitor she was tracking. In town, just as the Mafia might try to take over the city.

Heedless of Aryn's protests, Jie slipped between the dispersing crowds and trailed the trio. How ironic it was, that the pretty pink dress which would make her stand out back home was actually quite muted compared to the flashy clothes the locals wore.

The fake princess tossed a glass bead over to the man, her image instantaneously shifting to a young, dark-skinned woman who looked so similar to the other that they had to be related. The moment the man caught the bauble, he shrunk and transformed into the likeness of Princess Kaiya, only in the clothes he was already wearing. His form returned to normal when he slipped the bead into his pocket. Passersby gawked and pointed.

The magic couldn't be a coincidence. No, it was a clue tied to her mission. And clearly, with their cavalier flaunting, they wanted to be seen. Likely to attract someone's attention. It would be child's play to pick his pockets once they got back into a crowd, and Jie could use the bauble herself, to find out who they were trying to attract.

After winding through the wide, stone-cobbled streets, the group came to what looked like a market square, with dozens of fortunetellers set up around the edges. None of the dozens of people paid these charlatans any heed. Instead, they gathered around several huge, rectangular stones jutting out from the ground, forming what looked to be a circle. The three Aksumi jostled their way through the crowd.

Jie edged up to the closest spectator. "Why are there so many people here?"

The man looked down through his nose at her, his expression one of disbelief. "This is *the* Cassius Larusso. He's a confirmed descendant of Tatiana, herself. The best Diviner in the Estomar. Protector of the pyramid."

If she had a draka for every claim she'd heard in the crowds today, she could buy a ship and hire the crew to serve her for a year. Still, these Aksumi Mystics—the most powerful sorcerers in the world—had come straight to this Cassius Larusso. Maybe there was something to him.

She looked back the way she'd come. Aryn and his crew were nowhere to be seen. No matter, he'd said something about staying at the posh Regent inn. Surely it would be easy to find. She slipped through the people toward the front, to the edge of the megalith circle, right beside the Aksumi Mystics. Some exotic flower scented the females' hair.

Inside the middle of the circle stood a short rock column that served as an altar. Beside it, a handsome, dark-haired Estomari man twisted and turned the rings of a strange metal device. With a green embroidered longcoat over a black shirt and brown pants, it was clear his taste in clothes was much more subdued than his compatriots. His eyes—one brown, one blue—roved over a chart of some sort.

He looked up and gestured to three dark-haired, bronze-skinned warriors who wore high-collared long shirts. The heavy, curved swords at their sides marked them as Ayuri Paladins, the defenders of the South. This was the first time she'd actually seen one, up close no less, and they certainly didn't look like the mythical warriors of legend.

They had ordinary builds, nothing remarkable. The eldest was a woman, whose wrinkled skin, grey hair, and thin arms brought into question if she could possibly lift that heavy, primitive-looking blade, let alone wield it. The other two were men, one middle-aged and the other young. How strange it was for both Aksumi Mystics and Ayuri Paladins—not to mention a Cathayi half-elf—to be in the same, otherwise ethnically homogenous city. This was either a strange coincidence, or the start of a bad joke with an equally awful punchline.

The magic bauble was in the male's left pocket. Simple enough to retrieve. Sidling up to him, she started to tug the lacey gloves off for better tactile sense, but then thought the better of it. If it changed her image on contact, like the one she'd used back home, it would draw undue attention. She reached—

The female Mystic in the cotton robes clasped a jewel about her neck. Her head turned and her gaze locked on Jie. "Why have you been following us?"

CHAPTER 4:

Impulse

As a Paladin apprentice, Sameer Vikram strived to embody the virtues of the Gods of the Sun, Justice, and Martial Prowess, and the Goddesses of Wisdom and Compassion. Too often, the Goddess of Passion tempted him.

With his two masters flanking him in the renowned Cassius Larusso's megalith circle, it was all he could do to pretend he didn't still love Sohini. Sameer could barely contain his excitement in front of them. His heart skipped like a sling stone across the Shallowsea.

Larusso claimed he could find her in this strange, foreign land.

Ah, Sohini. She was descended from the Founder of the Paladin Order, who in turn could trace his lineage to Vanya, the first *Bahaduur*. Legend had it Vanya's martial skill almost equaled that of her lover and teacher, the Elf Angel.

Like her esteemed ancestors, Sohini had been unrivaled in her fighting prowess, perhaps the most talented among their class of Paladin recruits. She was so beautiful that all the other students were either jealous of or enamored with her. Sometimes both.

And against all rules, she'd chosen him. Sameer shuffled on his feet as Larusso's eyes—one blue, one brown—roved over a record of Sohini's birth date, time, and location.

"This is a waste of time." Master Anish, Sohini's mentor, scowled. His crooked nose and sharp eyes gave him the look of a hawk. Grey streaked his long black hair, which, like that of all Paladins, was tied into a topknot.

Sameer studied Sohini's famous master. Master Anish tapped the hilt of his curved *naga.* He'd been hesitant to consult a Diviner at all, but no doubt the guilt weighed heavily on him; assigned by the Paladin Council to investigate some Paladins who'd gone missing on their pilgrimage to the Estomari pyramid, he'd lost his own apprentice.

"Apprentice Sameer, still your thoughts." Elder Gitika's voice was calm as the Shallowsea. Unlike Master Anish's brow, which was furrowed from frustration, the only wrinkles in her forehead came from age. Her bushy white eyebrows stayed level. She exuded tranquility as only one of the greatest living Paladins could.

"I am sorry, Elder." Sameer curled his fingers in the *mudra* for apology. If only he could be so serene under such trying conditions. One day, maybe, he could become half the Paladin that Elder Gitika was. It was already such an honor to be mentored by her.

Master Anish nodded. "You must focus, feel the Vibrations of the World."

"I know it is difficult for you, Apprentice. It is for all of us." She placed a wizened hand on Sameer's shoulder. Elder Gitika was Master Anish's former mentor. She'd taken the first ship to this land of the fair-skinned as soon as the Paladin Council had received his news of Sohini's disappearance.

"Ahem." Signore Cassius Larusso cleared his throat.

The spectators outside the megalith circle fell silent, their attention now locked on him.

He pointed to the sky. "Your friend's signs are in transition, making the answer hard to pin down. What I can tell you right now is that her birth date, time, and location correspond to the missing Golden Flock, which will reappear during the Godseye Conjunction."

Sameer followed the Diviner's finger to the Iridescent Moon, now waning to mid-crescent. It looked smaller than usual, sitting just above the sparkling Dragonstone of the Estomar pyramid, much farther to the west of its usually reliable seat in the heavens. Legends claimed the Golden Flock constellation had appeared annually during the Era of the Orcs, disappearing after the War of Ancient Gods for seven hundred years, only to briefly reappear just before the Hellstorm, three hundred years ago. "When is the next time?"

Elder Gitika placed a reassuring hand on his shoulder again. "Patience, Young Sameer."

Sameer took a deep breath. Maybe one day, he could channel the Goddess of Patience as well as his master.

"In three years," Signore Larusso said.

Three years! Sameer's stomach sank. Risking the ire of his mentor, he asked, "Does that mean we won't find her until then?"

Signore Larusso stroked his thin, pointed beard. "The future is not set in stone; yet to alter what the hands of the gods plan to chisel may come at great risk. With a little more research into the skies over her birthplace, along with as many of her personal effects as you can provide, I can Divine at my other circle. It will reveal exactly where your friend has been, where she is now, and perhaps where she will go. I forewarn you, though, changing destiny may have unintended consequences."

Shivering, Sameer cast a sidelong glance at the two masters. Elder Gitika's expression remained serene as always, hiding whatever she thought.

Master Anish aligned his fingers into the *mudra* for apology. "Sohini was my responsibility. I will face whatever danger I must in order to recover her." He looked to Elder Gitika.

The elder had frequently reprimanded Sohini for her impulsiveness, and in private, Sohini criticized the elder for her stodginess. With more important matters back home, Gitika wouldn't want to join in anything more than a search of Tokahia and its surroundings.

And as her apprentice, where she went, Sameer would go too. His heart felt as if it was being torn in two. Part of him wanted to follow the elder, to absorb as much as he could from the greatest Paladin of her generation. The other part wanted—no, needed—to ensure Sohini's safety. Maybe Gitika would allow him to accompany Master Anish.

"I will do whatever it takes to help you," she said.

If not for the intervention of the God of Discipline, Sameer's jaw would've hit the grassy ground. The Goddess of Fortune must've thought of him when swaying the elder's mind.

Master Anish pressed his palms together and bowed his head. He fixed the elder with an adoring gaze. "Master, as I have said before, you do not need to trouble yourself. Please, return home and rest, and allow Apprentice Sameer to join me."

Elder Gitika's eyes fell on Sameer. "This mission, more than any other, will teach Young Sameer to temper his passions. He will need my guidance."

Sameer's chest squeezed. Of course his master would know his foible. If anyone could provide guidance, it would be the great Gitika. He would do anything to prove himself worthy of her... save for abandoning Sohini. Master Anish turned back to the Diviner. "Very well. We are staying at the—"

"—Seafarer," Larusso said. "Yes, of course I know. Do you have any of Sohini's personal effects?"

Sameer gritted his teeth as he looked between the two masters. Reluctantly, he opened the pouch at his side and withdrew a silver pendant with a cracked pearl. He proffered it to the Diviner. "This was her mother's only valuable."

Master Anish eyed him, then from his own pouch withdrew a long strand of hair. "This was hers."

Sameer's heart sunk. Why had Sohini bequeathed such a...personal... gift to her master? No, maybe he'd just found it on her pillow.

Her pillow? He was thinking too much about something so innocuous. Then again, why had Master Anish collected her hair?

Larusso took it. "Very good. I will send word tomorrow."

Master Anish pressed his palms together and bowed his head. "Thank—"

"Now if you'll excuse me." Larusso motioned them away. "I do not wish to tempt destiny, and it has been foretold that three Aksumi Mystics would seek me out at this hour, to learn of the whereabouts of their lost friend."

Sameer knit his fingers into the *mudra* of forbearance. So rude, to dismiss them so summarily. Perhaps the Northerners were so busy making money, they had forgotten common courtesy. He followed Larusso's eyes to the edge of the megalith circle, where two attractive Aksumi ladies and an older male waited.

One of the women looked to be engaged in an argument with a yellow-skinned Cathayi girl with pointed ears.

"I wasn't following you," the half-elf was saying as she withdrew into the crowds. "I just wanted to see the most famous Diviner in the Estomar."

Elder Gitika beckoned. "Come along now, Apprentice Sameer."

With a last look at the Mystics as they entered the megalith circle, Sameer hurried to catch up with his masters. The crowds parted to make way, pointing and whispering about the Paladins in their midst. Of course, even with the occasional pilgrimages Paladins made to the pyramid, darker-skinned Southerners were rare in this part of the world. Sameer hadn't seen any since they'd landed; until now, where seven had managed to converge in one place at the same time.

As they walked through the stone-cobbled streets, he imagined how Sohini must have felt among all the fair-skinned folk. She probably would have stopped at that dressmaker's shop to marvel at the colorful long skirts—much too hot for back home in the Ayuri Confederation, but perfect for the cooler climes here. Maybe she'd try on the silver bracelets and anklets at the jeweler's stall. She'd look beautiful, no matter what she wore.

Elder Gitika stopped short. Sameer stumbled and nearly ran into her. He'd been so busy daydreaming, he hadn't noticed. He looked around.

They'd turned into a narrow street. Up ahead, nine fair-skinned men brandished rapiers. Unlike everyone else in Tokahia, they didn't wear colorful clothes in the latest fashionable cut, but rather dark longcoats.

One stood a head taller than the rest, and was easily twice as broad. A jagged scar marred his forehead, and instead of a rapier, he held a single-edged sword of foreign make. "You've come back, eh, darkie?"

"Mafia," Master Anish muttered.

Raising her hands, Elder Gitika shook her head. "We don't want any trouble. We'll be on our way." She started backing up, and would have nudged Sameer if she hadn't sidestepped at the last second.

Sameer took a deep breath to settle his nerves. The Vibrations pulsed strongly here, even more so than at the ruins of the Ayudra pyramid where he'd trained. Something interrupted the energy field behind him, and he looked back. Four more men, larger and broader than even the Mafia leader, now blocked the other end of the street. Wielding longswords, they all looked to be in their early thirties.

"Masters," Sameer said. "There—"

"I know." Elder Gitika's hand rested on the pommel of her *naga*.

Master Anish leaned in and whispered in her ear, "These are the criminals who attacked me and Sohini."

Every second of every day, from the beginning of the world to the end, the Divine marriage between the God of Justice and Goddess of Vengeance waxed and waned. A Paladin was supposed to embody Him, using only as much force as necessary; but now She held sway over Sameer. If these thugs were responsible for Sohini's disappearance, they would pay. Spinning to face the men in the rear, he whipped out his own *naga* and charged.

"Sameer, come back," Master Gitika said, her tone more annoyed than frantic.

His blade glowed bluer than usual and the world slowed down. In that moment of mental clarity, the enemy's strategy became clear.

The two huge men on the edges fanned out, while the two in the middle backed up. Even a Paladin student would recognize the enfilade, and not care. To his right, the man swung his longsword toward his head, while the one to the left swept at his feet. They might as well have been slogging through honey.

Sameer dove between the arcs of the two weapons, landed in a roll, and came up to his feet. In the center, the two men's expressions slowly contorted into shock. One started to cock his sword back, but Sameer drove the *naga* into his gut. He shoulder-butted him while yanking the blade free. Even in slow motion, it felt like he'd thrown himself against a stone wall.

Dropping his sword, the man reached for the hole in his belly. Sameer spun out of a hack from the man beside him, while slashing at his midsection. The blade ripped through soft flesh. As both of the men at the center crumpled over, the ones to the flank turned to face him.

Before the one on his left could finish his turn, Sameer removed his head with a swift strike. Circling the *naga* over his head, he wrapped up the last assailant's thrusting arm between his elbows and his chest. The force would have dislocated a smaller person's shoulder and elbow, but the brute's sheer mass held firm. Still, the sword clattered from his hand, and Sameer dumped him to the ground with a sweep of his foot.

He set the blade at his throat and time returned to normal.

Back where he'd come from, Elder Gitika moved like a blur through two bandits. Five already lay writhing on the streets around her. Master Anish was disarming the last.

Awe mixed with guilt in Sameer's heart. How fluid and controlled they were, never dealing death when it could be avoided. He scanned the scene again.

The apparent leader, with the scar, was nowhere to be seen. How could that be? He couldn't have possibly fled to the next intersection, some fifty feet away, in such a short time.

The last two enemies fell to the ground in quick succession. Clutching her side, Elder Gitika kicked their weapons out of reach. "Where is the leader?"

Cold pricked at the back of Sameer's neck. Had that sensation been there before?

Master Anish looked around the groaning men, his brows furrowing. "I engaged him, but in one of my turns, he disappeared. I don't know how that is possible."

"You didn't mention Mafia," Gitika said through gritted teeth.

Master Anish held his hand in the *mudra* for apology. "I did not think it relevant."

The fact that these criminals had come back suggested it *was* relevant. Sameer nudged his captive with his foot. "Who are you? Did you kidnap Sohini?" If so, then Master Anish was right in not believing Signore Larusso's fanciful talk of conjunctions and missing constellations.

Still holding her side, Elder Gitika strode over and pointed at the dead enemies. "You were too impatient. You should have let us formulate a plan."

Master Anish nodded. "Yes, this is how I was separated from Sohini. She charged off into a group of them, and by the time I had dispatched my attackers, she'd disappeared."

Elder Gitika held out her hand. "More importantly, you have dealt mortal wounds to these men. Surrender your *naga*."

No! Sameer's stomach writhed at the thought. The weapon, whose *istrium* he'd collected on the slopes of Mount Ayudra, was no less part of him than his hand. He held it to his chest with one hand, while bending his fingers into the *mudra* of apology with his other. "But Master—"

Elder Gitika spoke through gritted teeth. "Recite the Mantra of Life."

With a sigh, Sameer bowed his head. "The *Bahaduur*'s power comes from the Vibrations of the World. The Vibrations comes from life. The *Bahaduur* must not take life unless necessary." He looked up. "Master, how was it not necessary?"

"Could you have incapacitated them without killing?"

Could he have? Possibly. It had just been easier to do it this way, and, if he admitted it, the mere possibility that they might've taken Sohini had fueled his anger.

Elder Gitika turned to Master Anish. "Can we incapacitate our enemy without killing?"

He pointed at the other men, some of whom gained their feet and fled. "They still live. Some may never wield a sword again, and this one will never walk, but they will live."

The last man he indicated, as large as the four Sameer had faced, snarled. "Just kill me, then."

Elder Gitika shook her head. "Crawl to your sword and take your own life, if that is your will." She locked her gaze on him and spoke in the *Bahaduur* voice of Command: "But first, you will answer my question."

"Yes, of course I will." The injured man's eyes glazed over.

It was easy for a great master to influence someone. Sameer set his hands into the *mudra* for admiration.

Elder Gitika wobbled on her feet, the Command apparently sapping more energy than it should have for a Paladin master. "Where is Sohini?"

"I don't know."

"Where did your leader go?"

"He has a magic bead. It makes him invisible."

Sinking into a defensive stance, Sameer jerked his head around. Was invisibility even possible? If so, and the leader was still there, the din from the bustling main street made it too hard to hear his breathing. Cold pricked at his neck again.

Elder Gitika's brows furrowed.

Master Anish closed his eyes and stretched his arms out by his side. "I don't sense anyone else here."

The hairs on the back of Sameer's neck stood on end. He looked from the first thug to the huge man he'd incapacitated. "What do you know? Where is Sohini?"

The brute cackled. "We sold her to a whorehouse. After she spread her legs for us."

Blood rushed to Sameer's face. Sohini had grown up in a brothel before her lineage and potential talent had been identified. He lifted his sword.

"Stop." Elder Gitika's voice rolled over him like an ocean wave.

Compelled, Sameer froze in place. He lowered his *naga* and bowed his head. "Forgive me, Master."

"He is baiting you," she said. "A dozen of them couldn't capture Sohini."

"But our Golden Scorpion could," the man whispered.

Traitors to the Paladin order! It wasn't possible, was it? Not in this city. Sameer looked to his master.

"I don't have the energy for a Command." Gitika shook her head and lifted her gaze to Anish.

He nodded. "Tell me, Mafia goon."

The Vibrations shifted, but the man's lips squeezed shut.

Anish sighed. "We've used it too much. He can resist now."

"There are other ways." Sameer tightened his grip on his hilt.

Frowning, Gitika extended her hand again. "Your weapon."

She was right. He'd violated the Paladin code. Chosen Vengeance over Justice, taking a life when it could've been avoided. He'd even been about to torture a man, all for Sohini. Bowing his head, Sameer proffered the blade. His hands trembled. The dwarves on Ayudra Island had hammered and folded it into the curved shape of the *Bahaduur* swords of old. For years, between lessons, he'd sharpened it on the smithy's steps.

She received it in two hands, as respect even for an apprentice's sword dictated. However, now that her left hand had moved from her flank, it revealed an expanding splotch of blood.

Sameer gaped. It wasn't possible for such an experienced Paladin to be touched by common thugs. "Master, you are injured!"

She winced as she passed his *naga* to Master Anish. Her hand returned to the wound. "Yes, Young Sameer. Perhaps I am getting too old. When we fought, I lost my connection to the Vibrations for a few seconds." She hunched over.

"That might be a nasty cut," a high-pitched voice called from behind.

Sameer spun around, hand reaching for a sword that wasn't there.

A Cathayi half-elf slunk into the alley. She'd been the one arguing with the Aksumi at Signore Larusso's megalith circle. She spoke Ayuri with a heavy accent. "I can clean it out and stitch it up for you."

There were Paladin Healers throughout the Ayuri Confederation, where confrontations with the traitorous Golden Scorpions occurred on occasion. There weren't any here. Maybe this half-elf, if she actually had skill, would be useful. Sameer exchanged glances with Master Anish.

The master's eyebrows furrowed together. He pressed his palms together in respect, but suspicion hung in his voice. "Why should we trust your skill?" *Or you*, his tone suggested.

She shrugged. "You can always go looking for a doctor, but who knows when you'll find one, and I'll do it for free."

"Why—" Master Anish started.

"Please," Elder Gitika said through clenched teeth. She unfastened the lower buttons of her kurta and opened it. Blood oozed from a finger-length cut.

Sucking her lower lip, the half-elf lifted her skirts and withdrew a flat pouch. She turned to Sameer. "Go fetch some strong alcohol. There's a tavern around the corner."

Was he an errand boy for strangers now? "Why?"

"I'm thirsty."

Heat flared in Sameer's head. This was no time to drink, not when Elder Gitika was injured.

The half-elf snorted. "No, silly, for the wound. And for your master. Now go."

Paladins used herbal liniments, not booze. Sameer looked to Master Anish, who nodded.

"Hurry." The stranger fiddled with a packet of powder.

* * *

If Jie counted the battlefield surgeries she'd performed in her life, she'd need to use both hands and feet, and maybe the wide-eyed apprentice's two hands and one of his feet, as well. Once this Sameer had returned with a red vintage that smelled stronger than White Lightning wine, she went to work.

Cleaning and stitching a wound came automatically, allowing her to think about all the intersecting threads. Especially when she ignored the master's winces and grunts.

Back at the megalith circle, she'd seen the Teleri agent with the forehead scar. He'd been the same one from the antique shop, watching them at the docks. Smaller than his brethren, she'd almost missed him. He had exceptional stealth skills, which marked him as a trainee of the clan traitor she'd been tracking. Him being here at the same time as Aksumi Mystics with a suspicious illusion bead couldn't be coincidence, though he'd gone off to stalk the Paladins. The Aksumi would be easy enough to reacquire in this city of fair-skinned folk, but a man trained in stealth would not. She'd trailed him just like he stalked them, watching as he acquired his Mafia goons along the way. Then the Bovyans joined in.

The fight between the Paladins and the criminals had been a thing of beauty, though her eyes hadn't been able to track it all. To think, none of the three skinny Southerners looked capable of ganging up on one Bovyan, let alone defeating several. Seven men had surrounded the old woman, and maybe, just maybe she would've been injured more grievously had the other master not intervened once he'd easily dispatched his two attackers. The injured men now fled, tails tucked between their legs.

Jie replayed the fight in her mind. One moment, the scar-faced leader had been there; the next, he'd disappeared. It might've been magic, but there was always the possibility he'd used Black Lotus Clan skills. If anyone could capture this Sohini, it would be someone like that.

She finished the last stitch and looked up. "Now, about your attackers. Let's find their leader. The one with the scar, who disappeared into thin air."

"We don't need your help." Master Anish waved her away.

She pointed at the fallen men. "These are Bovyans from the Teleri Empire. You can tell from their sheer size, and also their poor sense of fashion. In my experience, nothing good happens when they turn up."

"Well, they aren't talking." Sameer threw his hands up.

"Not with their mouths." She pointed at his captive's feet. "However, his muddy boots say that he's been down near the river."

The Bovyan gawked.

Elder Gitika leaned over, her eyes widening.

Jie knelt down and sniffed his breath. "He recently ate lamb with a tangy marinade. I don't know much about the food in this region, but I would remember the scent if I smelled it again."

The Bovyan covered his mouth.

"Why would you help us?" Master Anish's eyes narrowed.

"Would you believe me if I said I love a good mystery? No?" She flashed an irrepressible grin. "You aren't the only ones who lost someone in Tokahia. Those Aksumi Mystics back at the Diviner's megalith are looking for a missing member, too. Plus, I would like nothing more than to help a woman sold to a brothel. I'm off; the trail grows colder while we chat."

It wasn't entirely a lie. No, a Bovyan trained in Black Lotus ways, cavorting with Mafia just when the crime families were plotting to overthrow the city... as well as missing Mystics and Paladins who could turn the tide of a turf war... It was just too suspicious.

"Very well," Gitika said. "Let's go."

Jie held up a hand. "No, you must rest. Probably for a few days."

Anish nodded. "Come, Master. Let's go back to the Seafarer."

"Please Master," Sameer said. "Let me go with...with...."

"Jie." She started to curtsey in the local fashion, but then imitated the Paladins' greeting, pressing her palms together and bowing her head.

"The half-elf. Let me go with her." If Sameer's expression looked any more pleading, he'd be almost as cute as the Black Lotus temple dogs.

Gitika's gaze on Sameer was as evaluating as a certain clueless spy back home, calculating the blast volume for a firepowder keg. "Why?"

"To atone." Sameer pinned down his middle finger with his thumb, leaving the other fingers splayed. Since he probably wasn't practicing for a shadow-puppet show, it must be their peoples' *mudra* hand signal. "For justice, for all the girls taken into servitude."

"Very well. You must not engage in hostilities, except in self-defense. Anish, go with him. I can get back to the Seafarer myself."

Jie chewed on her lower lip. Wherever Bovyans went, hostilities seemed to follow close behind.

CHAPTER 5:

Duel of Wits

Brehane stood at the entrance to Cassius Larusso's megalith circle, her ribs aching from where Teacher Dawit had dug his elbow into her. Trying to get her attention. At first, she'd been so busy sensing the strong Resonance in this city, then thinking she'd seen the missing Melas in the crowds. When she'd looked back to confirm, she caught sight of the Cathayi half-elf sidling up to them. With all the distractions, she was just now noticing that this famous Diviner was a man.

A *man*.

Could that be possible? No. He was likely nothing more than the dozen charlatans they'd passed along the way, deceiving the unwary and the gullible. It had been easy to tell from the way their so-called Divining didn't so much as create a ripple in the Resonance, which was as strong here as near the pyramid back home. All hope of experiencing true Divining and perhaps merging it into her own magic dwindled.

At least this particular rogue was quite handsome. Unlike the other locals, who wore the most delightfully bright colors, he'd selected neutral greens and blacks for his longcoat, shirt, and hosiery. At first glance, his dull clothes seemed like a mark of poor taste, or perhaps poverty; but on further consideration, it was clear that the subdued palette must have been a conscious choice to bring out his good looks. He might very well be worth the conquest, even if he didn't have any real magic to absorb through coupling.

Now that the half-elf stalker had taken off after the treacherous Ayuri Paladins, most likely to pickpocket them, Brehane clasped the crystal about her neck and studied this Cassius Larusso.

Though the fair skin made him look sickly, his high, thin nose accented strong cheeks and full lips. His thin mustaches curled up, and a beard jabbed out from his chin, ending in the cutest point. Yet most striking were his eyes: one dark brown like coffee, the other like the Blue Moon. A dragon eye, like the Last Dragon Avarax and the evil sorcerer Rumiya, according to old legends.

Perhaps he did have magic. He did seem to know their purpose in being there; though maybe the tall fellow at the docks, the one with the scar on his forehead, worked for Larusso. He'd approached Teacher Dawit outside an antique shop and recommended this place. Maybe he'd sent a runner back to the megalith circle with advance information.

The way Makeda was eyeing him, like a sand devil stalking a rodent, she must've also been thinking of bedding him. If she managed to absorb any magic he might have, she'd no doubt use it to continue the oppression of the Biomancers. Brehane's chest tightened as if squeezed by a dragon's talons. She'd beaten Makeda into bed with Adept Melas and absorbed his younger, purer essence. She wouldn't lose to her here, either.

"Come in, come in to my circle." Cassius dipped in to a sweeping bow. "It is not every day that foreigners come looking for a lost friend, even rarer still that two groups would face the same conundrum."

Brehane snorted. No doubt the Ayuri were involved in some kind of treachery or backstabbing.

"A coincidence," Makeda said.

Cassius stroked his beard in a decidedly sensuous manner. "Destiny."

His words came out smoldering like a fireball. It was all Brehane could do to not fan herself. It took a second before she found her own voice. "We make our destiny."

"So we will." He winked.

By the Makeda's Eye! This man was brazen. Perhaps it was part of the act to bring in unsuspecting fortune seekers, like the *shermuta* back home who tried to lure women into paying for sex, using their pretty white teeth and all but their manhood exposed.

This Cassius accomplished the same filthy tricks fully clothed, with only a wanton smile. Back home, women would exploit him and other men would ostracize him for his loose morals. While every instinct screamed to take advantage of easy prey, Brehane's better senses warned to keep this *shermuta* at arm's length.

Until Makeda took his hands in her own. "I am Makeda, daughter of Kidist, and True Heir to the First Mystic. I trust your family is well?"

Brehane frowned as she clasped her necklace. The worthless *assama* had bandied about the True Heir moniker for years, even if it had no logical basis. Their shared maternal grandmother may have worn the First Mystic's pendant, but the heirloom had passed to Brehane's mother and now to her. Once she restored the Biomancers' honor, no one would question her legitimacy.

Still, try as she might to prioritize the mission of finding Melas, her eyes could only dwell on Makeda's hands, clasped with his. Whether he was a *shermuta* or not, she'd have to bed him before Makeda. The Pyromancer now squeezed her breasts between her arms, conjuring cleavage with a very different type of magic.

A grin formed on Larusso's face as his gaze dipped from Makeda's chest to their intertwined hands. "Pleased to meet you, Makeda, daughter of Kidist, True Heir to the First Mystic. However, the heavens do not wait for pleasantries." He looked up to Teacher Dawit. "I trust you have my fee of a hundred drakas."

As if a man would be trusted to carry money without spending it on something frivolous! Larusso apparently couldn't even Divine up some common sense. Brehane stepped forward and produced a heavy pouch. "Here, a hundred drakas."

Forehead scrunching up for a split second, Larusso released Makeda's hands and received the money. He hefted it in his palm. With a nod, he tossed it to one of the guards at the edge of megalith circle. "Now, you wish for me to find a missing person..." His eyes glazed over as he rocked back and forth. "Melas."

Makeda's gasp mixed in with the excited chatter of the crowd.

Still, the Resonance, so strong in this city, hadn't shifted. Brehane narrowed her eyes. There was no magic involved, at least none that she could experiment with and merge with her own.

Cassius' swaying stopped. "This master—"

"Not a master." Brehane shook her head. This rogue was indeed a trickster. "An adept."

"A linguistic subtlety, between your beautiful tongue and mine." He winked. "This *adept* does not wish to be found, for he has taken measures to protect himself from scrying."

Makeda pouted. "So you cannot help us?"

"Only the most skilled Diviner could." He paused, the effect quite dramatic, then grinned. "Luckily for you, I am the best."

Such arrogance! And there Makeda stood, batting eyelashes at him as if she were a pig in heat.

"I need to know about his birth. The date, the time, and the location."

Brehane exchanged glances with her companions. Such details held little importance for Aksumi men, whose birthdates were never added to the songs of lineage.

Looking from her to Makeda, Teacher Dawit sighed. "My friend Melas was born near Chenkar at midnight on the Full Moon Day of the seventh month, in the eight hundred and seventy-second year after the War of Ancient Gods."

Brehane stared at Teacher Dawit. Why would he know such minutia about Melas?

Larusso twisted and turned a spherical device of interlocking rings, set it over a map on the central altar, and spun it. Nothing he did used any actual magic; and as before, the Resonance didn't shift as he worked. Yes, his talent was in book learning, not true Divining.

He looked up. "Adept Melas was born under full White and Iridescent Moons, when Ayara's Eye was fully open. This indicates potential for power. Furthermore, at the midnight hour, the constellation of Fortuna, Goddess of Fortune and Opportunity, would have just risen over Chenkar. Adept Melas is a man of ambition."

Brehane snorted. In Aksumi tribal lands, males were pampered and treasured. What more could a man ask for? What ambitions could one have, save for depositing his seed in an appropriate wife, or protecting his family and clan as a warrior? If he were blessed with magic, maybe he could aspire to being a teacher. And in any case... "This tells us nothing about where we can find him."

"Oh, but it does." Larusso's grin, so roguish and compelling at first, was now clearly part of his act. "It tells us that he acted of his own accord, and wasn't taken against his will. As to where he is now..." He looked up at the late afternoon skies, where only the sun and the Iridescent Moon shone at this hour.

Again, there was no sign that he'd used the Resonance, only star charts and book learning. Brehane held up a hand. "What can you tell, when the stars have yet to come out?"

"Just because you cannot see them doesn't mean they are not there." He pointed to several spots in the heavens. "There, Nadea lounges on the shore of the silver sea, waiting for her love to return. Mortasi, God of Death, stalks the unsuspecting. And Kor the Hunter wanes, making this a hard time to search. They all govern our destinies."

Such gibberish, invoking gods and heroes. Brehane held his gaze. "Is that all you can tell us? That Adept Melas is ambitious enough to find his own fortune?"

"I can tell you where, just not exactly. The wards he used are powerful, so too much is uncertain. The gods have only revealed he is north of here. That could be as close as the marketplace over there, or as far flung as the Glacier. It will take time. Five, maybe six days. I offer you the hospitality of my home in the meantime."

The throng erupted into murmurs.

"Foreigners, in Signore Larusso's home!"

"What an honor!"

While Makeda was not exactly salivating, her eyes betrayed her thoughts: she was yearning for Larusso to explore her filthy cave with his pale snake.

Brehane's lips pursed. Handsome or not, the *shermuta* had yet to demonstrate any real magic. As such, this entire misadventure could be a waste of time which delayed her dreams of restoring the Biomancer clan's honor.

It was time to make this Signore Larusso squirm, to get him to prove he was more than a fraud wrapped in a pretty package. She turned to the others and spoke in the local language so he'd understand. "This swindler is not worth our time. I have yet to feel him manipulate the Resonance. Let us go and find someone who can really help us."

* * *

Cassius forced himself to maintain a smile. Fortuna seemed to have turned her naked back on him today. Never in his life had he encountered such hard-to-impress people. Still drained from gleaning the gods' secrets four times the day before, he hadn't wanted to use real Divining with the Paladins or these Mystics. However, if he didn't act soon, the opportunity to fulfill his end of the bargain with the Teleri would take flight like the Golden Flock and disappear. And with it, the chance to eradicate the Mafia and protect the pyramid. To prevent the orc gods from returning on their flaming chariots.

Not to mention, his end of the bargain was looking much better than he initially thought. Here was a chance to take one of these chocolate-skinned beauties to bed. Maybe both. Maybe at the same time. They looked so similar, they had to be related, and he had always dreamt of a threesome with twins. The three of them would be like the magnificent sandwiches Misha's tavern sometimes served: savory white chicken pressed between rich, moist pumpernickel.

"And since you are clearly not in want of wealth, return our money," the male was saying.

Talk of money shook Cassius out of thoughts of his other two loves, food and sex. It was now or never. Fortuna may have turned her back on him, but she still presented the opportunity of her perfectly rounded ass.

He sucked in a deep draught of the Gods' Whispers and took up the right hand of the second woman—the naysayer who had yet to introduce herself. The patterns on her palm lit up for him, and only him, revealing secrets of her past that even the best palm reader couldn't glean without the power of Divining. The vitality drained from his limbs, and it was all he could do to maintain a straight posture.

After an initial gasp of wonderment, the crowd settled into silence.

"Brehane, daughter of Dahnay of Bahir, First-born Descendant of the First Mystic. You are a spring child, born at noon on the new White Moon of the first month, twenty years ago. At the time, Ayara's Eye was closed and the Iridescent Moon was new. Such an auspicious birthdate represents a new beginning."

Clasping the curious crystal around her neck in one hand, Brehane's grip tightened on him. She gasped. "I felt it, the Resonance. You are a true Diviner."

He eased her fingers open. "At the time of your birth, Konkistor and Solaris faced one another over Bahir. You will be forced to make choices, many times over, between Good and Evil. If you choose Good, you will suffer, and beget a son of great power."

Her eyes rounded.

Beautiful as those dark eyes were, he focused on the fine glowing lines forming the constellation of Hunter Kor over her lifeline. "Your life will be one of pursuit. Of knowledge. Of fame. Of power."

A tentative smile formed on her full lips. "Will I succeed?"

"In the near future, yes." He looked at her left hand as the swirling colors on her palm began to fade, concealing her future. "That is all I can tell you for now."

Mouth twisted in clear jealousy, Makeda thrust her hands out. "Now me."

He had them. Fortuna danced in loops and whorls across his own palms. One pattern leaped out: Julia, his first and only love. His greatest mistake. Energy flickering, he banished the memories. The patterns twisted into gibberish. He shook his head. "I am sorry, Makeda, daughter of Kidist. Just like you tire when you call on your magic, the highest levels of Divining can tax me. The heavens do not divulge their secrets without a payment from my soul."

The two women nodded, though Dawit evaluated him through slitted eyes.

One last push with a few half-truths, and he'd be a step closer to wiping out the Mafia and bedding two pretty girls as a bonus. "A faint outline of Baell, the Warlock, intersects with your lifeline. I surmise that represents Melas, using his ward to hide from the eyes of the gods. The closer we get, the clearer he will appear in the signs around us."

Brehane looked to the others before turning back. "We would be pleased to have you accompany us on our mission."

He motioned toward his guards. "I must retire for the afternoon. Close off the megalith circle." He turned to Brehane and Makeda, and flashed the smile which had brought many a lady between the bedsheets. "You must be tired from your sea voyage. My manor is far superior to any inn you will find in Tokahia, and tonight I am hosting several of the city's prominent leaders for dinner. You will be my guests of honor."

Makeda, who had already succumbed to his charm, nodded so enthusiastically it conjured delicious images of what might transpire in the bedroom. Brehane, who'd eyed him with such suspicion at first, now gazed at him with adoring eyes. Even the dour teacher smiled, probably at the prospect of free food and lodgings. If only there were a way to house him somewhere else. Well, there was the guest room at the far end of the mansion...

Cassius kept his expression neutral to hide his excitement. He was one step closer to fulfilling his family's duty of protecting the pyramid. Not to mention, the way the two women looked at him and chattered excitedly in their own language, the question would not be if *one* would warm his bed tonight, but rather, if he'd enjoy a meal for three.

Now all he had to do was contact the Paladins, to tell them their lost friend was probably still in the city. Maybe she was, maybe she wasn't; it hadn't been worth expending real energy to confirm her whereabouts by listening to the Gods' Whispers. He'd soon be sending out his network of street urchins to listen to very different types of whispers. Still, the Paladins didn't have to know.

After all, it would be worth having three good warriors in the event Phobos and his Teleri friends proved to be untrustworthy, and stood idle while the crime families tried to take over the city and the pyramid...and unwittingly invite the orc gods back to Tivara.

CHAPTER 6:

Bodies of Evidence

Jie slipped behind Sameer and Anish as two of Prince Aryn's sailors passed. It was the third group of Tarkothi they'd run into on the way to the docks, all inquiring about a missing half-Cathayi elf in a pink dress. She borrowed a bonnet from a tailor's storefront display, and though flamboyant red, it didn't stand out as much as her elf ears. Certainly not among all the garish colors worn by the locals. It almost matched the gold-embroidered purple shawl she'd commandeered from a high-end boutique, which covered the cute pink dress.

Ah, the dress. A gift from Aryn, one which he'd stripped off her many times.

Poor Aryn. He was undoubtedly running worst-case scenarios in his head, worried she'd been kidnapped by Mafia, sacrificed by orcs at the pyramid, or who knew what.

Maybe falling in with Paladins *was* worse, since they looked to be on the crime families' bad side. Still, with a Bovyan agent involved, it was undoubtedly tied to her real mission of tracking down the clan traitor. If only she could send word to the prince, to let him know she was all right; but the vanishing spy's trail grew cold by the minute. Sadly, it looked like her time with Aryn had come to an end. Duty would keep her in Tokahia.

Once they'd bypassed Aryn's men, she paused to look over the eight-foot seawall at a muddy flat between two of the ship docks. The salt smell hung in the air.

"Well?" Sameer tugged on the sleeves of his long shirt.

She pointed at the jumble of footprints in the drying mud. "Our friends were here."

The Paladin master, Anish, shifted from foot to foot. "There must be a hundred sets of prints. They could be anyone's."

Such a doubter. Jie held her hands a foot apart. "Look at the size of those prints, and how deep they sank." She pointed to the tracks leading from the water to up along the seawall.

"Ooooh." Sameer's eyes were as wide as the temple guard dogs' when they begged for treats.

Anish's eyes narrowed. "How can you be sure it wasn't just another large man?"

Jie let her lip pop. "Heel print. The locals wear those ridiculous platform shoes, not the heavy boot that made this." Question was, what were the Teleri doing down there? "Come on, let's see where the tracks lead us."

They followed the trail for several dozen feet, to a set of stone stairs halfway between the docks.

"Dead end." Anish threw up his hands.

Ignoring him, Jie went down a few steps and studied the seawall. The mortar between the stones was stained to about waist height. She held her hand there. "When the tide comes in, the water level rises this high. Our friends had to have passed through while the tide was out, long enough for the mud to dry a little. I'd guess between two or three hours ago."

She climbed back up and intercepted the nearest sailor. She dipped into a curtsey; a showy, pointless skill acquired with plenty of practice around the Prince Aryn and Northerners over the last couple of weeks. "How long since low tide?"

The man scratched his head. "About three hours, maybe?"

She cast the Paladins a smug grin before turning back. "What do people do down on the banks?"

He shrugged. "Fish? Launch small boats?"

She turned back to the Paladin. "I don't think they were fishing, and the tracks lead away from shore. The tide has already claimed the traces of the boat they came in on."

"Like I said." Anish smirked. "Dead end."

"Not necessarily." Jie sniffed. Whatever combination of spices the Bovyan had stuck to his teeth, their aroma cut through the salt air and beckoned her now. A worthless elf father might have abandoned her in search of fun and adventure, but at least he gifted her with superior senses.

How bizarre she must have looked, snuffling like one of the Black Lotus temple dogs through the crowded waterfront. "The plague," she said to a woman who was staring with disgust, causing her to cover her mouth and run off.

Jie's elf nose guided them to a street vendor's cart, where layers of meat roasted on a vertical spit.

Unlike other merchants in their puffy, colorful clothes, the young man wore a plain white shirt with sleeves rolled up to expose bronzed, toned arms. A headband kept sweat-matted hair out of his face, and hopefully out of the food. "Roasted lamb gyros," he yelled, cutting slices from the rotisserie and piling them into a flatbread with some kind of chunky cheese and leafy green vegetables.

The Paladins crowded behind her, their noses scrunching up. Sameer's hand formed a *mudra.*

The vendor grinned. "I use my great-great-grandmother's secret marinade. It is the best roasted lamb in Tokahia. No, the best in the Estomar."

Like tarot card reader Roberto Romero, who'd claimed to be the best Diviner in the Estomar, there was no line for service. Perhaps the Estomari didn't define *best* the way the rest of the world did. Jie curtseyed. "Sir, some friends of mine highly recommended your stall. I'm trying to find them."

"I have so many patrons; you'll have to be more specific."

Jie looked over her shoulder at the non-existent line of patrons, then back. "Of course. My friends are big, with an appetite—and attitude—to match."

His face contorted for a split second before his broad smile returned. "The Teleri, yes. I didn't realize they had female friends."

Jie offered an apologetic smile. Of course, the Bovyans' reputation as rapists preceded them. She produced a silver draka, which she'd liberated from a pimp on the way over. "I use the term *friends* loosely. I'm just curious why there are so many this far south."

His eyes shifted left to right before he swiped the coin. He finished wrapping the gyro and gave it to her. "They've increased in the last year. The crime families recruited dozens as enforcers. Now, the Signores are hiring them as caravan escorts and bodyguards."

Jie sucked on her lower lip. The unspoken armistice Prince Aryn had mentioned earlier looked to have been replaced by an arms race, with beefy Bovyan arms as the weapons of choice. Strange, however, since they were cogs in the Teleri war machine. With every necessity accounted for and no individual ambition, why would they need money? "How long ago were they here?"

The vendor looked up at the Iridescent Moon, now waxing to its fourth crescent, just a few degrees from the dimming afternoon sun. "Not more than an hour or so ago."

Jie snickered. So the first thing the Bovyans did when coming ashore was eat. "So you know where they are staying?"

"I hear they hang out over in the tavern district. Neutral ground." He pointed up the road.

A broad avenue cut across the road, serving as a clear barrier between the clean and orderly shops and crafts district, and the rowdy chaos of taverns and bawdy houses. On one side, ladies and gentlemen discussed the latest fashions and arts; while on the other, sailors mingled with prostitutes, negotiating terms. It was similar to the port city of Jiangkou, where she'd last served the clan. It felt almost nostalgic.

Jie took a bite of the gyro. It was quite good, actually, the lamb more juicy and savory than the spicy sauces back home. She turned to her new friends. "Are you sure you want to expose your pureness to such a seedy environment, especially after dark? I can investigate myself."

Young Sameer clenched and unclenched his fists as he looked to Master Anish with puppy eyes. The boy was chomping at the bit to charge in and turn the place upside down. Given his fighting skill, he might very well succeed, even without his beloved sword. "I want to save Sohini."

"Wait." Jie held up a hand. All this talk of *saving* Sohini...something didn't add up. "I just watched you three dispatch fourteen men with ease. Just how could they possibly kidnap her?"

Sameer favored her with the kind of smirk usually reserved for a dimwit. "Our martial reflexes engage when we perceive a threat. If they'd taken her by surprise, or drugged her with gooseweed..."

Jie nodded. If she were going to try to take on a Paladin, she'd use a drug, too.

"Or, if she faced someone with superior *Bahaduur* skills. A Golden Scorpion." Sameer spoke the word as if it tasted like bitterroot tea. "Rumor has it a few have mastered the ability to block our Vibration-enhanced reflexes."

There was that word again, *Bahaduur*, which the Paladins used in lieu of *Paladin* at times. Jie searched his eyes. "What is a Golden Scorpion?"

Anish's measured tone sounded like a teacher explaining to a student: "People with our skills, sometimes even students or knights who abandoned our order, who were recruited by the aggressive kingdom of Madura."

Jie swallowed the last of the gyro. Before she'd embarked on her new mission a few weeks ago, she'd overheard spies from Cathay's neighbor, Madura, planning an attack on an imperial wedding. With her information, the clan had thwarted that plot.

"Because our powers are strongest around the pyramids," Anish said, "these disaffected or unattached *Bahaduur* come here to find work. It was my job to investigate if Madura was recruiting Scorpions here."

"Did you find any evidence of it?" Jie asked.

The master shook his head. "There are a few Maduran officials, possibly up to no good, but I never sensed a Golden Scorpion. I would have felt the aura."

Madura, operating here. Missing Paladins and Aksumi Mystics. A Mafia insurrection brewing. And Teleri spies with Black Lotus skills. A connection, maybe? She pointed her chin at the tavern district. "I'm going. You can follow me, if you want."

"I'm going with you." Sameer squared his shoulders. He looked to the master. "With your permission, of course."

"You may go," Anish said. "I will stay as rear guard, and sense the Vibrations from here."

Sameer pressed his palms together and bowed his head. Then he trailed behind her as she crossed the street.

The sound of drunken sailors echoed in the streets, while the musky scent of burning Ayuri gooseweed and alcohol fumes hung in the air. Light-bauble lanterns hung from lines between one- and two-story wood-and-stone row houses. Wooden signs hung over tavern doors, featuring such appealing names as the *Buxom Lass* and *Pirate Booty*. Outside of some stood men with black armbands marking them as the Signores' peacekeepers; others were guarded by thugs dressed in the dark coats of the Mafia. The two groups eyed each other with simmering anger, but stayed on their respective sides.

Though they lacked signs, several establishments were easily identified by the scantily dressed young women gathered near the entrances. They beckoned to passing men, some of whom stumbled into the buildings with little need of convincing.

"There," Sameer growled, pointing to the closest brothel. He started stomping over.

Jie grabbed his wrist. "Easy, sailor. If you go charging over, their lips will close faster than their legs will spread." She slipped her hand into the crook of his arm.

His body went rigid.

So... innocent. Jie smirked. "Relax. I'm not going to steal your virtue. Just follow along, and let me do the talking."

"Okay," he grumbled. He bent his fingers into a curious shape, and allowed her to pull him toward the brothel.

The three ladies of the night locked eyes on them. A blonde, in a blouse that revealed much more than it hid, beckoned. "Come, come, we are very happy to accommodate a couple in search of fun."

If Sameer's arms and legs could stiffen anymore, he might be mistaken for an embalmed Levanthi corpse. He started to speak.

Jie put a hand over his mouth. "My Ayuri friend is mute, and is very peculiar about his...appetites. He refuses to eat anything except home cooking." She winked. "You wouldn't happen to have dishes more to his taste?"

"Curry?" A prostitute with exotic red hair and more surface area than her clothes laughed. "We can certainly dress up, if that is what he fancies."

Sameer flushed an interesting shade of red. Jie stepped on his slippered foot before he could say anything. She bowed her head in what was hopefully an Estomari cultural show of apology and not acquiescence. "Unfortunately, he is snobbish and only deigns to eat authentic Ayuri cuisine."

Turning her head away, the third woman tossed brown locks over her bare shoulder. "We don't serve those dishes."

Jie produced a silver rupiya, borrowed from Sameer without his knowledge. All the women's eyes locked in on it. She flipped it through her fingers. "If you can tell me where I might find such a delicacy..."

The brunette reached for the coin. "The *South Seas*—"

The redhead shook her head. "That's Mafia-run. With all the trouble brewing, I'd avoid it. Now Signore De Lucca's... Go two blocks down, make a right. Second building on your right. Look for the lion crest."

Puffing his chest out, Sameer started in the indicated direction.

"Sorry, my friend can't control his hunger." Jie tugged him back, while pulling the rupiya just out of reach of the prostitute's hand. "Aren't you worried about tensions between the Mafia and the Signores affecting business?"

While Sameer's glare bore into her, the women laughed.

The redhead winked. "Nothing loosens a man's belt faster tonight than fear of death tomorrow."

Ignoring Sameer's reddening face, Jie sent the coin dancing through her fingers. "One more question before we go. Can you tell me how often Bovyans come to this fine establishment?"

The women looked among themselves, shrugging. The redhead lifted her chin to the silver piece. Jie flicked it in her direction.

With what could only be practiced skill, the woman caught it in her cleavage. Jie's stomach twisted in jealousy of the curves she lacked. In the corner of her eye, Sameer looked like he was about to faint. The redhead grinned at him before leaning forward and whispering, "They don't come to our fine establishment."

"Except for the small guy with the scar." The brunette drew a finger over her forehead.

Jie sucked on her lower lip. Unless there was more than one small Bovyan with a scar on his forehead, she must've been referring to the man who'd led the attack on the Paladins and then disappeared into thin air.

The redhead shook her head. "Yeah, but he visits all of the brothels. Word between the sheets is that none of the Teleri find their release around here, or even in the Mafia-held whorehouses."

Jie held up a hand. "I have it on good authority," if a gyro vendor could be considered an authority on anything other than food, "that they frequent this area."

The blonde waved a finger in ever-broadening circles. "Signore De Lucca hires some to guard his houses, but his girls say they don't entertain them."

Jie shuddered. Given the Bovyans' reputations, it was hard to believe they wouldn't jump at the opportunity.

"What about Isabella?" The redhead nudged the brunette.

The two others fell silent, their expressions darkening.

"What happened to Isabella?" Jie looked from one to the other and held up another of Sameer's silvers.

Sameer stared at the coin and patted his pouch. He started to open his mouth, but frowned instead.

The redhead pushed the coin away. "She came many years ago. An orphan girl that the mistress took in. There are too many in this city. She worked as a maid and learned from us. She would've started seeing clients weeks ago, but Signore De Lucca came and bought her contract."

Hot anger surged to the tip of Jie's ears. Girls—many orphans like herself, or maybe sold by desperate parents—were already virtual slaves in the whorehouses. Meanwhile, men like this Signore De Lucca bought and sold them like chattel, getting rich at the cost of women's bodies and dignities.

The blonde sighed. "We asked around with some friends who work for Signore De Lucca, but no one's heard from Isabella. They did say that Signore De Lucca has bought many trainee contracts from the pleasure houses, and even sent men out to the slums to recruit poor girls. None have ended up at his establishments."

Add finding Isabella to her to-do list. It might not be directly related to the Bovyan spymaster she was tracking, but orphans needed all the help they could get. The first step would be to visit the brothel where Sohini was last seen. Coincidentally, a place where Bovyans happened to be, and which Scarface frequented.

CHAPTER 7:

Disputed Lore

Everything about this foreign city fascinated Brehane. In their rush to reach Cassius Larusso's megalith circle before dusk, she hadn't had time to truly appreciate it. Now, riding in the most wondrous open carriage, pulled by actual horses, she marveled as the city drifted by.

Had she been walking on this late afternoon, she would've paused longer to admire the delightful mélange of colors that the people in this foreign city wore. Bright reds and yellows mixed with vibrant shades of purple she hadn't imagined possible. Frills and shiny buttons adorned their loose shirts and dresses. The Estomari reputation as craftsmen was on full display.

"It's horribly showy, isn't it?" Cassius' breath tickled her ear.

He lounged back in the red cushions of the seat, arms outstretched behind her on one side and Makeda on the other. Teacher Dawit sat across from them, his lips undoubtedly pursed at the Diviner's wanton display.

Yes, Cassius was unabashed at his own loose morals. Brehane tore her attention away from the intriguing city around them and back to this intriguing man. The Resonance had sung when he'd read her palm. Her hand had tingled, as if affected by a lost Biomancy spell her clan matriarch could only describe, but not invoke. He'd even divined the name of Father, who no one ever named. Yes, there was much to learn from Cassius Larusso.

No doubt Makeda had the same idea. How mortifying it would be if she rediscovered lost Biomancy spells first. She might've won in the Pyromancy ring; she wouldn't win their duel for the Diviner's body. Not when that dirty *assama* would use whatever power she gained to maintain the Pyromancers' hegemony, at the expense of the Biomancers.

Brehane studied Cassius' beautiful eyes, and especially his blue Dragon Eye. No matter how brazen he might seem, it was undoubtedly just an act for attention. There'd been many classmates and teachers like that, who led young women on, only to shy away at the last minute. If Cassius indeed wanted to give up his seed, he certainly wouldn't risk his reputation on both of them.

Of course, the missing Melas had surrendered to her charms, as had several others. Testing his willingness, Brehane placed a hand on Cassius' knee. Such a motion would make most men jolt back and demur. He froze. Perhaps the act had been too forward. Brehane's chest tightened.

Then he relaxed. His hand settled over hers, his fingers lacing between hers.

The tension in her chest didn't ease. No, now her heart hammered against its tight confines, and heat raced from her hand into her core. It was such an extreme sensation; more pronounced than the thrill of one-upping a malicious cousin.

Makeda's eyes darted to their intertwined hands before her glare settled on Brehane. Yet another loss for the dirty *assama*.

"Oh, look at the pyramid!" Makeda pointed at the top, its Dragonstone sparkling light blue in the darkening sky. It was the same color as Makeda's Tear at the university. However, unlike the basalt columns of the pyramid back home, this one was cream-colored, and had hard edges which spread to what appeared to be a square base.

Hand forgotten, Cassius nodded with enthusiasm. His tone carried excitement. "Yes, built by the orcs in ancient times as a temple to their gods. My ancestor, Tatiana, foresaw when their flaming chariots would depart, allowing our people to rise up against their masters. We are going to stop there first."

To think, he wasn't just a pretty face, but interested in history as well. Brehane would've clapped her hands together, but that would've meant untangling hers from the Diviner's fingers. Instead, she clasped the crystal hanging from her neck. "My ancestor, Makeda—"

"*Our* ancestor," Makeda growled. "For whom I am named. I am the True Heir."

"—was the lover of the Elf Angel Aralas." Brehane seethed inside at the interrupting *assama*.

"As I guessed, from the signs in the heavens." With that charming grin, Cassius looked down at their interwoven fingers. "Our destinies are as intertwined as our ancestors' were. After all, my progenitor, Tatiana, was also one of the nine loves of Aralas."

What? Brehane exchanged knowing glances with Makeda. At least in this they agreed: Cassius had it all wrong. The elf angel had taught men their humble place in the world by yielding only to Makeda, thereby imbuing her with magic.

Makeda snickered, her usual obnoxious bird titter. "The others were just Aralas' students. No more, no less."

"Only the great Makeda received his essence," Brehane said, "and therefore became the most powerful of his disciples."

Cassius' forehead furrowed. He opened his mouth, but then closed it. Like a good man, he knew when to be quiet. Still, he loosened his fingers from hers.

Brehane frowned. What had she said? Or was he playing hard-to-get? She withdrew her hand, crossed her arms, and looked up at the pyramid.

Unlike the bundled basalt columns back home, this pyramid looked to be made of smooth, seamless stone. However, the glittering Dragonstone looked just like Makeda's Tear. While the Resonance had lulled a bit on the sea journey, it pulsated just as strongly here as it did back home. Maybe that was why Adept Melas and the other missing Mystics had come here.

Did the strong Resonance make magic easier, as all the books claimed? Brehane would test that theory. With a sidelong glance at Teacher Dawit, she grunted out several syllables and opened her hand. A cold, purple flame sprung to life in her palm. Though fatigue crept into her limbs, the Pyromancy didn't drain her like it had on the ship ride over, where she'd used it to shut up a sailor who didn't know his place.

Cassius stared at her in wide-eyed wonder. "I am quite fascinated."

"Brehane is only a Biomancer. Watch what a Pyromancer can do!" Makeda's eyes lit up.

The blood burning in Brehane's cheeks was a reminder of her own Pyromancer heritage. How dare Makeda lie like that!

Teacher Dawit glared at the two of them, but the ugly *assama* waved him off. She barked out similar words in the language of Shallow Magic. A green flame danced in her hand, but shifted from red to purple and finally a luminous blue. She winked. "See? Like the color of your right eye. The Dragon's Eye."

"And yet, not as beautiful as yours." Cassius dipped his chin.

Brehane's chest squeezed tighter. In insulting her Biomancer tribe and flaunting her power, Makeda was winning the race to mount this most intriguing man. Well, if he thought dancing colors were impressive, wait until they both saw her latest experiment: fusing Pyromancy with the simple Biomancy spell.

Brehane snorted. Now, now. It would be foolish to reveal this magic to her rival over something so trivial. Not to mention, fighting over a man just distracted her from finding Adept Melas, and the ultimate goal of restoring her tribe's honor.

She turned to Cassius. "You must live here because the pyramid makes Divining easier."

The Diviner looked up from where he was ogling Makeda. "I've never left the city, so I wouldn't know."

"Never left?" Makeda arched that furry caterpillar of an eyebrow.

Cassius gazed at the pyramid. "It is my family's sacred duty to protect the pyramid. The elf angel's Last Command—"

Brehane recited the line from history: "*Keep well the pyramids, reminders though they may be of your enslavement...*"

"*...lest the orc gods return on their flaming chariots,*" he finished. "Most of the signores are descended from the heroes of the War of Ancient Gods, who swore to obey the Last Command. Unfortunately, despite the wealth their prestige has brought them, they no longer take it seriously."

She turned back to the pyramid. Up close, it appeared as if it were made of huge, smooth stones. On the side of the access road stood a grey metal statue, rising head and shoulders above passersby despite crouching on one knee, opposite hand to the ground. Its free arm was bent at the elbow, as if punching with its spiked knuckles. Its horned head had no nose or mouth, just lusterless crystal eyes. A beggar, head covered by a hood, huddled in its shadow.

She turned to Cassius. "What is that?"

He tore his gaze away from Makeda and to the statue. A smile blossomed on his pretty face. "These are the remains of Konkistor's Iron Avatar. My ancestor Helio, Seer for the last Arkothi Emperor, witnessed its descent from the heavens during the Hellstorm."

The Hellstorm! The statue didn't look three hundred years old, though it certainly resembled paintings of Maher, God of War. Brehane squinted. Puncture marks marred each of its major joints. "In ancient times, not even the elves with their sorcery and magic weapons could defeat Maher's Avatar. How could humans with no magic do such damage?"

Cassius searched her expression. "Helio's memoirs claim the Elf Angel Aralas returned that night and defeated the Iron Avatar with magic rapiers. It fell on this spot, and it was too heavy to move."

Teacher Dawit pointed to a series of jagged gashes on its calf. "These, too?"

He shook his head. "Over the last decades, Ayuri Paladins have come on pilgrimages to the pyramid. They test their *naga*s on it."

Brehane's shoulders tensed. Dishonorable Paladins. They'd betrayed her people before the

Hellstorm. Now they vandalized a statue. "Of course they would. They are nothing but rogues and bandits."

"No, no." Cassius waved his hands back and forth. "We allow it, and only in that spot. They pay a fee that funds the pyramid's honor guard. And in the event the avatar reawakens, or another one comes, we know what weapons can damage it."

Brehane pursed her lips. It was doubtful Paladins would risk their hides for anyone besides their own people.

As the carriage drew closer to the monument, the Resonance of the Universe quieted. A cold shiver crawled up Brehane's spine.

"You feel it, too." Cassius draped an arm over her. "I cannot Divine in close proximity to it."

Despite the satisfaction of seeing Makeda pout, Brehane shuddered. To be cut off from the Resonance, stripped of magic, would be horrible. "I would have the Paladins hack it apart and haul it away."

Cassius shrugged. "It's not bad, actually. Sometimes I enjoy the quiet."

She searched his eyes. Beyond his pretty face, the man was full of surprises. Still, when the carriage passed, the Resonance of the Universe returned, louder than ever. Her shoulders relaxed.

Kirala's book vibrated in Brehane's pouch in her lap, startling her. Teacher Dawit, Makeda, and Cassius all stared.

Heat rushed to Brehane's cheeks. She reached for the pouch, but paused. The book was her secret. She settled her hands in her lap, even if her fingers itched to see what was undoubtedly a new entry.

"Stop here," Cassius ordered the driver.

The carriage eased to a halt, providing a view of the pyramid plaza. Hundreds of men in shiny metal cuirasses and baggy red pantaloons stood in neat rows, poleaxes held at attention.

"Just why are we stopping here?" Makeda yawned.

Brehane glared at her. Leave it to that *assama* to be rude.

Ignoring Makeda, Cassius jabbed a finger at two burly men in black longcoats. "You there. You are not allowed in this district."

Brehane studied the two men. Nothing distinguished them from any other Estomari, save for their poor taste in colors.

Both of their eyes roved over the carriage, pausing on her and Makeda, then Dawit. They leaned their heads close to one another, whispering. They tipped their hats and skulked off back the way the carriage had just come.

"Who were they?" Brehane asked.

Cassius frowned. "Mafia."

It wasn't a familiar word. She tilted her head. "What is that?"

"Crime families. A blight on our beautiful city. They usually keep to their own territory, but they've been more brazen lately." His eyes stared off for a second.

Brehane gestured at all the soldiers lounging in front of the pyramid. Many leaned on spears, and some didn't seem to care about their disheveled armor. "Why don't those men run them off?"

"They are there to protect against orc attacks, not vagrants or thugs." Cassius laughed. "But that's a good idea."

Leave it to men not to go above and beyond their duty, nor to have the creativity to consider multiple tasks. Brehane rolled her eyes.

"One moment." Cassius wagged his fingers at the lines of soldiers, his lips moving. He then looked up, a scowl melting. "I need to gather information about the honor guard before tonight's reception."

On his signal, the carriage set off again. Brehane craned her head as the road from the pyramid lengthened, but the superstructure itself didn't seem to get any smaller.

"Here we are." Cassius gestured up ahead.

Brehane followed the motion. She gasped. So focused had she been on the pyramid, she'd missed the rows of enormous mansions, all surrounded by white stone walls rising to the height of a man. Back home in Bahir, she'd passed the villas of wealthy merchants and plantation owners, but even the largest of those was half the size of these grand concrete manors with vaulting decorative columns. And there were so many in one place.

Servants dressed in the same drab livery as Cassius opened a gilded gate, each bar spiraling upward and ending in a disk. The carriage wheels clunked over white pavestones on a path that led around a fountain until they arrived at the front doors.

The driver dismounted and opened the carriage door. Cassius slid past her and hopped out. "My lady."

Taking his offered hand, she jumped off. She pulled him toward the house, but he held firm. Turning in a circle, he took Makeda's hand as well. "My second lady."

Makeda pouted, putting her infuriatingly beautiful lips on full display. "Not your first lady?"

Cassius bowed his head. "Second only in seating arrangements, but equally first in my heart."

Forgotten in the carriage, Teacher Dawit frowned, no doubt jealous of this beautiful man. Perhaps he regretted not taking his chance to share his seed when he was still young and handsome.

A man emerged from the mansion with a tight bow.

Cassius nodded in acknowledgement. "How are the preparations for tonight, Patrizio?"

This Patrizio must be some kind of important servant. He straightened. "The dining hall is ready, and the chefs are almost finished in the kitchens, though they are waiting for you to taste things and put on any final touches."

Cassius' expression lit up, and he turned to face them. "I can't wait for you to try Estomari delicacies. You have some time before we eat, so please, rest and freshen up. Now, if you will excuse me, I must visit the kitchens. Patrizio, please take Mister Dawit, Lady Brehane, and Lady Makeda to their rooms and have the servants bring some wash basins."

Brehane clasped the jewel around her neck with her free hand. It was time to take a risk. She squeezed Cassius' hand. "Mister Cassius, won't you show me around your beautiful gardens?"

Cassius' eyes rounded, and he exchanged glances with Patrizio. "Patrizio, you go ahead with Mr. Dawit, and—"

"Take me, too." Makeda pulled Cassius' hand to her chest, and glared at Brehane.

Brehane gritted her teeth. The ugly *assama*. A forgetfulness spell might distract Makeda long enough for the two of them to get away for a private walk in the gardens, but she'd probably recognize the Neuromancy and use a counterspell. It would escalate into the petty magic squabbles Makeda had so enjoyed, ever since Brehane had taken the missing Adept Melas to bed. Ultimately, it would just tire them both out.

Cassius' cold, sweating hand in hers suggested they'd scared him off. Neither of them would be mounting him tonight. Then, he looked to Patrizio and lifted his chin. "You go ahead with Mister Dawit. I'll be right up with the ladies."

Brehane's heart flitted. There was still a chance. She watched as Teacher Dawit cast an unfriendly glance at Cassius before following Patrizio into the house.

Cassius looked from her to Makeda. "Are you sure you're not too tired?"

"Never too tired to see beautiful things, Mister Cassius." Brehane leaned into his shoulder and looked up through her lashes at Makeda.

"You're acting like a warthog in heat," Makeda said in their language.

Brehane smiled. "You're just jealous."

Makeda barked a few syllables while reaching into a pouch at her waist and flinging some sand.

The grains rained on Brehane, and she braced herself against the sleep magic with a quick grunt of a ward. Makeda had played the stupid prank often enough on her that she'd recognized the magic right away. The enchantment washed over her. Blood rushed from her head and darkness crowded the edge of her vision. She shot out a hand to catch...

...Cassius. His arm draped under hers. "Are you okay?"

How embarrassing, to be upstaged by Makeda, of all people. Brehane jabbed a finger at her. "This *assama* tried to make me faint."

Cassius looked between them and then smiled. "Now, now, no need to fight over whatever it is between you."

Was that it? No anger for attacking her with magic, no matter how mundane it might be? Brehane stared at him.

His expression softened. "Lady Brehane, you do not look well. Allow me to take you to your room to rest."

If Makeda's mouth could gape any wider, Brehane would stuff a Geomanced stone in. It was tempting as it was. Now, though, she had the advantage. She wobbled on her legs and leaned into Cassius. As he guided her up onto the manor's stoop, she looked back at her rival and stuck out her tongue.

Makeda's eyes narrowed. "No Neuromancy," she said in their language, before following.

As if Brehane needed to charm him. She'd already won. With Cassius' unnecessary support, they passed through the front door. Her home could've fit in the vaulting foyer, which boasted marble floors and a fountain in the center. A white stone statue of a half-naked woman rose from the rustling waters, the likeness to a real human unlike any sculpture in Aksumi lands. In her hands was a fist-sized globe.

Patrizio strode in, bowing.

Cassius recognized him with a nod. "I trust Mister Dawit is taken care of. Please take Lady Makeda to her chambers."

A frown cut across Makeda's face, but she reluctantly took Patrizio's gloved hand and allowed him to take her up a grand stairway of wood.

Leaving the prey alone with a predator.

Energy growing, Brehane smiled to herself as she studied the graceful lines and beautiful face of the statue, which bore a strong resemblance to Cassius. "Who is that? What is she holding?"

"That is my ancestor Tatiana, the First Diviner. She holds a Starburst, a gift from Aralas."

A starburst! With Brehane's interest in Dragonstones, she'd scoured the university's library to learn about them. In millennia past, when orcs and elves first battled for supremacy over Tivara, the elves had uncovered starbursts in glittering caves. These magnified the power of their magic, and almost turned the tide of the war until the Year of the Second Sun. She edged over to get a better look, though slowly enough that she wouldn't lose contact with Cassius.

"The same Helio who'd witnessed the Iron Avatar commissioned it from one of the premier sculptors of the time. It's been passed from father to son, in this house, for six generations."

Brehane searched his eyes. How strange it was, for a legacy to be passed along a patrilineal line. Whereas no one could question a mother's claim to a child, how could anyone be certain of a father? Though... "What happened to the Starburst? Is that still in your family?"

"No." He shook his head, and frowned. "When the Arkothi Empire conquered the Estomar, the Sorcerer Imperator took our starburst and set it in his crown."

She nodded in slow bobs. "The Crown of Arkos, which helped fuel the Sorcerer Imperator's magic."

"We call it the Crown of the Sundered Empire, lost during the Hellstorm." He gave a wry smile. "Arkothi peasants pine for the day when an Emperor returns with the crown."

"They've forgotten about the hundred years of war."

"More than a hundred. Now come." He withdrew his arm from under hers and took her hand. "The reception won't start for another hour. You should rest."

Cassius guided her up the stairs and down a hallway until they came to an open door. He released her hand, though a finger brushed across her palm and down her wrist.

The jolt might have stopped her heart if it weren't beating so rapidly.

He gestured toward the room. "Your room, until we begin our journey to find your lost friend. I will have Patrizio bring you to the reception once my guests arrive."

He started to turn.

Brehane seized his wrists and pulled him into the room. She kicked her shoes off as she backed over plush red carpets towards a fluffy-looking bed. He brought his face close, like an alchemist sniffing a potion. How strange. She kept backing up until she fell into the luxurious covers, pulling him down onto her. Unable to retreat further, all she could was turn her head to keep his mouth off her nose. Was he trying to eat her?

It was unlike anything a man should do during a bedding. No, even the most fervent of men would just lie there and be taken care of. Cassius, however... His lips brushed down her neck, stopping to peck every few inches before settling in the divot between her collarbones. Every nerve lit up, zipping down her spine like an Energist's lightning bolt. As his hands reached under her dress and swept across her bare skin, heat bloomed inside of her like a fireblast.

* * *

Brehane stared up at the smooth white ceiling as she lay alone, drowning in the cloud-like bed and her own failure. She might've been faking fatigue from Makeda's sleep spell before, but now she was exhausted from trying to get Cassius to spill his seed inside her. Never before had she failed to bring a man to climax in a few minutes, let alone a half hour. She'd mounted him so poorly, he'd even tried to rock his hips and set a rhythm. How humiliating.

He must've been equally disappointed. How could he not be? He'd left, maybe to try his luck with Makeda, leaving Brehane to wallow in self-loathing.

And for what? He didn't climax, so she couldn't Biomance whatever real magic he had. She was no closer to completing the mission, no closer to becoming an Initiate, no closer to rediscovering the higher levels of Biomancy.

This voyage was an utter failure so far. Except...she reached for her travelling dress, unceremoniously crumpled up to the side. He'd actually tried to undress her, but she'd removed it herself. She now pulled Kirala's *Dragonstones* book out and opened it.

The new illustration depicted Tatiana's Heart, which sat atop the pyramid. With countless facets and tapered toward the top, it looked exactly the same as Makeda's Tear back home.

While fascinating, it didn't help her in the quest to find Melas, or contribute to the revival of Biomancy. With a sigh, she rose out of bed and gazed at her naked form in an actual mirror that was taller than her. She was beautiful, with better curves than even the statue in the foyer. How could she have failed with Cassius? How—

What was the mark on her neck? She bent closer to the mirror to find a dark splotch on her skin. She brought her hand up to the discoloration. Right, that was where his lips had sucked, like an Aeromancer slurping up energy from the air. As strange as it was, it had felt good. By Makeda's Eye, it had felt better than good.

But he'd left a mark, like a Summoner etching a ward into a demon's flesh. How dare he? Power cackled in her fingers. It was time to punish the cretin.

CHAPTER 8:

Shades of the Enemy

As they left the whorehouse, Sameer growled at the impertinent little half-elf. "Mute? And you picked my pockets, didn't you?"

The shadows cast from the light-bauble lamps hanging above the streets made her grin look demonic. "Had you done the talking, we wouldn't have found anything out. Sometimes a little silver goes further than black and blue. Or red. Now come along." She waved back toward Master Anish, who hovered at the edge of the district.

His expression was inscrutable, and he showed no sign of crossing the street. That calm was everything a Paladin should be.

What Sameer should be. He unclenched his fists, unaware of having clenched them in the first place. Jie was right, of course. His heart sank into his stomach. Earlier, he'd slain three men in anger, almost killed a fourth. Even with the honor of being apprenticed to Elder Gitika, he'd failed to live up to the most basic principles of Paladinhood. The forfeiture of his sword had been well-deserved.

Still, it felt like he'd lost an arm.

"Perk up," Jie said. "We'll find your friend."

Right, Sohini. Squaring his shoulders, he took long strides in the direction the prostitutes had indicated. Drunken revelers made way for him. Most glared or made snide comments about his jammies—whatever jammies were—as he passed. They had to be close now.

"Wait, Sameer." Jie struggled to keep up with him. "Let's do it my way."

Her way entailed picking pockets, cavorting with prostitutes, and buying lamb gyros. Still, she'd done even better than the supposedly best Diviner in the Estomar in finding leads on Sohini.

"Fine, but hurry." Sameer loosened his fists again. Sohini had grown up in a brothel, and would've suffered her mother's fate had she not been discovered by the Paladin scouts. If this De Lucca held her as a sex slave, he'd better hope Sameer didn't have his sword back by the time they met.

He gritted his teeth. No, he couldn't think like that. Revenge wasn't the Paladin way.

Jie grabbed his arm again, just before they turned the corner.

His reflexes should've sensed it. So intent was he on rescuing Sohini, and reprimanding himself, he'd lost his focus. He'd never become a full-fledged Paladin, let alone a great master like Elder Gitika, if he kept failing at every aspect of Paladinhood. He took a deep breath and held an image of her in his mind. Patient. Dignified. His fists loosened. Again.

Jie peeked around the corner, then turned back. "A Bovyan is standing guard by the door. After your little escapade earlier, I would wager he already knows about you."

The gears in his head whirred like a dwarf steam engine. "Wait. The Bovyans we fought before worked for the Mafia. This one works for a signore. I thought they were enemies."

Jie nodded. "You're smarter than you've acted. The gyro merchant said both sides are hiring them."

"De Lucca is conspiring with the Mafia, then."

Jie sucked on her lower lip. "Hmmm. We can't count out that possibility. Maybe he's positioning himself for if the Mafia take over the city. As a dealer in flesh, he's closer to them than legitimate businesses like...fortune telling." Sarcasm hung in her voice on the last words, and she smirked.

"Signore Larusso was an honorable man," Sameer said.

"Sure." Jie shrugged. "What I don't understand is the Bovyans. Unless their coffers are dwindling, the Teleri Empire wouldn't just rent its warriors out. They want something bigger."

"Let's find out." He started toward De Lucca's whorehouse.

"Wait." Grabbing him, she lifted her chin back the way they'd come. "There's an alley. I'm going to see if there's a way in through the back. You wait here and watch the front door while I take a look around. In the very unlikely event that a commotion breaks out, get your master and come help me."

Sameer sighed. Relegated to a lookout. Maybe that was for the better. A voice in his head that sounded suspiciously like Elder Gitika advised patience. Setting his fingers into the *mudra* for wisdom, he closed his eyes and pictured her in his mind. So stately and calm. The vibrations of the world percolated through him, settling his nerves. Yes, this way—her way, the way of the Paladin—would yield better results than rushing headlong into a whorehouse.

He opened his eyes and watched as the impertinent half-elf slunk back and ducked into the alley. Had he not tracked her the whole time—and had she not been wearing the frilly pink dress—he might have lost her wispy figure, the way she moved through night's shadows. There was more to this little pickpocket than met the eye. She certainly had the skillset for her stated goal of solving mysteries, but it was doubtful her goals were as noble as finding missing people. For now, those objectives might intersect with his, but for all he knew, she could be just as mercenary as the Bovyans...or even the Paladin order's deadliest enemy: the Golden Scorpions.

He turned back to the corner and looked. The line of two-story concrete row houses looked elegant compared to the rest of the district, their architecture reminiscent of old pictures of the Arkothi Empire. The second building boasted columns supporting a triangular roof. Purple banners, each with a rearing golden lion, hung from the roofline down to the first story. A Bovyan in a dark surcoat stood by a heavy-looking front door. Four tall windows with actual glass flanked both sides of the door. Each framed a comely young woman, sensuously dancing in a revealing dress.

Setting his fingers in a *mudra* for modesty, Sameer shielded his eyes from the inappropriate behavior.

Maybe not so inappropriate. Sohini had excelled at belly dancing, learned in her childhood at a brothel, and she claimed it helped her sword-fighting skills. Considering she was one of the best warriors, perhaps it had merit. He snuck a peek.

A fellow with a sleeveless, embroidered longcoat and green stockings approached the guard. With his delicate hands and elegant manner, he looked out of place among the boisterous revelers. Unlike the other men in the streets, who whistled and jeered, he ignored the women, and tipped a hat adorned with a bright red feather to the guard.

With a thump of a fist on his chest, the Bovyan stepped aside and held the door open.

Sameer clenched his fists. The man hadn't so much as peeked at the dancing women, and the guard just let him in. He wasn't here for a tumble in the sheets. It had to be Signore De Lucca, who'd probably hired the

Bovyans to kidnap Sohini and force her into this horrible life. The voice in his head, which again sounded like Master Gitika, urged patience.

Yes, patience.

No—Jie had no way of knowing De Lucca was here, which could get her into serious trouble.

Or he was just rationalizing. Well, at the very least, he'd have to create a diversion. Sameer wriggled his fingers. Even without a weapon, he had the Vibrations to draw upon. They were stronger in this city, where a pyramid still stood, than around the ruins of the pyramid on Ayudra Island where he'd trained. A single Bovyan, armed or not, would be no match.

Squinting back, he found Master Anish in the same spot outside the district. Sameer motioned toward the whorehouse. When the master didn't explicitly gesture for him to stay put, Sameer turned the corner, marched past a few drunken sailors, and approached the guard. "I want to speak with Signore De Lucca."

With a smirk, the Bovyan crossed his arms and stepped in front of the door. He towered over Sameer. "The signore is not here. If you are not here to share a woman's company for the night, begone."

Elder Gitika might use a Paladin Command to influence the guard, but Sameer's own proficiency at the skill was poor. It would also leave him exhausted, whether or not it worked. He reached for the door. His martial reflexes kicked in just as the Bovyan raised a fist. To his perception, the punch hung in the air for eternity. It travelled so slowly that Sameer caught it, twisted his hips, and sent the brute tumbling to the ground. A swift heel to the temple knocked him out.

Time lurched back to normal. The women in the windows stopped dancing. A few pointed, while others covered their mouths. On the street, passersby paused and gawked.

Let them. Sameer pushed open the door and stomped into an airy foyer. It took up the entire front of the building. The ceiling vaulted high above, likely reaching the roof, like the audience chamber of a maharaja's villa. The women in the windows all fled up the staircases on either side of the foyer to a mezzanine. His feet sunk into the plush wool carpet, which undoubtedly came from his homeland in Vadara, given the gold-and-blue symbols.

Beneath the mezzanine, another Bovyan emerged from an archway. Gaze locking on Sameer, he drew a longsword. "If you know what is good for you, you will turn around and leave."

Sameer held up a hand. "I don't want any trouble, I'm just—"

The Bovyan's eyes locked on the front doors. The ones Sameer had left open, providing a view of the guard he'd knocked out.

The world slowed as the blade glided toward his outstretched hand. Sameer lowered his arm, out of the weapon's path. As the Bovyan trudged toward him with a sluggish backstroke to the neck, Sameer stepped in close. He drove his shoulder into the brute's elbow while catching his wrist. A pivot on his foot dislocated the man's elbow.

Time resumed to normal as the sword plunked onto the carpet and the Bovyan fell face-first. Grunting, he rolled over and cradled his elbow.

A female scream pierced the air.

Sameer turned.

By the archway stood a pretty woman in her thirties. Her lips trembled, but with a deep breath, she found her voice. "Good evening, kind sir. I am Elisa. Are you here to make a reservation for Prince Dhananad?"

How could she think he was associated with the leader of the Paladin's archenemies, the Golden Scorpions! Sameer glared. "I am a Paladin. I do not work for the Madurans."

She curtsied. "My apologies, kind sir. His Scorpion bodyguards have been making arrangements for the prince's...pleasure."

Steam might have been coming out of Sameer's ears, his head was so hot. The prince was here? With Scorpions? Had they used their powers to negate Sohini's, and captured her for their degenerate prince's pleasure? "The Scorpions are deserters to our order. They hide behind masks."

She curtsied again. "Again, my sincerest apologies. I just saw how skilled a fighter you were..."

By Vanya's sword, he'd let his passions get the better of him. Just like those vile traitors. Of course she'd mistake him for one of them. Conjuring a dignified image of Elder Gitika in his head, he bowed his head and set his hands into the *mudra* for apology. "De Lucca. Please tell him I am here to see him."

Lines formed across her forehead. "He's not here."

"I saw—"

Colors flashed from the mezzanine. Sameer looked up. De Lucca looked back at him, eyes wide. Sameer sidestepped the hostess. In three strides, he reached the steps. He darted up. De Lucca turned and ran toward the closest room as fast as the clopping wood soles of his platforms could take him.

Which wasn't very fast.

Sameer clamped a hand down on the man's shoulder and spun him around. "Where is Sohini?"

The man's mouth was gaping in a silent scream, but now he closed it and chewed on his lips. He cocked his head. "So-Who?"

"Sohini! The Ayuri lady. What have you done with her?"

"I...I am here to see Maria. I don't know any Ayuri whores."

Whore? After her childhood, Sohini would never willingly sell herself. Sameer tightened his fist. It was all he could do not to punch De Lucca into oblivion.

Flinching, the man put his hands up.

"Stop!" The hostess climbed the steps. "That isn't Signore De Lucca. He's just Maria's client."

Sameer took a deep breath and drew on the Vibrations to calm his racing heart. A Paladin wasn't supposed to fight in anger, only cool objectivity. His fist loosened. He'd almost punched an innocent—well, not exactly innocent—man. He would've let Elder Gitika down, yet again.

Maintaining eye contact, the mistress helped the man to his feet. "Your Ayuri friend came here several weeks ago, but she didn't stay very long."

Sameer blew out a sigh. Of course these people wouldn't be able to restrain a Paladin, even an apprentice, for very long. Unless they drugged her with gooseweed. It didn't grow in these lands, but its smell had hung in the air around the tavern district. "Do you know where she went?"

The woman shook her head. "I'm sorry, no. I just run this house."

A dead end. Or maybe not. Apparently, De Lucca had many houses. Drawing on the Vibrations, he Commanded, "Tell me where I can find Signore De Lucca." Energy drained from his arms and legs, so much that his knees wobbled. He fought to keep from collapsing. There had been too many syllables in the Command. He should've known better...had known better, when he'd confronted the Bovyan out front. It probably hadn't even worked.

Her eyes glazed over. "He's at a meeting over at Signore Larusso's mansion tonight."

"The fortune teller!" Sameer's fists squeezed so tight, his nails might've drawn blood. No wonder Larusso had given them the runaround. He was in on the prostitution ring with De Lucca and the crime families.

Limbs still recovering from his use of a Command, he trudged down the steps.

At the bottom, the Bovyan was unconscious and Jie was rummaging through his things. She looked up. "I talked to some of the women who work here. Your friend isn't in this house, but they think Signore De Lucca would know. He's at—"

"Signore Larusso's mansion."

Jie's eyes widened. "Yes. Perhaps you are smarter than you look."

Or maybe not. He'd knocked out one man, dislocated another's arm, threatened a third, been mistaken for a Golden Scorpion, and had to draw on Vibrations to accomplish the same thing the half-elf had through asking nicely. Still, she didn't have to know. He forced a smile. "Let's catch up with De Lucca at Signore Larusso's villa."

Jie held up a hand. "I doubt he will openly confess to kidnapping your friend. Let's split up: you and Master Anish visit Signore Larusso. I will investigate his personal office."

Sameer stroked his chin. It sounded like a good use of their limited resources. "Very well."

Jie slipped out into the night. Sameer took a last look at the foyer, the site of yet another one of his failures as a Paladin, and followed her.

Though she couldn't have been more than a few steps ahead of him, she was nowhere to be seen when he stepped out. He scanned the streets and found only groups of drunken men. With a shrug, he headed back to where he'd left Master Anish.

"Where is the half-elf?" the master's eyebrows scrunched together.

"She went to investigate Signore De Lucca's office."

Master Anish gave a slow nod. "Why?"

"We learned that Sohini stayed in one of Signore De Lucca's brothels, but she has since disappeared."

Master Anish's lips tightened.

"Also, it appears that Madura's Prince Dhananad is visiting Tokahia."

"What?" The master's eyebrows clashed in alarm.

"He frequents the brothel where Sohini was staying." Sameer's stomach churned. Prince Dhananad's reputation for depravity was well-known throughout Ayuri lands. "De Lucca is at Signore Cassius' villa. I would like to question him."

Master Anish nodded. "You go first. I must check in on Elder Gitika. I will rejoin you afterward."

CHAPTER 9:

Mixed Signals

Cassius greeted his guests in a haze, thoughts dwelling on the disastrous lovemaking with Brehane. If it could be called lovemaking. It had been too easy to get her into bed, with no smooth words or foreplay required. She'd resisted his kisses, ripped off her own clothes, and got straight to straddling him. Rarely had he failed to bring a woman to climax, but from the wrinkles in her brow and her pursed lips, Brehane clearly hadn't enjoyed the experience. Her luscious curves pressing against him when she collapsed after a futile half-hour did little to excite him.

"Signore Cassius?"

Cassius shook the fog out of his head. How absurd, to get tied into a knot over a woman. It wasn't as though he was seventeen again, when Julia had ripped his heart out, taken a part of his soul, and all of his money with it. He looked over to Patrizio, who'd just spoken.

Patrizio pointed with his eyes to the next guest, and mouthed, *Signore De Lucca.*

Cassius followed the steward's subtle gaze.

Dressed in a sleeveless longcoat made from Cathayi silk and Estomari lace, face powdered to smooth perfection, De Lucca made for a striking figure—despite his short stature and waifish frame—as he swept in ahead of his entourage. He eschewed a hat, allowing his long mane of black hair to tumble down his back. Keen, brown eyes glinted with the business acumen that had allowed the man to rise from poverty to Tokahia's social elite. His name had spread to other Estomari city-states as rapidly as that of the most elite Diviners.

Behind him sashayed in a dozen of his whores, as well as two Bovyan bodyguards. Those brutes in the manor… Cassius' gut tightened. They looked like bulls in a glassware shop, not to mention they were a reminder of the deal he'd made with the Bovyan, Phobos, to keep the Aksumi here for some nefarious reason.

Still, he and De Lucca clasped wrists. The signore's only piece of jewelry, a ring of brushed pewter, felt so icy on Cassius' forearm that he almost jerked back. Instead, he bowed his head as a host should. "Signore, welcome back to my home."

De Lucca laughed like a bow raking across violin strings at the wrong angle. "Many thanks for having me. I've brought some entertainment." He gestured back to his courtesans.

Cassius studied each one with forced nonchalance. They all had impeccable make-up and wore revealing yet classy outfits. Their smiles ranged from sultry to innocent, and they moved with a tasteful sensuousness. Unlike common streetwalkers from the Mafia-held sections of the entertainment district, they exuded elegance. No, these weren't normal whores, and they'd made De Lucca rich.

Still, even if there was little better in this world than the touch of a beautiful woman, there was no challenge in paying for it. Cassius glanced toward the top of the staircase. Brehane had yet to come down, probably disappointed by his poor performance. Then again, Makeda hadn't emerged either. There had to be a story behind their mutual dislike, something having to do with Pyromancy and Biomancy.

Not his problem. Let the Bovyans deal with it, whatever they had planned, and he'd be a step closer to eradicating the Mafia and their threat to the pyramid. He turned back to his guest. "Signore De Lucca, I hear you are constructing a new villa on the outskirts of town."

The Teleri guards stared. De Lucca turned his head, brow furrowed for a split second before his expression eased.

His high-pitched voice could pierce eardrums. "Yes. I want to start a plantation."

Cassius kept his face impassive. Fanaya the Farmer occupied an auspicious seat in the heavens, foretelling bumper harvests for the next few years. There would be more than enough food flooding the markets, making agriculture less profitable. Perhaps this young upstart should stick with peddling flesh. He bowed again and extended a hand to the banquet hall. "Make yourself welcome, Signore De Lucca. I—"

A swirl of black flashed on the mezzanine. Cassius looked up.

Makeda strutted to the top of the steps, the high slit in her black silk gown revealing a shapely leg sheathed in black fishnet hose. The dress' plunging neckline laid bare the valley between her breasts, and the tight waistline emphasized the sweeping curve of her hips.

Cassius' heart picked up a few beats. It would be a shame to turn her over to the Bovyans...but a small price to pay for exterminating the crime families and preventing the orc gods' return. He nudged Patrizio. "You chose nicely for her. I'm surprised it fit so well."

"*Fits* is hardly the word I would choose." Patrizio's gawk replaced his usual professional stoicism.

Makeda descended, one leg crossing the other, the sway of her hips mesmerizing.

A smile quirked on Cassius' lips, unbidden, as he followed every move. Of the two ladies, Makeda had been the more boisterous. An annoying trait, but that was now overshadowed by her physical perfection. If Brehane had been the antipasti, Makeda would be the main course tonight; and this time, he wouldn't fail to bring her to climactic bliss.

"Your mouth, Master Larusso," Patrizio whispered, leaning in.

Heat burned in Cassius' cheeks as he closed his mouth. Flashing his most smoldering gaze, he strode to the head of the stairs and extended his hand to meet Makeda's. "My lady."

"Your *first* lady." She grinned, chocolate eyes sparkling.

Her palm was so hot in his. He nodded. "Of course, my first lady. Please let me introduce you to—" He looked left and right. De Lucca and his entourage had already headed off toward the banquet hall. He pointed his chin at them. "Come, meet my guests."

An Estomari lady might tilt her head and bat her lashes, waiting for the man to offer an elbow, but Makeda tugged him along.

Perhaps forwardness ran in their family. Maybe she'd lead him to the bedroom this way, too. He looked her up and down as they walked. "The dress fits so perfectly, as if it were made for you."

"I had to make some adjustments." Her laugh might be confused for a donkey's bray, and in that, she might be more closely related to De Lucca than to Brehane.

It was all Cassius could do not to grit his teeth. "Oh? You are skilled with needle and thread, then?"

Her brows furrowed. "Of course not. Tailoring is men's work. I used a Transmuting spell to shrink it in some places, enlarge it in others."

Like the bust and hips. Apparently Aksumi sorcery had mundane uses. However, it was unlikely that the Teleri would agree to a war on the Mafia just to have Mystics make alterations to their armor and uniforms.

Perhaps the two Bovyans would show their hand when they saw his dark-skinned guests.

Indeed, as soon as they passed by the columns separating the central hall from the circular banquet room, the bodyguards flanking De Lucca stared. Fixing his gaze on her, one leaned over and whispered in the other's ear. Then again, if they were plotting, so were the Signores. Every single man was ogling Makeda.

If she noticed them, or even the orchestra playing their violins and cellos, she certainly didn't show any sign of it. Instead, she seemed more preoccupied with the transparent dome, which provided a stunning view of the heavens.

She gestured to it. "How is this even possible? What is it made of?"

Cassius waved at it. "It's the lens of a dragon's eye."

She stared at him, eyes wide and smile wider. "How?"

"In antiquity, the orcs turned on their dragon allies in the Dragonpurge. They slew the great dragon Grellax on this spot. His bones stretch below ground, from his tail at my megalith circle to his head here. The Elf Angel Aralas raised the lens and set it on these columns."

Her gaze swept over each column, nodding each time. "They are aligned the same way as your megalith."

He nodded. "You have a good eye."

She grinned and pointed to the mosaic floor, the hexagonal tiles depicting the continent. "The map is distorted. From the size of your city, you apparently believe yourself the center of the world."

"Of course not, my lady." He shook his head. Still, it was amazing she recognized the map at all, since the size of each region shrunk in relation to its distance from the city. Her homeland was a sliver at the edge.

She looked back up at the dome. "It's beautiful."

"Nothing but the best for my guests," he said. It was amazing she'd noticed the column alignment. It allowed him to glean the stars' secrets during these meetings, where so much of the city-state's policies were decided. Right now, Fortuna danced with the red star of Konkistor, indicating an auspicious time to discuss military affairs. He gestured toward his other guests. "Come, let me introduce you to the rulers of this city."

Her eyes shifted to the gathering, stopping on De Lucca's whores. They mingled among the signores, some sitting in men's laps, while others guided hands toward bare flesh. Now that the initial shock of Makeda's grand entrance had subsided, the men resumed their fondling. One of the courtesans fed a signore a grape, lip-to-lip, while another dabbed wine on her neck from a crystal carafe for her client to lick off. Stimulating certainly, but all paid for.

Cassius smirked. Whores' services weren't worth a bent copper. He studied Makeda's expression. Eyebrows clashing together, she pressed her lips tight. He leaned over. "Do not worry, my first lady. I will let the signores know that you are here as my guest. They won't do anything brazen."

"Brazen?" She cocked her head. "No, I am just shocked by how easily they succumb to their advances."

He laughed. "They are paid to."

Understanding bloomed on her face. "They are... I don't know the word in your language. *Shermuta*."

Disdain hung heavier in her words than the hammer which Derkin used to forge the world. Yet who could blame these women, who were forced into this life by circumstances often beyond their control.

"Cassius!" Wispy as a paperwood tree, Signore Bianchi stood next to De Lucca and one of the Bovyans. With one gaunt arm draped over a courtesan, he used the other to beckon Cassius.

Makeda's hand in his, Cassius guided her over the marble floors, around the long central table laden with wines, grapes, and cheeses. "Signore Bianchi, thank you for coming tonight. Allow me to introduce one of my special guests, Makeda, daughter of Kidist, from the Aksumi Mystics' Conclave."

The men's eyes roved over her, Bianchi's with unconstrained lust, De Lucca like an equine merchant at a Kanin horse auction. The Bovyan's expression managed to mix both sentiments.

Pit forming in his stomach, Cassius pulled her closer.

If Makeda noticed, it didn't seem to bother her. If anything, her look was disinterested.

"You have exquisite taste." With a sweeping bow, De Lucca took Makeda's hand and kissed it. "I have a sister who is close to your age. You will have to come and have coffee while you are here. Signore Bianchi imports the best coffee beans from Levastya."

Makeda stared at her hand in his before meeting Cassius' gaze. She turned De Lucca's hand over and kissed it in return.

The room went silent for a few awkward seconds. Low murmurs and giggles erupted.

Bianchi cleared his throat. "Cassius, we were just discussing the pyramid honor guard."

"Yes, I was just there earlier. I know you want to reduce funding, but they look horribly unprepared. The only thing they're protecting is their purse strings." Cassius tugged his beard. "We're becoming lax in our sacred duty. The old legends say if the orcs ever regain control of all the pyramids, they'll summon –"

Bianchi waved a dismissive hand. "Thousand-year-old fairy tales. There haven't been armies of Altivorcs or Tivorcs marching on Tokahia in three hundred years. They're just roving bands of mercenaries, and certainly no threat to the pyramid. The orc gods won't be returning on their flaming chariots any time soon."

Makeda nodded. "And the prophecies say the Dragonstones need to be removed from atop *all* the pyramids. Even if all the others fell into the orcs' hands, they could never capture the Mystics' university in my homeland."

With a sigh, Cassius pointed to the heavens. "The star of Konkistor, God of the Orcs, brightens. In three years' time, it will reach peak luminosity, coinciding with the Godseye Conjunction and the return of the Golden Flock. It augurs great change. We should at least maintain, if not boost, the honor guard until then."

Bianchi shook his head. "We have real, immediate problems. The other city-states aren't paying their fair share for the pyramid's protection. The local merchant guilds want a tax cut. Now, the crime families are trying to expand their influence. We can't afford to waste money to feed, train, and pay a thousand men to lounge around an ancient relic that nobody cares about."

Cassius snorted. "I have it on good authority that the crime families want to control the pyramid."

De Lucca waved his hand up and down in a calming gesture. "I agree with you, Signore Cassius. I proposed to Signore Bianchi that we maintain the honor guard, but use Bovyans."

The last thing Tokahia needed was more Bovyans. Cassius' protest died on his lips as his eyes fell on De Lucca's entourage.

"May I introduce Captain Baros." De Lucca gestured to his guard.

The enormous man thumped his fist on his chest. "Honored, Signore Larusso. I have three hundred men in my cohort currently working for the Signores. Another hundred are employed by the crime families, but their contracts expire between tomorrow and two months from now. Beyond that, I can request a thousand more. We will work for food and half the pay of your current honor guard. We will take care of our own training, and I guarantee you that no orc warlock or Mafia enforcer will get close enough to spit on the pyramid."

"See?" Bianchi grinned. "We can reduce honor-guard expenditures by over half."

Cassius stroked his beard. A handful of brutes in the city as bodyguards was manageable, and actually made sense if they lived up to their deal and wiped out the Mafia. However, inviting a small army sounded like a monumentally bad idea...especially considering that they believed they had a Divine mandate to conquer all of the Arkoth and the Estomar. "It would be a logistical nightmare to bring them all here, and uh, see to their needs."

Captain Baros waved a hand. "We have a battalion stationed in Levastya. It would be just a couple weeks' march. As for our needs...." His eyes drifted from Makeda to De Lucca.

"I will take care of it." De Lucca bowed. "The plantations I am building will house them and grow their food."

Cassius studied De Lucca's inscrutable expression. The upstart did nothing unless he benefitted. The question was, how would he benefit from having a large company of Bovyans in Tokahia? In his ambitions, had he played into the Bovyans' hands?

De Lucca smiled. He'd come out of nowhere—his birthdate, birthplace, parents' names, everything secret. He claimed to be descended from the heroes sworn to protect the pyramid, but no amount of Divining had revealed anything about his past or future.

Cassius would redouble his efforts to find out more. Perhaps the invitation De Lucca had extended to Makeda to meet his sister could yield more information. Sometimes, women's idle banter revealed more than the Gods' Whispers.

A hush fell over the room, followed by more pointing and quiet murmurs. Cassius looked.

Brehane stood at the entrance. If Makeda had been stunning, Brehane was nothing short of Divine. Her gown's rose-gold mesh accentuated her brown skin. The elegant design hinted at the curves he'd explored just a couple of hours earlier, without revealing too much. Give her a sword and bow, and she might be mistaken for Solaris' shieldmaiden, Deena.

Her deep brown eyes searched the crowd before locking on him. Her expression contorted into a scowl.

In contrast, his own lips tugged up at the corners. The unfulfilled confusion he'd felt before melted away.

Makeda released his elbow and stomped toward her cousin.

* * *

Brehane had been hesitant to attend Cassius' reception, because if he wasn't going to spill his seed in her, he was simply a distraction from her goal of finding Melas and eventually restoring the Biomancers' honor.

Still, the thought that Makeda might succeed where she hadn't drew her like a demon to a summoning circle.

Now she surveyed the room, feeling ridiculously plain in the monochrome gown she'd found in the dressing room. Although shiny, it lacked the vibrant colors of the jackets, stockings, and hats the men wore. Like peacocks, they drew the eye, no doubt to win the attention of the women here. They, too, sported the most delightful colors, though the clothes covered very little. Even the musicians, playing exotic stringed instruments, wore bright jackets and pants.

She felt frumpy and underdressed, like a merchant or laborer back home.

At least Makeda, now tromping over, looked equally dull, even if the cut of her black dress exaggerated her curves better than an illusion. Brehane wiggled her fingers, ready to raise a ward against whatever the *assama* had planned.

Something was wrong. Makeda's creased brows looked less competitive and more confused. She took Brehane's hands in hers, in a surprisingly sisterly gesture. "Cousin, I don't know what to make of this reception."

Brehane scanned the room again. The dozen men were audacious, hands all over the giggling women. Such a lack of modesty. "Me either."

"The men are *shermuta*."

No wonder they were so brazen. They were paid to be so. Still, Cassius must've contracted the cheapest brothel in all of Tokahia. Other than Cassius, the dark-haired one he was talking to, and the two enormous soldiers, the other men were generally plain-looking to downright ugly, with plump bellies that even their colorful clothes couldn't hide. If she ever stooped so low as to pay for a man, it certainly wouldn't be one of these specimens.

Makeda lifted her chin towards Cassius, now striding toward them. "Cassius said these women rule the city, yet it's those men talking about armies and Mafia."

Brehane snorted. If she were to ever hire a *shermuta*, she couldn't imagine talking at all, let alone about soldiers. Makeda was probably playing some trick again.

Then, Cassius arrived at their side.

"You warthog!" Brehane flared her fingers and wiggled them, ready to summon a cold fire again.

He stepped back, eyes wide. "Lady Brehane, I, we..."

With her other hand, she pointed at the mark he'd left on her neck with his lips. "What is the meaning of this?"

Makeda stared at it, eyes narrowing to slits.

His gaze shifted from the bruise to Makeda and back again. "My lady, in the Estomar, such marks are tokens of affection."

"Affection?" Makeda gasped. "You didn't..."

Brehane's forehead scrunched together. Such strange customs, but indeed, looking around, several of the women had similar marks left by these *shermuta*.

Makeda, on the other hand, had none. A smile pulled at Brehane's lips. "Yes," she said in the Aksumi language, "he has already given himself to me." No need to tell her she had yet to receive his seed and Biomance it into energy.

The steward, Patrizio, intercepted Cassius just before he reached them. "Signore, we need your presence in the kitchens."

Cassius shuffled on his feet, his eyes shifted from the far doorway, to the gathering, to them. "I would be a poor host if I had you follow me to the kitchens, but perhaps you shouldn't mingle with this lot without me."

Brehane looked back at the unappealing *shermuta* and the ladies. Even if a trip to the kitchens didn't get them any closer to Melas, and even though a woman didn't belong in a kitchen, it was far more appealing than having to fend off a bunch of homely men looking to earn a coin or two. "I will join you."

"Me, too," Makeda said. As though the ugly *assama* ever had interest in a man's job.

He led them around the side of the house to a stone building. Smoke trailed out of a hole at the top.

"None of the other signores will come near a kitchen." He pulled open the door, letting out a cacophony of chopping and sizzling noises, as well as the mouthwatering scents of unique spices.

The inside bustled with activity. Men *and* women chopped vegetables, carved slices of meat off some roasted carcass, and ran about with bowls of ingredients. One fellow stirred something in a pot next to a hearth at one end. Two male chefs worked around a square brick table with a metal top, scooping, mixing, and turning food.

"Food is life." Cassius' eyes sparkled with childlike delight. "Taking a necessity and transforming it into pure pleasure is magic in and of itself."

So bizarre to think in such a way; yet, watching him go around to each of the stations, tasting and adding spices, mixing and cutting, it was amazing to see a man with such passion for something. Every motion combined elegance and purpose. His expression lit up in a way that they hadn't when they'd made love.

Heat flared hot inside of her. Brehane would find a way to get him into bed again, and would do whatever it took to bring out the same passion.

He beckoned them over and held up a ladle containing some sort of soup. "My own recipe. I like to experiment with bringing different flavors together. Taste it."

Such a labor of love must certainly be delicious. And so like her own fusing of magical schools. In a way, they were kindred spirits. Brehane leaned in and blew away the steam. The single sip erupted in her mouth, caressing her tongue with a unique blend of spicy, savory, salty, and sweet. Her eyes widened and she met his gaze. "Amazing."

Cassius' smile warmed her even more than the soup, and in different places. Oh yes, he would be hers again.

Clucking her tongue, Makeda bent over, mouth open to the spoon.

With her fingers manipulating the Resonance behind her back, and mouthing words of magic that didn't normally go together, Brehane experimented with combining Hydromancy and Transmutation. If it succeeded, it would turn the soup to cat urine. Energy fled her limbs, but she forced herself to stand straight.

Makeda took a gulp. Her eyes widened, then she spat the soup out.

The entire kitchen staff paused in their work to stare.

Makeda's eyes raked from them, to Cassius, and finally Brehane. She fanned air into her mouth. "Hot, hot, hot!"

The delayed reaction was too obvious. Brehane stifled a laugh.

Makeda glared. "*Assama!* You heated the metal with Pyromancy, didn't you?"

So she was still trying to save face. Brehane crossed her arms. "Of course not. I'm just a plain Biomancer, and you're the incredible Pyromancer, remember? You didn't blow it first, did you? Admit it, your mouth can't handle hot." Or cat urine.

Makeda's face twisted into a telltale sign that she was about to cast a spell. Her fingers formed shapes that manipulated the Resonance.

Weak from the merging of magic schools, Brehane tensed up.

Then, Makeda's eyes shifted to Cassius' gawk. She lowered her hand, scowl melting into a forced smile.

Brehane's shoulders relaxed as a counter-spell died on her lips.

If Cassius' chuckle was any more nervous, he might be mistaken for a virgin about to be deflowered. He motioned to the kitchen staff. "Start serving in ten minutes. My ladies, let's not keep my guests waiting."

Brehane eyed Makeda. She was behaving, if only to make a good impression on Cassius.

As they approached the banquet hall, a commotion grew louder. At the entrance, Patrizio was arguing with a bronze-skinned man: the Ayuri Paladin who'd been at Cassius' megalith earlier that day. And where they showed up, trouble usually followed. He looked like he might punch the steward.

CHAPTER 10:

Pitter Patter of Little Feet

Jie peered around the corner at the two-story marble row house in the market district. Another small bribe, borrowed from Sameer's purse, had convinced one of Signore De Lucca's working girls to divulge the location of his office. The oval crest of the golden lion on a purple field above the door confirmed this was the right spot.

No lights shone in the windows. When she'd sent Sameer to confront De Lucca at the Diviner's villa, it was to keep De Lucca and his henchman distracted. That would leave plenty of time to rifle through the glorified pimp's records and find evidence of the Teleri spies she was tracking. And if there happened to be any clues to this Sohini's disappearance, it would ingratiate her to the Paladins.

Now, Jie just had to get past the decorative bars of the wrought-iron gate, and then the two Bovyan guards by the door. The first part would be easy, but the second... A distraction might draw one off, but certainly not the other, and in a fair fight she didn't stand a chance against a single Bovyan, let alone two.

She scanned the building again for any other insertion points. The second-floor windows on the front weren't barred, but first she'd have to get past the gate and soldiers without being seen. Up higher...that was it. Three chimneys jutted from the sloped tile roof. From here, they looked big enough for her to fit through, and no smoke wafted out of them, confirming that nobody was burning fires in this warm weather.

Creeping to the back alley, she examined the outer walls. The same decorative iron bars as those on the front gate covered the rear windows. The distance between them was much too narrow for even her slim build.

Unlike the marble in the front, the rear appeared to be a façade of flat stones, cemented to concrete. Her cat claws were back with her stealth suit on the ship—there was no telling what Prince Aryn would think if the crew discovered where she'd hid them—and all the tailor shops along the way displayed clothes which would be even more bulky and noticeable, even if they had anything that fit her. Meaning she'd have to make do with the pink dress, which both stood out in the moonlight and limited her movement. With luck, there was enough space for half-elf fingers in between the mortar, all the way to the top.

Perhaps this wasn't worth the trouble. Sameer's lady friend wasn't her problem, after all.

Then again, clan traitors training Bovyans were her problem, and De Lucca seemed to be at the center of the city's Bovyan infestation. Was he their unwitting tool, or the mastermind? A little snooping might reveal the answer.

She looked up the wall again. With a deep breath, she hiked up the dress and knotted it between her legs. She stuffed the slippers into her sash. Taking a dozen steps back, she took a running jump to the closest window and caught the bars. They provided an easy means of traversing the first dozen feet.

At the top of the window, she continued her ascent by finding the spaces between the stones with her small fingers and toes. It was surprisingly easy, the mortar having worn away over time.

Just before she reached the second floor windows, two people turned into the alley. She froze. Hopefully, it was dark enough that the pink wouldn't show, or at least the interlopers wouldn't bother to look up. They stumbled closer, taking their time.

"Is your eye all right?" one asked, voice slurred.

"Damn Bovyans." The other spat, a click against the wall suggesting a tooth had come out with the spittle.

The other laughed. "Don't taunt them next time."

"Bastards need to leave this town. I bet you a draka they're an advanced force, scouting us out."

Jie would make that same bet, but she wasn't about to share her opinion right now.

"Nah, their empire is too far away. Rumor has it this is the only city-state they're in."

"I can't believe the Signores not only let them come, but are actually employing them. Morons."

"The crime families hired them first."

"Well, they sure can fight, and the crime families are losing ground." The first stopped just beneath her and faced the wall. He lowered his pants and started to piss. The other sidled up and joined him.

Heavens, they just *had* to choose this building. Sweat gathered on her brow. Her fingers ached. And what was this? With her face close to the wall, the scratch marks near the border between two stones stood out.

Black Fist cat-claw marks.

Someone with a similar skillset had followed this path before. The hairs on the back of her neck stood on end. Definitely closer to the clan traitor.

When the men were done leaving their offering on the wall and continued down the alley, she resumed her climb. She'd be sure not to come down along the same spot and land in their puddle. At the top, the gentle pitch of the roof was easy to negotiate, though several of the ceramic tiles hung loose. The rows of rooftops followed straight lines, much like the capital's cityscape back home.

She made her way to the closest chimney and moved the flue cap. It was more than wide enough for her, though she'd end up filthy and track ash through the place.

Light bauble held between her teeth, she spider-climbed down the flue, finding sizeable handprints in the ash coating. Whoever had left the marks was likely larger than the average human, but smaller than a Bovyan. How long ago he'd passed was impossible to tell, but where she could, she placed her hands and feet in his so as not to leave a trail of her own.

She continued down, pausing at the wind shelf where a branch of the flue continued further down. It was much too narrow, even for her small size.

She'd have to settle with the second floor. Closing her mouth around the bauble, she shimmied past the wind shelf and landed in the hearth. She peered out into the large, windowless room.

Her elf vision picked out indistinct shapes, none moving. No sounds came from anywhere within earshot. She tongue-pushed the bauble back between her teeth and looked. Several quills and inkwells rested on a long table in the middle of the room. Eight chairs surrounded it. Shelves occupied every inch of wall space, save for above the door and hearth. Hundreds upon hundreds of books lined the shelves.

Where to start? Slipping her shoes back on, she tiptoed across the hardwood floors to a random shelf. The spines of the books were marked with some kind of code in the local alphabet. She wiped her hands on her dress, perhaps making them even dirtier given all the ash clinging to the fabric. She pulled a book out and opened it.

It was a ledger. Expenditures and income, meticulously organized in a blocky handwriting which suggested a stodgy person, with a meticulous attention to detail, and perhaps constipation.

Flipping through the pages, Jie unsurprisingly found no overt payments to Black Lotus Clan traitors, but quickly learned how to run a prostitution ring. Clearly, two years ago, Elisa from the Diamond House was De Lucca's most popular prostitute, though he stiffed her on payday. A significant amount of money went to a Don Acerbi for protection of the houses. A Mafia racket, perhaps. Or maybe even an expense mislabeled to hide the payment's true purpose.

A creaking, muffled by the heavy door and the floors, came from below. The first floor main entrance, in all likelihood, since there had been no sounds or scents to indicate anyone else was inside. Whoever was coming in now sure had late business. Jie froze and listened.

When the footsteps shuffled around downstairs, deeper into the building, she put the book away and selected the one to the left.

Surprisingly, unlike the first ledger, the dates went back in time instead of forward. Right; the Easterners wrote left to right, so their brains must work that way as well. Instead of prostitutes, this looked to document insurance and banking endeavors. Apparently, De Lucca had his fingers in many pies, his tracks covered by shell companies. If only a certain clueless spy were here, he could make sense of it all.

A few especially large income entries were written in a more haphazard hand, in runes that resembled neither the local alphabet nor the pictograms of her homeland, or even the loops and whorls of Ayuri script used in Sameer's country. It looked like no language Jie had ever seen.

She chose another book, several shelves to the right, labelled with a mix of the local language and the same runes as the first. As suspected, it detailed more recent transactions. The protection money payments to the Mafia had ceased, replaced by salaries to Bovyan mercenaries. Perhaps this related to what the pair in the alley had mentioned.

Footsteps approached, the sound suggesting a heavy person coming up the stairwell. A line of light and shifting shadows appeared under the door's threshold, and the thumping feet came closer.

Sliding the book back, she dashed on tip-toes back to the hearth.

A key fiddled in the door.

Kicking her shoes off and catching them, Jie climbed back into the chimney, settled on the windshelf, and shoved the light bauble into her mouth. Now it tasted like ash, and it took all her discipline not to gag.

The door swooshed open and feet trod to a bookshelf. Whoever it was withdrew a book and brought it to the table. A quill swished over the paper.

Ash tickled Jie's nose. A sneeze threatened to betray her position. She bit her lip.

Sand scattered on paper. Breaths puffed on pages. The book thumped shut, and the visitor swept it up and returned it to the shelf. The door opened and shut, and the lock clicked.

Jie dropped down and landed lightly on her feet. She blew several breaths out through her nose, clearing the irritant. Satisfied she wouldn't sneeze, she spat out her light and tried to track the footsteps in her memory. Her eyes locked on a book which jutted out a little more than before. A new code marked the spine.

Inside, the staggering transactions all related to Bovyans, and the construction of barracks and training facilities. There were mentions of contracts for girls, bought from several of the brothels she'd passed earlier in the night. Isabella, the trainee the prostitutes from the *Buxom Lass* had mentioned, had been purchased several weeks back. Perhaps she'd been bought specifically to entertain the Teleri. Poor girl.

After skimming several pages, there was no hint of dealings with suspicious clan traitors, nor mention of Sameer's friend, Sohini. Perhaps she was listed among the other prostitute records, but empires would rise and fall in the time it took to search all the documents.

Ear to the door, she listened. Whoever had entered the room before was either very quiet, or had left. She withdrew her lockpicks from the pouch strapped to her inner thigh. With a few expert twists, the lock yielded. Stashing her light bauble, she eased the door open and stepped out. To the right, the hallway continued toward two doors at the front of the building.

To the left, toward the back of the building, was another door, as well as a flight of steps heading down.

One foot in front of the other, she tested the floorboards for creaks. Unlike the castles back home, whose floors chirped like nightingales to discourage spying, these were silent.

A quick survey of the three rooms turned up more evidence of construction. The purchaser's office included lists of building materials, brothel supplies, and surprisingly, foodstuffs and gooseweed imported from Ayuri lands. The tidy accountant's office had the same metal device with numbers and dials that the *Intimidator's* quartermaster used. The scent lingering here belonged to the person who'd visited the records room.

It was time to find De Lucca's personal office. If he met with other merchants and dignitaries, it would undoubtedly be on the first floor. She headed to the stairs and paused at the top. Peering through the darkness, she looked down the steps, which led to the front door.

The office remained silent. She took each step slowly, testing for sound. At the bottom, marble floors stretched the breadth of the building. A scribe's desk faced the entrance, as well as several chairs. Several paintings graced the walls, though it was hard to discern the images in the green-and-grey hues of her elf vision.

She turned down the hallway, passing three doors to the left and the stairwell to the right as she headed straight to the pair of ornate doors at the back. The ostentatiousness of the elaborate designs suggested it belonged to someone who wanted people to know how important he was.

Definitely De Lucca's office.

Unsurprisingly, the doors were locked; but unlike the child's toy securing the door to the records room, this one was a complex, dwarf-made combination lock. Pressing her ear to the device, she turned a dial until she heard the soft whisper of a click. Thank the Heavens for elf ears! With a few more twists, the lock disengaged. The hinges whispered as the door slid smoothly open.

Inside, she closed the door behind her. The interior gears whirred, and the lock clicked. It appeared as if a simple lever disengaged the lock from this side. She withdrew her light bauble.

It was all she could do not to gasp.

If the double doors had been flashy, De Lucca's office could only be described as flamboyant. It took up the entire width of the building, with a mahogany sideboard along one side. Several glass tumblers sat on top. Two barred windows flanked a twelve-foot portrait of a thin, dark-haired man. If De Lucca had commissioned a painting of himself, then he was either incredibly handsome or harbored delusions of extreme grandeur.

In front of the portrait stood a large desk and a chair that might've been a throne. She tiptoed over and, careful to brush off ash and soot, jumped up onto the soft cushion. It was so high off the ground that her feet dangled. At the front of the desk sat a spherical crystal almost the size of her head, its bottom surface a flat grey.

It seemed to radiate cold, sending the small hairs on the back of her neck standing. Several letters were spread out in a haphazard manner around it.

While she could passably speak Arkothi, reading came slowly, especially given the ugly penmanship. One letter appeared addressed to a Don Acerbi, and it looked to be an ultimatum to sell all his brothels and gooseweed dens, lest he meet the sting of a scorpion. Those eerie creatures didn't live in this part of the world, but the Paladins had mentioned something about Madura's Golden Scorpions.

Another letter was addressed to a signore in the city-state of Lycium, thanking him for not paying for the protection of the pyramid. How strange. For someone who kept meticulous financial records, why would he not want to be paid?

She froze. The same strange script as in the records room peeked out from beneath the letter to Don Acerbi. She lifted the top sheet and scanned the runes.

Even if she didn't understand it, it was clear from the patterns that De Lucca himself had written the large income records in the upstairs ledgers. She could always use Sameer's money to bribe someone to translate it. She took a blank sheet and a quill and started copying the strange note as best she could.

Then, the sound of doors opening in a swift creak blared from a metal funnel in the wall at the front of the room. Like the ear horns the Black Lotus used to listen through walls, the device would allow De Lucca to hear his visitors.

Several voices erupted.

"He said she's in here."

CHAPTER 11:

Confrontations and Revelations

The most disconcerting part of Sameer's journey to Signore Cassius' villa had been trotting past the famed Iron Avatar in front of the pyramid. If he'd had his *naga*, and hadn't been in such a hurry, he could've tested his blade like so many Paladins in the past. Then again, he'd shivered so violently as he'd approached that he'd lost all connections to the Vibrations. The beggars there stared at him, except for the one cowering beneath a heavy cloak.

At Cassius Larusso's villa, he'd recovered his energy just enough to drain it all again trying to get past the guards with a *Bahaduur* Command. Now what was left guttered from trying to channel the Vibrations to bend the villa steward to his will. If only Master Anish had been there, with his more formidable skill, or better, Elder Gitika, herself. Had she been here, this would've been easy.

Just like she could've Commanded their assailants to flee earlier this afternoon, had Sameer not jumped into action. In the end, she was wounded. She wasn't here now, and it was his fault.

The steward sidestepped again, blocking his path out of the airy foyer. "I'm sorry, Sir Paladin. Master Larusso does not see clients after hours."

"I'm not here for a Divination. I want to see Signore De Lucca." Sameer glared at the steward, even as thoughts of Elder Gitika stayed his hand. Paladin code restrained him from initiating hostilities with an unarmed person. If only the man would make an aggressive motion, Sameer's combat reflexes would engage, albeit not as quickly given how heavy his limbs felt. Despite the fatigue, he should still be able to dash by.

"Do you have an invitation?" The steward's pursed lips said that he knew darn well Sameer didn't. "I am sorry, but this reception is invitation-only."

Frowning, Sameer craned to get a look at a large hall, where men caroused with scantily-clad women. Rumor had it that much of the city-state's policy was decided in gatherings like these, but it didn't look like any business was being discussed here.

At least, no legitimate business.

At the far end, Signore Cassius appeared, a stunning Aksumi woman on either side of him. On more careful inspection, they were two of the three Mystics who'd appeared at the Diviner's megalith earlier that day. The travelling robes they'd worn then made them look road-weary, but in their elegant gowns now, either might've been a maharaja's queen.

Perhaps they'd asked where the liveliest party in Tokahia was, or maybe the Diviner had hired them to entertain the men. No matter; the one in the breathtaking rose-gold mesh pulled Cassius through the party toward him. Her hostile glare sent the hair on the back of his neck prickling.

Shaking off the feeling, Sameer beckoned, even though his arm weighed like lead. "Master Cassius, a word please."

Everything went into slow motion as the steward reached for him. Sameer twisted out of the grab, spun around his attacker, and ended up on the other side. Time lurched to normal, with Sameer several paces closer to the banquet hall. He lengthened his stride, outpacing the steward in his stiff suit.

At the edge of the hall, Sameer skidded to a stop. Stars shone in the night sky above, clearly visible through the glass dome. He'd seen more glass in his afternoon in Tokahia than he had in his entire life back home, but the sheer size of this piece was bewildering. How was such a feat of architecture even possible?

"Welcome, Sir Paladin." Cassius dipped into a sweeping bow. When he straightened, he waved off the steward. "I have not had time to search for your friend, but will happily meet with you at my megalith tomorrow morning with more information."

Sameer pointed at the gathering. "I am looking for Signore De Lucca."

"Whatever f—" Cassius cast a sidelong glance at one of the dark beauties. "Of course you are."

Sameer studied the Diviner's expression, which revealed nothing but genuine confusion. Though De Lucca was here, he was just one of many guests, so perhaps Cassius knew nothing about Sohini's kidnapping. "My friend, Sohini, was seen at one of his brothels." The word tasted bad on his lips.

Cassius looked toward the gathering, his eyes locking on a short young man, flanked by two hulking Bovyans. Wine glass in hand, he was laughing with two men.

Cassius turned back. "I was going to tell you as much. However, she is no longer in his employ."

"Where is she?"

Cassius pointed up through the dome. "From Sohini's star chart, the Hunter holds hands with the Sage."

The cryptic language made no sense. "What do you mean?"

"She has gone on a journey to seek out answers to her questions."

Obviously, this man was a charlatan, coming up with ambiguous answers. "She was kidnapped!" He pushed past Cassius, who was not nearly as adept at blocking as his steward.

Conversation died. All eyes fell on him.

Sameer kept his focus locked on the thin young man. "Signore De Lucca!"

In turn, the waif stared at him, eyes wide.

"De Lucca!" Sameer jabbed a finger at him. "Tell me where Sohini is."

Two bodyguards—Bovyans, like the brothel guards—interposed themselves between him and De Lucca. One held out a hand. "Stay back."

The brothel guard had been easy to dispatch, but that was before using multiple Commands had sapped Sameer's strength. Not to mention there were two here, both armed with longswords.

Sohini needed him. He stood on his tiptoes and tried to look past the imposing men. "Your brothel manager told me she was at that house."

Cassius came up behind him. "Sir Paladin, please desist."

"It's okay, Signore Larusso." De Lucca stood and pushed the Bovyans aside. He was tall and thin, his long black hair flowing to his shoulders. When he spoke, his voice grated like the whine of sitar strings. "Sir Paladin, I assure you, Sohini came to my respected establishment of her free will."

Respected, indeed. "Liar. These brutes of yours kidnapped her and forced her into...into..." the word stuck into his throat.

If De Lucca's laugh were any more grating, the dome above would shatter. "I wish. I could have made a small fortune with her."

Sameer's stomach clenched tighter than his fists. Every nerve fiber screamed to punch this man, consequences be damned. "If she wasn't doing...doing...*that*, why was she there?"

"She was seeking refuge, and I hired her."

In two steps, Sameer's face was up against De Lucca's. He cocked his fist. "You bastard."

Time slowed a fraction as both Bovyans grabbed at him. Sameer seized their wrists, stepped back, and pulled them into each other. They collided and stumbled to the floor.

Single syllables dragged out in a foul language. He turned, just in time to see the Aksumi woman in the rose-gold dress point at him. Sticky fibers squirted at him. His guttering energy slowed his *Bahaduur* reflexes so much that they allowed him to perceive the sorcery, but do nothing about it. The threads tangled him up, like a fly ensnared in a spider web. The more he struggled, the harder it became to move. Time slowed back to normal as he tumbled to the marble floor.

The other Aksumi gaped, then turned to her companion and rattled off a litany of unfriendly-sounding words.

Cassius turned to the first, shaking his head. "My lady, we do not treat our guests like this in the Estomar."

She gaped. When she spoke in Arkothi, her accent was thick. "Signore Cassius. Long ago, the Ayuri Empire sent Paladins as emissaries to my ancestors, bearing gifts of peace. Little did we know they were the vanguard of a brutal occupation. The matrons they didn't slaughter, they held as hostage to force our clan against the other tribes. It all led up to the Hellstorm."

Blinking his eyes, Sameer tried to spit the cobwebs out of his mouth. This Mystic was holding a three-century-old grudge, and was clearly misinformed about the cause of the Hellstorm. Everyone in Ayuri lands knew it had been the last Arkothi Emperor unleashing a genocidal magic weapon, powered by demonic energy.

The Aksumi beauty in the black dress laughed, the sound akin to a donkey's bray. "Stop making excuses for your traitorous clan, Cousin. Admit they were too weak to repel the Ayuri. The other tribes were able to beat back the attack."

Cassius looked from one woman to the next, brow creased.

With the last of the webbing out of his mouth, Sameer wormed his way into a seated position. "Honorable Mystics, I am deeply ashamed by the actions of the *Bahaduur*. Please know we aren't like that anymore. After the Hellstorm, the Oracle of Ayudra established an order based on maintaining peace and protecting the weak. The Paladins are honorable and just."

The first Aksumi harrumphed. "It looks like you are more like your predecessors. You charged in, uninvited, and attacked Signore De Lucca."

Sameer's shoulders drooped as much as they could in the web. She was right. He'd let his passions get the better of him, just like the ancient *Bahaduur* succumbing to the Ayuri Emperor's rewards. Just like the Golden Scorpions who served Madura. Just like he'd done earlier today. His behavior would reflect poorly on Elder Gitika. He wriggled his hand into the *mudra* for regret. "I did. I have no excuse for my behavior."

The Aksumi's lip curled. "What did you hope to accomplish?"

"It is all right, my lady." Cassius stepped between them.

The Mystic's eyes narrowed, and she opened her mouth to speak, only to close it.

"Thank you for protecting me, Miss Brehane." De Lucca dipped into a bow. "I hope you would consider employment with me."

The Mystic—Brehane, apparently— looked from him to Cassius before shaking her head. "Thank you for your kind offer, but I have an important mission."

"*We* have an important mission," the other woman said.

"Unfortunate for me." De Lucca turned and knelt at Sameer's side. "Sir Paladin, I hired your friend for the most noble of causes: to lead my guards in an attack on the dens of powerful crime families in Tokahia."

Cassius sucked in a sharp breath.

"I don't believe you." Sameer shook his head. Master Anish had said nothing about attacking mob families, and Paladins would not normally engage in a power struggle in foreign countries. Still, fighting injustice did sound like a task that would appeal to Sohini. What if she'd tricked Master Anish and joined De Lucca? Then again, the Bovyan working for the Mafia claimed to have sold her into slavery.

De Lucca shrugged. "Why would I lie? Our city— indeed, most of the Estomari city-states—suffer from an infestation of crime syndicates. It's a fragile balance between the Signores' security forces and the Mafias' hired goons. Now, if I help you up, do you promise to behave?"

All muscles aching from his struggle against the webbing, Sameer let his body relax. With a sigh, he nodded the best he could.

"Can you free this noble Paladin?" De Lucca motioned toward the Mystics, never breaking eye contact.

The two argued among themselves for a few seconds before Brehane coughed out several guttural words. The threads thinned to brittle wisps and blew away.

De Lucca offered him a hand.

Taking it, Sameer climbed to his feet, his limbs exhausted from channeling the Vibrations and the struggle against the webbing. His head hung of its own accord, though he formed the *mudra* of gratitude with his fingers. "Did she succeed? Is she all right?"

"Yes, she succeeded, at first. Don Secca's syndicate is ruined. Don Russo's crime family is weakened beyond recovery." De Lucca's gaze turned severe. "However, she never returned from her third mission against Don Acerbi."

Never returned! Sameer's stomach twisted.

De Lucca patted him on the shoulder. "My surviving men said she was captured. I received a letter from the don, claiming that he was holding her somewhere outside the city. I'm sorry."

Could this be true? He turned to Cassius. "You said she was on a journey to seek out answers."

Cassius nodded. "So her star chart suggested. It appears she may have done so, in Signore De Lucca's employ. I will be able to tell you when I actually Divine."

Sameer snorted. Hopefully, Jie had already scoured De Lucca's office and found out more about Sohini's dealings with him. However, if he was telling the truth, Sohini was in a different kind of trouble than first suspected. "Where can I find this Don Acerbi?"

* * *

Cassius looked from De Lucca to Sameer, his head spinning from all these revelations. The citizenry had attributed the recent downfall of the Russo and Secca crime families to internal conflicts and an untimely turf war with the Acerbi Mafia. Nothing in the stars suggested a Paladin had gotten involved; and at the behest of Signore De Lucca, of all people.

No doubt, the self-serving flesh dealer was either tired of paying protection money for his brothels, or perhaps he was trying to acquire new ones for himself. Or, the way he looked at Sameer, maybe he was planning a pre-emptive strike on the crime families with a love-sick Paladin apprentice as the tip of the spear.

Maybe that was a good idea. If the Paladins could be manipulated into destroying the Mafia, the pyramid would be safe from their machinations. Not to mention, Cassius' own deal with the Bovyans through Phobos would be moot. He could still keep the Mystics here and win some other concession.

Was it worth it? His gaze shifted to the two arguing women. Beautiful as they were, Makeda was annoying. The way Brehane had gazed at him after tasting his cooking, however... Julia had never cared about this passion; only cared that she could get him to Divine for her, and buy her nice things. Brehane might actually see beyond the wealth and magic.

His heart fluttered, before he shook silly ideas out of his head. Philosophers waxed poetic about true love or undying love, but men like him knew such concepts were ways to make money off the foolish. Or sweet-talk naïve cousins into a threesome. No; given their mutual animosity, there was little chance for that.

Of course, this was all assuming Sameer survived an encounter with the Acerbi family in the first place. Cassius stepped forward. "Sir Sameer, Don Acerbi heads the most powerful crime family in Tokahia, and rumor has it that he is allying with other families. If you go there with the same brashness as you came to my villa, you will not survive."

Sameer shook his head. "You underestimate the power of a Paladin."

"They can't avoid spider webs," Brehane muttered.

Cassius flashed a glare at her before gesturing toward De Lucca's bodyguards. "Even with the help of Bovyans, Sohini did not succeed. I urge caution. Where are your masters?"

Sameer pointed at De Lucca's bodyguards. "Bovyans attacked us earlier. Master Gitika was injured and Master Anish went to check her stitches and dressings."

Even the Divine Accountant wouldn't be able to add all this up. Cassius turned to De Lucca. "Why would your men attack the Paladins?"

Eyes wide, De Lucca shook his head and waved both hands. "I never..."

Captain Robas, whom Sameer had earlier sent careening into his comrade, had since gained his feet. He now stepped forward and thumped his chest. "I can only speak for the men serving the Signores, but I assure you, no one under my command would attack Paladins. We have nothing but respect for their martial skill."

Cassius snorted. The Divine Accountant would have to find a way to balance out Bovyan respect for warriors with their disrespect for women.

Sameer snarled. "Your own man admitted to kidnapping Sohini and selling her to a brothel."

"He must be one who works for the Mafia families. By contract, we swear on the Last Testament of Geros to not discuss our employers' private business. However, I can tell you that none of us working for the Signores kidnapped her, and we certainly didn't sell her into slavery."

Cassius looked from Sameer to Captain Robas to De Lucca. The Last Testament was a canonical holy text for the Bovyans. Certainly, they wouldn't take an oath on it lightly. Perhaps it was worth expending energy to

Divine this Sohini's actual location, if only to protect his reputation in the event she turned up. Or to keep the Paladins from finding her, because then there would be no turning them on the Mafia.

He said, "If you are going to confront Don Acerbi, do not go into the lion's den. Go back to your masters at the *Seafarer*. Rest. I will Divine an auspicious time and a strategic location, and send word by the morning. The three of you have a better chance of surviving."

Sameer shook his head. "No. Now."

Cassius studied the fledgling Paladin. Even exhausted as he was, he was chomping at the bit to go after his friend—definitely more than friend, given his determination. There was an untold story here, one which a little Divining might unveil. Perhaps that personal history could be a way to manipulate him, as long as this Sohini didn't turn up soon. "Sir Sameer, Divining is not always so simple. I will have your answer tomorrow."

Sameer's posture slumped. "I can't bear the thought of her in danger. And so close. There has to be something I can do."

Behind them, Patrizio cleared his throat. "Master Cassius, a messenger has come for Signore De Lucca."

Despite the late hour, it came as no shock: the shower of shooting stars which had followed the one yesterday suggested surprise messengers. Cassius looked to De Lucca, then back at Patrizio, and nodded. "Let him in."

A heavy-set man stumbled into the reception hall and bowed. "Master De Lucca, we have an emergency. Someone snuck into your office. We have it surrounded and are waiting for your command."

Sameer's fists tightened. They'd cornered the half-elf, meaning he'd never learn any of the information she'd uncovered.

* * *

Brehane's eyes shifted from Signore De Lucca to the impatient Paladin, Sameer. Every instinct screamed that Sameer was just grasping at straws, like a man fretting over the possibility that his beloved was engaged in a tryst with someone younger and more handsome.

Then again, something about De Lucca felt off, beyond the exquisite, elf-like angles of his features. Perhaps it was the way the Resonance wrapped around him instead of joining with him. Or maybe his answers were just too glib. Still, if what he said was true, it meant that this Sohini was not where Cassius had said. That, in turn, meant his Divining was unreliable.

Her hand strayed to the jewel at her neck as she studied Cassius. No, she'd felt the Resonance when he'd Divined her past with unerring accuracy. One thing was certain: in a city where the governing authority struggled against criminal elements, those skilled in magic were disappearing. Lured here by the pyramid's power, perhaps they were working as mercenaries for one side or the other. After all, De Lucca had offered her a job, and had employed Sohini before.

"How did you do it?" Makeda shook Brehane out of her thoughts.

"Do what?"

"The webbing. It sounded like Transmuting, but there were other elements."

Brehane smirked. Each clan held such a rigid view of magic, they'd never think to combine Transmutation, Aeromancy, and Hydromancy into a single spell.

Makeda's lip curled. "*Assama*, you'd better—"

"Sir Paladin." De Lucca patted Sameer on the shoulder again. "I sent an ultimatum to the Acerbi family, demanding Sohini's release. I have no doubt the interloper in my office is one of their spies."

Sameer's expression tightened. "Allow me to go with you, then."

Sweat beaded on his abnormally pale brow, and his knees wobbled. His hands trembled. If Paladin skills were anything like sorcery, Sameer had clearly expended too much of his energy. He was willing to walk into certain death for his woman. It was like the epic ballads of sorceresses sacrificing themselves to save their man. The Paladin's dedication stood in stark contrast to his ancestors' backstabbing and lying. And since he was too foolish to be devious, maybe she'd judged him too harshly.

"Young Paladin," Cassius said, "if you accompany Signore De Lucca tonight, allow his men to deal with any threats. I fear you are too exhausted to fight anyone."

He was so considerate, caring more for Sameer's well-being than the young Paladin himself. Brehane fought hard to suppress a smile.

Sameer's face contorted into an expression that suggested constipation. "I will do what I must to find Sohini."

"I promise I will have answers for you by tomorrow. Don't throw your life away. As I just said, I will Divine her location tonight."

Brehane's pulse picked up several beats. Here was another chance to experience how Divining influenced the Resonance, and also prove that her faith in Cassius wasn't misplaced.

De Lucca patted Sameer on the back. "If you wait for word from Signore Cassius on an auspicious time to confront the Acerbi, I will send my Bovyans with you. However, I am going now. You must decide if you will accompany me, Sir Paladin." He pointed out of the mansion, where horses waited.

CHAPTER 12:

Opportunity In Disaster

It wasn't the first, and probably wouldn't be the last time Jie was trapped like a rat. Returning De Lucca's desk to the disorder in which she'd found it, she went to the windows and eased the heavy red curtains open. Unlike the wood shutters back home, these were made of actual glass. Outside in the alley, six Bovyans were pointing and chatting amongst themselves. The glass muffled the sounds too much for even her elf ears to make out the words.

The clack of boots on marble in the hall echoed louder as they approached the door. Maybe whoever it was knew the combination, maybe they didn't. She turned and reevaluated the window. It looked to slide open vertically, but then there were the bars, and then a half-dozen brutes. Hiding behind the curtain wasn't an appealing option. If the Bovyans flashed a light from the alley, they'd see her like the prostitutes dancing in the windows of De Lucca's brothel; and from the inside, it would be the first place she'd look if searching for a hidden spy.

The footsteps stopped outside the door. She zipped over to the fireplace and looked up. The space above the wind shelf might be just large enough for her to contort herself into, though the flue narrowed not far above it. There was little hope of getting much higher, let alone reaching the second floor. It would potentially be a long, uncomfortable wait.

Then again, it was better than the alternative, and she'd wedged herself into a space half this size in training drills at the temple, and waited there for a day.

Gears swished as someone fiddled with the door lock. Pulse racing, she squeezed up into the flue. Scrunching her knees against her chest and ducking her head, she fit in the space with just her arms dangling over the wind shelf. Never before had she been more thankful for a flat chest.

"Dwarf lock." The voice sounded like it came from a large person who'd just swallowed a bunch of rocks. "Do you know the combination?"

"De Lucca must have changed it. We sent word to him, but he's an hour away." The second man also sounded large.

"Not if he rides a horse," said the gravelly voice.

"He doesn't look like he'd be able to ride. Even then, it'll still be half an hour. I'll check the other rooms. You go find that Nightblade, he might be able to figure this lock out."

A Nightblade. Jie sucked on her lower lip. It sounded ominous. An assassin, maybe.

She uncontorted herself and slunk down. If De Lucca was the only one who knew the combination, she might have up to another half hour before they breeched the door.

The horn in the wall magnified the clacking of boots against marble. The footsteps, which tromped off in the distance. One set went up the steps, while the other pair went halfway down the hall and opened a door.

Perhaps this was a chance to get out. She ran to the office door and listened. When the footsteps turned into a side room off the hall, she flipped the lock lever. It clicked, much too loudly. She pushed the door open, wedged herself into the crack, and looked down the corridor.

The door into the closest of the three side rooms was open, a light shining out. Up ahead, the front door to the building stood ajar.

She dashed toward it. Escape! Unless—

The light in the side room grew brighter, and a shadow appeared on the wall. A large Bovyan stepped out, a light bauble lamp in his hand.

Jie skidded to a stop just before she careened into his massive side. She pressed her back to the wall. With *Mockingbird's Deception*, she mimicked the gravelly voice from before, and used a *Ghost Echo* to throw her voice in the direction of the stairs. "Up here!"

The soldier turned to the entrance and steps. Jie slipped past him and into the room he'd just left. The light turned down the hall, accompanying long, striding footsteps. Thank the Heavens he hadn't seen her. Even though she couldn't fault him for being tricked by Black Lotus techniques, she would nickname him Clueless. Once Clueless went up the steps, it would be a quick sprint out the front.

"Master Phobos, thank you for coming," a new, very deep voice carried from the front door.

"You won't thank me after I report your team's incompetence. You will make Signore De Lucca lose confidence in us."

A fist thumped on a chest. "Forgive us, Master Phobos."

"Never mind." Phobos snorted. "You say the intruder is a half-elf?"

Still trapped! Not only that, they somehow knew she was one of the handful of half-elves in the world. Had the soldier not emerged from the door at that time, she would've run right into these newcomers.

"So we were told." The same deep voice reached the entrance. He'd be nicknamed Deep Throat. "We've searched the building, save for Signore De Lucca's office. It has a combination lock."

"If she's in there, there's no way out." The last voice implied this Phobos was a large man, albeit smaller than the others. In fact, it sounded like the leader who'd tried to ambush the Paladins with the Mafia goons, before disappearing into thin air. If it were indeed him, he was freelancing for both the Signores and the crime families. Or maybe De Lucca was colluding with the Mafia.

However, the pimp's financial records suggested otherwise, which left a third option: the Bovyans had their own agenda. Either way, she was likely a step closer to the clan traitor.

"Stand guard by De Lucca's office door," Master Phobos whispered, apparently unaware that elf ears were much more acute than a human's. "I will climb to the rooftop and search from the second floor down."

Jie sucked on her lower lip. If this Phobos could climb to the roof, he was likely the one who'd left the marks in the stones and mortar, and the hand prints inside the chimney. Given the timing, he was probably also the *Nightblade* the first two Bovyans had referenced. Now there was a name to the assassins trained in Black Lotus Clan ways. Mix Bovyan fighting skills with Black Fist guile, and these Nightblades would be formidable.

Of course, the clan would never find out if she didn't escape. She eased the door shut, plunging the room into darkness that her elf vision couldn't penetrate. She withdrew her light bauble and scanned the surroundings.

Though lined with shelves like the record room, these volumes looked more like actual leather-bound books than ledgers. Two plush leather chairs flanked a table and faced a hearth on the far wall. Whether for guests or for De Lucca himself, the library looked like a retreat.

Given this room's placement beneath the records room, the flue was probably the one that had branched off of the chimney she'd come in through. She crept over and looked up. Like the fireplace in De Lucca's office, this one also had a small space above the wind shelf, perhaps large enough for her to squeeze into. Still, if this Nightblade Phobos was competent, he'd assume a half-elf girl could fit into it. For now, it was a last resort.

Up above, the sound of hands and feet working their way down the chimney echoed through the flue.

There was still a little time, perhaps enough to learn about De Lucca from what he read. She inched over to the closest shelf and held the bauble up to the books. Titles like *The Lips of Winter*, *The Lash and the Locket*, and *The Widow's Gentleman* were emblazoned on the spines. Such strange books for a glorified pimp to read.

She pulled *Lips of Winter* out and opened the page. The uniform, blocky letters indicated a press with movable type had been used to print this book. The content was nothing short of raunchy, graphically depicting acts that might make even Prince Aryn blush. Further examination of a few more pages revealed no patterns for a coded language, so the book was undoubtedly just what it appeared to be: erotic literature. Mass-produced, no less. Jie quickly stuffed it back into its place on the shelf.

Moving around the shelves, she took cursory glances at the titles. Warfare and military strategy, historical accounts, economics, botany, and animal husbandry were among the many genres included.

Whatever else could be said about De Lucca, he either had a wide breadth of knowledge or wanted his guests to believe he did.

Still, knowing of De Lucca's vanity didn't solve her current conundrum. There was no way out, and it was only a matter of time before the Bovyans came through with another sweep. Even now, the footsteps outside the door grew louder.

She made another quick scan of the room...then froze. Given where the near wall of De Lucca's office ended, the far wall here should've been another three feet back. Which meant there was likely a secret room, or maybe a stairwell heading into a basement. She pulled out thick books and tapped along the back of the shelves, each time eliciting a dull thud. On the third try, a hollow thump echoed. Given the proximity of the footsteps, her pursuers were not far from the door. Maybe they'd even hear it. Here was a secret door, but there were no clues how to open it, nor time to figure it out.

The footsteps were now outside the door. In five loping bounds, she made it back to the fireplace, wiggled past the wind shelf, and pocketed her light.

The door opened. Light shone in, casting shadows into the floor of the hearth.

"She's not in there. I just checked five minutes ago," Clueless said.

"I was watching the hall the whole time and didn't see anyone go in," said Deep Throat.

"Did you check the fireplace?" Nightblade Phobos asked.

Jie's heart leaped into her throat. Cornered, stuck in a fireplace. Given the precarious position, it was impossible to throw her voice anywhere but down.

Or up.

She angled her head up the flue. Again, she imitated Gravel Mouth's voice, currently unaccounted for, and threw it up the shaft. "Up here! In the record room."

It echoed through the chimney. Whether it tricked the men or just gave away her position, she'd find out in seconds.

The light flashed out. Footsteps hurried back out. One set. Two sets. Three.

Who knew, if the Nightblade was trained in Black Fist ways, maybe he'd thrown the sound of his footsteps just like she'd done her voice. She listened. No other sounds, but talented members of her clan could hold their breaths for four to five minutes.

She couldn't wait that long. They'd find Gravel Mouth in a minute or so. She poked her head down and did a quick scan. The main door remained open, and the little light that filtered in didn't reveal anyone there. Of course, Nightblade Phobos might still have his invisibility bauble, but there was no way to know. She dropped down and crept back to the secret door.

Running her hand along the frame, she found no buttons, levers, or latches that would disengage the door. What else could there be? A switch somewhere else in the room? Too inconvenient.

"I didn't call you," Gravel Mouth's voice said from somewhere on the second floor, definitely not the record room. "I thought that was one of you, calling me."

"The fireplace," Nightblade Phobos said from the steps.

Jie studied the books. While most had pristine spines, one had several smudges on it. She pulled it, eliciting a click behind the shelves.

The entire bookshelf whispered open. She had to jump back.

She ducked into the opening and looked along the back for any kind of lever or button to close the door. The footsteps grew louder. She found a switch directly opposite of the book she'd pulled, but before she could flip it, the door swung shut of its own accord. Pocketing her light bauble, just in case it shone through any part of the door's outline, she froze in place and held her breath.

"Check the fireplace," Nightblade Phobos said from the other side.

Footsteps clickety-clacked across the wood floors to the hearth.

"Nothing," Deep Throat said.

"Are you sure anyone was here at all?" Clueless asked.

"Of course. Someone imitated Preibus' voice," Nightblade Phobos said, irritation in his voice. "Keep searching. When Signore De Lucca comes, he might be able to tell if someone disturbed his things."

The voices and footsteps left again. By now, they must've been back and forth to this room so many times that they were bored.

Jie peered around. The indistinct greenish-grey hues meant her elf vision had kicked in, and that this secret room must not be too deep inside the building. The space was wide enough for her to stand against one side and extend her hand to the opposite wall, its length long enough for three half-elf girls to lay head-to-toe. Several sets of clothes hung at the far end, above a chest of drawers.

Perhaps De Lucca used this as a changing room, though it seemed odd he would not only dedicate a concealed corridor for changing clothes, but set it off of the library instead of his office. Unless there were another secret door there, as well.

She closed her eyes and brought up the image of De Lucca's office, of the wall adjacent to this room. Nothing looked like a secret door trigger; but then again, who would've thought to use a book?

Outside in the hall, boots continued to clack on the floors, back and forth, back and forth. Was that Sameer's voice among all the other conversations? The walls muffled the sounds too much.

For now, there was nothing to do but wait. She looked among De Lucca's clothes. The material felt slick like silk, but also stretchy. The color was hard to make out in the darkness, but it was certainly dull and monochrome, opposed to the flashy clothes the locals liked.

When she pulled the bottom drawer of the chest, it was heavy. With a stronger tug, it opened, revealing enough bars of gold to buy food to feed a small town for a year. The next drawer up had sheaves of paper, all with the same bizarre writing from his letters and ledgers before. One, though, was written in the local Arkothi script: a letter transferring ownership of all his assets to a Lucia De Lucca in the event of his death.

Jie slid the drawer shut, then opened the last one. Her eyes lit up. Two sheathed knives lay haphazardly in the drawer. If De Lucca's messy habits were any indication, he probably wouldn't miss a blade. She pulled one from its sheath and appreciated the serrations on the back end. Definitely a combat knife.

The trigger of the secret door clicked. How had she not heard anyone coming into the library?

The door slid open.

CHAPTER 13:

Broken

With more elephants than horses in Ayuri lands, Paladin training included only the basics of horseback riding. Sameer regretted that now, as he bounced up and down in the saddle. His knuckles blanched white from gripping the reins, and he sat as stiff as an embalmed corpse. If he had been tired before, he could now add a sore back, legs, and arms to his growing list of maladies.

Nearing the Iron Avatar by the pyramid had sent a chill through him, though thank the Thousand Gods it had receded as soon as he passed, leaving only the physical pain and exhaustion.

He would've loved nothing more than to go back to the *Seafarer* and throw himself into his bed. He should've stayed at Signore Cassius' villa until Master Anish arrived. However, he had no choice but to accompany Signore De Lucca, who now rode astride his horse as if he'd been born in the saddle. He might believe the Mafia had broken into his office, but of course it was

Jie who'd gone searching for any information about Sohini. Apparently the little half-elf wasn't as stealthy as she thought, and now it was up to Sameer to create a diversion to help her escape with any clues she'd uncovered.

So what if the Diviner and Mystics thought he was acting rashly out of love for Sohini?

A bump in the saddle jostled tender places. He looked to see the buildings around him rising higher, from the one-story daub-and-wattle dwellings along the dark streets on the outskirts of the city, to the two- and three-story concrete row houses in the lamp-lit downtown.

De Lucca's office was near the end of a line of row houses housing several trade offices and banks. Above the door hung the same golden lion crest that gave his brothel an official look. Several Bovyans stood by the entrance, while others were out in the street, scanning the rooftops. Of the faces Sameer caught in the dark, none belonged to the men who'd attacked them earlier in the day.

One of them jogged up and took De Lucca's reins with one hand, while thumping his chest with his other fist. "Signore De Lucca, we have searched everywhere except your personal office, and there is no sign of the intruder. We have eyes on the windows and door, and no one except our men have come or gone. She has to be in there."

"She?" De Lucca looked at Sameer and raised an eyebrow. "I didn't think the Acerbi would use a woman."

The Bovyan frowned. "Our messenger should've told you about the half-elf girl."

De Lucca started to suck in a sharp breath, but stopped.

Sameer buried a harrumph. As good as Jie thought she was, someone must've seen her sneak in.

Jaw tight, De Lucca swung out of the saddle and beckoned Sameer to follow him.

Sameer dismounted, nearly tripping when his foot stuck in the stirrup. Even on solid ground, his legs wobbled as he followed De Lucca past the iron gate and through the open double doors.

Illuminated by several light baubles, the foyer was large and airy. Opulent furnishings were arranged on the marble floors. Whatever else could be said about De Lucca, he had a flair for the showy. His taste for the glittery might rival the maharajas back home.

In comparison, Paladins didn't accumulate wealth. Sameer pictured Elder Gitika in his mind. Dignified. Austere. He locked his gaze forward as they moved into the hall, ignoring the expensive artwork. They passed by three rooms with open doors to the left: a privy, an office, and a library. A staircase rose to the right. A smaller Bovyan, his face and clothes covered in ash, descended the steps and met them at the double doors at the end of the hall.

Sameer watched him. Was this one of the men who'd attacked that afternoon? It was hard to tell through the dirt and shadows, and he didn't afford Sameer a direct view of his face.

"Master Phobos." De Lucca bowed. "What has your investigation uncovered?"

Phobos pounded a fist to his chest. "We heard her in the records room earlier, but my search turned up nothing. Your accountant had visited that room just a few minutes before we learned of the intrusion. He is upstairs now, looking to see if anything was stolen."

De Lucca's eyes narrowed. He then turned to the double doors. Shielding the complex lock from their view, he twisted a dial back and forth. The lock clicked. He reached for the door.

"Wait." Sameer stepped forward and pressed his palms together. He spoke loudly, so Jie could hear him. "If the spy is in there, she might be armed and dangerous. Allow me to enter first."

While providing only a side profile of his head, Phobos looked Sameer up and down before turning to De Lucca. "Signore, the Southerner doesn't even have a weapon. Allow my men to secure the room."

"Thank you for your concern for my safety, Sir Paladin." De Lucca tipped his hat, then turned to the Bovyan. "Master Phobos, please assemble a team."

Thumping his chest, Phobos beckoned several of the Bovyans.

Sameer shuffled on his feet. There had to be some way to get Jie out of there, even with his depleted energy. A Command? No, they'd barely worked for him so far, and he was too tired anyway. A distraction, maybe?

De Lucca motioned Sameer back. "Sir Sameer, I am going to have to ask you to wait here. Information about my many business dealings is in there, and I can't have just anyone seeing it."

"Of course." Pressing his palms together again, Sameer backed away. It wasn't as though he could fight a dozen Bovyans without a weapon, and certainly not when fatigue muted his connection to the Vibrations. Such an attack would quickly wear out his welcome in Tokahia and probably end all chance of finding Sohini. Jie was on her own, unless he could think of something on impulse.

Five more Bovyans assembled by the door. Phobos motioned with his hands at the men. "On my signal, Loras and Baris, open the doors. Torus, take point. You two, flank him and take the far corners. I will enter just behind while you two flank me and secure the near corners."

They all pounded their chest. It was all so formal, so exact.

Phobos jerked a hand to the door. His men executed his instructions with the perfection of a dwarf-made water clock, breaching the door and securing the room.

"Clear," Phobos called from inside. "She is not here."

Sameer blew out the breath he was holding.

De Lucca turned to him, eyebrow raised.

"All the suspense had me nervous." Sameer offered an awkward smile.

De Lucca studied him, but then squared his shoulders and strode in.

Sameer's stomach churned. Had he been suspicious? He craned around the threshold. The office was even more luxurious than the lobby. And cold. Not unlike the sensation near the Iron Avatar.

De Lucca walked over to his desk and stashed some kind of glass globe into the desk's compartment. Studying his throne-like chair, he brushed it off and sat. Then he studied the papers. He folded up one and stuffed it inside his longcoat, while organizing the rest of the letters, save for one, into a single stack. He turned them over and looked up. "Sir Sameer, you may enter."

Sameer stepped in and looked around. The cold from before now crept over him. It felt almost like the pricking on the back of his neck that he'd felt during the Mafia ambush, and later near the Iron Avatar.

He continued in. While the rest of the Bovyans stood at attention, Phobos was busy checking the hearth and then behind the curtains.

De Lucca proffered the letter he'd set aside from the others. "Here is a draft of my first ultimatum to Don Acerbi. Your friend delivered the final version."

As Sameer neared, the cold seemed to crawl through his veins.

No, not a cold. An emptiness. The Vibrations quieted. Was he the only one who noticed it?

Fighting to keep his hand steady, he received the letter. The Arkothi words came slowly:

Don Lucian Acerbi: Close all your brothels and opium dens, lest you meet the scorpion's sting.

The reference couldn't be coincidence. Could it be that De Lucca had made use of Madura's Golden Scorpions? Maybe he exchanged his prostitutes' services to Prince Dhananad for the Scorpions' help in defeating the crime families. It was time to test the theory. Sameer looked up from the letter. "Do you have scorpions in the Estomar?"

Laughing, De Lucca waved a finger in a circle. "As far as I know, scorpions only come from your homeland. I was referring to Sohini."

The cold emptiness continued to prick at the back of Sameer's neck. He set his fingers in the *mudra* for warding evil. "You shouldn't use that term. The Paladin Order's enemies are the Golden Scorpions."

"Oh?" De Lucca raised an eyebrow. "Sohini did not mention that."

How could she not? Sohini had always railed against the Golden Scorpions' perversion of *Bahaduur* skills for their own selfish gain. Or perhaps De Lucca was being evasive. For now, though, there was no choice but to assume he was telling the truth about her.

"Anyway," De Lucca said, "I want to rescue her. Go back to your masters and see if they are willing to accompany my men on an attack on the Acerbi's headquarters. I will send a man over in the morning."

Sameer clenched his fists. If only he could go now. Only he had no idea where the Acerbi were, and in his weakened state, he didn't stand a chance against an army of mobsters. Even at full strength, his swordsmanship didn't compare to Sohini's; and if De

Lucca had been telling the truth, she, along with several Bovyans, had lost their fight with the Mafia. No, he needed rest, and with no sign of Jie in the office, he wasn't needed here. He nodded. "Thank you, Signore."

De Lucca motioned to another guard. "Escort Sir Sameer back to his lodgings."

"That won't be necessary." Sameer turned on his heel and left. No sooner than he exited the office than the cold receded. The Vibrations returned. What was it in there that felt so wrong? Nobody else seemed to notice it, but then again, none of them were Paladins. His eyes darted left and right as he looked for signs of a half-elf in a pink dress.

Seeing none, he headed back to the inn on foot. Would Elder Gitika and Master Anish agree to assault a Mafia stronghold? The internal matters of a city outside the Paladin Mandate were none of their business. Still, Sohini was Anish's responsibility. And even with her detached objectivity, Elder Gitika had an incomparable sense of compassion and justice. Surely she would agree to rescuing Sohini.

One foot in front of the other, he tried to banish thoughts of Sohini and instead focus on his master. She was the paradigm of Paladinhood, everything he aspired to be. Patient. Objective. Dignified. He'd failed her in so many ways today. Gotten her injured, even.

Up ahead, a crowd had gathered around the *Seafarer* at this late hour. All were dressed in bedclothes, chattering and pointing at the two-story stone building. Sameer stood on his tiptoes and craned his neck to get a better view. Several men wearing the black armband of the Signores' police cordoned off the entrance to the inn.

"What happened?" Sameer asked the closet man.

"A murder!"

"What? Who?" Sameer's head spun.

Another man turned around. "I've heard that one of the crime families crossed into this district and killed a guest."

The first studied Sameer from head to toe. "Yes, the victim is one of your kind."

Sameer's heart leaped into his throat. Unless there were other Ayuri staying here, that meant either Elder Gitika or Master Anish had been killed. It didn't make sense. One Paladin master was more than a match for a dozen men. Two... He twisted and pushed his way through the throng.

At the front, a Bovyan with a black armband raised a staying hand, but then lowered it. "You can pass."

Sameer dashed past him and through the front door. Several men with black armbands came and went from the foyer. One was questioning the innkeeper.

"What time did you say they came?"

The innkeeper wrung his hands. "The third waxing gibbous."

Two hours before. Sameer's gut twisted.

"You were still awake?"

He shook his head. "They were very insistent and woke me up. When I got around to unlocking the door, they barged in."

"Which crime family?"

Sameer's fists tightened. A bad feeling settled in his gut.

The innkeeper shuddered. "The Acerbi, accompanied by someone in a featureless metal mask."

A Golden Scorpion! The mistress of De Lucca's brothel had said one was in town, making arrangements for Prince Dhananad. It was no surprise they were allied with a crime family. It would explain why Sohini hadn't returned from her attack—she would be no match for a powerful Scorpion, who might be able to block her power. Sameer cleared his throat. "Who was killed?"

The inspector turned and studied him. "One of your kind. Perhaps you can help us identify the body."

Sameer's stomach churned. Pushing past another man, he stormed up the stairs.

"Wait," the inspector called, hurrying after him.

Sameer turned into their shared room. Chairs lay overturned on the floor. A light bauble lamp lay on its side on a table. Paintings hung askew. Their clean clothes were strewn about. None of their weapons were anywhere to be seen. And on a bed...

The body was covered by a blood-stained sheet. From the smaller size...

No. This couldn't be happening. Bile rose in his throat. He staggered back two steps and put a hand on the table for support.

The inspector withdrew the sheet.

Elder Gitika. Throat slashed, bright eyes now dull and lifeless.

Sameer's world spun around him. Tears welled in his eyes. No, this couldn't be happening. This was all his fault, for having acted rashly in the ambush. "My master, Gitika, of the Ayuri Paladin council."

The inspector placed a hand over his heart. "I'm sorry for your loss."

Everyone's loss. But wait. He looked around. "Where is my other master, the male?"

"The innkeeper said he left at the second waxing gibbous, and planned to visit Signore Cassius Larusso."

Just as they had planned. If only he had stayed, both he and Elder Gitika together could've defeated a dozen treacherous Scorpions. Now, she was dead. Sameer staggered over to the bed and knelt by his master. Her energy had joined the Vibrations, and would one day coalesce into the spark of another human being, to learn whatever life lessons the Thousand Gods deemed appropriate.

Back home, all of her apprentices, past and present, would've bathed her body and dressed it in a pure white robe. Her *naga* would rest over her chest. Given her stature, all the nearby Paladins would've paid their respects before her body was cremated at sunrise. Just as the first Oracle had shattered his *naga* to represent the precedence of wisdom over martial skill, her apprentices would've broken her *naga* and mixed it with the shards of all the great Paladins' *nagas* in the Crystal Citadel.

In this faraway land, all of this was up to him. Tears blurred his vision. He brushed her lifeless eyes closed and folded her hands together over her belly. He looked around the room.

His stomach dropped into his gut. Neither her *naga*, nor his, were anywhere to be found. The damned Scorpions must've stolen them, probably to melt down and make those hideous masks. Fists clenched tight, he rose.

CHAPTER 14:

Whispers of the Gods

Cassius surveyed the dome room, wishing the last two signores would hurry up and leave so he could do some Divining. His gaze paused on Brehane and Makeda, apparently discussing the dome in their own tongue, from all that their body language revealed.

How he'd love to coax the both of them into bed, Brehane for a second time and Makeda for the first. Really, Brehane alone would be enough, just to redeem himself. And maybe, just maybe...

He shook the ridiculous notion out of his head. It was looking less and less likely, anyway. The only thing that spread faster than a good reputation was a bad one, and he was on the verge of earning the latter. If this Sohini was being held by Don Acerbi—which Cassius doubted, despite Signore De Lucca's claims—rival Diviners would spread rumors of how he hadn't been able to locate someone in his own city. Not to mention, he'd lose his opportunity to manipulate the Paladins into protecting the pyramid.

Now, this Signore party left little time to Divine both her location and an auspicious time for the Paladins to meet with the Acerbi family. And despite all previous failed attempts to Divine anything about De Lucca, his goals were becoming more and more suspect.

Motioning for Patrizio, he strolled over to Signore Bianchi, whose face was nuzzled in a courtesan's cleavage. "Signore Bianchi, allow my steward to take you to a guest room."

Bianchi looked up, his grinning face red and stupid.

With a nod from Cassius, Patrizio hurried over and helped Signore Bianchi to his feet. "Signore, allow me to pour you into a guest bed?"

Cassius turned to Signore Rossi, who had one prostitute in his bulky lap and another at his side.

"Signore Rossi, it is getting late. Your carriage is waiting outside."

Laughing, the man lifted the girl to her feet and struggled to stand.

Cassius lent him a hand and pulled him to the door. He gestured to another servant. "Have the dome room cleared, quickly."

The servant put two fingers to his forehead and nodded, then scampered off to direct the others.

Signore Rossi chuckled as he staggered, with Cassius' and the giggling woman's support. His speech slurred as he spoke. "I tell you, Signore Cassius, Signore

De Lucca's parties are more fun, but no one sets a table in your style. None have your mastery of spices. No plate compares to the feasts you serve."

"I'll take that as a compliment."

"Maybe if you let us share your Aksumi girls, it would be just as fun." Signore Rossi laughed so hard he broke into a fit of coughing.

Cassius cast a glance back at Brehane, who turned away from Makeda and locked gazes with him. They undoubtedly wouldn't be around for the next Signore reception, nor did he have any intention of sharing them with the Signores. To the Bovyans, for ridding Tokahia of the crime families, however...

The memory of Brehane's adoring eyes as she watched him cook surfaced. He shook it out of his head and reached the door. Taking a deep breath of the cool evening air, he cleared his nose of Signore Rossi's wine-heavy breath. The drunkard's covered coach waited by the steps, the driver jumping down from the seat to open the door.

One of the guards came over and helped Signore Rossi and De Lucca's two courtesans in. At least *he* would get his quim sandwich tonight, even if Cassius would not.

Cassius let out a long sigh as the coach set off into the night. He turned around to find Brehane and Makeda by the door.

Makeda took his hand and batted her eyelashes at him. Apparently she didn't care about whether his

Divining skills were suspect. "Cassius, are you ready to retire?"

His pulse notched up. If only he could! The Iridescent Moon waned toward full, when Heaven's Accountant claimed less of his soul from Divining...but if he could possibly get the both of them in bed at once, perhaps the task could wait until morning.

Brehane shuffled on her feet, her eyes going from their joined hands to meet his gaze. She neither frowned nor smiled. The local girls were easy to read and manipulate, but this one... Was a quick tryst possible?

He reached for her hand.

"Signore Larusso," a voice from the door called in a heavy accent.

Releasing Makeda's hand, he spun around.

The male Paladin master stood at the threshold, palms pressed together.

Cassius looked up at the Iridescent Moon, heading toward full. Almost midnight. "Master Anish. If you are coming to retrieve your apprentice, he already left with Signore De Lucca."

"I...with Signore De Lucca?" The Paladin master's forehead scrunched up.

"There was a disturbance at his downtown office an hour ago, and he convinced your apprentice that it might lead them to Sohini."

Master Anish harrumphed. "That is why I am here. Sameer is young and foolish, and I fear his emotional tie to Sohini will lead to his downfall. I must know her location, at once, before Sameer gets himself into too much trouble."

At once? A coincidence that he'd planned on Divining on this very question anyway. Even though he didn't have to reveal his actual interpretation, he could still milk the urgent request for a larger fee.

He looked from Master Anish to the two beautiful Mystics. On the Heaven's Accountant's balance sheet, the opportunity for a meal for three had been worth the cost of Divining at a more taxing time. Now, considering the additional fee, that pumpernickel chicken sandwich would have to wait. "I am very drained, but when the Iridescent Moon reaches full, I might be able to draw on enough energy to answer these questions. It will cost you."

"Do it." Master Anish's voice rolled over him like a tidal wave smashing into ships in the harbor.

Of course, it was a reasonable request. After all, he was going to do it anyway, albeit after a roll between Makeda and Brehane. Cassius turned and headed back to the dome room. Patrizio approached, all the while eyeing the Paladin master. "Signore Bianchi has settled in the guest chambers."

"Good. Bring me the large maps of the Tokahia."

Patrizio nodded and hurried off.

When Cassius arrived at the dome room, the servants were just finishing moving the tables and chairs to the storage room. The Divine Whispers rose to a shout in his ears, almost as intense as his megalith circle during a Full Blue Moon.

He looked up into the heavens. While the layman might appreciate the magnificence of a star-speckled night sky, the beauty of the stars lay in the mysteries they unlocked. Withdrawing Sohini's pendant that Sameer had given him, the strand of her hair from Anish, as well as two dice, he focused on the painted circle in the dome which showed the phases of the Iridescent Moon. Never tearing his gaze away from the moon, he wrapped the strand of hair around the twenty-sided die. There were only a few more minutes before it reached full, making Divining the most accurate and least draining on his soul. Patrizio had better hurry up with the map.

As always, the steward was reliable. He and another servant returned and stood at the edge of the floor mosaic map, where they unrolled the map so large that five men could lie on it.

Standing under the constellation of the Wanderer, which had been ascendant over Sohini's birthplace at her birth time, Cassius focused on the swirling colors of the Iridescent Moon. It was hypnotic as it waxed fraction by fraction, so much that he had to blink several times not to miss it.

Just before it reached full, he took a deep breath to suck in the Gods' Whispers. They surged through him. His fingers and toes tingled. He threw the dice onto the floor. The invisible hands of the gods guided them as they bounced in impossible curves over the mosaic floor map.

Somewhere behind him, Brehane gasped. "The Resonance," she whispered.

The dice and pendant tumbled through the Kingdom of Korynth and over several other of the Estomari city-states. They formed a triangle over Tokahia. The twenty-sider showed the symbol of Kor the Hunter, while the twelve-sider showed Kor's prey, The White Stag.

"As I suspected," Cassius said. "She is in Tokahia."

Brehane, Makeda, and Anish all crowded around, though they wouldn't understand the meaning: Sohini was still here in Tokahia, influenced by both Kor and the White Stag. How interesting a combination; one which meant she was both the hunter and the prey.

With the Gods' Whispers still coursing through him, he swept up the dice and pendant and returned to the spot under the Wanderer. He gestured toward Patrizio. "Lay down the city map, centered over Tokahia. Hurry."

The steward and the other servant rushed to the middle of the room and spread out the map.

Cassius cast the dice and pendant onto it.

Carried on the breaths of the Gods, the pendant ricocheted off the city map and took an impossible meandering roll off the map.

The dice, on the other hand, landed without a bounce, the twenty-sider in Mafia territory, showing The White Stag. The other fell right on top of the outline of a villa near the pyramid. Cassius counted the buildings.

His villa.

The shape of the building, with the dome room attached, should have made it obvious. The twelve-sider showed Kor the Hunter.

His head spun. The only other time he'd gotten such bizarre results was when trying to learn more about De Lucca. Now, with only two items on the city map, it was impossible to triangulate Sohini's exact location. There was no way to reveal this inconvenience without losing the ability to manipulate the Paladins. It wasn't as though he was going to tell the real location, anyway.

"Speak," Anish said, his voice again roaring like waves. "Tell me where Sohini is."

Cassius nodded. It was a reasonable demand. The Paladins had paid, after all. He leaned in and whispered, "She is here, in Tokahia. However, the three objects determine the range of her movement within the near future. With only two dice on the map, I cannot determine her exact location."

Frowning, Makeda said something to Brehane in their language. Brehane clasped the crystal around her neck. She shook her head.

They were doubting his ability, and if they left, the Bovyans wouldn't honor their deal to destroy the Mafia, and the Mafia would overwhelm the pathetic pyramid honor guard, and the orc gods would return on their flaming chariots... Everything was going wrong. Why had he even revealed his Divining failure, when it was so easy to come up with a glib excuse? He gritted his teeth. "It is like your missing Mystic," he lied. It was more like De Lucca. "Something prevents me from scrying her." He turned back to Anish. "I would surmise the Hunter, here on this very building, represents someone searching for her: you. The White Stag represents where she will flee to."

"Where is it?" Anish asked.

"In Mafia-held territory."

Brehane blew out a long breath. "Just like Signore De Lucca said."

Cassius gave a tentative nod. He was either confirming De Lucca's honesty, or reinforcing their trust. Maybe this wasn't a complete failure.

Anish's brows clashed together. "What did De Lucca say?"

"That the Acerbi crime family had captured her," Brehane said.

The Paladin turned to Cassius. "Is that what really happened? Tell me." Again, his voice felt like waves crashing on the beach.

"It is impossible to Divine at this time." Embarrassment washed over Cassius. Why had he answered the master's questions so honestly, again? How humiliating. Just after he'd saved his reputation, the Mystics would doubt his skill. He found them in the corner of his eye.

Brehane and Makeda exchanged glances, their expressions both contorted in disappointment.

Cassius clenched and unclenched his fists. If they didn't trust him, he wouldn't be able to keep them here long enough to fulfill his end of the deal with the

Bovyans; nor string the Paladins along until he could use them.

"Wait." He had to prove himself. He withdrew his star globe and twisted the rings to mark the current night sky. Sucking in another breath of the Whispers, his energy flagged. His head wobbled as his neck refused to support it. Fingers barely able to move, he tossed the globe toward the map. It floated in a gentle arc at first, but then dropped sharply. It landed right on Don Acerbi's headquarters, with the icon of the new Iridescent Moon facing up.

* * *

Brehane stared at the star globe, the symbols all gibberish. The shift in the Resonance still hung in the air and sang to her very core. The echo of the Paladin master's Command and Cassius' Divining felt like the aftereffect of a master Mystic's powerful spell.

It added more evidence to her theory of the similarities of magic.

Makeda would scoff at the idea. She hadn't been interested in experiencing this Divining magic, though she'd hung around, probably in hopes of taking Cassius to bed later. Now, she just yawned. She'd made it abundantly clear that the hostilities between the crime families and Signores wasn't their concern.

Perhaps a missing Paladin apprentice was just a diversion from finding Melas, but suspicion pricked at

Brehane's neck. Maybe it was more than just a coincidence that both had gone missing in the same city, a wondrous city; but other Mystic adepts had disappeared here, as well. She clasped her necklace and looked up from the star globe to Cassius.

Everyone else stared at him as well, all eyes expectant.

He was slumped over, panting, hands on his knees. His voice came out a weak whisper. "Noon tomorrow, at Don Acerbi's headquarters, is the most auspicious time to confront the crime families."

Brehane looked at the Paladin master. Lines formed on his forehead, and his jaw wiggled back and forth. What was he thinking? Casting a Neuromancy spell to read his mind would be too obvious, and her Ayuri language skills might not be good enough to understand his thoughts, anyway. Not to mention, such a difficult spell would drain her for days. She found Makeda in the corner of her eye.

The ugly *assama* looked to be lost in deep thought. She met Brehane's gaze. "So many missing people here."

Maybe she was smarter than she looked. Brehane turned to Cassius. "Besides Melas, the Mystic Council lost contact with two other adepts here. Is it possible the crime families are using them in their conflict with your government?"

"Paladins, too," Master Anish said. "At least six have gone missing. After I ruled out our rival recruiting them, I wasn't sure what had happened to them. Now, though, the evidence points to the Mafia."

Cassius might've already been pale from the draining effect of magic, but he managed to blanch even more. "I must inform the other signores. If the Mafia has hired the services of renegade Mystics and Paladin deserters, then they are even more of a threat to the city and the pyramid."

Makeda turned to her. "Cousin, I think this is now our concern."

CHAPTER 15:

Mistaken Identities

Gripping one of the knives she'd found in the chest of drawers, Jie set the light bauble behind her back. That way, whoever entered would only see her silhouette.

A thin young man stepped in, shading his eyes. A sleeveless longcoat made of silk and lace draped over his shoulders. Some kind of cosmetic foundation powdered his face to smooth perfection. Long black hair tumbled over his shoulders.

He looked like the portrait in the office. And, from the sound of it, Signore De Lucca was alone.

Every nerve tingled, muscles coiled and ready to leap. She flipped the knife into an underhanded grip.

"Sister," he said. "I'm glad you received my summons. I figured it was you trapped in here, though it's not like you to get spotted. I've sent everyone away."

Sister? The light at her back must've kept him from making out her features, and perhaps she had the same frame as his sibling. Or, he belonged to a clan like the Black Lotus. Could he, too, have been trained by the clan traitor? Jie lowered the knife, but kept the bauble behind her. Behind him, there were no other sounds from Bovyans tromping around.

He withdrew a folded sheet of paper from an inside pocket of his coat and proffered it. "Here's the report for Father."

What a strange turn of events, and definitely too easy compared to any of her past experiences. Not that it was worth complaining. Fighting the urge to bow Cathayi style, Jie tucked the knife into her sash. She took the letter and stuffed it into her dress where her cleavage would be if she had any.

"You are unusually silent tonight." He squinted at her.

She turned her head slightly, to keep him from getting a good look at her pointed ears. Never having seen or heard De Lucca's sister before, she had no way of using the *Mockingbird's Deception* to imitate her voice. "Sore throat," she croaked. Hopefully, that would provide a good cover. "I'll be on my way to deliver your letter."

She pocketed the light, plunging the room back into hues of green and grey. His human vision wouldn't be able to penetrate the darkness. Or could it? His eyes tracked her. He made no move to block her, and she slipped right by him, out of the secret room and into the library. Picking up pace, she took the longest strides her short legs could through the hallway. There still weren't any sounds of other people, though a Bovyan's back partially blocked the open front door.

Behind her, De Lucca's light footsteps trod through the library. Maybe he was suspicious. She had to get out before he called his guard to stop her.

Two paces behind the Bovyan, she modulated her voice to imitate De Lucca's. "Come here!"

As he turned around, Jie ducked low and twisted behind him. If she could rank the sweetness of the cool night air, she'd place it just behind the time after she'd gotten trapped by traitors in a saltpeter mine, and well ahead of escaping insurgents in the hold of a ship. None compared with making it out of a rebel lord's dungeon, naked, just before she blew up his castle with firepowder.

She dashed past the open iron gate and into the street, and didn't look back until she was in the shadows of the row house near the intersection.

At the entrance, De Lucca's head swept back and forth. She slunk around the corner and listened and searched for signs of Phobos, the unaccounted-for Nightblade. From what he had said, it sure looked as if the Bovyans had other plans besides just serving as De Lucca's hired muscle. He naïvely thought to use them against the Mafia, but it looked like they were playing him... But to what end? According to the pimp's financial records, there weren't enough to conquer the city. A Bovyan might be worth five normal humans—and when they fought in formation, no army had been able to repel them—but they'd need at least a thousand men.

With no sign of a tail, she dashed back toward the waterfront. The Paladin masters were staying at the *Seafarer*, and Sameer would hopefully find his way back there, if he hadn't first gotten in trouble turning Cassius Larusso's villa upside down. No, he would be all right, because that had been his muffled voice inside De Lucca's office earlier.

Periodically checking to ensure she wasn't being followed, she made her way through the moonlit streets. Now out of danger, she had to still her shaking hands. How lucky she'd been to avoid capture. In the end, it was almost too easy, with De Lucca just letting her go without confirming her identity in a brighter light. Not only that, but...

She withdrew De Lucca's message to his father and unfolded it. Even in the dim light, it was clear that it was written in the unreadable runes from before. A coded language, maybe. Perhaps it would reveal more about De Lucca's operations. Perhaps those Aksumi Mystics, with their magic, could find a way to translate it, though she'd hardly made a good first impression. Not to mention, their illusion baubles suggested they were somehow connected to the conspiracy back home.

The road to the *Seafarer* passed by the *Regent*, the three-story stone behemoth of elegance where Prince Aryn and his entourage were staying. Columns rose to arches, covering balconies. On her way to De Lucca's office earlier in the evening, she'd slipped past some of the prince's men, out searching for her. Her heart squeezed. Aryn must be distraught at her disappearance, and it would be nice to let him know she was okay. Heavens, it would be nice to give up on this silly chase and share what was undoubtedly a comfortable bed.

Alas, duty came first. The Aksumi and their illusion bauble of Princess Kaiya, searching for a missing master. Paladins, too, looking for a lost comrade. And Bovyans, specifically the Nightblade Phobos, who could apparently climb walls and moved with stealth. The convoluted web of connections couldn't all be coincidence, and no doubt she was a step closer to uncovering the clan traitor.

She cast a longing glance at the *Regent*, whose curtained glass windows were all dark. Behind one on the third floor, Aryn slept, hopefully alone and worrying about her. She continued down the road.

Up ahead, light orbs illuminated a small crowd, dispersing from the front of the *Seafarer*. At this late hour, it couldn't be anything good. A fight among drunken ruffians, maybe.

Then Sameer stumbled out the door. Perhaps it was the light, but he looked abnormally pale for someone so dark.

Jie slipped through the departing townsfolk and came to his side. "What's wrong?"

His eyes fell on her with little focus. Then, recognition bloomed on his face. His voice managed to tremble as he intoned her single-syllable name. "Jie."

She nodded. "What happened?"

"Elder Gitika...she's dead." He set his fingers at an angle.

Dead? Jie'd cleaned and stitched the old woman's wound. There was little chance of infection, and even if there had been one, it wouldn't have killed so fast, unless... "Poison?"

He shook his head. "No. They cut her throat."

They... "The Bovyans?"

"The Acerbi crime family."

Jie gawked. It was the family De Lucca had threatened with a scorpion sting. Maybe they'd launched a pre-emptive strike. Still, how could a bunch of mobsters defeat two Paladin masters, even if one were wounded? No, they'd need a Paladin to fight a Paladin, and there was one unaccounted for. "I think you need to consider the possibility that Sohini works for the crime family."

Sameer's face, pale up to now, flushed an interesting shade of red. "Never. She would never do such a thing."

Jie held her hands up and took a step back. "Consider this: I saw your master overcome several Bovyans—the best-trained soldiers in the world." Albeit not the smartest. "I can't believe a bunch of ruffians could scratch her, let alone overcome both her and Master Anish. And where is he?"

Sameer's voice cracked. "Just as we planned, Master Anish had left to meet me at Signore Cassius' villa. It was a phase before the attack. She was injured and tired. And alone."

Lucky timing on the part of the Mafia, to catch an injured Paladin by herself. Jie snorted. No, there was no such thing as luck, and nothing he'd said ruled out Sohini. "I still don't think a bunch of thugs could beat her."

"The innkeeper says they had the help of a Golden Scorpion."

Jie's head spun. With the Mafia and Signores, this city's power dynamics made little sense already. Now, Madura's anti-Paladins were thrown into the mix. Perhaps the Mafia was hiring Golden Scorpions to escalate their fight with the Signores. Still, something didn't add up. "What did the Mafia have to gain by attacking her?"

"I don't know." His eyebrows knitted together. "De Lucca says he sent Sohini to attack the Acerbi family, and they captured her. Maybe they knew we would try to rescue her, and launched a pre-emptive attack."

"All right. Still, I can't believe it is just luck that they attacked when your master was wounded, alone, and undefended. You have to consider that someone is helping them. Who knew Master Anish wouldn't be there, and who benefits from her death?"

His brow furrowed. "Nobody knew we'd be coming to this town, not even Master Anish."

Jie snorted. It was a town full of Diviners, so somebody had to know something. They might even be able to solve this mystery...if their magic was real in the first place. Really, she'd trust Black Lotus forensics over fortune-telling any day of the week. She pointed her chin at the *Seafarer*. "Come on. I'm going to check out your room."

He followed her, tentatively. Inside, men wearing the black armbands of the Signores' police looked to be wrapping up their investigation.

The apparent leader waved toward Sameer. "The priestesses of the Temple of Mortasi are coming to retrieve the remains."

Sameer's hands formed an unfamiliar *mudra*. "I must clean her corporeal form so it can be cremated at dawn."

"They will clean the body, but..." The inspector shuddered. "Only the evil are cremated, to purify their remains."

"I need to see her first," Jie said. "Sameer, take me to your room."

He nodded, and when the inspector gestured them through, she followed him up the stairs.

Inside the large room, the investigators had already mucked up the crime scene. There was no telling if the muddy footprints belonged to the attackers or law enforcement. A shattered ceramic cup lay overturned, its contents seeping into the floor.

Her eyes locked on the body lying on a bed. She pulled back the sheet. The old woman lay on her back, her legs straight and arms by her side, as if asleep. The gaping throat wound had been poorly executed, hacked instead of slashed, most likely with a large weapon. It ruled out any of these Nightblades.

There were no other injuries, save for the one she'd sewn up earlier in the day. No smell or skin discoloration suggested poisoning. When Jie placed a hand on the belly, it was warm. She moved one of the arms to find it still pliable. The crime must've occurred within a couple of hours.

She beckoned the inspector. "Is this how the body was found?"

Staring at her wide-eyed, the inspector harrumphed. "Of course. The only ones who would touch a dead body are the priestesses of Mortasi."

And Black Lotus adepts. She pointed to the master's throat. "Whoever it was used a heavy weapon, not a knife. I don't think a bunch of ruffians could sneak up here without making enough noise to catch her unawares. It's possible they killed her first and put her body on the bed, but..." Her eyes strayed back to the broken cup.

She went over and knelt by the fluid stain. Wiping a finger across, she sniffed it. It was sweet. "What was she drinking?"

"Tulsi tea," Sameer said. "It helps relax someone so they heal faster."

Perhaps it was too relaxing. If only there was enough for her to taste. Jie sucked on her lower lip. "If not Sohini, what about Master Anish? Can you trust him?"

Sameer's jaw gaped wide. "Of course. The council chose him, specifically, to prevent those who gave up their Paladin training from joining Madura's Golden Scorpions. He is beyond reproach."

Was he? He'd been against seeking out the Diviner's help, or accepting Jie's assistance. Sameer lacked the objectivity to even consider it. "Your master was killed by a large hacking weapon, like an axe...or a Paladin *naga*."

Sameer scowled. "Both hers and mine are missing. The attackers likely used them, or a Scorpion used his sting. The weapons are similar."

Certainly a possibility, but... Jie headed out of the room.

"Where are you going?" Sameer called.

"To talk to the innkeeper." She made her way down the steps, Sameer's and the inspector's footsteps hurrying after her.

In the foyer, the innkeeper was speaking to a middle-aged woman. "If word gets out..."

Wringing her hands, she nodded. "No one will ever stay here again."

With a sidelong glance at the inspector, Jie cleared her throat. "I hear a band of Acerbi thugs came through here. How many were there?"

The innkeeper exchanged glances with the woman and counted on his fingers. "Eight? Maybe nine?"

"Any Ayuri among them?" She tilted her head toward Sameer, just in case they forgot what an Ayuri looked like.

The innkeeper looked at him and cocked his head. "I...I don't think so. Unless it was the person in the mask."

Jie studied his expression. The answers were vague, but his disconcerted facial expressions and body language didn't indicate lies or treachery. "Was the one in the mask male, or female?"

"They were wearing a *mask*." The innkeeper squinted at her like she was feebleminded.

"You couldn't tell from their, uh...body shape?"

The innkeeper's expression went blank. "I...I didn't notice. I must've been looking at the mask."

"What were they wearing?"

"I really don't remember." The innkeeper shook his head.

The inspector harrumphed. "I already asked."

Jie looked around and raised her voice. "Did anyone else outside see the attackers?"

Only blank stares greeted her.

She turned back to the innkeeper. "Were there any other guests here?"

He shook his head.

All dead ends. She turned to Sameer. "The Scorpion might come back, and you don't have your sword. If your master went to Signore Larusso's, we should go meet up with him."

"What about Elder Gitika's body?" Sameer gestured up the steps. "In the absence of family, I should be the one to clean it."

Jie studied him. His forlorn expression looked like the Black Lotus temple dogs when they got scolded. With a sigh, she nodded. "I will help you."

Sameer's lips first rounded, then turned up into a smile with an uncharacteristic warmth. He bowed his head, and formed his hands up in the *mudra*. "Thank you."

"I'll go get some water and cloth," she said.

"No, wait." He held up a hand. "We need a mixture of milk, yogurt, clarified butter, and honey."

It didn't seem like time for a snack, and who knew how to clarify butter? Jie raised an eyebrow. "It's midnight. How will we find that?"

Sameer's shoulders slumped. "Then flowers. Collect them to scent water, which has to be boiled first."

Now it was Jie's turn to round her lips. Apparently, the aforementioned food was meant to cleanse the body. "All right, you go with the innkeeper to boil some water, I'll go out and find some flowers."

Outside, the crowds had dispersed. She looked around. There wasn't much foliage at all, but a patch of dandelions grew between some pavestones. Back home, herbalists would prescribe them for fighting infections, but they'd have to do. She picked those, and caught sight of dawn-blooming everblossoms growing next to the inn. Used for women's issues, they would bloom too late to be decorative, but maybe they could still infuse water with a sweet scent. She grabbed those as well, and went back into the inn.

She returned to the room and found Sameer alone, contemplating his master's body, which was draped in a fresh sheet. Not even the famous poets of the Yu Dynasty could capture in words all the love and respect pregnant in his gaze.

He looked up, expression hardening. "We need to align her north-to-south, with her head to the south, but I'm so confused by the direction of the Iridescent Moon. It's not where it is supposed to be."

Jie nodded. When she'd first travelled out of her homeland, it had been disconcerting to find the Iridescent Moon, which never moved from its seat in the heavens, in a different spot. Of course, Black Lotus training included many ways to find directions on cloudy days. She pointed south.

While Sameer pushed and pulled the bed so it was at the right angle, she dropped the flowers into a bucket of steaming water. The pungent scent of dandelions mingled with the sweet aroma of everblossoms.

"Thank you." His hands formed up in a *mudra*. Then he dipped a white cloth into the water and unshrouded the body to the shoulders. Chanting in Ayuri, in what sounded like some kind of prayer, he glided the cloth over her face. Though he was smiling, tears glassed over his eyes.

He finished washing her shoulders and arms, then wetted the cloth, uncovered her legs, and cleaned those too. Still chanting, he took special care to scrub between her toes. He looked up and passed her the cloth. "Please clean her torso. Chant a mantra while you do so."

A mantra? She raised her eyebrow at the Ayuri word.

"It's like...a prayer. Something you recite."

Black Lotus recitations were mnemonics for toxin names, pressure points, heraldry, and the like. None seemed appropriate for the gravity of the situation. Instead, she chanted the poem of the clan's three famed young masters. The Architect, Surgeon, and Beauty had all died on a secret mission just before she was born, and the entire clan mourned and venerated them. With Sameer's back turned, she undraped the body and washed it.

Emotionally, it shouldn't have been much different from cleaning the wounds of live people, or modifying corpses with make-up to make a death look less suspicious. Still, Sameer's chants weighed on her shoulders.

Halfway through, Jie's ear twitched. The door to the inn had creaked open downstairs. Footsteps crept up the stairs. Mafia, coming to finish the job? Or the Golden Scorpion? She palmed three throwing spikes. "Sameer, someone's coming. Close the door."

He turned around and reached for his *naga*, which wasn't there. He stumbled toward the door.

The footsteps came closer, the length of their stride and echo on the wood floors suggesting an average male. The Mafia would've sent several men, so maybe it was the Scorpion. Jie cocked her spikes back, ready to throw.

Just before Sameer reached the door, his male master, Anish, turned the corner. He froze in place, hand on his hilt. Then he relaxed. "Sameer! And...Jie. How are you...here?"

Jie scrutinized him. "Where else would I be?"

"It's late, wouldn't you be back...wherever you came from?" His eyes strayed down, then widened. He ran over and knelt by the body. "By the Thousand Gods! What happened?"

Sameer came to his side. "Mafia enforcers, assisted by a Golden Scorpion, killed her."

"So there really is a Scorpion operating here." Master Anish's voice cracked. He looked up, tears in his eyes, hands set in a *mudra* of sorrow. "If only I had been here."

The grief in his tone and expression were either genuine, or worthy of a renowned stage actor. Perhaps Sameer's assessment of him was correct. Which meant unlucky timing. Anish had left her alone, and Sameer hadn't even needed him at the Diviner's villa. Jie looked back down at the dead elder.

"We should find Prince Dhananad and his Scorpion guard." Sameer turned to Jie. "Can you find out where he is staying?"

Jie nodded. It shouldn't be hard to track down a flamboyant foreigner...one coincidentally linked to the three famed Black Lotus masters.

"Not yet," Anish said. "We don't know how many Scorpions he has at his disposal. There might have been one when we faced the mobsters earlier, blocking Elder Gitika's power. We are tired, and you don't even have your *naga*. It would not be wise to rush in."

Jie looked from Anish to Sameer. Rushing in was Sameer's specialty, but hopefully he would listen to a master.

"Then what do we do?" Sameer's hands clenched and unclenched.

Anish bowed his head toward Gitika's body. "For now, we finish what you started." He extended his hand toward Jie.

She pressed the cloth into his palm.

"Thank you." His head bobbled. A long sigh escaped him as he set about cleaning the body. "I was Master Gitika's apprentice, too."

Sameer nodded. "What was your fondest memory?"

"We were in Vyara City," Anish said, dabbing the master's eyelids. "She was negotiating peace with Madura's Grand Vizier when young Prince Dhananad was kidnapped. The Madurans accused us of treachery."

Jie held in a gasp. Unbeknownst to anyone but the clan, the Black Lotus' three famed masters, using the guise of trade negotiators, had been involved with that plot against Prince Dhananad. "What happened?"

"Master Gitika saved me, single-handedly holding three Golden Scorpions at bay." Wistfulness hung in his voice as he cupped her lifeless cheek. "The impasse broke when the Last Dragon awoke from a thousand years of sleep and flew over the city, on his way to the Ayudra pyramid where he stole our people's Dragonstone."

Feigning awe, Jie nodded. It had all happened a year before she was born, and despite the fact that all the young masters had died soon after, their actions had secured a trade deal which had profited her homeland.

Anish turned to her, eyes intense. "We need some cord to tie her big toes together, prayer beads to wrap her hands into prayer, and a garland of flowers for her neck. Also a lot of wood, and a place to cremate her by the sea. Can you go find all that before dawn?"

More flowers, more tasks to do. Somehow she'd gone from elite spy, to prince's bedmate, and now to errand girl. Still, he'd asked politely, and this was a chance to get away from his scrutinizing stare. Outside, the Iridescent Moon waned to half, indicating three hours until dawn. With a sigh, she bowed her head and headed out.

CHAPTER 16:

Farewells

As if possible Mafia recruitment of gifted foreigners to assault the pyramid wasn't headache enough, Cassius now had to put out a literal fire, lest the rest of the signores complain about all the chaos caused by his clients. Every jolt of the carriage's wheels over uneven pavestones sent his headache from annoying to excruciating. He'd been in such a rush, he hadn't even gone through his morning ritual of consulting star charts to gauge the day's risks and opportunities.

He squinted to where the sun glowed red, not far above the horizon. The star of Arcea, the Traitor, hung unseen over it, suggesting those on righteous paths would face betrayal. Was his path righteous?

Of course it was. The pyramid was at risk, and with it came the potential danger of the orc gods returning on their flaming chariots.

He sighed. It was much too early in the morning, after a late night of Divining, to be righteous. His arms might now be draped over Makeda and Brehane on either side of him, but neither were naked and sated. Instead, they wore their white Mystic robes. The male, Dawit, unseen since the afternoon before, had wanted to come, but Makeda ordered him to stay behind at the manor.

The scent of burning wood and something unfamiliar filled his nose. Cassius blinked several times. A line of smoke curled up from behind the seawall, not far ahead.

"Over there," he ordered his driver.

The smoke smell grew stronger as they passed through some of the old villas, until they at last came to a sandy beach where fishermen often tied down small boats.

He stumbled out of the carriage and, not bothering to help Makeda or Brehane this time, shouldered his way through the crowd of fishermen, city watch, and fire brigade members gathered at the top of the seawall. Many had covered their faces with colorful cloth.

A pyre of driftwood and planks burned on the sand, just a dozen paces away. Both the Paladin master and the apprentice stood nearby, palms pressed together, chanting. And beside them...

A girl, in a frilly but filthy and torn pink dress, whose style had been all the rage years ago. Pointed ears poked through her long, dark-brown hair. An elf, perhaps? They rarely left their secluded valley realms. The last one on record to visit Tokahia was the golden-haired one who'd fought the Iron Avatar outside the pyramid on the night of the Hellstorm, three hundred years ago.

The girl looked directly at him for a few seconds before turning her attention back to the pyre.

He sucked in a breath. By Ayara, she was stunning. Exotic. Not just elf, but part-Cathayi as well, given her honey-toned skin.

Alas, she was much too young. Maybe a segment of De Lucca's clients wouldn't care about her age, but Cassius would have to wait a few years. Or maybe a decade more, with the longevity of elf blood. He shook out the thought.

"Signore," the fire brigade chief said, joining him. "Every time we try to approach, one of the Ayuri blocks our way."

Cassius nodded, then took the steps down to the beach. "Master Anish, Sir Sameer, this type of open fire violates our city ordinances. Just what are you doing here?"

The two Paladins continued their chanting.

The half-elf beauty walked over and curtseyed with the grace of a cat. Her Cathayi accent lilted, adding to her charm. "Signore Cassius."

She knew his name. Of course she did. He swept into a bow, but then pointed at the bonfire. "This is against the law."

"The Ayuri are sending off their departed master."

So they were sending a signal? Cassius squinted out to sea. There were no signs of a ship, nor did the harbormaster's office have record of one scheduled to disembark at this hour. "The Gods' Whispers did not speak of early ship departures today."

"Not *that* kind of departed." Shaking her head, the girl curled her index finger.

He stared at the finger and cocked his head.

She sucked on her lower lip—such a cute gesture—and drew a finger across her throat.

Cassius' jaw might've been in the sand. *That* kind of departed. The pyre wasn't a signal to the old master… He peered into the flames. Something blackened and suspiciously human-shaped burned on top of the wood. Bile rose to his throat, and he covered his mouth.

Straightening, he looked over his shoulder. Makeda and Brehane were just descending the seawall, and thankfully, couldn't have possibly seen his moment of weakness. He cleared his throat, as if that would dispel the foul taste in his mouth.

The half-elf smirked for a split second. "They were insistent on cremating the body at dawn."

Cassius tore his gaze away from the body. "What…what happened?" He regretted the words as soon as they left his mouth.

"Surely the great Signore Larusso knows everything that happens under the stars." The half-elf raised an eyebrow.

Curse every god. Exhaustion was throwing him off his game today. He gestured to the sun. "When Tivar, the Deceiver, shrouds the sun in his veil of red, one cannot trust the Gods' Whispers."

"Riiiight." She winked. "The Mafia attacked her last night."

"I see." Cassius nodded in slow bobs. Was this part of the crime families' strategy to seize the pyramid? Perhaps they had tried to recruit the old master, too, and killed her when she refused. He waved the fire brigade chief over, then pointed to the buildings past the seawall. "Lucian, is the fire a danger to the buildings?"

Lucian nodded. "Yes, but many of the structures in this district are the concrete buildings from the old days, and the others have stone facades. With no breeze, the danger is low. If it were closer to some of the crime family districts, I would be more concerned."

"Very well. Keep watch on the fire, make sure it stays under control."

Lucian gestured to some of his men and hurried off.

Cassius turned back to the pretty girl. "The Paladins are clients of mine. They didn't tell me they had a companion, Miss...?"

"Jie." Her eyes flicked behind him before meeting his.

Cassius looked over his shoulder, tasting the foreign name. *Jyeh.*

Brehane and Makeda traipsed across the beach, the latter muttering in their language as she held her robes up and stared at the sand like a cursed soul forced to walk across Mortasi's bed of glass shards and hot coals.

He turned back to her. "I am sure I would've heard of a half-elf in Tokahia."

"I'm surprised you didn't Divine my arrival." Her grin was mischievous, in an adorable way. "The sun wasn't red when I landed."

"You!" Brehane marched through the sand, pointing at Jie.

The half-elf put a finger on the tip of her nose and blinked. "Me?"

"You were following us yesterday, before you went after the Ayuri Paladins." Brehane snarled a word of magic. A purple flame flared in her palm.

"Brehane..." Cassius looked from Mystic to half-elf. All these people's paths were intersecting, and nothing in the stars had hinted at a convergence. Damn that shooting star from a few days ago, throwing everything off. Now, it looked like Brehane was about to roast Jie, probably before the fire brigade could douse her.

* * *

Had Jie known the Mystics would appear his morning, she would've stayed out of sight. Now, the one with the plain robes looked like she planned on starting a second pyre, with half-elf blood as the fuel.

Up close, the flower scent in their hair fogged up Jie's brain. Shaking her head, she waved her hands back and forth. Hopefully the Mystics couldn't detect falsehoods or read minds. "You misunderstand. I was just headed to Signore Cassius' megalith circle, when I saw an acquaintance. Then it turned out to be you, with the magic bead."

"Do you know the girl in the image?" Eyes brightening, Brehane snuffed out the flame. She exchanged glances with her companion, who wore fine silken robes and enough jewelry to open her own shop.

Rich Girl shook her head.

Brehane's lip curled. Whatever their silent argument was, it looked like Brehane had made up her mind. She reached into her pouch. Her face and complexion transformed into the idealized version of Princess Kaiya... The same image Jie herself had assumed, with a similarly mysterious magic bauble, just weeks ago.

The Diviner, whose narrow eyes and drooping head suggested either a hangover or a long night, if not both, now sucked in a sharp breath.

Brehane—the fake princess—held out her palm, revealing a glass bauble. Just like the one Jie had used to thwart a rebellion. Its size and shape was the same as all the light beads the Mystics made and sold in every corner of the continent.

Jie looked her up and down. It was such an exact copy, it must've been created by the same person. Of course, the Mystics didn't have to know about that. At least, not yet. "You look like a famous painting of the princess of Cathay. How did you come by this magic?"

Even if Brehane now looked like a pretty version of Princess Kaiya, when she spoke, her voice didn't begin to compare with the princess' melodiousness. "It was infused with an illusion by our missing adept, Melas."

Yet another missing person, and unless Aksumi Illusionists all used the princess' generous court painting as practice, the missing person was undoubtedly connected to the failed coup back home. "Is he here in Tokahia?"

Brehane looked to Cassius and raised her eyebrow.

Cassius pointed north. "The stars say he is north of here. How far, I am not sure. It could be as close as that house, or as far as the Teleri Empire."

Some Diviner. Suppressing a snort, Jie studied him. "How about Sohini? Any luck with her?"

Cassius' eyes flicked to the Paladins. "Didn't the master tell you?"

"Tell me what?"

"I Divined last night, at his request. Sohini, too, is somewhere in the city."

Jie looked to Anish. He'd said nothing about this. Still, it was possible that what Sameer said was true, that Signore De Lucca had sent Sohini to attack the Acerbi. It also didn't discount Sohini working for the Mafia. That made the attack on the Paladins more plausible, starting with... She turned to Brehane. "Would an Illusionist be able to magic up a bauble that makes the holder invisible?"

Rich Girl, who'd looked bored up to now, snorted. "Maybe three hundred years ago, before the Biomancers betrayed the Illusionists. Since then, none have been able to invoke invisibility, let alone imbue that magic into a bauble."

Brehane glared at her, then turned back. "If anyone could do it, it would be Melas. Invisibility is easier than recreating all the detail of a new face." She held out the bauble in her hand again.

Melas. Nightblades, trained by a traitor. All had contributed in some way to the attempted coup in Cathay, and all were connected to Tokahia. Maybe the plan had been hatched right here. Or maybe it was just a coincidence. The local Mafia would have no reason to interfere with Cathay. Jie sucked on her lower lip.

She let it go with a pop. "A Bovyan using an invisibility bauble joined the Mafia in attacking the Paladins. Perhaps Melas is a mercenary, hiring his skills out to the highest bidder, and that bidder happens to be the Bovyans who work for the crime families. The Mafia is the common denominator."

Brehane sucked in a sharp breath and exchanged a glance with Rich Girl.

The Diviner, whose hangover didn't prevent him from trying to sneak a peek down Rich Girl's neckline, cleared his throat. "I told Master Anish that the most auspicious time to meet with Don Acerbi would be noon. The best place, at his headquarters."

Jie looked up at the Iridescent Moon, now waning toward its second crescent. Five hours until noon. But going into the lion's den sounded like a recipe for disaster. "Why would you want to do that?"

Cassius cocked his head and winced. "Signore De Lucca was going to send some of his Bovyans with Sir Sameer to confront Don Acerbi and demand Sohini's release."

There was enough doubt in the Diviner's tone to suggest he, too, thought it was a bad idea. Jie looked to the Paladins, still chanting. Perhaps Don Acerbi had Sohini, or maybe De Lucca was looking to escalate the turf wars, using a brash Paladin apprentice and his master. After last night's encounter with Signore De Lucca... She patted her chest, where the letter he'd given her was hidden. It might reveal his motives. She turned to the Mystics. "Can Aksumi magic translate written foreign languages?"

Rich Girl turned up her nose. "Of course."

Jie pulled out the letter. "I need this translated. In return, I will help you find your missing Illusionist."

Rich Girl harrumphed. "I doubt you can help us."

Jie tilted her head to the Paladins. "I found out more about their missing apprentice than the greatest Diviner in the Estomar."

If Cassius had looked dopey before, his mismatched eyes now glared at her.

She waved her hands and grinned. "Not you. I meant a tarot-card reader we met."

Brehane peered at the sheet. "What is it?"

Revealing what it was would inevitably lead to questions of how she got it. The answer would probably fuel the Mystics' suspicion that she was a pickpocket. Then there was Signore Cassius, who might very well be De Lucca's ally. It was time to lie. "A crime family message to De Lucca."

Cassius' eyes drew into sharp focus. He reached for it. "How did you get ahold of it?"

She pulled it out of his reach as she prepared a new lie to drive a wedge between him and De Lucca. "From the men who attacked the Paladins yesterday."

He turned to the Mystics, his haggard expression transforming into that of a rakish playboy. "Please, my lady, translate it."

Both reached for it, but Jie passed it to Brehane, who'd been less of a turtle's egg.

Brehane turned her shoulder, avoiding Rich Girl's grab, like the games of keep-away Black Lotus children played, albeit with sharp objects. She unfolded the letter with a whip of her wrist.

Rich Girl's eyes went from the strange runes to Jie. "What language is this?"

Jie shrugged. "If I knew, I would've found someone who could read it already."

Rich Girl harrumphed and looked back.

Cassius looked over Brehane's shoulder, his chin nestled on her neck. She flashed a smug smile at Rich Girl, who frowned.

The Diviner might be handsome, but certainly not worth acting like a pair of cats in heat around. Jie suppressed a snort. "Um, the letter?"

Brehane knelt and placed the paper on the sand. Producing a crystalline prism from a pouch, she set it atop the sheet. She then spoke a three-second string of words which sounded like the temple dogs fighting for scraps. The prism glowed, and the words on the paper swirled into yet another foreign script. Her eyes roved over it.

Jie leaned in. The new squiggly lines made no more sense than the runes. "What does it say?"

Brehane started to speak, but Rich Girl interrupted and said, "*Father—*"

"Father?" Cassius cocked his head, and winced again.

Brehane nodded, and looked up at Jie. "Are you sure this is from De Lucca to the crime families?"

Looking over her shoulder to make sure the Paladins weren't paying attention, Jie turned back and shrugged again. "That's what the man we dispatched said, but who knows? Maybe he lied. What else does it say?"

Rich Girl cast a triumphant glance at Brehane. "It says, *Father: Plans are proceeding on schedule. I've convinced most of the signores to support using Bovyan mercenaries to protect the pyramid.*"

Jie looked to Cassius. From his expression, perhaps the smell of smoke was coming from his ears, not the funeral pyre. He and De Lucca must be rivals. "Who is De Lucca's father?"

Cassius shook his head. "No one knows."

"Except the Mafia, apparently, since he sent the letter with one of their thugs." It didn't matter that it was a lie, just that it would get her close to the creator of the illusion bauble—and therefore, the conspiracy back home.

Cassius turned to Rich Girl. "De Lucca said he wanted to introduce you to his sister. Sometimes, girl talk can reveal even more than the Whispers of the Gods."

Jie's ears perked. De Lucca had confused her for his sister the night before.

"That's of no interest to me." Rich Girl waved a dismissive hand. "I am going to go talk to Don Acerbi."

Brehane stared at her. "Stupid *assama*. What do you hope to accomplish?"

"I will ask them nicely about Melas." Rich Girl threw her hair over her shoulder.

Whatever else anyone could say about Rich Girl, no one could accuse her of being a coward. A fool who might be walking herself into a prostitution ring, maybe, but not a coward. No matter what happened, she'd provide the perfect diversion for a little reconnaissance, to see if Melas had any dealings with the Mafia. In any case, as much as she wanted to see what De Lucca's sister looked like, Jie didn't want to risk another meeting with De Lucca himself. "I'll take you there."

Of course, she'd have to figure out where *there* was.

Cassius favored her with a raised eyebrow, then turned to Rich Girl. "It will be much safer to meet De Lucca's sister."

Rich Girl pointed her chin at Brehane. "Let my useless cousin engage in idle chit-chat. Come, elf girl." She beckoned with a flippant jerk of her head.

"Take some of the watch with you!" Cassius waved furiously at some of the men in black armbands.

Rich Girl wasn't waiting. She picked up the hem of her robe and marched through the sand toward the seawall.

A captain of the watch came and bowed. "Yes, Signore?"

"Take a squad and follow her, Julius! She's going to Don Acerbi." Cassius' voice sounded frantic, yet he did nothing to stop Rich Girl.

The incredulous look on Julius' face would've inspired caricature artists for the next century, if they'd seen it. "Signore, the families would see it as a violation of our truce."

"Do it, but don't be aggressive." Cassius turned to Jie. "Please, keep an eye on her."

Jie nodded, even if she'd only do so as long as babysitting didn't conflict with her own agenda. She motioned to the chanting Paladins. "Let them know I'll be back."

Cassius nodded like an agitated seal she'd seen at one of the ports.

She started to hurry after Rich Girl, but paused. "What's her name, by the way?"

"Makeda."

Makeda, like the name of the first sorceress in history. It even sounded rich. Jie hurried after the ten members of the city watch. Maybe they'd know where to go, and she could pretend to be guiding.

When they caught up with Makeda, she was tapping her toe. "Come on, fools."

Julius frowned, but took the lead. Jie strode by his side as they traced the waterfront road. Near the entertainment district, he turned up a broad street lined with brightly colored row houses. He and the rest of the guards slowed, their steps becoming uncertain. They must be getting close, given their reticence.

That, and the handful of eyes which tracked them from several of the windows. Outside the centermost house, which boasted a stone façade painted a nightmarish orange, two men in grey longcoats placed hands on their hilts.

Feigning an air of certainty, Jie pointed at them. "Don Acerbi's."

Makeda turned to the watch. "You are all unnecessary. Stay here."

While Makeda walked to the door, Jie inched back to the side street, to see if there would be an alley behind the building.

CHAPTER 17:

Kindred Spirits

Sitting next to Cassius in his carriage as it wound up the waterfront road, Brehane looked at Signore De Lucca's manor. The blush of dawn reflected in the marble columns and façade. How many Geomancers would it have taken to shape such a marvelous structure? Though not as sprawling as Cassius' villa, it still dwarfed any building in Aksumi lands. A large purple banner with a gold lion hung from a third-floor balcony.

The short ride from the beach where the Paladins were cremating their master hadn't provided much time to analyze Makeda's actions. Was it bravado? The dirty *assama* wasn't lacking in that, and it certainly wasn't charity. Bravado, that was it. Trying to show off to the Diviner that she was in charge.

Cassius hadn't seemed to care. He now rested his head on his palm, and his wincing looked like a man losing his virginity to an aggressive, middle-aged woman. The late night and true Divining must've taxed him. She'd pestered him with questions afterward: not just to learn more about his magic, but also to prevent him from taking Makeda to bed.

The carriage rolled to a stop outside a wrought-iron double gate, whose bars twisted up into lion crests. Two Bovyans in chain hauberks stood motionless outside.

Brehane sighed. Makeda might consider talking with Miss De Lucca idle chit-chat, but no doubt, learning who De Lucca's father was would get her in Cassius' good graces. And perhaps this sister was the brains behind the signore's rise to prominence.

The driver came out and opened the door. Cassius stumbled out, then turned and held out his hand. His voice lacked all the enthusiasm of the day before. "My lady."

Brehane took his hand and hopped out. Though the Bovyans' eyes were set forward at first, their gazes roved over her. It had been a common occurrence, perhaps to be expected given the rarity of Aksumi in the city.

"Kind sir," Cassius said. "Please inform Signore De Lucca that Signore Cassius wishes to speak with him."

One of the Bovyans came out of his statue-like stance, like an automaton the Artificer clan matriarch once demonstrated. He motioned toward the manor. Across the small courtyard, up some stairs to the front door, a young man dressed in a black longcoat jerked to attention. He turned and rapped on the door.

The Bovyan who'd gestured snapped back to his statuesque pose. Nothing moved. It was like waiting on a

Pyromancer ritual to finish, where something might explode if someone budged a fraction.

Then, another man with curly brown hair emerged from the manor and crossed the courtyard. He came to the gate and bowed. "Ah, Signore Cassius. What an unexpected surprise. I will inform Signore De Lucca of your arrival. In the meantime, come in."

When he opened one side of the gate, Cassius took her hand and guided her through. No matter how often he'd done this, the strange custom took a while to get used to. The steward ran ahead while they followed at a slower pace.

Up the marble steps and between the columns, they came to the entrance. Bowing, the young man opened the door and extended an open hand. Brehane looked to the Iridescent Moon. There were only three hours until Cassius' recommended time of confronting the Acerbi. She turned and entered.

The foyer, walled with shiny wood panels, might have been a quarter the size of Cassius', and lacked a stairway despite the height of the house. Their footsteps echoed across the black-and-grey tiles as the man guided them through an archway to the left.

Large windows allowed the morning sun stream into this new room. The man motioned them to plush chairs of a carved dark wood. Cassius guided her to one, then rounded a low table and plopped down in the other.

She sunk into the cushions, which felt almost like clouds. What magic was this?

"Please wait. I'll be back with some coffee." The man's shoes clacked off toward another room.

Coffee? Brehane looked to Cassius with a raised eyebrow.

Elbow on the chair's arm, the Diviner leaned over and rested his head on his palm. His eyes were closed.

Brehane cleared her throat.

His eyes flapped open. "My lady?"

"What is coffee?"

"A drink I could use right now." If his grin could get any feebler—

"Signore Cassius, welcome, welcome," Signore De Lucca said from the archway. Like the night before, he was impeccably dressed in a red-and-orange longcoat and yellow stockings; but today he wore no make-up to mute his fine, almost elf-like features. If his ears were pointed, he might be mistaken for a half-elf. He bowed. "And Miss Brehane. Thank you again for protecting me from the Paladin apprentice last night. To what do I owe the pleasure?"

"Signore De Lucca," Cassius said, climbing to his feet. "Thank you for seeing us with no notice."

De Lucca's high-pitched, grating laugh sounded too similar to Makeda's as he flashed a smile. "Of course. How could I not want to meet with my savior?"

Each of Cassius' nods made it look like a Neuromancer was trying to control his body. "Yes. Please forgive the early hour, but last night, I was Divining. A rare, fleeting situation augurs an auspicious time for new ideas, new beginnings, and new authority. Solaris ascends, while Chaos flees into shadows. Perhaps having Bovyans guard the pyramid is a good plan. I'd like to discuss it with you."

Rubbing his hands together, De Lucca grinned. "With no other signores? My, my."

Brehane favored Cassius with furrowed brows. He'd said nothing to her about pyramids, just that she needed to learn more about De Lucca's father from his sister.

Cassius' grin was so brittle it would break with a light tap. "Not every ear needs to hear the Gods' Whispers. Perhaps we should speak in private? Perhaps you would introduce your sister to Miss Brehane?"

"Of course, of course." De Lucca looked to her. "If you'll excuse us. My staff will bring you coffee, and I'll have my sister come entertain you."

Brehane watched them leave. How strange it was for men to discuss business, leaving women for idle talk. Or in this case, finding out about De Lucca's family. Once she'd progressed in Neuromancy, she could just pry the answers out with mindreading, but for now, she'd just use a charm spell. She watched the archway.

A servant came back bearing a silver platter which held ceramic cups with bizarre ears attached. Bowing, he set it on the table. "Cream or sugar?"

Brehane leaned forward and studied the drink. A rich aroma, like Geomancers tilling fresh earth, rose up in curls of steam from the dainty cups. Her eyes widened in excitement. "What is it?"

The servant's smile looked more condescending than polite. "Coffee. Imported from the Levastyan Empire."

As she reached for the cup, he twisted it so that the ear faced her. He muttered something unintelligible under his breath. "Take the handle, my lady. Otherwise you'll burn yourself."

She pinched the loop, lifted the cup, and sniffed. By the Tear of Makeda, it smelled amazing. Closing her eyes, she sipped it. Heat flowed through her, like the channeling of a Pyromancy spell. Then, energy surged up her spine, as if she'd Biomanced a man's seed.

The servant bowed and left, leaving her with the cup. She drained it, then took the other on the platter.

"Ahem," a female voice said from the archway.

Brehane looked up.

Standing there, open book in hand, was a homely young woman with hair the color of goat butter. Her forlorn expression screamed of loneliness. With a stick-thin arm, she took the hem of her frilly purple dress and curtseyed. "I am Signore De Lucca's sister, Lucia."

She looked nothing like De Lucca. Taller than him, she had broad shoulders. Her blunt nose and prominent forehead looked nothing like her brother's exquisite features. Despite ;her stout constitution, her wan complexion made it appear as if a Biomancer of old had stolen half her energy.

It would be too easy to use magic on her. Brehane feigned a sip from the empty coffee cup, then choked out the words of a charm spell.

The Resonance shifted with her words, rippling out from the syllables she'd invoked. It should've bent Lucia to her will; instead, the waves just absorbed into the girl. Brehane cleared her throat of the fake cough.

"Are you all right?" Lucia asked.

"Yes, thank you." Heat flared in Brehane's cheeks. Setting the coffee cup down, she stood and walked over. She took the girl's bony hands in her own. A grey ring sent a lance of cold, like a Hydromancer's ice dart, up Brehane's spine.

She withdrew and cleared her throat. "Greetings. I am Brehane, daughter of Dhanay. I trust your family is well?"

The girl raised a painted-on eyebrow. "My family?"

It was a standard Aksumi greeting, yet foreign to these light-skinned folk. Brehane attempted a smile. "Forgive me, this is how we introduce ourselves in my homeland."

"Oh. Not much to say about my family, it's just me and my brother."

This was easier than using magic. Still, the information conflicted with the half-elf's letter addressed to their father. "I'm sorry to hear that."

"You couldn't know." Lucia gestured to the chairs. "Please, sit."

Plopping into the cushions, Brehane snuck a glance at the leather binding of Lucia's book.

Perhaps her eyes hadn't been subtle enough. Lucia held it up, making the gold Arkothi lettering easier to read. *Taken by Pirates*.

Apparently, this Lucia was a woman of intellectual depth. Brehane nodded in approval. "What is it? The journal of someone captured by the Pirate Queen?"

If her reading showed intelligence, her giggle was as vapid as that of a young man vying to catch the attention of a woman. "No, no. It's fiction."

"Fiction?"

"Made-up stories. They've been all the craze since a local inventor took apart and reassembled a Cathayi printing press. My brother has a huge collection of fiction at his office."

Brehane's head rose and dropped in slow nods. "So it is a story teaching morality?"

Lucia's head swept in equally slow shakes. Chewing on her lip, she looked from the book to Brehane. The internal struggle written on her face looked like an Aeromancer trying to control a tornado. At last, she flipped a few pages and offered the book. "Here."

Taking the sacred tome in hand, Brehane looked at the words. *He drove in and out... Her back arched...* She looked up. "This is spectacular! Except it seems the author got the roles all wrong. Shouldn't the heroine be flogging the strapping, bound boy?"

Lucia giggled again. "I am sure there is a market for that kind of book, but I have never seen them in my brother's collection."

Smiling, Brehane clasped her hand. "Find that book. Or write it yourself. Get your brother to print and export these books to Aksumiland, and he'll get even richer."

Lucia flashed a grin and winked. "I'll be sure to find some for you."

They were virtually blood sisters. Brehane couldn't control her grin. "Back home, we say children are a reflection of their mother. Clearly, you and your brother are knowledgeable. Did you get your love of reading from your parents?"

Smile drooping, Lucia shook her head. "My parents were just peasants. They were illiterate."

"Still, they must have ingrained a strong work ethic for your brother to come so far."

Lucia's head shook even more. "My father worked hard, for sure, but it was back-breaking labor."

It didn't seem possible. Brehane looked at the fine furnishings. "Then how did Signore De Lucca build his business empire? He had to start somewhere."

Lucia leaned in and lowered her voice. "Let me tell you a secret: Rafael isn't my full brother. Nobody knows who his real father was."

It would explain why the two looked so different. "Not even your mother?"

With a sigh, Lucia circled a finger over her ear. "She was stricken by madness. She said the strangest things."

"Please, tell me."

Lucia looked over her shoulder to the entryway, then shrugged. "I guess anyone back home could tell you. She claimed an angel impregnated her."

Brehane covered her mouth. The only time angels had come to Tivara in the past was during the War of Ancient Gods, to teach humans magic so they could overthrow their orc slave masters. Could it even be possible? De Lucca did have exquisite features. "What do you think?"

"Well, truthfully, he doesn't look like anyone else in our village."

Brehane rubbed her hands together. "A handsome visitor, then."

"Nobody ever visits our village."

"Except angels, apparently."

Lucia leaned back in her chair and laughed. Hers sounded much more pleasant than De Lucca's. "Yes, except angels."

Brehane kept a smile transfixed on her face. With no father in the picture, perhaps the half-elf had gotten the letter from someone else.

Lucia leaned forward and rested her elbows on her knees. "There's more to the story. Mother said she had twins, but nobody ever saw the girl. Mother claims the angel came and claimed her right after birth."

They were either the ravings of a madwoman, or the...what was the word? *Fictional* origin story of some great heroine from the past. Sometimes they went hand in hand. "Well, your brother must've had some talent and luck."

"Both. And he needed both, because of his small size and girlish features. The other boys bullied him, until..." She let out a long sigh. "I remember the day clearly. I was working in the fields, and he'd gone to check his rabbit traps. Instead of a rabbit, he came back with a crystal this big."

The spread-out fingers of Lucia's hands formed a sphere. Brehane sucked in a sharp breath. The only gemstones that large were the Dragonstones atop the pyramids.

"We came to the city, where he sold it. He used the proceeds to buy and sell spices, and he got rich."

It didn't seem possible that one gemstone could lead to so much, unless the young De Lucca had an eye for doing business. "Do you remember where he sold the gemstone?"

Lucia shuddered. "That is also a mysterious story. Not long after, the jewelry store that bought it burned to the ground, killing the owner. The gemstone resurfaced years later in a flea market. By then, my brother was rich, and he bought it back. It sits on his desk in his office as a reminder of his good fortune."

Through the windows, movement flashed near the gates. Brehane turned and looked into the courtyard.

The iron gates flung apart, and Teacher Dawit strode through with two of the watchmen from before. Like any man, travelling exhausted him, and no doubt he found the foreign city intimidating. He hadn't come to the banquet the last night, but he looked refreshed now.

Back toward the foyer, the door swooshed open. Rapid footsteps clicked across the tile. The doorman scampered past the archway. Brehane exchanged glances with Lucia.

Cassius and De Lucca reached the foyer at the same time as Teacher Dawit and the watch.

De Lucca's jaw went rigid. "Julius. What is so urgent that you disturb us?"

Julius bowed. "Signore Cassius, the Aksumi girl was captured by Don Acerbi. They said if you want her back, her cousin would have to fetch her herself."

Captured! As satisfying as it would be to just leave Makeda in the hands of the crime family...

Cassius looked through the archway, his gaze meeting Brehane's, before turning to Teacher Dawit. "How fortunate you are here, now."

Julius shook his head. "We went to your villa, and your steward said you were coming here. Her teacher accompanied us from there. Still, we lost valuable time, and the Mafia said the teacher could not come. Only Lady Brehane."

Cassius looked at her again, then back at the watchman. "What about the half-elf?"

Julius shared a disdainful look with his comrade. "She disappeared before the Aksumi went into the Acerbi's den. We haven't heard from her."

Brehane frowned. All doubts disappeared. This Jie was definitely a rogue.

Teacher Dawit beckoned her. "You must go, Brehane. I know you don't like her, but she is heir to the Pyromancy clan, not to mention your cousin."

"You mustn't." Cassius shook his head, eyes wide. "The Mafia are ruthless."

Brehane rose. Maybe they'd try to capture her, too, and she'd never used magic in a real confrontation before.

"Julius, detain her." Cassius motioned to the guardsman, then met her gaze. "It's for your own safety."

"She must rescue Makeda." Dawit interposed himself, fingers twitching. Adorable for a scryer, a man no less, to think he could actually make a difference.

Julius, however, stared at his wriggling fingers with wide eyes.

Cassius' expression darkened. He looked at her and sighed. "If you go, then I will too. With guards."

De Lucca, who'd all but disappeared, cleared his throat. "Cassius, you mustn't. Nor the watch. It will escalate the conflict with the crime families. Things are already so tense. They will send armies of their enforcers to attack us."

Cassius chewed on his lip. His shoulders slumped. "You're right."

"I will definitely be joining you," Teacher Dawit said. "I don't care what they say. Let's see them stop me."

So assertive, for a man! It was almost cute, like a child puffing out her chest and demonstrating a simple cantrip to her mother for the first time. Still, he might provide a distraction. Maybe his Neuromancy could charm a few mobsters.

Cassius straightened. He sucked in a deep breath, then let it out. The Resonance shifted as he drew a card from a pocket in his longcoat. He held it out, revealing a man in armor. "The Paladins. It will soon be an auspicious hour to confront the Acerbi in their own den. Take them with you."

A knot formed in Brehane's stomach. The *Bahaduur* had betrayed her people in the past. Now she'd have to trust them.

* * *

Cassius watched as Brehane and Dawit headed to the door. Uneasy standoff between the Signores and Mafia be damned, he needed to go with them. Needed to protect Brehane...er, his investment.

And what horrible timing! Had this been just a few hours later, he could've turned Brehane over to Phobos, and the Bovyans would've wiped out the Mafia.

With the Gods' Whispers still resonating through him, he drew another card from his deck, so as not to waste the leftover energy.

Death.

His own.

The Knight card had already been drawn. Unlike his duel with the enforcer days ago, there was no way to change this future. To join in the confrontation this time would end in only one way. He drew another card to be sure.

A lithe girl with wings. Arcea, the Betrayer. He peered out the window, where the sun rose higher towards Arcea's star.

* * *

With Master Anish singing at his side, Sameer watched as the last of the charcoals reduced Elder Gitika to ash and bleached bone. His voice was hoarse from chanting, and after a night without sleep, every nerve screamed at him to rest.

He couldn't. Not now, not with Sohini possibly held by a Golden Scorpion and his Mafia allies. Signore Cassius had promised to Divine an auspicious time and place to confront the Acerbi family, but he had come and left with the Aksumi. Jie had left, as well, accompanying the city watch somewhere. That had been two hours ago, and the crowds had thinned to just a few of the fire brigade.

"Master Anish, Sir Sameer," Cassius called from behind.

Sameer took one last look at the pyre, exchanged nods with Master Anish, and turned around.

Standing at the top of the seawall, Cassius looked even more haggard. At his side, Brehane wore plain white robes instead of the gorgeous dress from the night before, but she still glared at him in suspicion. Apparently, she wouldn't be letting go of a three-hundred-year-old grudge anytime soon. An older Aksumi male hovered a little behind.

Master Anish sucked in a breath.

"Sir Paladins," Cassius said. "We have a convergence of coincidences that not even the heavens could foresee."

It was an unexpected statement from someone always so certain about things. Sameer met his gaze. "Do you have news of Sohini?"

The Diviner motioned toward Master Anish. "I told the master that all clues suggest she is held by Don Acerbi, and the most auspicious time and place to confront them is noon, at their headquarters."

Glaring, Master Anish let out a hiss.

When he didn't speak, Sameer pressed his palms together and bowed his head. "Thank you."

"Not only that, Makeda went to confirm if Sohini was there, and they took her captive as well." Cassius gestured toward the Mystics. "This is the convergence I speak of. If you join forces with the Aksumi, you have a greater chance of success."

Brehane shuffled on her feet. "You must be trustworthy. The Mafia demanded I go alone, and if they see all of you coming, they might hurt Makeda."

It didn't seem like Brehane would mind, given the hostility evident in the way the two female Mystics glared at each other the night before. Sameer turned to

Master Anish. "You can use a Command to keep them from harming her."

Master Anish's head bobbled. "Shouldn't you be the one practicing Commands?"

Sameer's shoulders drooped. "I'm too exhausted, and there might be a Golden Scorpion there."

CHAPTER 18:

Confrontations

For Jie, borrowing dark clothes from a nearby tailor's shop and infiltrating the Mafia den had been second nature. Criminals and spies were nearly cousins, and the crowded gambling hall had been easy enough for even a day-three Black Lotus initiate to lose themselves in. It might've been a family reunion. Now, though, she was trapped under a large table, dodging the shuffling feet of the Acerbi leadership.

And Makeda's.

Jie suppressed a snort. She'd been cornered more times on this one trip than in the last couple of years combined. After sneaking into the Acerbi headquarters through the back kitchens, she'd soon found out all the row houses were actually connected inside, and most of the interior space was a cavernous gambling den. She'd clung to the shadows and found this room on the mezzanine, only discovering that it was the boss' meeting room when he and his underlings came in with Makeda.

And she hadn't come in as a prisoner. Nor had she broached the issue of Sohini or the missing sorcerer.

The Mystic laughed now. "I don't care what you do with her. I just want her necklace. And she can never leave Tokahia."

The door creaked open, and a voice called in. "Don, the sorceress is coming, and she's not alone."

Jie sucked on her lower lip. Not alone. Maybe, just maybe, Brehane stood a chance.

* * *

Brehane's heart raced as she, Teacher Dawit, Sameer, and the Paladin Master Anish approached the center building in a long row of brightly-colored, connected houses. Cassius had stayed back at the insistence of Signore De Lucca, who worried Signore involvement would lead to an all-out war with the Mafia.

Four of them against an entire den of mobsters didn't sound as smart now as it had before. They didn't even have the surly half-elf; not like she could do much more than pick their pockets. And who knew if Cassius' suggestion of a noon attack was auspicious or not? At least the Resonance was as strong here as any other place in this fascinating city. With Makeda's life at stake, they'd need every advantage.

All of this, for a worthless cousin who'd tried to sabotage her at every opportunity. Brehane shook all the curses out of her head, ignoring the stares of the ruffians and lowlifes walking on the seedier side of the entertainment district.

Standing by the front entrance, two burly, fearsome men in black longcoats eyed them with nothing but disdain. How brazen these criminals were, carving out their own section of the city, where their word was law. And soon, she'd come face-to-face with the woman running this operation.

When they reached the heavy wooden door, she read a sign on the wall. *No Diviners.*

One of the brutes held out a halting hand. "Only the Female Darkie can come in."

Shoving his way to the fore, Sameer pressed his palms together. "We also have an appointment with Don Acerbi."

The two men exchanged glances before the first one grunted, "Don Acerbi is indisposed. Go away."

Master Anish waved a hand at them. "Stand aside."

The Resonance echoed from him, feeling much like a charm spell. The two men stepped away from the door.

Brehane clasped her crystal. How amazing! Paladin powers could replicate Aksumi Neuromancy. This was yet more evidence that her theories, gleaned from all her research of the different forms of magic, was true. She looked to Teacher Dawit, who gave a tentative nod.

Sameer yanked the door open, allowing boisterous noise and the stench of burning gooseweed to waft out. He stalked inside.

Armed only with an attitude, the kid apparently had a death wish. Maybe he was trustworthy, maybe not; but for now, with both Makeda and Sohini captive, their goals aligned like some of Cassius' stars. Brehane followed after him with the others.

The noise petered out. Her eyes took a few seconds to adjust to the low light, but when she looked, she had to suppress a gasp.

It was one giant room, connecting all the houses on the block. Walls had been knocked down, replaced by wood columns that vaulted all the way to the roof. Several dozen men sat around tables, their card game stalled as they stared at the newcomers. How strange it was for men to engage in such idle pastimes, instead of taking care of hearth and home.

Equally disconcerting were all the scantily-clad, pretty girls circulating among them, carrying drinks and food—*serving men.* They, too, froze in place.

A flash of dark skin whisked by in Brehane's peripheral vision. She turned. Was that the missing Melas? No, it was a drunken patron, watching with unfocused eyes.

Brandishing a club, a particularly large man stomped toward them. "Get out, Darkies."

Sameer continued, undaunted. When the brute swung the club, the young Paladin's movements blurred, merging with the Resonance. The man thudded to the ground, disarmed and moaning.

Now the young Paladin held the club.

Chairs screeched back. Men sprang to their feet. Knives flashed.

This was a bad idea. Brehane backed toward the door. "Sameer, there are too many."

The enemies surged forth, angry war chants on their lips.

Brehane's hands trembled. Flaming darts might kill one mob enforcer, but she wasn't supposed to use lethal force, and there were so many of them. A foxfire...no use. A sleep spell! She eyed a pack of goons, closing fast. Her mouth felt like cotton. The syllables to invoke even that simple magic died on her lips.

Teacher Dawit grunted several words of Aeromancy and pointed at the vanguard. A thunderclap erupted, splintering tables and sending cards fluttering like a swarm of butterflies. A dozen thugs lay on the ground, unconscious.

One convulsed at Brehane's feet. Bile rose in her throat, even as she gawked. Dawit had never displayed such power before. He'd always been the demure Neuromancer, using no more than the basics of the other schools. By the Tear, he wasn't supposed to *know* more than the basics.

The second wave of men held back, mumbling among themselves. One's eyes locked on Teacher Dawit. He cocked his arm back and flung the knife.

Brehane's heart leaped into her throat. The whirling blade might've been traveling in slow motion, the way time seemed to slow. A shield! All she had to do was take a step forward and invoke a single syllable. What was it? Just one stupid word.

Teacher Dawit's mouth opened in a scream. Now there wasn't enough time to raise that shield—

Master Anish's *naga* swept into the path of the knife and knocked it out of the air with a clang.

The mobsters all froze, wide-eyed, before one—no, two—jumped forward.

"Stop!" A rotund, middle-aged man in a bright longcoat stood on a staircase, pointing. "Men, put away your weapons."

The ruffians hesitated, then tentatively sheathed their knives. Several helped their fallen comrades.

Brehane's stomach heaved, and it took all her willpower to swallow the rising bile. She'd been totally useless in this fight. Couldn't even remember the words to an easy spell that could've protected Teacher Dawit. Performing rote patterns in combat drills or warding off Makeda's dirty tricks didn't begin to compare to using magic when there was a real threat of harm. Her shoulders sagged. Some descendant of the First Mystic she was.

The fat leader descended, the steps creaking under his weight. Several fearsome men followed behind him, while more joined when he reached the landing. He motioned to an alcove near the back. "Bring our guests to my niche."

With derisive glare, another mobster strode over and jerked a head toward the alcove. "This way."

Sameer folded his hands in front of him and followed a goon through the tables. Patrons and enforcers alike grumbled as they passed, while the women worked to clean up spilled drinks and pick up overturned chairs and tables.

Head spinning, Brehane could only stare. Everything was wrong in this culture. Men didn't know their place. Women didn't claim theirs. And there, groaning in a leather couch, was a slob of a man. How could a man, let alone one so fat, inspire others to follow?

Yet eight men guarded him, hands on weapons.

His eyes met hers, then swept over the rest. "I'd extended an invitation only to her."

Master Anish pressed his palms together. "Don Acerbi, greetings. I am Anish Mohta of the Ayuri Paladin Order."

Brehane found Sameer in the corner of her eye. The young Paladin was clenching his fists so tight, the knuckles turned white. Whenever his missing mistress was involved, he could barely contain his rage.

Don Acerbi placed two fingers on his forehead. "Anish Mohta of the Ayuri Paladin Order. My men have seen you around the city on and off for at least a year, always sticking to Signore territory. What are you doing, disrupting my place of business?"

"I am here to demand the release of my apprentice, Sohini, and to retrieve the swords of my master and my other apprentice."

The don pursed his lips. "I don't know about any swords, and I've never heard of him. This So-whatty."

"*Her.*" Sameer took two steps forward.

The men around the don formed up, knives and clubs in hand.

The words, what were the words? And the hand motions…. Fingers manipulating the Resonance, Brehane uttered several syllables and waved. Three of the men to Don Acerbi's right collapsed in sleep, while two more wobbled. She staggered, too, as her energy flagged from the effort of casting the spell without sand or rose petals as a medium. At least she had succeeded this time.

Don Acerbi grunted. "Enough. Shedding blood is bad for business, but I've sent word to two hundred of my foot soldiers. They'll be converging here soon, and I suggest you not be here when they arrive."

"Stand down, Sameer." Master Anish beckoned to the apprentice.

Sameer arranged his fingers in a pattern, but maintained his glare on the don. "I was told you have Sohini."

"And I told you, I have no idea who she is, unless she's one of the Ayuri whores we brought up from the South. I don't know any of their names." His flippant tone was anything but dissembling.

Whore…whatever it meant, the Arkothi word sounded close to their word for a four-legged furry pet, or an irrigation ditch. Brehane placed a hand on Sameer's shoulder. It felt cold, and his body shook so much it was stirring the Resonance.

Master Anish opened his mouth to speak, only to be cut off by Sameer. "Signore De Lucca sent her here to demand you close your brothels. Then, last night, your men murdered my master. You have my sword, and hers."

Expression contorting into genuine confusion, Don Acerbi's gaze swept around his men. "What is this boy blabbering about? Did anyone kill his master?"

A thin man with spectacles at the edge of the alcove placed two fingers on his forehead. "Don Acerbi, we received no reports of hostilities at any of your places of business last night."

As nonchalantly as she could, Brehane scrutinized the don. These Northerners' expressions were too hard to read.

Don Acerbi looked up, smirking. "See, Darkie?"

Sameer jabbed a finger at him. "Your men came to the *Seafarer* last night."

"That's Signore territory." Don Acerbi laughed without mirth. "Maybe you should be asking *them*. Now take that finger out of my face before I have my men break it, then chop it off knuckle by knuckle."

A shiver ran through Brehane, a feeling of cold as the Resonance shifted.

"The Signores aren't criminals!" Sameer clenched his fist.

Don Acerbi's laugh guttered. His expression darkened. "Tell me, boy, what is the difference between a businessman like me, and the Signores?"

Sameer opened his mouth, then closed it.

Don Acerbi harrumphed. "Why is it that both Signore De Lucca and I deal in the pleasures of the flesh, and yet he is somehow a noble and I am considered a criminal?"

Sameer waved at the guards. "You enforce your will with fear."

"And you think the Black Armbands don't?"

"The pyramid," Brehane said, clasping her necklace as she remembered what Cassius had said. "The Signores are sworn with the Divine mandate to protect it, to prevent the orc gods returning on their flaming chariots. You Mafia families are ganging together to take control of it."

"Nonsense. The pyramids and flaming chariots are fairy tales, and I know nothing about our families banding together." The don waved a dismissive hand. "The Signores just want to scare people into paying taxes for an expensive, meaningless honor guard, and skim money off the top for themselves."

"Enough." Master Anish motioned at Don Acerbi. "Where's the Ayuri girl? Tell me."

The Resonance shook at his words. Don Acerbi's eyes glazed over. "At one of my brothels. *The South Seas.*"

A low growl rumbled in Sameer's throat, again shaking the Resonance of the Universe. Thankfully he didn't have a weapon, because he might've cut Don Acerbi down right then.

The Resonance shifted again, the source of the disturbance unknown. The cold sent goosebumps erupting over Brehane's skin.

Don Acerbi's gaze faded, but then regained its focus. "Kill all the Southerners."

Brehane's heart leaped into her throat. How did that happen?

The don's guards stomped forward, knives in hand. Back in the main room, more weapons rasped from sheaths.

CHAPTER 19:

Blaze of Glory

Crouching on the bar along the back of the gambling den, Jie's jaw dropped at the sudden change in atmosphere, from tense to downright hostile. Don Acerbi must've decided to honor his deal with Makeda, and had been stalling to get his men in position to capture Brehane.

Jie thanked the Heavens she was now wearing clothes more suited to sneaking and fighting. They might not be her stealth suit, but at least it wasn't that silly pink dress. Once the commotion erupted downstairs and the don and his men rumbled out of his office, she'd tailed them, huddling in their shadows. Then she crept through the back door to the kitchens, and hid behind maids who brought beer and wines to the guests. Now, these poor women were screaming as they fled from flashing knives and rapiers. Gambling patrons, too, cowered under tables or dashed for the front exit.

The turn from heated discussion to armed confrontation had started with a simple question from Master Anish. The Paladin master now moved like a blur among the thugs, avoiding stabs and slashes, counter-attacking with vicious hacks of his *naga*. The mobsters might as well have been standing still—at least until they fell to his blade. And if the Paladins really believed in some code, it wasn't showing now.

Sameer, too, deftly bobbed and weaved through the skirmish. He'd liberated a rapier from a fallen man, and now swept it through the air in broad arcs. The pair's fighting style appeared to focus on avoidance and single, incapacitating chops to exposed targets; though the rapier's thin, light, double edge did not seem as suited to the approach as the heavy, curved *naga*. Unlike the fight the day before, and unlike the master, Sameer was using the flat of the blade. Either his deceased master's words had gotten through his thick skull, or he was just incompetent with a foreign weapon.

Jie scanned the crowds for Brehane. The Mystic might not trust her, but that didn't mean she should be betrayed into a life of slavery and humiliation at the hands of the Mafia.

Guttural words chopped through the air. Jie turned to their source.

Around Brehane, several of the criminals crumpled to the ground. Her shoulders looked like they carried a pair of invisible ship anchors. Two of the don's guards rushed toward her, and all she could do was stare at them.

Jie hurled several ceramic mugs, which smashed into the attackers' faces. Brehane's head turned, and she met Jie's gaze. Jie waved her toward the exit. "Escape! Your cousin betrayed you!"

Brehane stared back with no sign of understanding. Perhaps weak human ears couldn't pick out a shout amongst all the crashing, shattering, and screaming.

Yells rang out from closer to the entrance. Jie turned.

Dawit flung spells left and right, searing assailants with fiery darts, dropping them into sleep, and sizzling some with arcs of lightning. The mobsters now held back, pointing their weapons at him while looking for others to attack.

Jie made a note not to trifle with angry Mystics, or try to pick their pockets again. It was amazing to think that, outnumbered as they were, the Southerners were holding their own. Only Brehane seemed to be at risk. Jie looked back to where the Mystic had been.

She wasn't there. Captured?

Jie scanned the crowds of screaming people. There, near the back, Brehane picked her way through the throng, craning her neck. What was she searching for? Jie tracked the Mystic's eyes.

Don Acerbi. Surrounded by several of his men, the rotund crime boss was working his way toward the steps to the mezzanine.

Brehane was losing ground on him as she ducked out of sight of mob enforcers, only to pick up Don Acerbi's trail again.

"By the steps," Jie yelled, pointing. "Don Acerbi is getting away."

Sameer and Anish stared at her, then at each other, before following her finger.

Not far from the entrance, Dawit barked out several guttural sounds, all ominous enough to send a chill down Jie's spine. He pointed. She followed the gesture.

A blast of fire erupted from the steps, sending chairs, tables, and people flying. The scent of sulfur and smoke hung in the air, like spent firepowder.

Jie blinked away the orange glow behind her eyes and looked. Where Don Acerbi had been standing with his guards, there were now several piles of charred flesh. Other people lay burning, while still others ran like screaming human torches. Flames licked at the stairway and across the floors, spreading up wooden beams.

Heavens, what kind of idiot used fire as a weapon in an enclosed space full of wood, with only two exits?

Heat and smoke filled the room as the conflagration spread through the wood framing, columns, and beams. What had started as a panic of gamblers trying to avoid a fight now became a stampede as the terrified crowd fought to fit through the front door. Some pounded away at the boarded windows.

Scanning the crowd, Jie found Brehane and shouted in her broken Ayuri, "This way, there's an exit at the back!"

Brehane shook her head. "I need to rescue Makeda."

Poor girl, didn't know her cousin had wicked motives. Jie shook her head and shouted, "She betrayed you!"

Hand cupped by her ear, Brehane squinted and wagged her head. "What did you say?"

Frail human ears. Jie scanned among the panicked faces. Where were the Paladins? "Sameer, Anish!"

The Paladin master was nowhere to be found. At the edge of the spreading fire, Sameer was pulling one of the serving girls to safety. His eyes lifted and paused on Jie.

With one hand she pointed at the rear door, while with the other, she waved him over. "The back exit is safer."

Sameer ushered the girl in the direction of the back door, but then turned back to help others. The boy would get himself killed. Even now, the heat blared in waves through the inferno. Smoke hung in the air, and undoubtedly in his lungs.

Ripping a strip of cloth from her shirt, she covered her nose and mouth. She looked to where Brehane had last been. No sign of her, and no way to warn her again about Makeda.

At the front, Dawit, face contorted in what could only be described as malice, grunted more guttural words. Thunder clapped, then rumbled through the room.

Ears ringing, Jie looked at the source. Bright sunlight flooded in through a gaping hole in the front wall. Wood, stone, and people lay strewn in a semicircle around the opening. Panicked gamblers trampled over each other as they fled for the new escape route.

The wood frame groaned, and the rafters splintered. Between the fire and Dawit's magic, the building's structure wouldn't last long. Scanning the room again, Jie found Sameer helping another woman. Jie leaped off the counter and landed in a crouch on the wood floors. Staying low beneath the smoke, she darted to help the brave, foolish Paladin.

Who was the greater fool?

A horizontal beam above snapped. Jie sidestepped before it crashed down on top of her. The engineer tasked with connecting the interiors of these row houses probably never predicted Mystics going on a rampage when he drafted the renovation. When she reached Sameer, she grabbed his arm. "Come on, the building is going to collapse."

Sameer's wide eyes stared back at her. A look of recognition bloomed on his face. He pointed at the edge of the fire, where several men now stirred and coughed in their ensorcelled sleep. "We need to help more people."

Those men were as good as dead. She waved to the ceiling, now crackling as the wood split. "Can your Paladin skills keep this place from collapsing? No? Then get out! There isn't much more time." She took the girl Sameer was helping by the hand.

Anguish painted Sameer's expression as he looked back at a man with spectacles who was pinned by a column. He'd been at Don Acerbi's side before. He must not have followed the don to his fiery death by the stairs.

His wide, panicked eyes met theirs. "Help!'

"I'm going to save him." Sameer pulled out of her grasp.

Foolish boy. Jie pulled the young woman along. "This one can be saved. If you get crushed by beams, roasted by fire, or suffocated by smoke, it's your own fault."

* * *

Sameer had no intention of getting crushed, roasted, or suffocated in the inferno, but he couldn't let that man—gangster or not—get either burned to death by the fire or buried beneath the rubble. Around him the screams continued, albeit less loud as many of the people had escaped, and others were claimed by the smoke and flames. Yet more were claimed by Master Anish's *naga*. He hadn't used the flat of his blade.

As Sameer dashed back to the fallen beam, he considered what had just happened. He should've kept his cool, shouldn't have antagonized Don Acerbi; but the sudden change in the crime lord's demeanor couldn't have been explained just by his anger at Sameer. No, Master Anish had already used a Command and eased the tensions. Then, there had been something unsettling in the Vibrations, a cold which had made the hairs on the back of his neck stand on end. Just like when they'd fought the mobsters the day before.

Now, he knelt over the trapped man, one of Don Acerbi's henchmen.

"Help me," the man whispered through gritted teeth.

Sameer nodded. How, though? Pushing the beam, as big around as his head, would do nothing to free the man; and with the rubble one end, there was no chance of lifting it. The heat from the fire flared on Sameer's face, and smoke clogged the air.

"This will hurt," he said. Borrowing the Vibrations and envisioning the center of the beam, Sameer lifted his hand and aimed at a spot on the wood, right over the man's chest. If he could channel enough energy, he could split the timber. If the God of Justice favored him, it wouldn't kill the goon in the process. If the Goddess of Vengeance guided his hand...

Sameer took a deep breath...

And choked on the smoke. His shoulders heaved as he coughed several times. A column broke with an ear-splitting snap and fell toward him.

Paladin reflexes took over, and he sidestepped the column before he joined the henchman, pinned to the floor. Focusing again, he raised his hand and struck the beam with his palm.

The wood splintered and snapped in half.

By the Thousand Gods, he'd done it! And really it hadn't felt like Justice manifesting in him, but rather Justice *and* Vengeance. The latter cut, while the former restrained.

Sameer pulled the man free. Draping his arm over his shoulder, he worked toward the back entrance. Flaming debris crashed down around them, his Paladin skills slowing time enough that he could dodge. Smoke burned his eyes and throat.

Light from the open door filtered through the ash. Though thin, the man was so heavy it was slowing him down. The entire ceiling was collapsing behind them. With three more steps, they burst through the opening.

While other people fled through the alley, Jie waited for him.

Jie beckoned. "Come on."

Sameer pulled the man to the far end of the alley. It probably wasn't far enough away, but for now, he didn't have any more energy. He hunched over and coughed.

"To the *South Seas*."
"Why?"

Jie sucked on her lower lip for a second before answering. "To save your lady friend. We can ask around to find it."

Sohini! Sameer straightened and looked over to the man. "Are you well enough to get away?"

He nodded. "Yes. I am Don Acerbi's accountant. I can get you into the brothel."

Jie looked back toward the building. "Did you see Brehane?"

* * *

Brehane followed Jie's example and tore a piece of cloth off to cover her face. Flames burned everywhere, and smoke blurred her vision. Still, she had to rescue Makeda, and maybe even uncover the source of the shift in the Resonance which had caused Don Acerbi to attack.

Don Acerbi... He'd been running to the steps when Teacher Dawit had thrown a fireball in that direction, starting the conflagration.

A fireball! From a Neuromancer. A man, no less. It shouldn't have been possible.

She craned around piles of burning rubble to look at the stairs. Charred corpses lay strewn about. Bile rose in her throat. It was one thing to use magic at the academy, and something completely different to use it *on* someone, under duress.

Makeda was likely at the top of those steps. Perhaps she was gagged and bound, unable to use

Pyromancy to control the raging fires. It would be ironic for a Pyromancer to die that way. It would be even more ironic if Brehane rescued her.

She took a quick look around. Everyone who could had already fled. The yells and screams had quieted, replaced by crackling wood and snapping flames.

Feeling the Resonance, Brehane barked out words in the language of Aksumi magic. The Pyromancy in her blood coursed through her. With a sweep of her hands, she opened a path in the flames.

Her vitality guttered as she worked her way through, pressing the flames down with waves of her palms and the force of her will. Maybe with a few years of practice, she'd be able to put fires out altogether. She at last weaved by the mobsters' bodies, burned beyond recognition, to the head of the steps.

Behind her, the flames roared again, blocking the escape route she'd just made. She spun around.

On the other side of the wall of flames stood Makeda, grinning. "This is not the way I had planned to recover our ancestor's necklace, but if you die, nobody back home will miss a dirty Biomancer."

"What are you saying?"

Makeda snarled out foul sounds. Flames erupted in her palm. "The Pyromancy clan sent me on this mission to make sure you never returned."

The Pyromancy clan? Brehane's jaw dropped. Was this the matriarch's idea? Or Makeda's? When she found her voice, she said, "I came here to rescue you."

"And in doing so, you fell into my trap. I'd hoped Teacher Dawit would witness the Mafia doing the dirty work for me, but nobody will know now."

So Teacher Dawit knew nothing of it. Still, no matter their mutual dislike, it was hard to believe Makeda would do something so horrible to a fellow Mystic candidate. A cousin, no less.

Teeth bared, Makeda hurled the flame in her hands.

Barking out guttural words of magic, Brehane waved her hand. Just like in the drills they practiced. The air crackled as bright flakes of fire dispersed around her shield spell. Her knees buckled, but held. She'd been so stupid, expending so much energy to control the fire before; now Makeda would overpower her.

Makeda swept a hand through a fire and pointed.

A fire dart sped toward Brehane. It was just like the scripted Pyromancy drills they did day-in, day-out. She spat out foul syllables. The hissing flames froze inches from her chest. With a sharp exhale, she repelled them. The vitality in her limbs guttered. It took all her effort to focus past the blurring edges of her vision.

Growling out more sounds, Makeda swept a blazing hand into the path of the dart, absorbing it. Her eyes flickered red in the flames. She stepped through the wall of fire, which surged through her and coalesced at her hand. She extended her palm, which blazed with a fire stronger than even the one from the duel.

Brehane staggered back, but slammed into the stairwell. What vitality she had left wouldn't be enough to ward off Makeda's magic, let alone reinforce the fireshield with a Hydromancy spell. If only she had more power to draw on. Like Makeda had drawn on the fire.

Pausing, Makeda grinned. "Once you are gone, I will take the crystal that rightfully belongs to me."

As candidates, they were equal in power in all schools of magic, save for that of their clan blood. Makeda could draw on the most devastating school, while Biomancy was left only with one pitiful spell. If only Brehane had been born to the Pyro… Wait—her mother had been one of the most powerful Pyromancers before betraying the clan by marrying a lowly Biomancer. With a quick sidestep, she dodged Makeda's palm strike.

Makeda pulled her hand back and shrugged. "You're only delaying the inevitable. Tonight, I'll take Cassius' seed, which also belongs to me."

A different kind of heat flared in Brehane's face. Anger? Jealousy? She ducked under Makeda's flaming swipe and scuttled to the side. If Cassius knew about this treachery, surely he wouldn't share his…

Seed… Biomancing could shift energy from one person to another. What was that spell, if not a combination of schools? Transmutation of seed, Biomanced into power. It was time to test her theory that all magic was related. Only now, it wasn't just the clan's honor at stake. It was her life.

Makeda growled out more words, gathering more Resonance in her spell than any fireshield Brehane could conjure with her flagging energy. The blazing hand thrust forward.

As the palm pressed into her, Brehane dug her toes into the ground as she would the bedsheets when she brought a man to release. She arched her back. The guttural words of fire absorption and seed Biomancy escaped her lips.

Without burning, Makeda's magic flames surged through Brehane. So did something else: something invigorating, like hot wine on a freezing day. Like peaking during intercourse with a man, receiving his seed and feeling the power surge up her spine.

Brehane opened her eyes.

Wobbling on her feet, Makeda gawked. Her skin looked dry and sallow, with a fine wrinkle that hadn't been there before, radiating from the edge of an eye. A strand of white streaked in the waves of her ebon hair. She rasped out words of Pyromancy and held out her hand, but only sparks fizzled. "Dirty Biomancer..."

A smile formed on Brehane's lips, unbidden. It had worked! At least some of her theories were correct. She'd just improvised Biomancy and Pyromancy together, and absorbed some of Makeda's Pyromancing vitality.

With renewed energy, a fire flared in Brehane's hand on her command. She thrust her hand at Makeda's cowering form.

And stopped.

As much as Makeda deserved punishment for her betrayal, they were still family. They shared the same blood, which allowed them to master Pyromancy. She snuffed the flame out. "Go. Anywhere but the University. If I ever see you again, I'll drain what's left of you."

Eyes wide, Makeda took several steps back, turned, and ran to where a collapsed wall allowed a way out.

Brehane coughed as the smoke clung to her lungs. Left uncontrolled, the fire would probably spread to the adjoining blocks and burn much of the city to the ground. She ran through the flaming rubble, following the same path as Makeda. Wherever splintered rafters and beams raged with flame, she Pyromanced them down as much as her energy would allow. Perhaps with practice, she could Biomance fire itself into power.

Reaching the opening, she ran through into what looked to be the back alley. At the far end, Sameer and the half-elf were helping a man hobble away.

Dashing faster on reinvigorated limbs, Brehane caught up with them on the side street.

Sameer turned to her, his expression surprisingly concerned for an Ayuri Paladin. "Did you find Makeda?"

Brehane pursed her lips. Apparently the treacherous *assama* hadn't come this way. Had Teacher Dawit conspired with her? From what Makeda had said, probably not. "No, have you seen my teacher?"

"Over there." Jie pointed.

Brehane followed the finger.

Teacher Dawit beckoned from half a block away.

Brehane's insides squeezed up. Would he have enough energy to confront her after using so much magic in the gambling den? She hung a step behind the half-elf and Paladin. "Where are you going now?"

"The *South Seas* brothel," Sameer said, "to rescue Sohini."

The boy was single-minded. Why would a woman need rescuing from a brothel, unless she was spending all her money? She looked up to Teacher Dawit, who was strolling over as if he hadn't just unleashed devastating magic.

"There you are," he said. "Did you rescue Makeda?"

Brehane studied his expression. There was no guile there, only concern. He must not have known about the Pyromancer plot against her. She shook her head. "Come on, we're going to help the Paladin rescue his lady friend."

He frowned. "You are just a student, not even a candidate yet. You do not give me, a teacher, orders. Not here. I'm not going anywhere until we find Makeda. You don't even like the Ayuri."

Didn't she? Sameer had proven reliable, for a man and for a Paladin. Not only that, it would provide an opportunity to experience how he shifted the Resonance when he fought. "I am going to help him."

"No," Dawit said. "This is none of our business. We are here to track down Adept Melas, and he was neither with the Acerbi, as the Diviner claimed, nor at the brothel. Come."

Brehane's eyebrows clashed together. "You are a man. Teacher or not, you do not give me orders."

His lips tightened. The expression was not one of anger, but one of scheming. Since when did Aksumi men scheme? Did he know about Makeda's plans after all? Maybe he was going to lead her into a trap. Would it be safer to keep him close, or get as far away as possible?

CHAPTER 20:

First Aftermath

Trudging back to his carriage, head still heavy from fatigue, Cassius wondered if Brehane had gone to her death, and he was unwittingly complicit. But had been no stopping her, and the tarot cards suggested that she had to go, and he could not. At least she was protected by a Paladin master and apprentice, a Mystic teacher, and maybe the mysterious half-elf.

Still, in his many years of Divining, never had the messages been so ambiguous. The Traitor card, combined with the climbing sun about to meet the Traitor star, portended multiple betrayals.

Who would betray whom? There was no love lost between Makeda and Brehane, but it seemed more like a petty squabble. The Paladins? Would one of them turn on Brehane? They had no reason to. The half-elf Jie? The cards he drew marked her as a viper in a nest of snakes, interpretation ambiguous. Or were there other untold betrayals waiting to happen, making noon an auspicious time for the Paladins to parlay with the Acerbi?

He had to protect Brehane. If not because she was beautiful and enchanting, then because she was the key to pitting the Bovyans against the crime families, and eliminating their threat to the pyramid. He lengthened his stride.

"Signore Cassius," De Lucca called.

Cassius looked up from the pavestones.

De Lucca beckoned from his own carriage. "We had not yet finished discussing the Bovyans."

Cassius would've grinned if it wouldn't make his head ache so much. Even in his mental fog, he'd been able to talk De Lucca in circles, giving Brehane time to find out about the De Lucca family from the whoremaster's homely sister. Knowing how his father connected to the letter Jie had acquired might reveal more about his goals than the Gods' Whispers had so far.

Curses! In his torpor, he'd forgotten to ask Brehane about her conversation with the sister. Sighing, he met De Lucca as he climbed down from the carriage.

"So, are we in agreement that hiring the Bovyans as pyramid guards will save us money?"

Cassius would've shaken his head if it didn't feel like his brains would leak out. "The Bovyans weren't even around when the Elf Angel gave us the sacred duty. They never suffered slavery under the orcs. They can't understand the importance of protecting the pyramids. Not only that, they believe it is their people's Divine mandate to bring all the North to heel. I don't trust them, and neither should you."

"Does it matter? As long as we carefully set out their terms in contract, and keep their bellies full and their loins empty, they will do what we say. That's the way they are."

So naïve! Cassius snorted. "How can you be so sure?"

"Watch how today unfolds. Every last Bovyan's contract with the crime families expires today, and their new contract begins with me."

Cassius' heart just about leaped into his throat. That's what made noon an auspicious time. De Lucca was creating a future just as Cassius did with the merchants. "You plan to suppress the crime families."

"Not just suppress. Wipe out." He turned his hands over, examining his perfectly manicured nails. "I've been pitting them against each other for months now. Weakening them. Making them ripe for the Bovyans to squash beneath their capable boots."

Cassius shook his head, sending flares of pain into his temples. Phobos had conned him. The Mafia had never been a serious threat to the pyramid, and the Bovyans were going to attack them whether or not Cassius kept Brehane in Tokahia, anyway. They'd secure the Signores' good will, who'd then vote to hire them as pyramid honor guard. And still... "Even if that were the case, there aren't enough Bovyans currently in the city to take on the entire Acerbi family."

"Maybe not." De Lucca's grin looked like that of a sadist at a brothel catering to those tastes. "But I played another card."

Another card... Cassius jaw dropped. "You never sent Sohini to Don Acerbi's, did you? You never even met her."

Clucking, De Lucca shook his head. "The Gods' Whispers don't all reach your ears, apparently. Yes, Sohini came to me, seeking refuge. From what, she didn't say, but she apparently has a soft spot for prostitutes. I told her about the crime families' treatment of their whores, and she helped undermine some of them. I did tell her about Don Acerbi, but I never saw her again after that."

"But you did send the Paladins, by telling them Sohini might be there."

The sadistic grin returned. "And, because of your rash Aksumi friend, I was able to send a pair of Mystics, as well. You, of all people, should know the benefit of getting others to do your dirty work."

Cassius' lips pursed. All of his arrangements were negotiated in secret, yet it seemed like De Lucca knew. Still, it might work out for the better. The Mafia, long a thorn in the Signores' side, weakened. Brehane and Makeda, not in any real danger from the don.

Or were they?

Horns blared out in a sequence. The pattern repeated, closer this time. A fire.

Cassius squinted in the direction from which it came. Thick curls of smoke rose in the distance, much larger than the line of smoke from the makeshift funeral pyre the Paladins had made. It looked to be coming from the entertainment district.

In the general direction of the Acerbi stronghold.

Brehane. With a quick glare at De Lucca, Cassius darted to his carriage and climbed in. He tapped the driver's shoulder and pointed. "To the entertainment district. Hurry."

The driver snapped the reins. The carriage lurched into motion, perhaps leaving Cassius' brains behind, based on how his head hurt.

De Lucca yelled over the rattle of wheels on pavestones. "You'll thank me for this, when the crime families are gone. You'll trust the Bovyans, and it will save us all money."

Trust the Bovyans? Maybe they'd prove themselves true to their contracts, but no doubt they'd find ways to twist them, like a snake-tongued barrister. De Lucca clearly didn't realize they'd undoubtedly replace the Mafia as a threat to the city. To the pyramid. Maybe they were the ones responsible for the fire.

And Brehane and Makeda were caught in it.

"Faster," he urged the driver. Though, with his fatigue he would be useless to help, beyond barking a few orders.

The driver snapped the reins, and the horses picked up pace. If Cassius' head had hurt before, the rapid bumps and jostles now made it worse. The sound of panicked shouts grew louder. The scent of smoke thickened. The trickle of men with soot-covered faces became a rush. The fire horns blared, but less frequently.

He waved a member of the fire brigade down. "How far have the fires spread?"

The man stopped. "It's contained to Don Acerbi's headquarters."

Don Acerbi's territory was full of wooden buildings. It didn't seem possible for a fire to be contained so quickly. Even the fire brigade leader had worried about the district. Cassius tracked the aqueduct lines. One serviced the area, but the average time for the fire brigade to mobilize wouldn't have allowed them to control the fire so quickly. He tipped his hat, and motioned the driver to continue.

Though smoke hung heavily in the air around the Acerbi headquarters, the flames looked to be limited to a single block. The walls and roofs had collapsed, leaving the row houses a mass of jumbled beams and rafters. With their faces masked against the smoke, fire brigade members formed a line, passing water buckets to douse the rubble. Several bodies lay in the street.

Cassius' stomach roiled. Were Makeda and Brehane among the dead? Covering his mouth, he jumped off the carriage and tentatively worked his way to the first body.

A member of the fire brigade ran over and dipped into a bow. "Signore, the fire is under control."

Cassius nodded. "Good work."

"It wasn't just us. One of the Aksumi used her magic to weaken the flames. I've never seen the like."

Relief washed over Cassius. Makeda must have helped with her Pyromancy. "Where is she now? Was she with her cousin?"

The man shook his head and shrugged. "We saw only her, and she ran off with the Paladins."

Cassius' heart sunk. Even though Makeda must be safe, Brehane was unaccounted for. With the fire brigade member following, he went over to the first body.

It was a local man, his face and garish clothes smudged by soot. He hadn't burned to death. The next couple of men looked the same. Each time, Cassius' stomach roiled, threatening to rebel.

"Signore Cassius." The male voice carried a thick accent.

Cassius looked up from another victim to find the Aksumi Mystic. His heart sunk into his stomach. "Master Dawit. Have you seen Makeda and Brehane?"

"Brehane escaped."

A weight, like the Forger of the World's Anvil, lifted off Cassius' shoulders.

"Thankfully, Makeda is not among the dead I have seen so far." Dawit gestured toward the string of bodies behind him.

Thankfully, Cassius would not have to look at those bodies, now that Makeda and Brehane were both accounted for. "The fire brigade said that Makeda helped them."

Dawit's forehead scrunched up. "That doesn't sound like her."

"Well, that's what they said." Cassius snuck a look at the dead. "The victims don't look burned at all."

"The smoke burns your lungs." Dawit tapped his chest.

Cassius shuddered. The idea of dying, unable to draw a breath...he added smoke inhalation to drowning and hanging on his list of ways not to die. "Where did you see Brehane?"

Dawit's lips pursed. "Here. She went with the Paladins to one of the mobster brothels."

Could it have been Brehane, not Makeda, who helped the fire brigade? Or maybe they were together. "Which brothel? Why?"

"The *South Seas*. Still chasing after the Paladin girl."

That brothel belonged to the Acerbi. Perhaps some of what De Lucca said about Sohini attacking the Acerbi held a kernel of truth. "Why did Brehane go with the Paladins?"

Dawit harrumphed. "She wanted to help them."

Cassius cocked his head, sending a sharp pain flaring in his skull. "I thought she hated the Ayuri."

"I thought so, too."

Cassius looked to the skies. The Betrayer might not be visible now, but at this time of day, it still hung close to the sun. More betrayals were bound to happen. If he weren't so exhausted, he might listen to the Gods' Whispers. His gaze shifted to the smoldering remains of the Acerbi den. Hopefully, Makeda had escaped and was with the others.

"I am going to the *South Seas*," Cassius said, gesturing to the carriage. "Would you like to ride with me?"

"I am going to stay here and make sure Makeda isn't among the dead. I'm sure the Teleri will be more ingratiated to you if you deliver both of them, alive."

Cassius stared at the Mystic. The old legends of the Great Wars told of Aksumi plucking thoughts from the minds of those around them. Now, it looked like Dawit had uncovered Cassius' own treacherous plans.

CHAPTER 21:

Realizations

Despite the fatigue from a lack of sleep and overuse of the Vibrations, and his heartbeat throbbing in his temples, Sameer strode ahead of Jie, Brehane, and Master Anish. He couldn't get to the *South Seas* soon enough, to save Sohini from whatever the Mafia had done to her.

Unfortunately, Giovanni, the late Don Acerbi's accountant, still hobbled from his brush with death. They'd already taken five minutes to cover what should've taken two. Had he not promised to guide them there and get them past the brothel guards, it would've been faster to leave him behind.

He would've been safe with Dawit, who'd kept up his search for Makeda. When asked if she'd seen her cousin, Brehane's lips sealed tight.

Even as most citizens fled away from the conflagration, men from the fire brigade carrying pole hooks and buckets of water ran toward the smoldering mob headquarters. They slowed his progress toward the *South Seas* even more, as he paused on the side of the street to let them pass.

Stumbling to a stop, the accountant pointed down the row house-lined street. "The don's men!"

Less than two blocks ahead, two dozen ruffians with determined expressions jogged down the middle of the street. Despite De Lucca's claim of Bovyans working for the Mafia, there were none. Pedestrians made way, pressing themselves against the buildings on the side.

Tired as he was, Sameer tightened his grip around the rapier. It was far too straight and thin to execute many of the *naga* techniques. Still, it was better than being unarmed against so many.

Giovanni pushed Sameer's hand down and looked to the others. "Let me handle it."

Sameer's jaw clenched. They'd saved him, but that didn't mean the criminal wouldn't turn on them now. They continued walking half a block before Don Acerbi's men ran up.

"Mister Atalia," one of the men tipped his hat. "What is going on?"

"An attack on the headquarters!" Giovanni turned and pointed back in the direction they'd come. Plumes of smoke still ribboned up.

The men nodded and hurried to the gambling den.

Sameer sighed. What had they done? How could Dawit have been so careless to start the inferno with his sorcery? Most of the buildings here were made of wattle and daub, and stone, but if they were anything like the mob den, they had wooden supports. If not for Brehane's magic calming the flames, maybe the entire city would be reduced to rubble, for all he knew about fires.

"There weren't any Bovyans in that group," Jie said.

The accountant scratched his chin. "Maybe they are protecting the brothel. There are certainly plenty on the don's payroll."

"Or maybe," Brehane said, "clients want to enjoy strapping young men like these Bovyans."

What? Sameer joined in the others in staring at the young Mystic, who just shrugged. Everything about her self-assured tone suggested she wasn't joking.

Jie turned back to the accountant. "How many Bovyans work for the Acerbi?"

"Twenty-two." Giovanni gave an emphatic bob of his head.

"How is it none were guarding the don?"

"He has a trusted inner circle, and he preferred to keep them at the brothels to keep order, since everyone knows better than to start trouble at his headquarters. Until you came along."

Sameer snorted. Honor among thieves.

Jie flipped a curious black dagger with a serrated edge in her hand. "That means we will encounter them at the *South Seas*."

"No, wait." Giovanni coughed and held up a finger. "Now that I think about it, I think their contracts expired today..." He looked up at the Iridescent Moon, now waxing to its first crescent. "At noon."

Maybe that was why Cassius had recommended the noon hour. Resuming their walk, Sameer turned to Master Anish. "What happened, Master? After you Commanded Don Acerbi to speak, I thought the issue was resolved."

Brehane nodded. "I sensed it, a shift in the Resonance. Similar to our charm spells."

Master Anish stroked his beard. "Yes, I felt it, too. Something compelled the don to order the attack. His mistake. He and his henchmen got what they deserved."

Sameer turned and gawked at him. "What about the innocents?"

"Gamblers." Master Anish shrugged. "The world won't miss them."

Sameer's stomach churned. How uncaring. How...un-Paladinlike. "I don't think—"

"There." The accountant pointed. "That is the *South Seas*."

Sameer followed his finger. The building stood two stories high, and like most of the buildings in this district, was made of off-white wattle and daub. No sign marked it as a brothel, nor were there any imposing guards or dancing girls by the open door like at De Lucca's establishment the night before. His heart leaped into his throat. At last, they'd find Sohini.

"Strange," Jie said. "Where are the guards?"

Giovanni shook his head. "It is out of the ordinary."

"I'll go first and scout it out." Jie sprinted to the building, her short legs moving deceptively fast.

Even with his energy flagging, Sameer rushed after her. Sohini needed him.

He burst through the entry just a few steps behind Jie. His boots clacked on the wood floors, but beside that, the only sounds were women sobbing. He looked around. Beyond the foyer, there was a long hallway, as well as steps leading upstairs. Jie had already disappeared into one of the side rooms.

If she was going to check downstairs, he'd go upstairs. His pulse quickened as he took the steps two at a time. They creaked beneath his weight.

On the second-floor landing, he picked the closest door and ran in.

Two young women, with dark hair and a skin tone just a shade lighter than his own Ayuri people, huddled together on a bed, their shoulders shaking as they cried. Both wore drab robes with translucent veils. The outfits would've resembled the holy vestments of the Levanthi pious if they hadn't been so skimpy.

He knew that only because his family had hired a Selastyan refugee to do housework, and her husband had been an exiled high priest. Their son had been a good friend, and Sameer had visited their home in the ghetto and experienced their poverty firsthand. Perhaps these Levanthi women were refugees as well, forced to sell themselves. Sameer averted his gaze and cleared his throat. "Excuses me, misses. I'm..." Looking for Sohini, but these poor girls... "Are you all right?"

"The Bovyans," one said, accent thick. "They betrayed the don."

Sameer scratched his head. There hadn't been any dead mobsters in the halls or on the stairs. "What happened?"

"They took Bella and Sarah."

"Where?"

The women exchanged terrified glances and shook their heads.

Sameer's jaw clenched. "What about Sohini?"

"Who is that?" The second's forehead scrunched up, and she looked at her companion.

It's not like there could be that many Ayuri here, and the don couldn't have lied under a Paladin Command. Sameer tried to keep exasperation out of his voice. "The Ayuri woman."

"Oh." A look of recognition bloomed in their expressions. "We could never pronounce her name. Sarah. The one the Bovyans took."

His heart sunk. They must have her drugged, or bound, or who knew what. She always seemed just out of reach... "How long ago?"

"Maybe half an hour ago."

They couldn't have gotten far in such a short amount of time. "I'll be back to help you." He pressed his palms together and darted out.

* * *

Brehane took in the foyer with wide eyes. Fading frescoes depicted fair-skinned men and Southern women engaged in the act of intercourse; yet it looked all wrong. One picture depicted a couple rutting like dogs, while another had the man mounting the woman. This was not the way it was supposed to be, yet Brehane couldn't turn away.

Of course. This was a fetish brothel, where some women, tired of following the natural order, experimented with submission. The *shermuta* here were trained to take the dominant role, while the woman grunted and moaned beneath them. Perhaps this one catered to visitors from the South, like her. No wonder Sameer wanted to save his lady friend from engaging in such perverse behavior.

With a reassured nod, Brehane followed the sound of sobbing girls. They were undoubtedly acting out some sick fantasy. She peeked into a room, likewise decorated with vulgar frescoes. Two young women with honey-toned skin like Jie clung to each other. Their breasts nearly spilled out of roughspun dresses cut, dyed, and embroidered to resemble Cathayi gowns. Makeda's Tear, this brothel wasn't as twisted as she thought. After all, it wasn't abnormal to enjoy the company of another woman, though Brehane had never had to pay for it.

Still, it was hard to tell which one was the client and which was the *shermuta*, and they didn't seem to be engaged in any erotic activity. Nor did any of the murals depict women together.

The prettier one looked up, her voice cracking. "Who are you? Did the don send you?"

Brehane shook her head. "The don is dead."

"Dead?" The other, who had dragon tattoos, beamed with a wide smile. Relief? What a strange reaction. Pulling up the dress to cover herself, she turned to the prettier one. "Does that mean our contracts are satisfied?"

Contracts? Brehane's head spun. It was all too confusing. Maybe this couple wasn't client and *shermuta*, after all. "Where is Sohini?"

"So-who-y?" The prettier one tilted her head.

"The Ayuri girl."

The brunette's mouth formed a perfect summoning circle. "She was upstairs, but I thought I heard her leave with the Bovyans."

Oh no, Sameer would be crushed. But why would she go with the Bovyans?

The blonde shuddered. "They took Maya and Eira, too. We couldn't stop them. No telling what those brutes plan to do to them."

Brehane clasped her crystal. It didn't make sense. "What would they do?"

The tattooed one looked at Brehane like she was a six-headed demon dragged from the pits of Hell by a Summoner. "What men do to women."

What men do to women... Brehane gasped. The truth she had been denying this entire time, despite all the evidence, was now unmistakable. In this foreign land, gender roles were corrupted. Turned upside down in contempt toward the natural order. Men ruled, women served. All the poor women she'd seen at the Signore party, in the gambling den, and in the brothel were playthings. Sameer's lady friend, Sohini, was likely reduced to the same fate.

Which also meant... Brehane gasped. Cassius saw her as a conquest.

The two girls exchanged glances. The tattooed one met her gaze. "What do we do now?"

How to answer? Brehane certainly didn't understand the ramifications of contracts here.

On the other side of the door, Sameer dashed by.

One foot in front of the other, Brehane turned and stumbled out after him.

* * *

Sitting on a creaky cot, Jie patted the Cathayi prostitute on the back, wondering why the Bovyans had turned on Don Acerbi, and also why they'd taken only the one girl, Jovanna. Surely the four of them guarding the joint could've taken eight, one over each shoulder.

"How old is Jovanna?" she asked, her home tongue sounding strange in her own ears after weeks of not speaking it.

The woman's answer wobbled through her choking sobs. "Fourteen. Her parents died and she had to provide for her younger brothers. She just came to us a few weeks ago."

So young; but in this trade, horrible men often had a taste for the nubile.

Sameer popped his head in. "Hurry up, Jie, the Bovyans just left. They have Sohini and some girl named Bella. Do that thing with your nose."

As if she were one of the temple guard dogs. Jie harrumphed. Not like Sameer could offer her a treat. Disentangling herself from the prostitute's clingy grasp, she rose and followed Sameer and Brehane out. Anish and Giovanni all waited outside.

She met the accountant's eyes. "What is so special about Jovanna?"

"Jovanna..." His forehead crinkled and his eyes stared up into his skull, comparing receivables to payables in all likelihood. His expression blanked. "A beauty, that one. A virgin. Don Acerbi had started an auction for her maidenhood."

Face contorting into an interesting expression, Brehane blew out a sharp breath.

Jie sucked on her lower lip. It was a common practice in Cathay's Floating World, as well: a beautiful girl's virginity sold to the highest bidder.

Sameer tapped his foot. "Come on, Jie. They have a half-hour lead on us."

Jie waved him off. "What about Bella?"

"Bella..." Giovanni made the same face, one which she'd love to slap. "She's been with the don for eight months, but she's rather plain. She's made the don seventy-two drakas."

Not even enough to pay for Signore Cassius' fortune-telling services; so why would the Bovyans pick her? "And Sohini?"

Giovanni cocked his head. "I've never met her."

"Sarah," Sameer said, fists clenching. "Hurry up."

"Sarah, she's the Ayuri girl." Giovanni nodded. "Very popular among for those looking for an exotic treat."

Jie snuck a glance at Sameer.

His face was flushed bright red underneath his bronze complexion. "We need to go now."

"Wait." Jie held up a hand. "If we know why they took those three…"

"Five," Brehane said. "Maya and Eira."

"What about them?" Jie asked.

Giovanni tapped his chin, which would have been a cute gesture if it didn't belong to a foul mob accountant. "Some are prettier than others. They all have varying profitability."

Jie released her lip with a pop. The girls were all different races and ages. So far, nothing connected the ones who'd been taken. Unless… "Do they see clients during their special time of the month?"

The accountant looked as if he'd sucked a lemon. "No."

"Can you think of any time when their revenues drop?

Giovanni drew figures in the air, the motions forming a chart and numbers. "Considering when their income dropped every month, I would say they bled recently. Maybe even now."

The man could keep track of so many details, like a certain clueless spy back home. Thank the Heavens the latter used his talents for more noble goals, like assassinating rebels. "I—"

Sameer tugged her sleeve. "Come on, they just left half an hour ago."

"Shhh." Jie waved him away. His urgency was ruining her concentration. The Bovyans had taken five girls total, one a virgin. The others had just finished their monthly bleeding, which meant... She studied Giovanni's expression, looking for any sign of a lie. "What do you do if a girl gets pregnant?"

"An herbal mixture of some sort." Giovanni stared into his skull again. "Based on the financial accounts, I'd say cloves, princess lace, and periwinkle, mixed in wine. I don't know the specifics, but I could find out."

Jie looked among her companions.

Both Anish and Sameer's lips pursed.

Brehane's face contorted. "Barbaric," she muttered.

Barbaric, but it was all clear. "The Bovyans are looking for breeders."

Sameer's face paled. "We must hurry."

Anish held up a halting hand. "No, Sameer. Your judgement is impaired."

Jie couldn't disagree.

"Master," Samer said. "It's your apprentice, Sohini, we are trying to save. Not to mention all the other girls."

Anish shook his head. "Without Elder Gitika to rein you in, I can't control you. You will be tempted to use your power in ways you should not."

Brehane clasped her necklace. "Don't worry, Sameer. The rest of us will rescue your lady friend."

CHAPTER 22:

Contractual Matters

Sameer's chest squeezed so tight, it felt like it might crush his heart. With the death of Elder Gitika, Master Anish was now his master, at least until the Council reassigned him. To disobey a direct command would mean expulsion from the order, and with that, no further development of his *Bahaduur* skills. He might never see a *naga* again, except maybe on the receiving end.

He closed his eyes and summoned an image of Elder Gitika. A paragon of Paladin ideals. His master, his real master. Whose body he'd cleaned just this morning and sent off into the next world. What would *she* do?

She might not have sacrificed Paladin ideals just to rescue Sohini. On the other hand, she would protect the innocent, Ayuri or not. Whore—no, prostitute, as the half-elf said—or not. That was the Paladin way.

He opened his eyes and faced Master Anish. "My first duty is to protect the innocent girls."

Master Anish's lips curled into a...smirk? But the frown that followed was clear. "I am sorry, Apprentice Sameer, but I will be forced to recommend expulsion. I would command you to surrender your *naga*, but it is already in the hands of some Acerbi mobster."

Sameer's shoulders slumped. Like his master, his *naga* was also gone. There was no telling what evil deeds some criminal was using it for.

He straightened and turned to Jie. "Please find Sohini."

The half-elf was already kneeling by the road, running her finger over the stones. "The prints are hard to follow, but..." she sniffed the air and pointed. "I think they headed that way."

Away from town.

Brehane nodded. "I think De Lucca said the Bovyans were housed on the outskirts of town."

"That would be a good place to start." Jie sniffed again. "The prostitutes will slow the Bovyans down. Their perfume was pretty thick in the brothel, but it is quickly dispersing here."

Beckoning Brehane, Jie trotted away. The Mystic tailed after her.

The two of them wouldn't have a chance against so many Bovyans. Sameer held back a sigh. Perhaps this was the end of his life as a Paladin, but it was worth it, if he could help Sohini escape her ordeal. He might no longer be a Paladin in name, but he could still live as one. He might never wield a *naga* again, but he could still embody justice. Again holding an image of Elder Gitika in his head, he bowed one last time to Master Anish, then followed after the half-elf.

Even if the prostitutes were slowing the Bovyans down, they still managed to stay ahead. Jie had to stop every now and then and backtrack. Eventually, she shook her head and claimed that the other scents of the city were masking the trail. Scanning the cobbled roads gave her no insight into the correct direction, either.

Every time he was about to give up hope, they ran into more passersby. When she asked if they'd seen the Bovyans, some nodded and pointed, while others shook their heads and shrugged. Sameer's pulse raced faster and faster with each delay. At this rate, the Bovyans would reach wherever they were headed first.

The two-story row houses gave way to one-story ones, and eventually to unconnected hovels. At the edge of town, the road changed from paved stone to hard-packed dirt.

Jie's eyes lit up. She pointed to the tracks. "Look at the size of the bootprints."

Sameer followed her finger. There was nothing there beyond the scatter of dust in the ground. He frowned.

"There, silly. Some of the dirt has been displaced by their heavy feet."

Sameer leaned over and squinted. Whatever the half-elf saw, it didn't look like footprints of any sort to him.

She threw up her hands. "Sixteen Bovyans in all. I would assume the girls are too light to leave a trail, or maybe the Bovyans are carrying them. In any case, this is the way, I'm sure of it."

Sighing, Sameer looked down the road, which crested over a hill. Like the route to Signore Cassius' mansion, it was lined with green rows of tilled land, dotted with wooden farmhouses. Besides whatever tracks Jie thought she saw, there was no sign of sixteen large warriors and five young women. "They must have gone into one of the farms? Unless they are on the other side of the hill?"

Jie nodded. "They'd have to have a ten-minute lead on us to get on the other side of the hill. I'll run ahead to the hilltop. You can start checking the farms."

They were closer. They had to be. Soon, he'd be reunited with Sohini. If he couldn't be a Paladin, at least he could make sure she stayed one.

* * *

Jie's short legs made her the worst candidate to run up the road, but then again, she'd know how to process whatever she saw better than Sameer once they got to the top. He'd likely charge down the hill without even looking.

So run it was. At the top of the hill, she paused and caught her breath. Whoever had decided to make a road over a hill instead of around it needed to experience Black Lotus torture.

Then she saw it.

A walled compound laid another *li* down the road, surrounded by a few farms. There were four separate structures within. Just outside its gates, twenty-some Bovyans escorted nearly fifty smaller women. The distance made it impossible to pick out Sameer's darker-skinned friend from the rest.

Jie dropped to the ground. She withdrew a dwarf-made spyglass she'd borrowed from a closed store, and looked again. With the magnified view, it was clear that there were five distinct groups, each with four Bovyans and between three and nine young women. Sure enough, in a group with five girls, one had the bronze skin of an Ayuri. Curiously enough, given Sohini's Paladin skills, they hadn't bound her. Maybe they'd forced her to take gooseweed to mute her Paladin skill.

Jie sucked her lower lip. It wasn't just the South Seas which had been betrayed. Five, if not more, of Don Acerbi's brothels had been hit. It all made sense now: the Bovyans had guarded those brothels over several months, so they'd picked out potential candidates to kidnap and were waiting for a chance to steal them away.

As she counted the Bovyans already inside the compound, she froze on one near the door to the center building. Her suspicions were right. Smaller than the rest, one Bovyan had a scar on his forehead. Nightblade Phobos! The spy trained in Black Fist ways. The one who'd made a practice of visiting all the brothels, according to the prostitutes she'd talked to that first night with Sameer.

Now, what to do? It probably wouldn't be hard to infiltrate the compound. The surrounding walls were only the height of a man, with plenty of finger and toe holds between the stones. There were several hiding spaces, between the well, stables, a kitchen, and other buildings. Of course, there might be more than one Nightblade, and that would make things a little more difficult.

She looked back in the direction she'd come. Sameer was still half a *li* away, just leaving one of the farms. If she went ahead, he'd undoubtedly follow once he saw the compound. Then again, even if she waited and told him not to follow, he still would, charging in with rapier flashing. If he was going to make a scene, it could be a diversion to take advantage of; better to coordinate with him so he made said diversion at the right time. And hope he followed the plan.

Unlike last night, at De Lucca's brothel.

With a sigh, she studied the layout carefully, looking for innocuous insertion points and gauging the guard posts' lines of sight. The Bovyans guided the women through the front gate and took them into a central two-story building made from concrete.

Sameer's footsteps, heavy despite his cloth shoes, came up behind her. When she signaled him to get down, he dropped to the ground and squirmed up to her side.

She passed him the scope. "This is where they took your friend. I counted twenty-two Bovyans in total, and the forty-six women they brought in. The number of structures suggests there could be more of both. The compound could house a hundred or more people."

Sameer was already scrambling to his feet.

Jie yanked him down. "Let me scout it out. If this Sohini is as good a fighter as you say, I can probably get her out."

His shoulders drooped. "I can't just sit here and do nothing."

Brehane wormed up beside them. Given how she'd frozen up in the melee of the Mafia den, she might not be reliable if a fight broke out.

Jie gestured to the closest farm to the compound. "The two of you, get closer and wait for my signal. It will be the sharpest whistle you have ever heard. That'll let you know I found Sohini."

"Then what?"

"I need you to create a diversion so I can get her out."

Sameer frowned.

Jie snorted. "Trust me, it will work better than you charging in, without your own weapon, and trying to take on at least twenty Bovyans."

"Wait," Brehane said. "You ask him to trust you. What is your stake in this? Why are you helping? You are more than a pickpocket, aren't you?"

Jie blinked innocently. "You wouldn't believe it's for altruistic reasons?"

"Now that I think about it," Sameer said, "you appeared yesterday, right after the Mafia ambushed us in the alley. How do I know you don't actually work for them, or the Bovyans, and have been trying to ingratiate yourself with us, only to lead us into a trap?"

"I'm actually proud of you for thinking that." Jie chuckled. Maybe the Paladin wasn't as naïve as he looked. "You have no way of knowing, unless Brehane here can read minds."

Brehane clasped her necklace, frowning. Like Sameer, she didn't know how to hide her thoughts, and she clearly couldn't magic up a mind read.

Which was good. The less they knew about Jie, the better. For now, a convincing half-truth would have to do. "You're right, I am a spy; but I don't work for your enemies. I'm investigating how your illusion bauble is tied to the Bovyans. Maybe even De Lucca, though I suspect they are just using him. If helping Sohini gives me a diversion where I can learn more about the Bovyans, then I'll help Sohini."

"Fine, we'll do it your way." Sameer set his fingers into some *mudra*. Regret, perhaps.

"Just don't try to attack them, unless I give a second signal. That means I need you to help me. Most likely, I won't have to use it."

Sameer just stared at her, gawking.

Standing, Jie brushed the dust off her shirt and pants. The tailor she'd borrowed them from wouldn't be getting them back clean. She trotted down the road, keeping eyes on the compound as it grew larger with her approach. At the closest farm, she ducked by a well. Looking back toward the crest of the hill, she beckoned and pointed at the ground in front of her. Sameer might be too dense to understand that it meant for them to come this far, but Brehane had proven to have a good head on her shoulders, even if she froze under pressure.

Jie turned back to the compound. Besides the two Bovyans guarding the gate, there hadn't been any other sentries; but if she were the one in charge and had a Nightblade as an asset, she'd hide him in a high vantage point, regularly scanning the perimeter. The main building's rooftop, maybe, or the barracks.

She worked her way around toward the back, keeping low beneath the roof's line of sight. With a running jump, her hands reached the crest of the wall. Toes finding purchase between the rocks, she climbed up and peeked over the top.

This position was closest to the stables, which blocked the view of her insertion point. She slid over the top of the wall and dropped down to the ground. When she made it to the stables, she squinted through a knot in the wood walls. Two horses munched on hay.

Jie shuddered. Her last experience with horses had entailed riding back and forth between a port city and her homeland's capital. Her butt hurt just thinking about it. She crept along the wall and looked around the corner.

Several Bovyans came and went from the front of the central building, whose rear door faced her now. A stone-lined well stood between there and the stables. She waited until a soldier passed and then, staying low, dashed across the open area to the well.

From this angle, only someone at the rear of the main hall, or looking from the stables, would see her. The windows, paned with real glass, were all curtained. She stood up—

The rear door opened.

Jie dropped.

Footsteps approached, the swishing sound of a dress and the weight of the steps suggesting someone too light to be a Bovyan.

She peeked around the edge.

A young woman in a roughspun shift approached, one hand carrying a wooden bucket, the other cradling a heavy belly.

Ducking back, Jie shuddered. Her guess had been right: this was a rape camp, like the many spread throughout the Teleri homeland. All these poor girls, subjected to such horror. How could the Signores allow this to happen in the Estomar?

If only there were a way to free all these women, instead of just Sohini, and burn the place to the ground. Then again, the girls would probably just return to a life of sexual servitude at the hands of the Mafia.

The pregnant woman retrieved water and waddled back to the central building. She had to be at least five months along. No matter how depressing their life must've been before the camp, at least they'd had a semblance of choice then.

Checking the windows again, Jie stood and slunk to the building. Heavens, a night reconnaissance would be safer. This was about as foolish as the time she'd tried to infiltrate a rebel lord's saltpeter mine.

She went to a window close to the back door and peered between the crack of the curtains. It opened into a long central hall. The newly-arrived girls sat around long rectangular tables. Unfamiliar women in various stages of pregnancy, none more than five or six months, mingled with the newcomers.

At one table, a blonde woman, perhaps in her early thirties and wearing a black dress, scribbled notes. Sitting beside her was one of the new arrivals—a plump brunette—nodding. After their brief exchange, muffled by the window, the brunette stood and went to another table with several stacks of paper.

When she sat, a Bovyan across the table slid a sheet of paper in front of her. She nodded several times. She pressed her thumb into an inkstone, then made her mark at the bottom of the sheet.

Oh, to hear what was being said. The Estomari-made glass muffled sound, even for her sensitive elf ears. Inside, however... Jie stared at the back door. It was probably too risky to actually go in. She looked back in the window.

Sohini stood next in line at the first table. Up close, she was pretty, but not beautiful, with dark bronze skin and rounded features. Perhaps she and Sameer shared a relationship that went beyond skin deep, enough that he'd do anything to save her. Even give up his dreams of Paladinhood.

It was time for that diversion. If Sameer and friends raised enough ruckus in the front, she could slip in the back. Rescue Sohini, and maybe ask one of the pregnant ones if they knew where Nightblade Phobos stayed.

She slunk along the side of the building. Making sure the coast was clear, she dashed to the well, then to the stone kitchens. She set two fingers on the side of her mouth and blew out an ear-splitting whistle. By the time she made it back to the window near the back door, the compound had roused to life. Shouts relayed orders throughout the camp.

Jie peered between the curtains again. One of the Bovyans was pointing toward the front. Several of the soldiers now stood, weapons in hand. The women looked about, confused expressions on their faces. The black-haired girl sitting at the first table stood up, and Sohini took her chair. It looked like they were continuing with the registration process.

Voices shouted in the yard. "It sounded like it came from the kitchens."

"Or somewhere nearby, on the east side of the compound."

"Start there, but sweep the entire grounds."

Jie would need to get inside before they came here, which meant Sameer had to start that diversion soon.

"Check over there," a deep voice called from the front of the building.

Jie's palms sweat. *Over there* could mean here...

"Open up!" Sameer's voice carried from the compound entrance.

Jie looked back through the window. From the narrow space between the curtains, it looked like only one man guarded the front door, while the other was speaking with the black-haired girl.

Footsteps came closer.

Staying low, Jie opened the door and slipped in—

Only to almost run into a Bovyan butt. The limited line of sight had kept him hidden, and of course they'd guard both the entrance and the exit.

Using the *Mockingbird's Deception* to imitate one of the voices from outside, she used a *Ghost Echo* to throw the sound through the crack in the door. "Help!"

Without practice, the pitch came out just a little too high, but up to now the Bovyans had proven themselves poor at sorting sounds out.

The man swung around, and Jie stayed low and slipped around to his back. When he pushed the door open and stormed out, she turned and took in the room.

There were only tables and chairs, and no places to hide. Thankfully, the blonde woman at the first table and the Bovyan at the second had their backs to her, and she was below the line of sight of the front door sentry. Up to now, none of the young women showed signs of having spotted her. A flight of stairs near the back headed up.

She crept up right behind the seated blonde woman and sank low. One table over, Sohini's brown legs shone from beneath her *sari*.

The Bovyan's voice was gruff. "And you understand that, after you give birth, you will nurse many different babies for six months?"

"Yes." Sohini's accent was thick, even with that one word.

"You will never be harmed. Your room and board will be provided for, and at the end of your term, we will pay you five gold drakas. If you agree to this, sign here, or mark here with your thumb."

A contract? Jie rose just enough to peak over the blonde's shoulder, to the other table. Squinting, she zeroed in on the sheet Sohini was pressing her thumb into.

It was too far away, even for elf eyes, and written in Arkothi no less. Still, why wasn't she signing with a quill? Certainly Paladins were taught how to read and write, and Sameer had been able to read. Which meant...

The Ayuri woman probably wasn't Sohini.

The woman's head bobbled as she pressed her palms together. If her accent could get any thicker than Sameer's or Anish's, it would be molasses. "Thank you. I will bear you a strong son and serve you faithfully."

Ducking down, Jie sucked on her lower lip. Maybe these women weren't kidnapped. Perhaps they'd willingly come to the breeding ground. And why not? They were apparently prostitutes, and this new job provided stable housing. With five gold drakas at the end of it all, an enterprising woman could start her own business.

In the meantime, for just five drakas and the cost of housing and feeding the women, the Bovyans got a future soldier. De Lucca's deal, if it went through, already covered much of these costs, but what did he stand to gain from it? Was he breeding a personal army? Or were the Bovyans exploiting his ambitions so as to establish a foothold for their evil empire? Nightblade Phobos' words from the night before suggested the latter.

The Ayuri girl came to the blonde's table and sat. She set some papers down.

"I am Doctor Myra. I'm here to see to your medical needs."

A doctor. A female one, no less, working for the Bovyans. Jie shifted and studied the woman's side profile.

A couple fine lines radiated from the corner of her eye. She had a strong jawline and a high-bridged nose. Her olive complexion and brown eyes suggested she'd come from somewhere in the Arkothi North. She picked up the papers, revealing the brown tattooed outline of the Teleri Empire's nine-pointed sun on her wrist. "I see your name is Laja. I'm going to ask some questions about your health."

It didn't take a genius to know where this line of questioning would go. The girl wasn't Sohini, and the fact that the Bovyans used female doctors was quite the revelation. Jie crept back toward the rear exit.

A quick peek out the window revealed Bovyans patrolling in a search pattern. Leaving through the rear door would be much too risky. With the front door guarded and enemies swarming the rear, there was only one way out.

She darted to the stairs and tiptoed up.

CHAPTER 23:

Ulterior Motives

Cassius' head jerked, rousing him from his nap. The steady whir of carriage wheels over the smooth pavestones had lulled him into sleep, but the vehicle now jolted to a stop.

"Signore," the driver said, his voice trembling. "We are surrounded."

Cassius took a quick look. A burly mobster was fighting with the driver over the reins. Two others, armed with rapiers, were climbing up to the door, their boots scraping on the running board.

The exceedingly short nap had given him just enough clarity to realize his mistake. A signore, entering Mafia territory alone, was an inviting target.

"Kill the signore!" the mobster at the right door yelled.

Cassius twisted and kicked it open, sending the man flying. The open door revealed another goon.

Cassius stood and drew his rapier and dagger. The higher vantage point gave him a good view.

Five enemies total, only one standing on the right side as the other he'd kicked struggled to get up. With two quick steps, Cassius leaped and stabbed with the sword.

The man raised his blade to block, only to leave an opening for Cassius' dagger to thrust between his ribs. He staggered back, hand over the spurting blood.

Before the other gained his feet, Cassius stabbed him in the thigh, the man's scream piercing the air.

Now, the green-clad one from the left side stood in the carriage, while the other, dressed in orange, rounded the back. Cassius strode to meet him, parrying a stab and riposting with a thrust of his own. The man was talented, responding with a flurry of thrusts and swipes.

The flash of steel and garish orange cloth pushed Cassius back, back toward the one in green atop the carriage and their two wounded comrades. To be caught between them would mean certain death. Even now, the one in the carriage was jumping down.

Cassius feigned an injured left arm and provided an opening.

As planned, the mobster lunged for it.

Cassius spun out of the way, while redirecting the man's stab into the green-clothed goon's gut, just as he landed on the ground.

As the first stared at what he'd just done to his comrade, Cassius slammed the pommel of his dagger into his temple. He crumpled to the ground.

Cassius paused to reevaluate. Four men, dead or incapacitated, and the other...

"Drop your weapons, or your driver dies."

Cassius looked over.

The loyal driver, bless his heart, had refused to let go of the reins, and the big mobster had yanked him close enough to set a dagger point at his throat.

Cassius lowered his weapons. "Just let him go. We didn't do anything to you."

The man growled. "You attacked Don Acerbi's headquarters. This is war."

Cassius' stomach knotted. The crime families usually fought among each other, but the dance of rogues in the skies always suggested they had an agreement in place for the unlikely event that the Signores tried to suppress any one family. An all-out war would devastate Tokahia, and leave the pyramid unprotected. That's why he'd always insisted on moderation in dealing with the Mafia, and also why pinning it on rogue Bovyans had made sense.

Now, Signore De Lucca had loosed the first volley. Whatever insanity drove him to risk ending a truce which made everyone rich, how he'd done it actually made sense. Cassius shook his head. "We are not your enemy. It's the Bovyans. They are trying to weaken both our sides so they can take over."

The mobster's brows furrowed. His dagger tip remained pressed into the driver's neck, and the driver hadn't thought to just let go of the reins and scuttle back out of reach.

Really, Cassius could run away at any time, but good, loyal carriage drivers were hard to come by. He sheathed his weapons and took several steps closer with his hands raised. "It's true. Our security forces weren't involved, and even now, our fire brigades are putting out the fires. We need to work together, for our city's sake."

The man's expression tightened. He pointed his rapier at his fallen comrades. "Then why did you hurt them?"

Cassius swatted the closest horse in its flank.

With a whinny, it reared. The reins ripped out of the mobster's hands.

"Go, go!" Cassius yelled.

The driver snapped the reins and the horses set off. They brushed the mobster to the side, sending him tumbling to the ground.

Lunging forward, Cassius whipped his rapier out and drove it into the man's sword arm. He dashed to catch up with the carriage, which had come to a stop half a block away. Cassius started to look over his shoulder, then thought the better of it. He'd fought in self-defense, and to protect the driver. Those men would likely survive their wounds, anyway.

Cassius climbed back aboard and patted the driver on the shoulder. "Good job. Are you all right?"

The driver nodded. "Yes sir. Thank you, sir."

"Good. Let's get out of here. To the *South Seas*. If any more mobsters try to stop us, just run them over next time." Cassius settled back into his chair and pondered the situation.

The Bovyan, Phobos, had lied when they'd made their deal the other day. The Mafia families were never a threat to the pyramid, but he'd exploited Cassius' Gods-ordained duty to protect it in exchange for turning over Brehane. But why? Or was it just a distraction, to hide their real goals? And what motivation did Signore De Lucca have for attacking the crime families? He stood to lose a lot if the city fell into civil disorder. In fact, even if they did overcome the Mafia, De Lucca's brothels might suffer if his patrons thought the former Mafia whorehouses were now safe, cheaper alternatives. Maybe...

Cassius' eyes fluttered open as the carriage jolted over a large rock on the hard-packed road. He blinked several times, then turned to find the Iridescent Moon now waning to its second crescent. He'd been so tired he'd drifted off in hostile territory. He must've been asleep for more than a half hour. At least his muddled head felt nominally better. A little more rest, and maybe he could Divine, once.

He coughed several times. With the recent dry weather, the carriage wheels and horse hooves had kicked up dust. They'd left the city center and driven to where two-story gambling dens and brothels flanked unpaved roads. It was quiet, even for an early afternoon. No Mafia enforcers stood outside the doors. Perhaps most had organized and counter-attacked the Signore-controlled districts.

Cassius' chest squeezed. The mansion might be protected by his guards, but the megalith circle...

Up ahead, a single figure strode through the otherwise empty street, sun at his back. The scene was reminiscent of the popular novels which depicted showdowns between a single hero and single villain.

"Stop," Cassius told the driver. His hand tightened around his rapier hilt. This person might very well be another villain.

The carriage slowed. The person drew closer, and his hand made no move toward the large blade at his side.

Cassius blinked.

It was the Paladin Master.

Tipping his chin, Cassius waved him down. "Master Anish! Where are Brehane and Sameer?"

The Paladin looked up and slowed a step. Then, head bobbing, he motioned behind him. "They are chasing Bovyans to Signore De Lucca's plantation."

"Whatever for?"

Master Anish harrumphed. "My fool apprentice thinks the Bovyans have Sohini."

"You seem certain they don't."

"I might be more sure, if your Divining worked better." The Paladin pressed his palms together and started off.

"Master Anish," Cassius called, hoping to avoid a repeat of the last Mafia attack. "Rest your feet. Come ride in my carriage."

The Paladin afforded him a scathing glance. "I have other business to attend to."

Cassius sighed. Even if he hadn't gained the Paladin's protection, at least this encounter saved him a trip to the *South Seas*. He motioned to the driver. "Head to Signore De Lucca's new plantation."

With a nod, the driver turned the carriage down another street. Up ahead, six Bovyans in chainmail marched in the middle of the street. They had no marks revealing whether they worked for the crime families or De Lucca, but the all evidence, as it came together in Cassius' foggy head, suggested they had their own agenda.

They broke formation to make way for the carriage.

Cassius waved to get their attention. "What are you doing here?"

The leader came closer, revealing Captain Baros from the banquet the night before. His eyes roved over the carriage before he thumped a fist on his chest. "Signore De Lucca ordered us to disarm the crime families and establish order."

"Just six of you?" Cassius raised an eyebrow.

"We have two hundred men sweeping through the mob territories."

Two hundred! All obeying Signore De Lucca. Captain Baros had said something about four hundred total Bovyans in the city. De Lucca had wanted to bring a thousand more to protect the pyramid. Housed in his barracks, fed by his plantations, entertained by his whores. Perhaps his goal wasn't just to eliminate the Mafia, but to take control of the entire city-state and surrounding lands, using a small army of Bovyan mercenaries. Or, the Bovyans were just manipulating De Lucca to gain a foothold in the region.

For now, though, they would make this foray into Mafia territory safe. Cassius dipped his chin. "Thank you for all your hard efforts in enforcing the law."

Captain Baros thumped his chest again. "It is our pleasure, Signore. Bringing order to chaos was our Divine mission."

And yet, they'd served both the Mafia and the Signores. No doubt they had plans of their own. Perhaps they were the threat to the pyramid, and De Lucca was their unwitting means of allowing them to take it without force. Their other Divine mission was conquest of the sundered Arkothi Empire, including the Estomar.

CHAPTER 24:

Redemption of Sorts

Wondering what the half-elf had planned after her shrill whistle, Brehane stood beside Sameer outside the compound as a Bovyan opened the heavy wooden gate. The Paladin apprentice fidgeted, staring as if the gate couldn't open any slower.

It budged just wide enough to frame the hulking brute. He studied both of them, his eyes finally fixing on her. "What do you want?"

What did they want? Jie had said to cause a distraction and sent the signal, but hadn't specified what. Brehane bowed her head. "Signore De Lucca invited us to visit his plantation."

"Signore De Lucca?" The Bovyan's face contorted even more than a Transmuter could accomplish in clay. He looked over his shoulder. After a second, he turned back and opened the door a little wider. "You may come in, my lady. The Ayuri may not."

If this compound really was a pleasure house for Teleri soldiers, walking right in, alone, didn't seem like the brightest idea. Especially after she'd learned how vile and corrupted their culture was. "On second thought—"

Sameer sidled past her. The Bovyan reached for him. Like at Cassius' mansion the night before, he moved like a blur, slipping right by. He disappeared into the compound.

The Bovyan turned and gave chase, leaving the door unguarded. Shouts erupted inside.

Brehane stared at the opening. After expending so much energy on calming the burning Acerbi building, she might not have enough energy to escape if the need arose. And arise it probably would.

Still, Sameer would need help. Foolish Paladin. Foolish, noble Paladin, who'd risked his life to rescue as many people as he could from the conflagration. He was nothing like the treacherous *Bahaduur* of the past. She squared her shoulders, pulled the door open, and strode in.

Inside the walls, four Bovyans surrounded Sameer, his little rapier looking like a toy compared to their hefty longswords. More Teleri swarmed out of the barracks. In moments, they'd engulf him like a Hydromancer's wave.

He didn't move as fast as before, yet the Teleri might've been slogging through webs the way he dodged their attacks. Though he misused his rapier, he twirled it in arcs so fast that it looked like a solid, curving wall.

Brehane turned to the onrush of Bovyans from the barracks. So close to the pyramid, the Resonance coursed through her, replenishing her. Unlike her reaction to the chaos of the Mafia den, the words and motions of magic came easily. She splayed her fingers and growled out the syllables which would combine Transmuting, Geomancy, and Aeromancy. Her vitality flickered.

Webbing shot out from her fingers, wide enough to envelop the first three men. They stumbled to the ground, while the five behind them careened into the first rank. Another few managed to jump to the side, but many still slammed into their comrades.

Energy flagging, she blurted out more words of sorcery. More sticky strands sprayed out from her hands, pasting another Bovyan against the barracks door. Three, four—no, six—had managed to avoid her webs, only to meet Sameer's blade.

The door to the barracks thumped and buckled, but held fast under her webs. She'd done it! Casting spells under duress, where she'd failed just hours before. Her chest filled with pride. And relief.

With the lull, Sameer hunched over and panted. His head turned to her, and nodded. "Thank you."

A grin formed on her lips, unbidden, as she strode over to him. Who would've thought a Mystic and Paladin, enemies three hundred years ago, would work so well together?

Teleri writhed around him, moaning through clenched teeth. Their weapons lay scattered out of reach.

None appeared dead, with most suffering cuts and stabs to their limbs.

She pointed to them. "You spared them all?"

Straightening, Sameer nodded. He held up the rapier and twisted it back and forth in the sunlight. "It looks quite fragile, but slapping with the thin blade or raking with the tip makes it easy to incapacitate an opponent without causing fatal injuries. Even if the council expels me from the order, I will strive to live like a Paladin."

Noble and foolish, indeed. She studied his earnest expression.

The barracks door thumped again, louder this time. The webbing stretched, and it looked like some of the fibers were fraying.

She turned back to him. "Now what?"

"I'm going to find Sohini." He marched toward the central building.

The door to it swung open, revealing a Bovyan armed with a longsword.

Sameer held his hand up to her. "No webs. I need to get in."

She snorted. "I didn't think you needed help against one."

The two warriors met, and in just a second the Bovyan was sprawled on the ground. Sameer kicked the man's sword out of reach. In three steps, he'd entered.

She started after him, when the Resonance shifted. She stopped in her tracks and looked around.

The door to the barracks flung open...not from her webs snapping, but rather from them *disappearing*. She gaped. How had that happened? Bovyans couldn't use any magic.

And now, several of their eyes were locked on her.

The only way to gain time was to seal them behind the doorway. She splayed her fingers again and grunted out the web spell. The Resonance shifted again, and her threads dispersed into wisps as soon as they left her fingers. Her energy guttered, her knees wobbling against the strain.

Why was her magic failing? Even at full strength, her repertoire of spells didn't include fireblasts or lightning bolts. Fire darts and ice bolts could only affect two or three at most.

Heart racing, she turned and darted toward the door to the main building. It would be safer with Sameer, though maybe she'd just get in his way.

The door slammed shut.

Brehane yanked at it, but it held firm. Over her shoulder, the Bovyans were checking on their injured comrades, but several were striding toward her. She raked her gaze across the compound. To the right stood a well and stables; to the left, a single-story wood building.

Maybe on a horse, she could keep the Bovyans running around in circles. Not like she'd ridden a horse in over a decade. She ran toward the stables. Behind her, the Bovyans didn't appear to be in any rush to catch her.

And why not? As long as they covered all the exits, she and Sameer were trapped.

Inside the stables, the earthy scent of hay and horse assaulted her nose. Her stomach roiled as her eyes adjusted to the lower light. There were at least eight stalls, with tack and harness hanging from nails on the wall. The nickering and neighing of horses was reminiscent of minor demons dragged from Hell by Summoners.

She hurried over to the first stall. The horse inside had no saddle or tack. Nor did the horses in the next few stalls. Did they not wear it at all times? They all looked agitated, ears pinned back and tails swishing. If only she were a Kanin shaman, with their supposed ability to influence animals.

The stomp of boots came closer.

Stomach twisting, she ducked into an empty stall.

What a stupid idea, coming to the stables. Now she was trapped, and there was no telling what the Teleri soldiers would do to a trespasser.

Light footsteps crept through the middle of the stable. Why would a Bovyan even bother trying to sneak in? Maybe they thought she had more magic to draw on.

It was time to bluff. She opened her fingers and took a stance which projected much more confidence than she felt.

The stall door started to creak.
Her heart lodged in her throat.
The door swung open, revealing...

Nothing.

Shoulders sagging, Brehane blew out a breath of air. The Bovyan must've waited, expecting her to throw a spell. She listened.

More boots clopped near the entrance to the stable. "She came in here."

They hadn't even entered? Then how had the door opened?

Now though, they were coming this way. She straightened and arranged her face in the most ferocious expression she could muster.

Bovyan boots came closer. "Not in any of these."

A warm, firm body pushed up against her back. A hand clamped over her mouth.

Her heart, which had settled from her throat back into its rightful place only seconds ago, just about stopped.

"Shhhh." The voice tickled her ear. Something cold pressed into her neck. The Resonance shifted.

Above the stall doors, a Bovyan face appeared and peered in.

Every muscle locked up.

He looked right at her. Then his head shook, and he turned away. "Nobody here, either."

Nobody? Brehane raised her hands, only to not see them.

"Do another sweep outside." The bootsteps hurried out.

Brehane's muscles relaxed. Her body materialized out of thin air.

The hands on her shoulders spun her around.

Nothing was there.

Then a human form blinked into existence, hand in his plain grey robes.

Melas.

He looked older than before, with white streaking through his tight black coils. His broad nose and large lips made his eyes look even smaller.

"Teacher Melas," she said, clasping his hands. "What are you doing here?"

"I've been watching you, ever since I heard of your arrival in Tokahia."

"I thought I saw you! Near Cassius' megalith. And then in the Mafia den."

He nodded. "You always were talented."

"You knew we were here. Why didn't you reveal yourself?"

His head turned in slow shakes. "And risk capture? Makeda would happily drag me back to Sodorol in chains for breaking the Conclave's rules."

Makeda's ambitions knew no end. Brehane shuddered. Then again, she herself had planned to bring Melas back, and take her rightful place at the university. There was no other way to restore the Biomancer clan's honor. "Then why did you help me now?"

"When you came here with the Ayuri, I knew you would get in trouble."

"You followed us here?"

Wetting his lips, he opened his mouth, then shut it, then spoke. "Yes. You don't know what the Teleri do to women. They are breeding an army here."

Brehane's head spun. This society was so backward. Women were reduced to objects of pleasure, to be used. Then again, her own people did the same to men back home. No wonder Melas didn't want to return. How could she force him?

At the same time, how could she give up on her dreams? Her hand strayed to her jewel. "Will you not return to the university?"

His eyes followed. "Why would I? Why would *you*? You've felt it, haven't you? The power of the pyramid has allowed me to experiment with my magic, without some useless matriarch or master looking over my shoulder, trying to steal my work. I am rediscovering the old Illusionist skills."

She sucked in a sharp breath. He was right. And if he'd accomplished invisibility and the First Mystic knew what else, perhaps she could do the same with Biomancy.

His grin spread wide as he nodded. "Yes. Imagine: an Illusionist and Biomancer, whose tribal conflict before the Hellstorm led to the loss of our respective clans' magic, working together to revive it. After I teach you everything they would at the university, we will learn as much as we can here. Then, we can travel to the pyramid in Arkos and expand our skills even more."

Brehane's heart soared. As a teacher, Melas knew the fundamentals of all the schools. Instead of going back to the university and playing by the Conclave's rules, and clawing her way through all the obstacles they'd put up, she could return as a full-fledged Mystic, ready to restore the clan's honor. She nodded. "Yes, yes! Let's save my Ayuri friend and get out of here."

"It's too risky." He waved his hands and grunted out some sounds. The Resonance shifted.

"What did you do?" she asked.

"I made you invisible."

She held up her hands.

They weren't there.

"Can't we help him like this?" She raised an eyebrow, though he wouldn't see it.

He shook his head. "If you try to attack someone, the spell will dissipate. Take my hand."

It was hard, when her own hand was invisible. With a few attempts, her palm found his. He grinned, then reached into his robe pocket and blinked out.

"How?" she asked.

Melas' disembodied voice spoke: "I infused a bead with invisibility. I can save energy this way. Come on." He gave a tug.

The first few steps felt strange, until she stopped looking at the ground. He guided her out of the stables and back through the compound. Bovyans swept through the grounds, yelling as they searched.

"He's inside," said one.

"Still no sign of the female," another yelled.

Her pulse picked up a beat. Melas' hand squeezed around hers.

They made it back to the front gate without a problem, where a wagon with a rectangular wooden back waited. Several Bovyans loaded crates through the wagon's back door.

Dressed in a formal black surcoat, a smaller one with a scar on his forehead pointed. "That one goes in back. We'll need quick access to it when it's time to take the pyramid."

Brehane gasped. Heads turned toward them, and hands reached for swords.

* * *

Sameer looked among the dozens of screaming young women, who huddled in groups of three and four around rectangular tables. None much older than fifteen or sixteen, they all stared at him in fear.

In fear? They were captives of rapists, while he was here to help them. And though there was a single Ayuri girl here, it wasn't Sohini.

An older woman with blonde hair rose from a table near the back and put out her arms to shield a woman behind her.

At the adjacent table, a Bovyan stood and pointed at him. "You! You are trespassing."

Sameer squared his shoulders. Maybe these women had come to see their captors as saviors. "First release these ladies."

The older woman curtsied. "Sir Paladin, I am Doctor Myra. I tend to these girls' health needs. I assure you, they are all here of their own free will."

Several of the girls nodded.

How could it be? Sameer turned to the Ayuri and spoke to her in their native tongue. "Is it true? Did you choose to come here?"

The girl gave a tentative bob of her head. "Yes, Sir Paladin. We were all prostitutes, trapped in a life of debt and servitude to the Mafia. The Teleri offered us a means of escaping that life. Once we have a child, they will pay us enough to start a new life, or even hire us to sew their uniforms and cook their food." She reached over to the table and held up a piece of paper.

Sameer stalked over and read it, the Arkothi words coming slowly. It was basically a contract for the girl's womb. Heat rose to his head. "Come with me, I will help you escape this life."

She shook her head. "And then what? I have no home, no money. I'll just end up in another brothel."

His heart sunk. How unfair was this world, where a girl saw an injustice as fair. And there was nothing he could do about it. He didn't even know what he was going to do with himself.

The front door pushed open. Several more Bovyans crowded in, blades bared. The girls, who'd relaxed, now huddled together again.

A middle-aged man in De Lucca's purple livery pushed through the soldiers and pointed at Sameer. "Surrender."

Maybe he could fight through, maybe he couldn't, but armed conflict would risk these young women. Sameer turned to the doctor. "Doctor Myra, I am looking for another Ayuri woman. Sohini."

The doctor shook her head. "Laja is the only Ayuri here. I swear it."

Shoulders slumping, Sameer knelt and set the sword on the floor. He laced his fingers above his head.

Several of the Bovyans surged forward. They pulled his hands down and manacled them behind his back. Hauling him to his feet, they dragged him toward the door.

He gave no resistance as they led him across the yard, toward the front gate. "Where are you taking me?" he asked.

His captors said nothing, instead gesturing to a wagon outside the walls.

CHAPTER 25:

Unexpected Allies

The building's concrete walls were thick enough to muffle the commotion outside in the yard, even with Jie's keen elf ears. She looked down the second-floor hallway, which was lit only by the windows at the top of the stair's landing and all the way at the other end.

Rafters ran across the hallway ceiling, exposing wood planks. Dozens of doors lined either side. With almost all of them open, Jie darted from doorway to doorway, catching glimpses of young women in various stages of pregnancy inside the rooms, sewing and patching Bovyan uniforms. She counted forty-three girls by the time she came to a closed door. The sign, hanging at convenient height for a human, read *Doctor* in Arkothi script.

No doubt there'd be insights regarding the Teleri operation here, and possibly information regarding the Nightblades. At the very least, given its position in the building, it had a window which would allow for an escape.

Unsurprisingly, the door was locked. Like all the others she'd come across in this city, the lock's simplicity would make it easy enough for a beginner Black Lotus trainee to handle. Jie withdrew her picks. With a few deft twists, the lock yielded. She pushed the door open and slipped inside to the small room, then locked the door behind her.

She crept over the soft carpet, past the cot, and looked at the desk in front of the window. Sunlight streamed in, spotlighting a folded letter resting above another letter, next to an inkwell and quill.

She studied the window. Made of glass like the others, it had two offset wood frames with grooves and ropes. Such a foreign concept! From the look of it, it likely opened vertically. She gave it a slight test, and it rose several inches with ease. A breeze whispered in through the crack, threatening to blow the papers off the desk.

Jie closed the window and scanned the contents of the first letter. The bold, blocky script likely belong to an equally confident individual.

My Beloved Myra,

I trust that all proceeds as planned, and your charges are in good health. If this model works, perhaps we can copy it in lands we annex in the future. The First Consul will soon visit Tokahia to meet with the Madurans, and it will be up to you to convince him of its validity.

Here, we are making progress with roads and logging. Unfortunately, our barbaric breeding practices continue, and the resentment grows among the natives. I await your arrival.

Altos

Jie chewed on her lower lip. There was just too much to digest. A Bovyan addressing a woman as beloved, when they typically loved only their motherland. The First Consul visiting this city. And wherever the writer was, the empire was building roads and logging. She turned to the doctor's letter, written in a neat cursive.

My Dear General:

Your strategy of contracting prostitutes was brilliant. They have no objections to the process, and so far, thirty-two are pregnant and the nursery interior nears completion. As expected, your men have been disciplined, and I have not had to report any of them. I regret that my efforts to find someone for our purposes have failed. I've also been told that the First Consul will not be coming.

I look forward to when I can join you.

Myra

Jie's brow furrowed. Not only did a Bovyan general love a woman, but apparently, the feelings were reciprocated. Or maybe it was like the Court Concubine Syndrome of her homeland's previous dynasty, where some courtesans in the large harems supposedly fell in love with the emperor. Still, the letter made everything clear: the Bovyans were breeding an army in Tokahia.

Yet, there was no mention of Nightblades.

Footsteps stopped right outside the door. A key thrust into the lock.

Jie lifted the window.

It screeched and stuck, only a hand-width wide. It wouldn't raise or shut.

The lock clicked.

Stifling a curse, Jie scanned the room. Under the bed was too obvious, and unlike De Lucca's office, there were no fireplaces.

The door started to open.

Jie dashed towards the far corner on her tiptoes, then pop-vaulted between the corners to the ceiling. She wiggled between the rafters and froze just as the doctor, Myra, stepped in.

The doctor's eyes swept over the room before her head fixed on the open window. "Phobos, you bastard. I know you're in here. That's why I sabotaged the window."

Phobos, the Nightblade from De Lucca's office! He had been in the compound right before her insertion, but had been unaccounted for since.

Apparently, he stalked the doctor, and she clearly wasn't fond of him, from the way she put her hands on her hips. "I don't care if you work for another department, I'm going to report your ass for harassing me." She knelt down and looked under the bed. Brows creasing, she stood, her gaze roving the room, but predictably not looking up.

This was too easy. All Jie had to do was wait for the doctor to leave.

The doctor looked up, and their eyes met. She gasped.

Jie pushed herself out of the crevice and drew De Lucca's knife as she dropped to the floor. She pressed the flat of the blade to the doctor's neck, just as the latter's mouth opened.

"Who are you?" the doctor asked in a whisper.

Jie listened. No more footsteps echoed in the halls. "One of Phobos' spies," she whispered.

The woman's brows clashed. "Since when do the Nightblades train women? Half-elf women, at that."

Foolish on the Nightblades' part, to not use females, but not surprising given the Bovyans' all-male culture. Jie snorted. "You seem to know enough about them. Tell me what you know."

Eyes narrow, the doctor shrugged. "They are Consul Haros' own spies: he recruited Bovyans too small to become shock troopers, and had them trained in acrobatics and spying."

By the traitor Jie was tracking, if the doctor was telling the truth. Jie lowered the blade, but kept it at the ready. "Where?"

"Somewhere in the Teleri heartland. I don't know. I'm just a doctor."

"A Teleri doctor. A woman doctor, complicit in gang rape." Jie pulled the doctor's sleeve up, revealing the nine-pointed sun tattoo.

The doctor pulled the sleeve down. "Do you know what this mark means?"

"It means you work for them."

"In a twisted way, yes." The woman's lips pursed. "Every girl in the Teleri Empire's lands gets one at age eight. It's blue at first, but once she begins her monthly bleeding, it will turn red. That's when their census takers know it is our time to go to the mating compounds."

Jie shuddered.

Searching her eyes, Doctor Myra sighed. "We've heard of people trying to alter the tattoo, but the dye invariably turns red. Deep in the Teleri heartland, where the Bovyans have ruled for two hundred years, it is so ingrained in the culture that the girls view the Bovyans as dashing, heroic figures. They believe it is their patriotic duty to have a healthy boy."

It didn't seem possible to be so brainwashed. Jie shook her head.

The woman traced the circle in the middle of the star. "Once we give birth, the tattoo will turn brown of its own accord, and will temporarily change back to blue when chasteberry juice touches it. It's proof that we've done our duty, and that we can return to our lives. To get married to non-Bovyans, and have daughters, to repeat the process all over again."

Though Jie lowered the knife, she jabbed a finger at the woman. "How can you participate in such savagery?"

The doctor's gaze shifted to the ground. "My city, Mirkos, was conquered by the Teleri almost fifty years ago. It was especially hard on the first generation. My grandmother and mother refuse to talk about it."

Jie nodded. She'd used her body to gain information on more than one occasion, and it still felt dirty.

The woman held up the tattoo again. "Though I never knew them, I have both a Bovyan brother and son somewhere. Maybe both are alive after all these years of constant war. I have to hope the Bovyans are not all evil. I'd like nothing more than to see the Teleri Empire change or fall. But until then, I will do my best to take care of the soldiers and women under my care."

"Is that why you are telling me about the Nightblades?"

"Yes. They're a dangerous asset. The First Consul's private army, which he must've developed in secret for years before we ever heard of them."

"Why in secret?" Jie asked.

"Subterfuge isn't the Bovyan way. They're a blunt force instrument. The Nightblades are a scalpel."

Just like the Black Lotus back home. If the doctor was telling the truth, it would explain how the Teleri Empire had expanded so much in the last year. Jie spun her finger in a wide circle. "What is going on out there?"

Understanding bloomed on the doctor's face. "You are with the Paladin."

Jie kept her expression impassive. Apparently, the doctor didn't know about Brehane. "What about him?"

"He surrendered, and the Bovyans are taking him to Signore De Lucca's office."

Foolish Paladin. All he had to do was create a diversion. Brehane had to have more sense, but of course she wouldn't be able to control him if he thought he could save Sohini. Now, Jie had to try to rescue him. "Where is Phobos?"

The doctor shook her head. "I wish I knew. He usually spends time at his antique shop, but when he's here...well, he could be anywhere, doing the First Consul's dirty work."

Jie gestured to the bed with her knife. "I'm sorry, but I'm going to have to gag you and tie you up."

"And then what? You'll try to sneak through a fortress on high alert?"

Jie snorted. "I've made it out of tougher spots."

The woman held her hands out. "I'll make it easy. Take me hostage, and we'll walk out the front gate."

If someone would've told Jie that the day's activities would include burning a gangster den down before noon, breaking into a Teleri breeding compound around mid-afternoon, and then finding help inside... She suppressed a gawp. "Get your bedsheet and hold it up."

The doctor did as told.

De Lucca's knife passed through the cloth as if it were water, making no sound. Jie studied the amazing blade for a moment before sheathing it. She twisted the length of cloth and bound the doctor's hands in front of her. "This will make it more convincing, and keep you out of trouble." And make things easier, if the woman decided to betray her.

With the taller doctor in front of her, Jie headed through the hall. A commotion erupted as trembling, gasping, and crying women, many in various stages of pregnancy, came to the doorways.

"Let the doctor go."

"Please don't hurt her."

So the doctor was well loved. Jie kept her expression grim, lest the charade be exposed.

The doctor waved her bound hands down. "It's okay. No one will get hurt."

The women followed them down the steps into the main room. Six Bovyans drew longswords and blocked the front and back doors. The collective gasp of the new recruits might've sucked all the air from the room.

"Clear your weapons and make way, or the doctor dies." Jie twirled the knife with a flourish, then reached up and pointed it at the base of the doctor's neck.

The soldiers lowered their blades. Jie motioned them all to one side, to keep the doctor between them and her. She donkey-kicked the front door open and pulled the doctor out.

In the yard, Bovyans stopped in their tracks and stared. Jie gauged the distances between them. If things went badly, there were still two gaps in their positions she could take to the wall.

"Just keep calm," the doctor whispered.

Jie snorted. "Do I look nervous?"

"Do you? I can't see you." Mirth carried in the doctor's voice. They were now just two dozen steps from the gate.

A crossbow string twanged from the left. A bolt whizzed through the air.

Jie shoved the doctor forward, out of possible harm. The bolt zipped right where a certain half-elf's head would've been had she kept backing up. Whoever pulled the trigger was a sharpshooter. She tracked the trajectory to its source.

On the barracks roof, a dark-haired young man with a honey complexion cocked a repeating crossbow. Too large to be a Cathayi and too small to be a Bovyan shock trooper, he fit the doctor's description of a Nightblade—though not Phobos. He took aim with the same kind of weapon that had been used to assassinate a lord back home—the incident which had started her mission to the North.

Here was another piece of the puzzle.

One which would be impossible to investigate now, with a Bovyan now pulling the doctor to safety and others closing in.

The crossbow twanged, cocked, and twanged again. Two more bolts flew. The second's tip glinted in the sun—it wouldn't hit her—but the first came straight at her. He was baiting her to jump back, probably into the path of the second.

Jie rolled forward, the first bolt wooshing by her ear, and into the shin of a charging soldier. He tripped over her, and she came to a stop as another Bovyan raised his sword to hack her. Her knife sliced through his leather boot, flesh, and Achilles tendon as if it they were made of lard. He screamed, and his chop thudded into the dirt.

Jie popped back onto her feet, just as the crossbow twanged again. Sidestepping the thrust of the next man, she seized his arm, twirled on a foot, and pulled him into the bolt meant for her. He hit the ground with a thump.

Four shots, and if the weapon was the same model as the one used in the assassination, its magazine held twelve bolts. Four Bovyans now stood between her and the gate. One pulled the gate shut.

"Stop," the doctor yelled. She waved her hands up and down at the sharpshooter. "The men..."

Jie didn't wait to see if he'd listen. She charged his position, a good sixty feet away. His crossbow lined up with her and he pulled the trigger. She sidestepped and continued her advance, the bolt hitting somewhere behind her.

He emptied his magazine in an arcing spray of death.

Now just thirty feet away, Jie froze, limiting her exposure to one bolt. It flew true. She shot her hand out, caught it, and rolled backward with its force. Two, five, six more tips lodged into the earth around her.

She windmilled up to her feet, catching a glimpse of the gawking Teleri soldiers well behind her as she landed.

The Nightblade dropped to the ground in a kneel, one fist to the ground and a single-edged straight sword in hand. Everything about him screamed Black Lotus Clan, though she'd seen every initiate who'd come through the Temple in the last twenty-plus years.

As much as she wanted to question him, at least sixteen Bovyans now ran toward her. She reached into her sleeve and whipped out three throwing stars with a backhand spin. The Nightblade rolled to the side, but the arc of one of the stars caught him in the gut. He crumpled to the ground with a grunt.

There was no time for interrogation. Jie resumed her sprint to the closest wall. The Bovyan's longer legs gained ground on her. With a leap, she caught the top of the wall. Just avoiding the swipe of hands at her ankle, she scrambled to the top and took a quick glance back into the compound, then up the main road.

Bovyans were still running toward her, but none thought to head back out to the gate. Up the road, a covered horse-drawn cart, flanked by six Bovyans, crested the hill, kicking up a cloud of dust. Sameer was probably inside. There was no sign of Brehane anywhere. No scent of her hair perfume, no tracks from her slippered feet.

Jie dropped down and raced to the front gate. With a last loving glance at De Lucca's wondrous knife, she lodged it into the door's frame. The blade slid through wood with ease, the hilt sealing the door shut.

Jie sighed. Such an amazing weapon. Though if what the doctor said was true, they were taking Sameer to De Lucca's office, where at least one more of those knives waited for liberation.

* * *

Cassius' eyes fluttered open as the cart lurched to a stop. With his energy so low, he must've dozed off yet again, on their way to De Lucca's Bovyan compound.

"Signore, Bovyans." The driver pointed up ahead.

Cassius focused on the column of soldiers marching double time beside a horse-drawn, covered wagon. They sure looked to be in a hurry.

By the Gods, what was he thinking, risking himself against the best soldiers in the world? Was it because he wanted to bed Brehane again? A gut feeling said she was in trouble, and it had to do with the Teleri who had wanted him to turn her over to them.

He peered into the heavens, where the late afternoon sun still drowned out all the stars. Only the three moons shone in the sky, revealing none of the Gods' secrets. Maybe it was worth drawing a tarot card, but the hair prickled at the back of his neck. No, the same gut feeling from before said he'd need to save his Divining energy for later in the day, and the Bovyans before had recognized the Signores' authority.

For now, at least. Cassius' gut said they were exploiting De Lucca so as to bring a small army into Tokahia, and conquer the city without actually fighting.

As the vehicles drew closer, the warrior at the head of the column met his gaze.

Cassius waved him down, then said to the driver, "Stop."

The driver nodded and reined the horses back. The carriage slowed to a halt.

The Bovyan leader strode up. "Yes, Signore?"

"I heard there was some trouble at your plantation," Cassius said. "In my capacity as signore, I was coming to investigate."

The man's eyebrows clashed together for a split second. "How did you know?"

Cassius swept into a flourishing bow. "I am Signore Cassius Larusso, descendant of the First Diviner, after all." And, with Sameer looking for Sohini, there was little doubt there'd been the equivalent of a Cathayi fireworks show at the compound.

"Just an intruder. Nothing we could not handle."

An intruder. Just one. Surely, a Bovyan wasn't smart enough to give a misleading statement, and they were rumored to be honest to a fault. And if they only knew of one, it was most likely the brash Sameer. Cassius lifted his chin at the approaching wagon. "What do you have in there?"

The Bovyan looked over his shoulder, then back. "A delivery for Signore De Lucca, from his compound."

Cassius stared at the wagon. It could be anything back there: food, wine, Brehane... He closed his eyes and gauged his strength. He was still too weak from the night before. With the Iridescent Moon not yet waxing to half, Divining without a token of hers would sap him. If only he'd kept some kind of memento from their tumble in the sheets, it would be so much easier.

The Bovyan started to turn on his heel.

"Wait," Cassius said. It couldn't hurt to ask. The worst thing that could happen would be a refusal. Hopefully. "May I see what is in the wagon?"

The leader scowled. "It is none of your concern."

"I thought you worked for the Signores now. I am ordering you to show me." Cassius stood.

A sword swept out of the Bovyan's scabbard. "We are contracted by Signore De Lucca. This is his personal matter."

Surely a Bovyan wouldn't draw on a signore unless the cargo was important. Cassius appraised the column, now close enough to spit at. The men marched with such precision, their chainmail hiding rippled arms as large as his own leg. Six mobsters had been hard enough, and these were the best soldiers in the world, short of the Paladins. It didn't take Divination to know that fighting with them wouldn't end well.

He flashed a broad smile and returned to his seat. "Give Signore De Lucca my regards."

Thumping his chest with a fist, the Bovyan sheathed his sword and returned to the head of the wagon.

Cassius listened and watched as it passed. The rear door was closed. The wagon jolted as one of the wheels ran over a stone.

"Ooomph," came a muffled voice from inside, along with the sound of rattling crates and jostling bottles.

Cassius tightened and loosened his fists. Whose voice? It was hard to tell if it was male or female through the door. Was Brehane inside? He scooted over to the front bench and leaned over to the driver. "Turn the carriage around and follow that wagon."

The driver pointed to the fields at the side. "Signore, we would have to go off the road in order to circle around. I'm worried the wheels might catch in the soft soil."

"Do it."

With a nod, the driver snapped the reins. The carriage lurched forward. In the time it took to pick up speed, then start the circle, all the stars could have fallen from the heavens. Still, the driver's concerns about the wheel catching didn't seem to be—

Cassius lurched forward in the carriage as it jerked to a stop. The horses complained with neighs. The Trickster's Ass! A wheel had stuck, just as the driver had warned. He looked over his shoulder.

De Lucca's wagon was well in the distance, and he wasn't much of a runner.

"The horses," came a high-pitched voice.

Heart leaping into his chest, Cassius spun back around.

The half-elf girl, Jie, pressed her fist into her palm. "They're taking Sameer back to De Lucca, and not for tea."

Cassius nodded. A compound full of Bovyans was too much for an apprentice. "What about Brehane?"

Jie shook her head. "I don't know. I didn't see any sign of her after I broke into the compound, but her faint scent lingers here."

Chest squeezing, Cassius looked up and down the road. Surely he or Jie would've spotted Brehane. Which left the Bovyan carriage as the only place she could be. He gestured to the driver. "Unhitch one of the horses. I'm going to ride."

CHAPTER 26:

Masters of Deception

Fog muddled Brehane's head, her shoulders ached, and her arms buzzed with numbness. She was lying face up, arms pinned beneath her on a bed. Blinking several times, she started to pull them out, only to feel rope biting into her wrists.

Her heart lurched. The foggy head; it was the after-effect of a sleep spell. She took a deep breath to try to clear her mind. What was the last thing that had happened?

They'd passed through the courtyard and front gate, where Bovyans were loading crates into a wagon. When the smaller one with the scar on his forehead spoke of attacking the pyramid, she'd gasped, and inadvertently revealed herself. Then, all had gone black. No, Melas had uttered something first. A spell. A familiar one, but what? Fragmented dreams of rocking and pitching, like the ship ride over, came back to her.

Now, though, all was still. She turned her head to get her bearings. All was black, like... She sensed the Resonance, which pulsed in slow beats. Melas had cast a darkness spell.

Why? She'd agreed to learn with him, to mutually help one another progress in their schools of magic. He must not have trusted her.

She focused on the sounds.

From not far away came sniffling. A woman, from the sound of it.

"Who's there?" Brehane called.

The whimpering stopped. "Brehane?" The naggy voice, more whiney than before, belonged to Makeda.

"Yes. Makeda, what is happening?"

"*Assama*, it's your fault this happened to me."

Always trying to blame someone else. Brehane snorted and sidled away. "I was just protecting myself. You tried to sell me to the crime families and steal my birthright." She gasped. The jewel wasn't hanging from her neck. "*Assama*, you took it, didn't you?"

"No," Melas said. "I did."

He uttered a foul sound. Lights flared, chasing away the darkness.

Brehane's eyes seared from the sudden change. She blinked several times and tracked the voice.

Melas leaned against a doorsill, grinning so wide his white teeth might've been the source of light. He held up her jewel from his neck.

Heat surged to Brehane's head. The *assama*! She struggled again, her wrists again chafing on the ropes. She looked around.

She was lying on an enormous bed with fluffy blankets, much like the one she'd taken Cassius on. The room was quite big, with a large window overlooking the harbor. An enormous mirror hung on the opposite wall. Several oil paintings in elaborate frames depicted fair-skinned beauties, idealized and naked.

Makeda, too, was naked, sitting on a green cushioned chair with her hands bound above her head to the chair's decorative frame. Her legs were splayed wide, ropes lashing her knees to the armrests. As before, the luster of youth in her skin was gone, making her look five years older.

"Biomancy?" Melas' gaze had followed Brehane's, but now shifted back.

Despite Makeda's betrayal, guilt pitted in Brehane's stomach. Her merging of Biomancy and Pyromancy had stolen Makeda's youth. She had to help her escape, and that started with finding out more. "Where are we?"

"My room in one of Signore De Lucca's pleasure houses."

So Melas was associated with De Lucca. "How did we get here?"

"I am an Illusionist, after all." Melas' smile stretched wide. "I made you look like a crate, and we hitched a ride back with the Bovyans."

The smug *assama*. "What for?"

"With your adventures in Tokahia so far, I thought you would've guessed what happens in these places." Melas tilted his head at Makeda. "She was even better than I remember from years ago, but I guess that is what happens when things follow the natural order."

Makeda burst into tears.

The twisting of Brehane's gut squeezed all the guilt out. Instead of being a proper man, Melas had become like a Bovyan. "You... you..." There was no word for forced intercourse in their language, and her brain couldn't remember the word in Arkothi.

Melas laughed. "As for Makeda... What do you think, Brother Dawit?"

Dawit stepped in from the next room over, grinning.

Brehane gasped. The two might have been working together this whole time.

"I trusted you," Makeda spat through her tears.

"It was my first time with her, so I have no basis for comparison." Dawit ambled over to Makeda. "In Aksumi lands, as much as I wanted her...both of you, really...I had to play demure and subservient. It's so unnatural back home. Here, a man can be himself."

Brehane's heart raced. This was all wrong. Coupling was supposed to be initiated by a woman. Men weren't supposed to want it at all, unless seduced by the sweet words and beauty of the perfect woman. Managing to sit up in the soft bed, she struggled with her bonds again.

"Why the resistance?" Melas asked. "You were so eager in the past. Quite the ravenous beast. Brother Dawit, I think you'll enjoy it."

Dawit stroked Makeda's cheek. "I'm spent for now, but I'll be sure to taste it before our trip."

Trip? With fear coursing through her, it was too hard to think. "Where?"

"I told you." Melas smirked. "Arkos."

What was it with Arkos? The pyramid there? "Why?"

Dawit brushed a finger down the middle of Makeda's face. "The Teleri Empire offered us a million drakas to deliver a female descendant of the First Mystic to Arkos. I wonder if they'll pay double for two."

A shudder climbed up Brehane's spine. "Why do they want us?"

Melas shrugged. "That's not my business, and now that we have Makeda, you are more valuable to me for something else: I need you to help me learn to Biomance female energy into male energy."

Brehane shook her head. "It's not possible."

"Of course it is. You always liked to experiment with magic. It was quite nifty what you did, making those webs."

"Making webs and reversing Biomancy are totally different. It just isn't—"

"Shhhh. I have something that can help." Melas held up a book.

With her curiosity piqued, all fear drained out of her. "What is it?"

"A Cathayi book about what they call the *Dao*. It explains that if a man can reach his peak, but not spill his seed, he can draw out a woman's energies. The Cathayi emperors have practiced it since the War of Ancient Gods. Before the current Dynasty's Queen Regent overturned the natural order, they once had entire harems to draw on."

Was it even possible for males to draw from females? Nothing in Biomancer legends spoke of it. Cathayi magic was limited to artistic expression, so whatever the *Dao* did, it couldn't involve the transfer of life energy. Could it?

Possible or not, if there was a way out of this predicament, it might work to play along. Brehane nodded with as much enthusiasm as she could fake. Maybe it wasn't faked? "Let me see the book."

"Ever the student." Grinning, Melas strode over. He held the book open.

The words were written in wavy Cathayi script, one which Jie might be able to read; or one which she could with a translation spell. The pictures depicted the side profile of a man and woman, with an arrowed line looping down the center of their bodies, then back up their spines. When he flipped to a new page, it showed a coupled man and woman, their lines merging.

Brehane sucked in a sharp breath. It was visually similar to the Biomancy spell for converting male seed into energy.

Melas turned to Dawit. "A million drakas is more than we'll ever need. Brehane is more useful to our growth of magic."

Which undoubtedly meant coupling with the two of them. Something which had seemed like a game years ago. Now, both were disgusting. They'd already forced themselves on Makeda. Brehane's stomach lurched.

Still, playing along might be the only way to escape and spare Makeda from an even worse fate. Even now, the poor girl was crying.

"Go to the first page," Brehane said, feigning excitement.

"So enthusiastic!" Melas laughed. "She's forgotten all about Makeda."

Brehane looked up from the book and curled her lip. "No, not forgotten. She betrayed me. The Bovyans can do what they want with her."

Makeda wailed.

If only Brehane could provide some comfort, to say she was lying, she would. Even for a rival. "We will all grow powerful. We can return to Aksumiland and overthrow the Conclave."

"Treacherous *assama*," Makeda spat.

"Says the one who tried to sell me to the Mafia." Brehane forced a cruel smirk.

Melas exchanged glances with Dawit, then mirrored her grin. "I think we can untie her."

Stroking his chin, Dawit studied her expression. "Hmmmm."

Brehane projected her most ambitious smile.

Looking back at Melas, Dawit shrugged and nodded. "She always was single-minded."

"All right. You untie her; I'll leave this book with you to study while I finalize arrangements with the Pirate Queen's ships."

Pirate Queen? That must be how they were going to Arkos.

Setting down the book, Melas turned and headed out of the room.

Dawit left Makeda's side and took his time strolling over to the bed. He sat down beside Brehane and twirled his finger in a circle. "Turn around."

Brehane shifted so her hands faced him. Her arms had regained sensation. Once she was free…

His hands brushed down her shoulders, pausing to grope her breasts before reaching her wrists and fiddling with the ties.

It took every bit of discipline not to tense up at the violation. She'd be free soon enough. But then what? He was physically stronger, and his magic more powerful. Far more powerful.

Once the rope came off, she shook her hands. Her fingers tingled as warmth returned. She motioned to the book. "May I?"

Dawit was already back by Makeda's side. She squirmed as much as the bindings would allow.

He looked back, expression lurid, and nodded. "Don't leave the room. I'll be watching you."

Brehane hid her shudder. No woman, not even a betrayer like Makeda, deserved this fate. She swept up the book and retreated to a corner. Even though she opened the book, she didn't even look at the pictures.

After all, those fascinating images wouldn't help with the invisibility spell.

Brehane thought back, remembering the sounds Melas had made, the way his hands had moved, and the way the Resonance shifted.

Hopefully, Dawit wouldn't recognize her attempt to mimic it. She spoke the words and waved her hands. The Resonance shifted. Her energy flickered.

Turning his attention from Makeda, Dawit looked directly at her.

Brehane found her hands, still visible. She shook her head. "Even with the translation spell, the book doesn't make sense."

With a grunt, Dawit turned back.

Maybe she had enough energy for one more attempt. She grunted out the syllables and manipulated the Resonance with her fingers.

Her hands disappeared. All vitality drained from her.

Makeda gasped.

Dawit turned around. His eyes widened.

With what energy she had, Brehane had already tiptoed toward the doorway. She might have no way of defeating Dawit, but maybe she could get help.

* * *

The wagon slowed to yet another stop, stirring Sameer from his meditation. The first time had been when the Aksumi male had gotten off with a storage chest. Given how he'd been at the Teleri compound, he was likely the one who'd provided the invisibility bauble for the Bovyan who'd been involved in the attack the first day. He was probably also the one Brehane was looking for. The next several stops, they'd loaded up bodies— Mafia enforcers, judging from the dark clothes. The stench of voided bowels had sent his gut churning.

Now he opened his eyes. The wagon door opened from the outside, letting in light and glorious fresh air.

A Bovyan stood there, beckoning. "We have arrived. Get out."

Sameer rose, taking care not to bash his head on the ceiling. Huddling over, he shuffled to the back and jumped out. The clean air filled his lungs. Meditation had rejuvenated him, and even with bound hands he landed with ease. He blinked several times in the late afternoon sun.

The block of two-story buildings looked familiar. Above one hung a purple banner emblazoned with De Lucca's gold lion. Of course. It was the signore's office, which he'd visited the night before. It looked different in the daylight. More opulent, with vaulting columns and frescoes.

Sameer's shoulders relaxed. De Lucca had been nothing but helpful, so perhaps this wouldn't be so bad. Surely he would forgive the misunderstanding.

Four Bovyans flanked him as they passed through the iron gates.

Dozens of soldiers watched him from the front door. Like the ones at the compound, two Bovyans wore the same De Lucca purple longcoats; but several more to the left were dressed in formal black surcoats emblazoned with the nine-pointed, gold Teleri sun, above burnished steel cuirasses. On the right, bronze-skinned Levanthi soldiers wore lamellar armor and turbans, which must've been hot in the afternoon sun. The black scythe on their white banners marked them as Levastyans.

Guards at his side, Sameer passed into the foyer. If last night had been chaotic, the building today looked to be running with the efficiency of dwarf gears. Several men in De Lucca livery took silver platters of sweets and tea to the rooms down the hall. Sameer's escort seized his elbows, stopping him. Looking up from some kind of ledger, a man at the front desk stood up and marched toward De Lucca's office.

He returned. "Signore De Lucca will see the Paladin now."

The guards led Sameer past the side rooms. In the first sat several bronze-skinned men with pointed beards and mustaches, swathed in embroidered white robes. Levanthi, dressed in the white robes of the Levastyan Empire's Akolytes.

The Bovyans prodded him along, but Sameer glanced into the library.

Captain Robas, from the banquet last night, sat straight in a plush chair. The small, scar-faced Bovyan, from the ambush yesterday morning, stood next to him. Both wore the same formal black surcoats as the men at the front, and the platter of sweets went untouched.

Just who did Scarface work for? Given his smaller size, he might've been the ash-faced Phobos from last night. Sameer's head spun. He clenched his fists, as if that would loosen the bonds around his wrists.

"When will your men assail the pyramid?" Scarface asked in a low voice.

"When the second battalion reaches it," Captain Robas said. "They cleared the Mafia district faster than expected, so I would guess before dusk."

"Good. It will be easier to arrange the Mafia bodies under the cover of darkness."

Sameer sucked in a breath. The Bovyans planned to capture the pyramid. He had to warn Signore De Lucca of the betrayal.

One of his escorts shoved him in the back, toward De Lucca's office. The air didn't feel cold, like it had the night before.

Inside, De Lucca leaned back on his enormous chair, turning a metal box the size of a head over in his hands. "Sir Sameer."

"Signore De Lucca." Sameer held up his bound hands. "Am I your prisoner?"

Face impassive, De Lucca motioned to the guards. One untied the knots.

Sameer shook the numbness out of his hands and fingers. "The Bovyans. They plan to attack the pyramid."

"Oh?" De Lucca's tone displayed no concern.

Sameer pointed back down the hall. "I just overheard them. Captain Robas and the small one who worked for the Mafia..." Unless the scarred one worked for De Lucca? It might've been him last night, here in the office. "You can't trust them."

De Lucca studied him for a moment. "I'm not sure what to do with you. On the one hand, you and your friends eliminated Don Acerbi. What's left of his organization is in shambles."

Anger burned in Sameer's cheeks. "Was that what this was about? Getting rid of your rivals? Did you really send Sohini there?"

De Lucca's grin couldn't get any smugger. "No."

Emulating the God of Patience, Sameer took a deep breath to keep him from lunging over the desk. "You said she came to you, seeking refuge."

De Lucca shrugged. "That's what she told me. I can't tell you how much of that is true. I suspect she was trying to kill my guest." He pointed his chin to the door.

Cold pricked at the back of Sameer's neck, like the day before when the Mafia had ambushed them. He looked over his shoulder.

A man with long, oiled dark hair and a thin pointed beard ambled into the room. He, along with the masked aide a few steps behind, wore the high-collared longshirts ubiquitous in Sameer's homeland. If the rich burgundy robes with gold borders didn't give away where they were from, the gold scorpion emblem emblazoned on their right breasts marked him as from the evil kingdom of Madura. A Paladin *naga* hung at his side, singing with the Vibrations. Singing with...

Sameer gasped. It was *his naga*. In the hands of a filthy Maduran. Its song was unmistakable. Heat raged in his head. He jumped to his feet.

Time slowed as the Bovyans reached for him. Sameer sidestepped their grasps and pulled the dagger from one's belt. He lunged for the Maduran.

Cold flared in him. Time resumed. With blinding speed, the masked aide leaped forward, swept the *naga* from his hip and clanged against Sameer's weapon.

Sameer's hand wrung as he watched the blade fly from it, clattering across the marble floor. He looked back, tracking the *naga* from its tip at his neck to its wielder.

The mask was featureless, revealing only the wearer's dark eyes behind two slits. It marked a Golden Scorpion, a former Paladin recruited by Madura. Their masks were supposedly made from the re-forging of their Paladin *nagas*.

Yet this one still had a *naga*. He now removed his mask.

Master Anish.

Sameer's gawked. How could it be?

"Master Anish," De Lucca said from his desk. "I have yet to thank you for telling my men about the half-elf interloper last night."

Sameer's eyes went from the signore to the man he'd once admired. "Why?"

The traitor smirked. "She was too smart. I was worried she would deduce who I was."

"I'm still trying to figure out who *she* is." De Lucca laughed, a grating sound.

Cold seeping into his bones, Sameer eyed Master Anish's *naga*. The Vibrations felt so distant, so far out of reach.

The other Maduran laughed. "Surrender, boy. You have no chance against Anish. He has achieved such mastery, he can mute your Paladin skills."

That would explain the cold sensation and the dulling of his combat reflexes. Sameer studied the vile traitor. "That's how Elder Gitika got injured yesterday."

Master Anish shrugged. "Someone so powerful... I could only weaken her combat reflexes a little, but it was enough that the mobsters and Bovyans could injure her."

Anger and sadness buzzed in Sameer's head. "Why?"

"To separate you from her. To keep her from guiding you to Paladinhood."

The bastard! Sameer's face burned hot. "It wasn't the Mafia that killed her, was it?"

"Of course not. An army of pathetic mobsters wouldn't stand a chance against her, even wounded." His scoff transformed into a genuine expression of remorse. "It was me. A sad but necessary sacrifice. She should have never come to Tokahia."

"If it was you, and not mobsters, then how did the innkeeper—"

"I just planted that suggestion in the weak-willed man's head. Just like I did Don Acerbi to get him to attack us in his den. It's a more powerful skill than a Command. A skill taught to the Golden Scorpions by Madura's former Grand Vizier. A skill I can teach you, if you join us."

Sameer's head spun. Madura's former Grand Vizier had used Dark Arts to preserve his life for centuries before disappearing almost thirty years before. To think he'd corrupted *Bahaduur* abilities with his evil magic. One which would corrupt a soul. Sameer knocked the *naga* away from his neck and lunged for Anish. "Traitor!"

In a blur, the master swept a foot out and slapped Sameer in the back of the head.

Sameer tumbled to the ground, face-first. The sword tip was again at his throat.

The other Maduran snorted. "This one looks too foolish to be recruited."

"Your Highness," Master Anish said, "despite his lofty goals of Paladinhood, Young Sameer is brash and ruled by his emotions. He is a perfect candidate."

Your Highness? The Maduran was Prince Dhananad himself.

Turning over and scuttling back out of reach, Sameer hung his head. It was too true. He'd been so blinded by trying to rescue Sohini, he'd missed the obvious. Now, it was all making sense. "You're the one responsible for all the missing Paladins. Sohini found out, didn't she?"

"Her, again?" The traitor didn't pursue. He just grinned. "Do you want to know why I had a lock of her hair?"

Sameer's fists clenched tight. The bastard had forced himself on her. Taken her against her will. It had to be. He jumped to his feet and lunged for Anish's neck. Time slowed.

It wasn't supposed to. Not if Anish had blocked his power.

Anish backed away, moving fast, but not blindingly so. His eyes widened.

He'd left Prince Dhananad unprotected.

Sameer reached for his *naga* at the prince's hip. Dhananad's hand moved much too slow to prevent from losing the blade.

The weapon felt so right in his hand, its Vibrations merging with his own. Sameer chopped and hacked.

Anish dodged each blow, and circled himself into a protective position by the prince.

"You fool!" Prince Dhananad screeched. "He could've killed me!"

Sameer found himself by the office door. Taking several deep breaths, he disengaged. How foolish he'd been. He could've taken the prince hostage. Instead, he'd let emotion dictate his actions. Elder Gitika would be so disappointed in him.

Signore De Lucca cleared his throat. "I hate to ruin your entertainment, but Prince Dhananad and I have business to discuss."

The Paladin traitor took several purposeful strides forward.

Sameer turned and fled. Anish didn't know where Sohini was, and it was foolish to keep fighting someone with the skills of a Scorpion master.

"After him!" Prince Dhananad yelled. "If he doesn't join, kill him."

CHAPTER 27:

Illusions

Jie had once thought nothing could be worse than riding a horse; that was before having to ride without a saddle, clinging to Cassius' back on their canter back to the city. Though he rode well, he was so tall that she couldn't see over his shoulder. Not to mention, if it wasn't his hair whipping in her face, it was his long jacket billowing into her nose.

The Bovyan wagon had a good lead on them, and by the time the horse had reached the outskirts of Tokahia, they were nowhere to be seen. Cassius couldn't appear any more frantic, the way his head turned side to side as he checked every one-story wood building and brightly-dressed pedestrian on the main road.

If she didn't know any better, she'd assume he actually cared about Brehane. Harrumphing, Jie scanned the surroundings as they passed. At this hour, people were headed home.

There, in a patch of dry clay that had gathered where the pavestones dipped...

"Stop," Jie yelled over the rush of wind.

Cassius looked over his shoulder. "We're losing time. You told me the doctor said they were going to De Lucca's, so that's where we'll find them."

"We'll lose even more time if we ride in the wrong direction. I don't think they are going straight to his office. Let me look for clues."

He brought the horse to a stop. "What—"

Jie shimmied off the horse with about as much grace as a duck on dry land. When her feet hit solid ground, she could've knelt down and kissed it. Instead, she loped toward the spot they'd passed.

Passersby chattered, talk of the Acerbi fire on every lip. Almost everyone discussed the crime families' attack, and how only the heroic Bovyans had been able to vanquish them. Rumor had it that the remnants of the Mafia had taken control of the pyramid, and that the Bovyans were now marching there to finish them off.

She stepped in front of a pair of laborers, who were just expressing their hopes for more Bovyans to protect the city.

"Have you seen a wagon with nine Bovyans guarding it?"

They shook their heads.

Taking note of the direction those people had come from, she went to the patch of dry dirt. The slightest imprint of a wagon wheel and a partial bootprint passed through it. She knelt down to examine the tracks.

Fresh. Definitely a Bovyan-style boot. Angling toward a turn two intersections down the road, though *not* toward De Lucca's office.

She pointed in the direction opposite the laborers. "What's that way?"

Cassius spoke as if he'd sucked on bitter melon. "High-end whorehouses."

There were so many brothels, it was amazing there was enough seed to keep the population from declining. Jie snorted. Now, why would the Bovyans be headed that way? Surely not for a tumble in the sheets, since they had an entire breeding compound where they didn't have to pay. "The Bovyans must've had Brehane. Maybe they are selling her to a brothel."

Cassius, already fair-skinned, paled even more. The man seemed as obsessed with Brehane as Sameer was with Sohini. Men.

"Does De Lucca have a place there?" she asked.

Cassius scowled. "I don't keep track of all his endeavors."

"I'm guessing that's where they'd take her. We'll look for his banners." She gestured for him to follow.

Walking with as long a stride as her short legs would allow, she scanned and sniffed. A slight trace of the flower Brehane used to scent her hair hung in the air, almost hidden by the odor of sweaty men and women.

With Cassius on the horse behind her, she broke into a trot, following as the scent grew stronger. One-story buildings gave way to two-story stone row houses, and the sour stench of boisterous laborers gave way to the flowery perfumes and musky colognes of the chattering wealthy.

It all overwhelmed Jie's senses, burying Brehane's smell. She turned back to Cassius. "I've lost her scent."

He stared at her, wide-eyed. "Have you been following her smell? What are you, a bloodhound?"

It wouldn't be the first time—and probably not the last—that she'd been compared to a watchdog, bloodhound, and in Prince Aryn's case…she shook the image out of her head. "It was a sweet fragrance, but there are too many around here. Let me ask around."

Cassius held up a finger.

She ignored him, and instead hurried up to a pudgy merchant in a blazing orange longcoat. A pretty girl hung on his arm. "Excuse me," Jie said, "have you seen Aksumi around here?"

He looked down his nose, favoring her with a look as if she were a fly that had landed on his crumpet. With a harrumph, he shouldered past her.

Palming his coin purse, Jie silently thanked him for his donation. But it didn't get them any closer to finding Brehane. She turned to Cassius—

Who was off his horse. With a charming smile, he was clasping the very same merchant's hand.

The merchant was bowing his head. "Signore Cassius, it's such an honor. Thank you for your help. The

Pirate Queen's marauders ignored Antoli's ships, just as you said. My glassware is safely on its way."

Cassius dipped into a flourishing bow. "The Gods' Whispers never fail."

Jie raised an eyebrow. The Gods' Whispers didn't seem to be telling him about Brehane.

"May I recommend a fine house?" The merchant pulled the giggling girl closer.

Cassius waved his hands. "I've come for a client, but I'm having a hard time finding him."

"The great Cassius Larusso?"

"Alas, the White Stag is hidden behind the Eye of Ayara, while Kor, the Hunter, is distracted." Gesturing to the heavens, Cassius leaned in with a sidelong glance at Jie. "I tried to warn her this was an inauspicious time to search."

Jie sucked her lower lip. Surely this merchant wouldn't buy into such an obvious con.

The merchant looked back at her, his lips rounding into a circle, then back at Cassius. "I haven't seen any around here, but ask that street urchin, Odi. He knows everything that happens around here."

Cassius shook his head. "Odi's birth hour, too, is dominated by the White Stag. If he wishes to remain hidden, not even the Gods' Whispers will reveal his location."

Just ask for directions, Jie mouthed to no one in particular.

"You can find Odi pimping his girls, over by the Orchid Fountain." The merchant pointed down the street, then laughed. "Today, I can say I beat the Great Diviner."

"And yet, you won't," Cassius said, grinning like a snake. "Because the Gods' Whispers will tell me the next safe shipping company, and I will tell you."

"Of course." The merchant dipped into a bow, then headed off with the giggling girl.

Jie watched until he'd walked out of earshot, then turned to Cassius. "You have no idea who Odi is, do you?"

Cassius searched her eyes for a moment, his expression inscrutable for those who couldn't scrute.

Jie could. Without a doubt, Cassius was just better at conning unwitting victims than the rest of the charlatans and fakes in this city. With a snort, she scanned the streets. "Where is the Orchid Fountain?"

"Hurry up." For the first time, in his own city, the great Diviner was taking the lead in finding his lost Mystic. He pulled his horse along, his long strides hard for her short legs to keep up with. The rush left little time to follow up on clues that flitted by.

Several blocks and three turns later, they arrived at a circular plaza. An oily-looking youth hurried from one passerby to the next, pointing back at the skimpily-dressed young women huddled by the stone fountain in the center of the plaza. Predictably, it was shaped like a bearded orchid, with water pouring from between its petals. The connotation couldn't be coincidental.

The youth—Odi, no doubt—locked eyes on Cassius and approached. "The Great Diviner, Cassius Larusso. Let me tempt you with one of my orchids."

No doubt, Cassius weighed the loss of his reputation as a Diviner with his urgency to find Brehane. As amusing as it would be to watch his discomfit, Jie pushed forward. "Odi," she said.

"My, my, what a pretty little jewel we have here." He reached for her chin.

She seized his hand and twisted his wrist.

"Ow, ow!" Odi buckled to his knees. "Let go!"

Jie added more pressure, while grinding her thumb across the back of his hand to ignite flares of pain up and down his arm. "Aksumi. Where are they?"

Eyes wide, Odi jerked his thumb repeatedly down one of the avenues which spiraled out of the circle. "De Lucca's guest house. Five blocks that way."

Jie released him and started in the indicated direction.

"I thought so, bitch," Odi said under his breath, wringing his hand.

She turned back and glared.

He shriveled back.

Satisfied, Jie beckoned Cassius along. Right where the street exited the avenue, drainage from the fountain had formed a mud patch. Wagon tracks passed through, as did huge bootprints, leaving a trail well into the pavestones. Not one block away, Brehane's hair scent carried on the wind, just strong enough to pick out from the other smells.

Several blocks up ahead, a dark-skinned male zigzagged through the streets, pausing every so often to look around at the surrounding two-story row houses. It wasn't Dawit, and unless there were several Aksumi males roaming the streets, this was the missing Illusionist.

He snarled as his eyes locked on a house between them.

Jie followed his gaze.

Besides the blue row house with fat hedges, nothing was there.

Or was there? A blur...

* * *

Being led around like a child by an impertinent half-elf, who resorted to violence, Cassius would consider himself lucky if the day ended with his reputation intact. Still, Brehane, the only woman who'd appreciated his magic and cooking more than his money, was worth it.

He shook the silly, useless, sentimental thought out of his head.

She was worth a good roll between the sheets. And the Teleri might offer him something more.

Now all they had to do was find her, based on the extorted lead of a pimp, and said half-elf's nose. He looked up at the heavens, where the sun still drowned out the dance of stars. He'd lied about Hunter Kor and the

White Stag to the merchant to save his reputation, but it was true that their seats in the heaven would make Divining exceptionally taxing on his soul's future.

It wasn't worth anything the Bovyans could offer.

But maybe it was worth seeing her beam again as he Divined. Or even when he cooked.

Closing his eyes and reaching for his cards, he took a deep breath of the Gods' Whispers.

"Cassius." Jie shook him out of his process, tugging him toward the side of the street.

The horse had other ideas, holding its ground.

She motioned with jerks of her head.

He looked in the indicated direction. An Aksumi male was waving his hands in circles, his lips making sounds that were too far away to hear. He pointed.

Cassius followed the gesture.

Brehane appeared out of thin air, huddled near a row house hedge, trembling. Her Mystic robe was smudged with dirt. She looked at her hands as if they didn't belong there, and then back at the man.

Cassius' heart leaped into his throat. He jumped onto his horse and spurred it into a gallop.

Ridiculous.

Why was he doing this? She was just another con in a long list of them.

The Aksumi man's eyes locked on her. His grin widened.

Brehane wobbled to her feet, hand outstretched. She barked out guttural syllables and pointed. Flames darted at the man, but he swept his hand up, dispersing the attack into a wall of fire.

Dozens of passersby froze, pointing and chattering.

Cassius was now just a half-block away. He drew his rapier and pointed it forward as if it were a spear.

Brehane splayed her fingers and webs shot out. The strands passed through the man, and he dissolved into nothingness.

Where had he gone? Cassius brought his horse between her and where the Mystic had been.

"Cassius!" Brehane's smile was as brilliant as a second sun.

His heart pattered as he stretched his hand out. "Come on!"

The spectators screamed.

The horse reared, nearly throwing him.

Dropping his sword, Cassius threw his arms around the horse's neck. He looked back.

The Mystic stood a few feet behind a lion. It prowled towards them, teeth bared in a snarl. It roared.

Cassius blood froze. The beast must've escaped the colosseum. The rapier would be useless against such a monstrosity.

The horse skittered back, despite his best attempt to control it. Citizens fled, shouting and screaming.

"It's not real," Brehane yelled. "It's an illusion."

Cassius shook his head. The beast's mane rippled as it crouched low, ready to pounce. Its claws glinted in the sunlight. It even had a smell. It couldn't possibly be fake.

Brehane grunted out foul-sounding words and pointed. She crumpled to the ground.

The lion blurred for a split second before regaining its shape.

Cassius could only gawk. It *was* just an illusion!

Now if only the horse would understand it. The poor animal reared again. Cassius' balance lilted. He lurched to wrap his arms around—

The ground rushed up. He slammed into it. Pain flared in his arm, hip, and head. He tried to draw in a breath, but just choked.

Then the half-elf was there. She stared at the wide-eyed Mystic, right through the lion, which blinked out of existence.

The man barked out more magic. Three of him appeared.

Jie froze for a split second, but then cut-stepped to the far left's flank. In the same motion, her dagger—which looked suspiciously familiar—cut through him, and he disappeared just like the lion had.

Head spinning, Cassius clambered to his feet and staggered over to Brehane.

Knees to the ground, she was bent over, head lolling.

He looked over his shoulder.

The Mystic was gone. Sniffing the air, Jie's head raked back and forth.

Chest squeezing, he turned back and brought an arm under Brehane. "Wake up!"

Her eyes fluttered open. She leaned into him.

Her body was so warm and soft. He brought his free hand up to brush the hair out of her face. "Are you all right?"

"Exhausted." She patted at her neck, where her crystal was missing. "Just exposing his illusion drained me."

"I assume that was your missing friend?" He looked over his shoulder again, just in case the Mystic reappeared.

"Clearly not a friend." She flashed a feeble smile.

His heart fluttered. Fluttered? Nonsense! It couldn't be.

Her expression stiffened. "He and Dawit kidnapped Makeda. We have to stop them before they take her to Arkos."

He swallowed hard. No wonder Dawit knew about the Teleri offer. Instead of playing along, he'd decided to collect some reward himself. Cassius rose, picking up Brehane as he did.

"Why Arkos?" Jie asked. "Wouldn't it be easier to deliver her to the Bovyans here?"

"Low risk, low reward," Cassius said. "In any case, we need to rescue her. Do you know where they are keeping her?"

Brehane pointed down the street. "It was a row house, maybe two or three blocks away."

"We'll need help." His dagger in hand, Jie was sniffing the air. "Dawit killed several mobsters and destroyed the Acerbi headquarters with a single fireball. We'd never know where the Illusionist was, or if it was the real him if we did see him."

"Sameer could help," Cassius said. "By now, the Bovyans have taken him to Signore De Lucca's office."

Jie looked up at the Iridescent Moon. "I think you're right. Luckily, it's not far from here."

Cassius stared at her. "How do you know?"

She snorted and pointed to the west. "How don't you? We can't be any more than a *li* away."

Cassius pursed his lips. A *li* could be a passus or a league. Somehow, Jie knew his city better than he. "I will talk to De Lucca, and negotiate for Sameer's release."

Jie nodded. "I'll get Prince Aryn's marines from the *Regent*."

CHAPTER 28:

Hunter Kor And The White Stag

The Bovyans, Levastyans, and Altivorcs had not tried to stop Sameer as he fled out of De Lucca's office. Thank the Thousand Gods that Paladin reflexes enhanced combat and not running, because his youth and longer legs kept him in front of Master Anish.

If only Sameer knew where he was going. He sidestepped a cursing merchant, then side-slipped between a young couple. From the woman's scream and the thuds to the ground, Anish must've barreled right through them. Sameer looked over his shoulder.

Indeed, the traitor was disentangling himself from the man and woman, and picking himself up off the street. There might be a chance to escape!

Sameer turned back.

A horse-drawn carriage was crossing right in front of him.

He dropped and skidded under the carriage, bruising his knees on the pavestones before rolling at the last second to avoid getting crushed by the wheels. Blowing out a breath, he jumped up and glanced back.

Whatever ground he'd gained on Anish from the traitor's crash, he'd lost it now. He resumed his sprint, dodging a street vendor pulling a cart of silverware, a juggler, and a pregnant woman.

Where to?

He had no money of his own, and De Lucca's place wasn't an option anymore.

That left the Diviner, Cassius. Who knew where he was? Not like Sameer would know how to get there from here.

A scream pierced the air from behind.

"Sameer!" Anish barked.

Sameer stole a glance over his shoulder.

The turncoat had one arm wrapped around the pregnant woman's neck, and his *naga* blade resting over her swollen belly. The featureless mask of a Golden Scorpion now covered his face.

Escape, or surrender? It wasn't even a question. Sameer skidded to a halt. The weight of defeat weighing on his shoulders, he hung his head. He turned and trudged back, resigned to his fate.

"Still a Paladin." Anish snorted. "You will be hard to convert, but convert you will."

Sameer looked up and glared. "Never."

Anish shoved the woman away and swung his blade.

Time slowed just enough for Sameer to jump back. He swept his *naga* out in Anish's path.

Moving twice as fast, Anish twisted out of the way. His sword cut across Sameer's shoulder.

Pain flared there, and then again on his forearm. The offensive had come so fast, yet they hadn't bitten deep. Only nicks. Another slash stung his other arm. Dodge and block as he might, he just couldn't stop the flurry of attacks.

Anish disengaged. "You are skilled, but not enough to fight a Master Scorpion. Not unless you let your emotions guide you."

Sameer took a deep breath and conjured an image of Elder Gitika in his mind. No, he wouldn't surrender to emotions. The Vibrations were so strong here, stronger than on Ayudra Island where he'd trained. With calm, he could tap them to defeat this traitor. With another breath, they surged through him. The chatter of pointing onlookers melded in.

Time slowed again as the *naga* swished at him. Slower than the last engagement, slow enough to evade. He slipped and ducked the next two slashes and chopped with his own blade.

It missed his mark, and pain bit into his thigh, then his flank. Anish's *naga* became a blur, nicking him in three more places.

Anish stepped back and removed the mask. His lips tugged into a smirk. "Pathetic. Gitika thought so highly of your potential. She'd be so disappointed."

Holding the most painful of the wounds, Sameer took more deep breaths. He wouldn't be goaded into anger.

Anish moved like a blur as two somethings flashed in the sunlight in front of him. He turned.

Sameer followed his eyes.

Jie was charging in, knife in hand.

Anish chuckled. "Your new friend? Watch her share Gitika's fate."

No, others shouldn't die. Sameer leaped in and chopped at Anish's head.

The master ducked under and swung at Jie.

The half-elf stopped just out of range, and circled. Of course she was too smart to engage a superior fighter with a longer weapon.

Sameer's heart soared. Here was a chance to survive this. He just had to maneuver Anish so his back faced her. He took another deep breath and felt the Vibrations course through him.

Anish's *naga* swept in lazy arcs, baiting him.

Pretending to take the bait, Sameer surged forward, but then sidestepped the traitor's slash and countered with an attack of his own. Anish turned, his side exposed to Jie, but she was moving in slow motion in comparison. Sameer chopped again as he moved to a flanking position. Anish shifted again, his back now to the half-elf. Sameer pressed forward, pushing Anish back. His belly met the *naga*'s edge in a flare of pain.

Jie's stab travelled so slowly, as if she were moving through water. The tip was a hairbreadth away from the base of Anish's neck.

Anish spun away from both the dagger and Sameer's upswing. His elbow smashed into Jie's temple. She crumpled to the ground. He disengaged again, grinning. "Smart, boy. You almost had me." His blade came down.

Sameer swept his own into the path of the attack. The clang reverberated through his arms; but his forward surge pushed Anish back. For now, Jie was safe.

Interposing himself between her and the traitor, Sameer held his stomach. The cut had severed the skin, but hadn't reached muscle. A surgical strike, meant to inflict pain but not incapacitate. The traitor was just too powerful and skilled.

It was hopeless. Sameer dropped to his knees, bent his head forward, and set his *naga* on the ground. "I surrender. Follow the prince's orders and kill me, but spare Jie."

"Giving up so soon?" Anish snorted. "Don't you want to know how I have Sohini's hair?"

Sameer looked up.

That same infuriating grin crossed the traitor's face. "Ah, you do. Well, De Lucca has been lying to you. We have Sohini tied up in one of his whorehouses. What you've wanted for years, I've tasted more times than you can imagine."

Fire raged in Sameer's head. He snatched up his *naga* and lunged.

The first chop nearly caught the traitor in the neck. Eyes wide, the treacherous scum twisted out of the next blow. Blade clanged on blade as Sameer pressed into him. The cold that had pricked at the back of his neck had subsided, and the Vibrations felt so close, so easy to draw on.

Panting hard, Anish shoved him back and held his blade at the ready. "You feel it, don't you? The Paladin order has lied to you all this time, claiming that calm lets you feel the Vibrations. See? That training teaches you a detached objectivity. Justice, without feeling, because of some arbitrary code created by a fallible man just two centuries ago."

A lie! Face ablaze with anger, Sameer stared at his *naga*, which glowed a light blue as the Vibrations coursed through it. "Before the Oracle, we were nothing more than mercenaries. Using our gifts for our own selfish gain."

"You don't need a code to use your gifts as you see fit. See? By following your emotions, you have overcome my block on your connection to the Vibrations."

Sameer raised his blade and started—

"Stop." Sohini's voice crashed into him like a wave.

All the heat drained from his face. Cool washed over him. How beautiful her voice was, even in Command. He'd almost forgotten what it sounded like. He turned.

Wearing a dark cloak, Sohini strode down the street, both hands set in the *mudra* for calm. She looked more mature since they'd last met, but still beautiful. Long black locks framed her perfectly oval face and cascaded down her shoulders. Her deep brown eyes, so full of enthusiasm in the past, now bore a hint of sadness.

Sameer could only gawk.

Her eyes searched his. A smile formed on her lips for a split second. Then she shook her head. "Master Anish is baiting you. Don't give in to your emotions. Not like I did."

Sameer gawked. It couldn't be possible. Sohini was the most talented, most disciplined Paladin student in a generation. He shook his head. "You didn't…you didn't become one of them. Did you?"

"I was close," Anish said with a laugh. "I broke her, but not enough."

Relief washed over Sameer. Not all was lost.

Studying his expression, Anish shook his head before turning to her. "I was worried the Diviner might find you."

"I hid by the Iron Avatar."

Sameer gaped. Had she been the one who'd cowered back when he passed by the night before?

"Smart. Your intelligence is one of the reasons the Scorpions want you." Anish donned his featureless mask. "You all have weaknesses. For her, it is her need to protect whores."

Sohini lifted her chin, defiant. "You helped that foul prince do horrible things to that poor girl."

"And instead of protecting her with your *Bahaduur* skills, you reacted in anger."

Just like Sameer had.

Sohini hung her head.

The betrayer looked to him. "Your weakness is her. I was unable to convert her, but I would've succeeded with you. Until she intervened. Now, I have you both."

Sameer raised his *naga*. All his wounds screamed. "You can't beat both of us." If only Jie were conscious and could help.

"Wait." Sohini stayed his hand.

"He's the one who's been turning Paladins. We need to stop him." Sameer tugged free and charged.

Cold crept over him. Time didn't slow. The Vibrations felt still, like a ship's sails on calm seas. Even so, Sohini flanked Anish. She moved like a normal person, while Anish blurred between their coordinating attacks. Anish's *naga* streaked in solid arcs.

Pain bit into Sameer's wrists and arms. All shallow nicks which sliced skin and nicked nerves, but didn't damage muscle. Still, every move he made burned with pain. He buckled to his knees, using his *naga* to keep himself from crumpling over.

Anish shoulder-butted Sohini, sending her flying back onto her rear. Her *naga* clattered away.

The traitor stepped back and snickered. "See? It's just as Gitika said: with Paladin skills, you can incapacitate without killing."

Wounds burning, Sameer pushed himself up with his *naga*. Cold pricked the back of his neck. He looked up at the pyramid in the distance. The Dragonstone at its top pulsed, but whether with the Vibrations or not, it was hard to tell. So close, yet the Scorpion Master muffled his connection to it.

Anish shook his head. "Such determination." He zipped in and swung his blade.

Sameer's *naga* went flying from his wringing hand. Without its support, he fell on his face.

Anish knelt down and lifted his chin. "You won't join us?"

"Never." Sameer would've shaken his head, had it not been held in the master's grasp.

"Then you will join Elder Gitika in death and rebirth." Anish lifted the sword.

Sameer gave him a defiant glare.

"Stop!" Sohini screamed. "Let Sameer go, and I will join you."

A grin spread across the traitor's face. "You were always the one we wanted. If you swear loyalty to Madura, I will spare him."

She pressed her palms together and bowed her head.

No. This couldn't be happening. Sameer struggled to break free of the traitor's grip. All the cuts across his body flared. "Don't do it, Sohini. I'd rather die than for you to become one of them."

"No, Sameer. I couldn't live with myself if you died because of me." Shaking her head with a sad smile, she walked toward Anish.

"No!" Sameer lurched forward, only to get yanked to the pavestones.

"Kneel," Anish said.

Sameer looked up.

Sohini sank to a knee.

Anish set his blade on the top of her head. "Swear your allegiance to the Golden Scorpions of Madura."

"No!" Sameer crawled forward.

"I swear." A tear trickling down her cheek, Sohini pressed her palms together and bowed her head.

His own vision blurred with tears. This couldn't be happening. Everything Sohini despised, she would become. Sameer staggered to his feet.

Anish returned his sword to his side. "Now, my apprentice, we have a mission: to escort Prince Dhananad to Arkos, for his meeting with the Teleri First Consul."

Weaponless, Sameer blinked away the tears.

Sohini seized his arms and threw him over her hip.

He hit the street with a heavy thud, not far from the half-elf. His eyes hazed over as Sohini followed Master Anish away.

CHAPTER 29:

To the Bitter End

Outside of Signore De Lucca's downtown office, Cassius helped Brehane off the horse. His heart might've fluttered from the way her ample breasts had pressed into his back on the ride over, but her arm's tight grip around his chest had nearly choked out his breath. Thank Solaris the canter through the streets only took a few minutes.

When her feet touched the ground, her tight expression relaxed. She looked so beautiful, the way the wind swept her coarse hair. "Will Signore De Lucca let Sameer go?"

Cassius cast her a reassuring grin. "He is first and foremost a businessman. I'm sure we can strike a deal." Whether they could do so before Dawit and Melas escaped with Makeda...

Two Bovyans dressed in De Lucca's purple livery stood guard by the front door. They stepped together to form a living barrier as Cassius climbed up to the stoop.

Cassius bowed. "I have an appointment with Signore De Lucca."

One of the brutes shook his head. "The signore is attending to important business. Begone."

Cassius kept his expression calm, even if anger roiled his stomach. There was no time for this silliness. "I am Signore Cassius Larusso. The city's business can't wait." He took a step forward.

Both guards reached for their longswords.

Behind him, Brehane grunted out feral sounds. Sand sprayed past. Both men crumpled to the ground, asleep.

"Thank you, my lady." Cassius turned and dipped his chin. He swept into a bow and held the door open for her. "After you."

She flashed a smile, which made her all the more beautiful. It was hard to believe the horrible sounds of her magic could come from such a lovely face. Her legs wobbled as she entered.

He followed after her...and skidded to a halt. Brehane seized his arm.

Six Altivorcs formed a rank to the side of the foyer. Standing half a head shorter than a man, their muscular frames might've been twice as broad. Scraggly black hair made the blunt features on their turquoise faces all the uglier.

None of their species had come to Tokahia since the Hellstorm, when they'd marched on the pyramid. Now, with their chainmail and broadswords, it didn't look like they were here for noble reasons. In all likelihood, De Lucca had been too blinded in his ambitions to realize they would do anything for the gods to return.

The steward stood up behind the desk. "Signore Cassius, welcome. I'm afraid Signore De Lucca is indisposed." His eyes darted to the Altivorcs, then back.

What did that stare mean? No matter, time was running out for Makeda.

"I will only be a moment." Cassius strode toward the back office, clasping Brehane's hand.

"But..." the steward held up a hand, but just watched them pass.

The Altivorcs stood so still they might've been statues.

Open doors to the library and antechamber revealed they were empty. Up ahead, the double doors to De Lucca's office were likewise open, allowing voices to echo through the hall.

"All goes as planned," De Lucca was saying. "We've made arrangements for the Madurans and Levastyans to meet the Teleri First Consul in Arkos."

Cassius stopped in place. What was De Lucca doing, brokering deals for the Teleri? Maybe it was in return for them providing Bovyans as pyramid guards.

It was time to warn De Lucca that the Bovyans had ulterior motives, probably the occupation of Tokahia. De Lucca was inviting conquest. Expression tightening, Cassius started toward the office...and froze again.

"You have done well, Carlo," spoke a sonorous, accented voice. "The King will be pleased."

Carlo was De Lucca's given name, but king? The only realms which used that title were the Nothori realms of the northwest, and the Eldaeri Kingdoms in the north. Before the latter's empire sundered over a century ago, they'd tried to conquer all of the Estomar; now, they seemed content to transport trade goods. And of course, they were mortal enemies of the Bovyans, both races claiming to be the Chosen People of Solaris.

De Lucca sounded smug. "It might take a little more negotiating, but I'm sure the Signores will approve the Bovyans as pyramid honor guard, after we frame the Mafia for slaughtering the local guards. Once I hear that their operation is complete, I will cap the pyramid myself."

Cassius' blood ran cold. It wasn't the Bovyans plotting. No—given the Altivorcs in the foyer, and the heavy accent of the voice speaking of pleased kings, De Lucca was making deals with the infamous Altivorc King. In his foolishness and greed, he either didn't care about the pyramid prophecy, or perhaps... He turned to Brehane. "I think De Lucca wants the Altivorc gods to return on their flaming chariots."

Her eyes widened.

Though every fiber of Cassius' being urged caution, protecting the pyramid was his family's Divine mandate. De Lucca was a scrawny little man; devious, but certainly not a fighter. "You put the Altivorcs to sleep, I will handle De Lucca." Drawing his rapier, he charged in.

A cold rolled over him, and the Gods' Whispers quieted to near inaudible. He stuttered to a halt.

De Lucca sat on his tall chair, turning a metal box the size of a head in his hands.

Across the desk, an Altivorc turned and looked at Cassius. Unlike his ugly brethren, this one was handsome, like an angel. Perhaps an angel of death.

"Signore Cassius," De Lucca said, shaking his head. "I thought it was my steward traipsing around out there. I'm afraid you have heard too much. For that, you will have to die."

The Altivorc jumped to his feet, sending his chair flying back. Drawing a broadsword, he barked out several foul sounds toward the hall. Heavy boots marched from the foyer.

De Lucca set the box down and flipped a serrated knife over in his hands. The scrawny traitor wouldn't stand a chance with the weapon's short reach.

Cassius deflected the Altivorc's hack and spun past him. Kill De Lucca, and the threat would be removed.

De Lucca hadn't even risen from his throne.

It would be dishonorable to run a sitting, unarmed man through, but easy was always better than risky. Cassius stabbed.

With a sweep of the knife in his hands, De Lucca sheared through the rapier blade as if it were made of paper.

Cassius' hand didn't even hurt from the impact. He held up what remained of his weapon. Longer than a dagger, but shorter than a gladius, it still gave him better reach. He reached for his dagger.

It wasn't there.

Of course: Jie had taken it from him earlier.

* * *

Brehane's stomach knotted as Cassius exposed his back to the Altivorc. He was so intent on killing De Lucca, he'd abandoned all caution and charged in. It was so unlike everything else she'd ever seen of him. Rather dashing, actually.

And maybe that was for the better. No child could help but cry when told of the horrors mankind suffered when the Altivorcs controlled the world. If their gods returned...

Cassius stabbed and chopped with his castrated rapier, but De Lucca looked almost bored, sitting while deflecting and parrying with his knife. Thank the First Mystic the Altivorc hadn't engaged.

The Resonance, so strong outside the office, was no more than a whisper here. Using as much as she could draw on, she channeled Neuromancy with soft words and gentle gestures of her hand. She pointed at De Lucca to finish casting the charm spell. Vitality seeped from her limbs.

He didn't so much as look at her, continuing to avoid Cassius' attacks with nonchalant grace.

Barking out words of Pyromancy, Brehane pointed. Fire darts streaked toward De Lucca...

And dissipated, as if De Lucca had cast a shield right on his skin.

How could it be? An Estomari shouldn't have been able to use magic to shield himself, nor had he made any of the gestures or sounds required to do so.

Her energy guttered, and neither Pyromancy nor Neuromancy had worked on him. She grunted out more words of magic, combining several schools of magic. There was no way he could resist. A thin wisp of web undulated past Cassius toward De Lucca.

It separated into thin strands over his body.

The way the Resonance was muted...it was just like when she'd tried to cast a charm on his sister. Brehane bent over, supporting her now-onerous weight with trembling hands on wobbling knees. Nothing she threw at him was having an effect. Without her necklace to help reinvigorate her, it was becoming harder and harder to draw on the Resonance.

The Altivorc interposed himself between De Lucca and Cassius, and now pushed Cassius back with hacks of his broadsword. It clanged against Cassius' blade.

From the hallway, the other Altivorcs were now rushing in, broadswords raised.

With her last reserve of energy she swept her hand toward them, flinging some sand she'd collected in the streets. Singing out words of Neuromancy, she unleashed a sleep spell. The draining effect buckled her knees, and she collapsed. With a hand on the ground, she held herself up, panting.

The two in front stumbled to the ground, unconscious. The next four veered around their fallen comrades. They ignored her and fanned out around Cassius.

Cassius disengaged from De Lucca and circled in place, eyes darting from the surrounding Altivorcs and back. He raised a pleading eyebrow at her.

The message was clear. He couldn't take on so many enemies, and he needed her help. Yet she knelt, gasping for air, no magic on her lips. She shook her head.

The handsome Altivorc leader stepped back while his four underlings charged in. Broadswords hacked at Cassius, forcing him back toward the window beside De Lucca's chair.

All was lost. Her necklace, heirloom of the First Mystic, lost to Melas. Makeda, lost to the Teleri.

And her tribe. She'd been their best chance to restore the Biomancers' honor.

No, there was still hope. She just needed a few minutes to regain some energy. Enough to put the rest of the Altivorcs to sleep. She cleared her throat. "Please, Signore De Lucca, we won't tell the Signores of your plan. Please let us go."

De Lucca held up a hand.

The Altivorcs took a step back, but kept their weapons trained on Cassius.

This was their chance. The Resonance echoed in her core, slowly restoring her. Not enough to cast a sleep spell, though. Not yet.

Setting his knife down, De Lucca steepled his fingers under his chin. "Signore Larusso will never agree to it. It's his family's Divine mandate."

"Spare Brehane, and I will surrender." Cassius lowered his blades and bowed his head.

"My, my," De Lucca said. "I would never believe Cassius Larusso would sacrifice himself. Funny what love can do."

Love? Did Cassius love her? She stole a glance at him.

He was chewing on his lip. He looked up. "Swear it, Brehane. Swear that you will leave Tokahia, and that you will take everything you have heard here to your grave."

A chance to live. A chance to recover her heirloom and rescue Makeda. All she had to do was betray Cassius' trust. Curse the slow trickle of energy! She rose to her feet. "I... I..."

"You have three seconds," De Lucca said. "One."

She looked at Cassius.

If he could nod any more violently, his head might wobble right off.

"Two."

She *might* have enough for a sleep spell, but with such low energy and without sand or rose petals to help mediate the spell, she'd have to draw on her base energy. At best, it would knock her unconscious. At worst, it could cripple her magic forever.

"Three."

Brehane swept her hand at the Altivorcs and barked out the sleep spell. Vitality drained from her limbs. Her vision faded black at the edges.

The last thing she saw was a single Altivorc collapse, while the others charged at Cassius.

* * *

With Sameer's arm draped over her shoulder, Jie wobbled toward Signore De Lucca's office to meet up with Brehane and Cassius. From there they'd get the Tarkothi marines and rescue Makeda.

Her head ached from Master Anish's elbow, and everything looked blurry. Sameer had shaken her out of her stupor, but none of what he'd said about scorpions made sense. Still, he'd agreed to help assail the sorcerers' hideout... Catch the Illusionist, and she'd be one step closer to the attempted coup back home.

The poor boy winced with every heavy step. It didn't look like he'd make it to De Lucca's, let alone be able to fight. Still, he soldiered on, and they at last made it back to the site of last night's misadventures.

"They're here?" He looked at her incredulously.

On the stoop, a thin man in De Lucca's purple livery was shaking two unconscious Bovyans. From the look of it, Cassius' and Brehane's courtesy call hadn't been particularly courteous.

Jie unslung Sameer's arm from her shoulder. "I think Cassius must've asked for you, and then gotten into a fight when De Lucca claimed he didn't have you."

"No. De Lucca is dealing with the Bovyans, Madurans, and Levastyans. They might be in trouble."

Sameer straightened and picked up his pace. Though his stride lengthened with each step, he was still slow. "Go on without me, I'll catch up."

Jie was already well ahead. The servant stood and held up a finger, but she slipped right by him and into the foyer.

Clashing metal echoed in the hallway.

Jie broke into a sprint, passing the library. One of those marvelous knives might be in there, but Cassius and Brehane might not have that much time. Up ahead, the doors to De Lucca's office were open, providing a view of the man himself lounging behind his desk, head turned to the scuffle on the right.

She surged through the doors, Cassius' dagger in hand, and...

Froze.

Brehane struggled on all fours. Two Altivorcs lay on the floor beside her, chests rising and falling in sleep. Three more had pushed Cassius to the window, and he was doing an admirable job fending them off with his broken rapier. One already lay dead—or sleeping—by his feet. An Altivorc Prince, handsome despite his teal skin tone, stood back, barking orders.

Jie's head spun. The last she'd seen these humanoids, they'd chased her in Cathay's imperial palace. What were they doing in Tokahia?

De Lucca's eyes met hers. "Sister! Did Father send you to set the capstone? I am capable of doing it myself."

Sister? Apparently, his vision was just as bad in the bright bauble lights as in the darkness of his secret room last night.

The Altivorc Prince spun and met her gaze. Pointing, he snarled something in a guttural language. His minions turned from Cassius and looked at her.

De Lucca's eyes widened. With a stammer, he growled out syllables that sounded similar to the Altivorcs.

All four Altivorcs, with their prince in the lead, left Cassius staring as they moved toward Jie.

"Teleri are marching on the pyramid." Cassius pointed in the wrong direction. "De Lucca plans on capping it."

Not that such things mattered to her. Especially not with four Altivorcs loping toward her, fangs bared and broadswords raised. They charged past Brehane and right at Jie, as if she'd shaved their mother's butt at one time or another.

Her pitiful little dagger might as well have been a sewing needle, for all the help it would be against swords. She ducked under the first hack, but the prince's stab kept her from closing. The third's chop sent her scuttling back several steps toward the door. The fourth tried to flank her, but she sidestepped low with an arcing slash to the inner wrist, in the gap of his bracer, and to the back of his knee, in the opening between his boot and his chain tunic.

He bellowed. His broadsword slipped from lifeless fingers, and she caught it as her body twisted.

Heavy, it forced her to hold it two-handed, and set the dagger between clenched teeth. She lifted it against another attack, only to have the clashing reverberation send it flying from her grip.

She jumped back from the prince's slash, which pushed her to huddle against the wall. The two others hacked down at her, and there was nothing she could do.

This was it. An inglorious end to an orphan half-elf. She'd die, without a clueless spy ever knowing she was gone. She closed her eyes.

Metal clanged above her.

She opened her eyes and looked to see Sameer's faintly glowing *naga* between her and what should've been her death. In a blur, he beheaded one and lopped off another's leg. Black blood sprayed every which way.

Only the prince remained uninjured. The one she'd maimed huddled on the ground, holding his wrist. One, missing a leg from the knee down, writhed on the floor. Jie slipped under the prince's chop, rolling to the dead Altivorc, snatching up his knife, and bouncing back to her feet.

The prince jumped to the right, putting her between him and Sameer.

"Go." She gestured toward De Lucca. "Help Cassius."

Brandishing his sword in tight circles, the prince studied her. He must've really cared about his underlings, given all the hate burning in his gaze.

Jie flipped the orc's knife into an underhanded grip, but then paused. She examined it. Its form was exactly the same as De Lucca's, though it wasn't as light and balanced.

The leader surged forward with hacks and slashes. Jie bobbed and weaved, avoiding the attacks as she closed in. Reaching the prince's flank, she seized his sword arm in the crook of her elbow. She swept a foot to the back of his ankle, while scissoring her free arm in the opposite direction, knife blade-first.

The knife didn't cut through his tunic, but his shoulder dislocated with a pop. He fell backward, head slamming into the floor. Jie finished her spin, dislodging his sword. Dropping down, she plunged the knife into his throat.

She looked up to reevaluate.

All the Altivorcs were dead or incapacitated. De Lucca was on his feet, hand on the metal box on his desk. Cassius held back, while Sameer advanced with his *naga*.

* * *

Sameer held his *naga* at the ready, but there was no reason to harm Signore De Lucca. Though he'd treated with Prince Dhananad, he'd actually hidden Sohini from Master Anish. Maybe...

"Where are you sending Prince Dhananad? To Arkos? Tell me, and I'll let you live."

"Is that the Paladin way? Would you kill me?" De Lucca laughed. "*Could* you? Let's find out."

Time slowed as Sameer sidestepped De Lucca's stab. Even though all of Master Anish's cuts still burned, the pain had subsided. The Vibrations surged through him.

De Lucca moved so slow, it was too easy. Sameer avoided all of his attacks, finally sending the signore sprawling with a shoulder-butt. He raised his *naga*. "Tell me, where is Prince Dhananad going?"

On his rear, De Lucca backed out of reach. His eyes betrayed no fear, despite his inability to match the Paladin's speed. He scrambled to his feet next to his desk.

Sameer advanced on him. "Answer me!"

De Lucca opened the lid to the metal box, then reached in and withdrew the spherical crystal with the grey bottom half from the night before. Cold swept out from it like a wave, stilling the Vibrations.

No matter—even without the Vibrations, Sameer had survived against a Golden Scorpion.

"The Whispers of the Gods," Cassius said from where he knelt by Brehane. "They're silent."

Eyes wide, hand in the fold of her robe, she nodded.

Ignoring the pain from Anish's cuts, Sameer swung his *naga*.

De Lucca ducked under it, then sidestepped the follow-up stab, grinning the whole time.

"The crystal." Sameer stepped back to catch his breath. "It's blocking my power."

Cassius nodded. "That's what he will use to cap the pyramid."

De Lucca laughed his obnoxious laugh. "You don't have to be a Golden Scorpion to slow a Paladin down. Or to neutralize a Diviner who might try to get the upper hand in negotiations. You—"

Jie materialized from under the desk and swiped the sphere out of his hand. Slipping away from his grab, she snatched up the box and ran.

The Vibrations flooded back into Sameer's limbs. He raised his *naga*.

De Lucca wiggled the grey metal ring off his finger and cast it to the side. He lunged forward with a stab.

Time didn't slow...or did it? De Lucca attacked at the same speed as a Paladin student, while Cassius moved as if swimming through honey. Turning his body, Sameer avoided the attack, and nicked De Lucca's forearm. Sameer's downstroke dragged a shallow wound across his thigh.

De Lucca grimaced. His knife met Sameer's *naga*, leaving a notch in the blade, and his backstroke sliced through Sameer's sleeve without a sound.

Sameer disengaged and assumed a defensive position. He studied his weapon. Made from an alloy of *istrium* fused with steel, it was the hardest substance short of a diamond. And yet, De Lucca's knife had left a rent. It wasn't severe damage, but enough that the dwarf smiths in Ayudra would have to repair it.

"Be careful, Sameer." Cassius held up his severed rapier. "His knife can shear metal."

"Thanks for the forewarning," Sameer muttered.

De Lucca surged forward in a whirlwind of attacks. With their speeds near even, it forced Sameer back into Cassius.

Sameer tackled the Diviner, pushing him out of harm's way, and popped back up to his feet. He waved away Jie who'd come back without the box, and now was helping a groaning Brehane gain her feet. "Stay away! He's too dangerous."

Too dangerous, even for all four of them, working together…

De Lucca lunged in again. His knife zigged and zagged, pushing Sameer back.

* * *

A Dragonstone! No sooner than De Lucca had opened the box and revealed the orb, than Kirala's book in Brehane's inner pocket buzzed. The Resonance around them had gone silent, only to return when Jie swiped the box and ran off with it.

Now, exhausted as she was, Brehane's head spun from trying to keep track of the duel between De Lucca and Sameer. As soon as the signore had slipped off the ring, the Resonance shifted yet again. It coursed through him, just like it did the Paladins when they fought.

Even though he wasn't Ayuri, and only Ayuri could channel magic into fighting.

His speed surged, as if energized by lightning, and the slashes and stabs of his knife became blurs. Even Sameer with his superhuman speed barely kept pace.

The ring.

It had protected him from magic, but had prevented him from drawing on what Sameer called the Vibrations. Now he could fight like Paladin, despite not being Ayuri. The Resonance danced between and through him and Sameer, their interaction a symphony. Was De Lucca combining magic, like she did?

If only she had enough energy to cast a spell, to...

She sucked in a sharp breath. There was a chance; she just had to get close enough to the circling duelists without getting dissected by De Lucca's knife.

For a split second, De Lucca's back was to her.

She shot out her hand, only to miss.

"Get back!" Sameer said, deflecting a stab at her with his *naga*, and spinning between them.

Cassius pulled her back, but she wriggled out of his grasp. She swatted at his grabby hand, all the while trying to time how De Lucca and Cassius were darting, stabbing, slashing, and sidestepping.

Whatever happened, it was too fast to see, but their effect on the Resonance fell into a predictable pattern. Sameer slammed backward into the window, shattering the glass. He was holding a spot on his belly, where a splotch of red grew.

De Lucca paused, his back again to her.

She lunged at him.

He spun so fast it didn't seem possible.

Still, she careened into him. They tumbled to the ground. Though it hadn't happened as she'd planned or hoped, she was straddling him, his right wrist caught in her hands. His knife...

She stared at it. He wasn't as strong as say, Cassius, but even with her two hands against De Lucca's one, the blade edged closer and closer to her.

This was it.

The Resonance of his fighting magic reached a crescendo, its pattern prickling her nerves. The words of Biomancy and Electromancy surged through her. She arched her spine and let go of his wrist.

The knife plunged into her flank. Pain seared through her...

But so did his energy. Flooding from the wound, through her core and into her limbs, it felt like the result of a good night's rest.

The luster in his eyes faded; the sheen of his skin dulled. He shoved her off, but he struggled to rise. When he finally gained his feet, he hunched over, hands on his knees.

Brehane gasped. Despite the vitality flowing through her, his knife had cut into her side. Blood stained her robe in an ever-growing crimson stain.

※ ※ ※

Cassius looked from Sameer to Brehane to De Lucca. The young Paladin slumped in the window frame, leaning against the bars. Brehane lay on the floor, holding her side and panting.

De Lucca stood straight and flipped his blood-stained knife into a reverse grip. Gone was the luster of his skin. White now streaked his mane of black hair. When he spoke, his voice sounded weaker. "Well, Signore Larusso. It is just you and me, and you don't have the skill to beat me. My secret will die with you."

Secret.

Secrets. The Gods' Whispers swirled around them, having shifted as soon as De Lucca had removed his grey metal ring. It was as if they wanted to reveal even more about the upstart signore, after all these years of being pent up.

All Cassius had to do was ask. He closed his eyes and sucked in the Whispers. What little of his energy he'd regained from the Divining last night yielded a myriad of images.

A pitiful existence, trapping rabbits. Disdainful whispers among peasants. And then, an impossibly handsome Altivorc Prince coming to deliver the gemstone that Jie had run off with.

"Divining, are you?" De Lucca lunged forward with a slash.

The attack came fast, but not Paladin fast. Cassius jumped back to avoid it, even as images blurred over his normal vision.

De Lucca was looking himself over, but a future image of him stabbing, feinting, and jabbing again overlapped the present reality. Behind him, a certain half-elf was concealed by the window's curtain.

To change the future would cost some of Cassius' soul, but it was better than dying here and now.

The stab came, and Cassius blocked it with his broken rapier. When De Lucca feinted, Cassius jumped in and pressed De Lucca to the window.

Jie pounced from behind the curtain. With three swift motions, her knife jabbed into the base of De Lucca's skull, slid by the side of his neck, then raked across his throat.

De Lucca's eyes widened as the pupils rolled up into his head. His strangled gasp choked out blood. His body crumpled to the floor. The Gods' Whispers around him quieted.

In three long strides, Cassius went to Brehane and knelt by her. He tried to pull her hand away so he could inspect the wound. "Are you all right?"

Brehane gave a curt nod.

Jie batted his hand away. "Stick to conning the unwary, and leave the surgery to someone who knows what they are doing. Go get some of the booze from the side table."

Growling, Cassius did as told. He checked Sameer on the way, and was relieved to find him breathing. He returned with some expensive brandy.

CHAPTER 30:

Unfinished Business

Cassius sat alone at De Lucca's desk, flipping through several documents. He ignored De Lucca's body, which lay draped with a cloak where he'd fallen, alongside the dead Altivorcs. Sameer and Brehane were being treated by a physician at a clinic several blocks away, while Jie had gone to fetch De Lucca's sister, Lucia.

Before she'd left, though, she'd disappeared into De Lucca's library and returned with the contracts he was perusing now. No doubt she'd pocketed any number of trinkets along the way, but what she'd unearthed would keep the pyramid safe from Altivorc machinations.

"Signore Larusso," a throaty male voice said. "What happened? And what are you doing here?"

Cassius jerked his head from the papers and looked around. Nobody was there, but the voice... "Master Phobos."

"At your service." The small Bovyan materialized out of nowhere, his hand leaving the pocket of a formal black tunic emblazoned with the nine-pointed star of the Teleri Empire.

"To answer your question, the Signores are on their way over here to discuss him..." Cassius pointed his chin at De Lucca's body. "...and the orders he gave the Bovyans to attack the pyramid and frame the Mafia."

"We execute the stipulations of our contract. It's just business." Face impassive, Phobos strode over and lifted the cloak, then looked back. "So, De Lucca is dead."

"Yes." Cassius shook his head in contrived dismay. "Slain by Altivorcs. A pity."

Snorting, Phobos searched Cassius' expression. "Right."

Cassius flipped through a sheaf of documents. "It appears that four hundred of Captain Baros' Bovyans have contracted with De Lucca Enterprises for at least a year."

"And?"

Cassius held up a single sheet, the one Jie had given him first. "It appears his sister, Lucia De Lucca, is now the owner."

"She is a vapid girl, with no idea how to run the late Signore De Lucca's business."

"The Gods' Whispers..." or Brehane... "tell me that Miss De Lucca will place the businesses' operations in a trust, governed by the Signores. We command you to help maintain order in our fair city's new, post-Mafia status quo. You will report to the head of the watch immediately."

Phobos snorted again. "You will, of course, maintain the terms De Lucca established? Maintenance of our compound, food, and salary?"

It felt as if a stone hung in Cassius' gut. The Bovyans here, with women provided as breeders. But there was no way around it, without risking an attack. "Of course. A contract is a contract."

"Well, you will have to summon Captain Robas." Phobos shrugged. "I am just a businessman."

"Riiiight."

Phobos grinned. "Speaking of business, what about the deal we made the other day? When can we expect you to deliver the Aksumi girl to us?"

Cassius studied his nails. "You presented the terms, but we never agreed. I do appreciate you eradicating the Mafia, but you really should have confirmed it. I am a man of honor, and a handshake would have sufficed."

"Again, your reputation proceeds you." Phobos leaned over the table. "How about another deal, then. Take the Aksumi girl to Arkos. If you reach there before her masters bring her friend, then my country will deliver a letter of credit for a million drakas to your bank."

A million. How many zeroes were in that number? Six? Seven? Even at six, he could live in luxury for the rest of his life. Indeed, this must be the wealth that the Divination at their first meeting hinted at.

And the risk of death, as well.

"That's a long way to go." Cassius' lips pursed.

"That's why we are paying a million."

"My family is entrusted with watching over the pyramid *here*."

Phobos grinned. "It won't go anywhere while you're gone."

Was it worth it, to go into the Teleri heartland? His brother Marcus would meet his demise in the frigid Northwest in two years—there was no way to avoid it without Cassius dying himself—bringing the profitable relationship with the Pirate Queen to an end. Working for the Teleri this once would help allay the loss of that revenue stream. All he had to do was turn Brehane over.

His gut twisted for a split second, before other memories surfaced. If he wasn't careful, Brehane would be his next Julia; only this time, instead of losing money, he could very well lose his life.

Phobos extended his hand. "How about that handshake?"

Cassius stared at it. "What happens if the Aksumi deliver Makeda first?"

"Then the reward will be two hundred and fifty thousand."

Still a sizeable amount. And of course, Brehane planned on going to Arkos, anyway. Phobos named the terms as *taking her*, not *delivering* her into the hands of the Bovyans. There'd be plenty of time to decide what to do. Cassius took Phobos' hand and shook it.

EPILOGUE:

Friends and Enemies

Haros Bovyanthas didn't believe he was born to a virgin, nor that he was destined to end the Bovyan Curse. What mattered was that enough of his peers did believe that.

He was surrounded by them now. Consuls, Keepers, and Prospecti dressed in formal black togas with gold borders all chanted as he knelt in the central hall of the Shrine of Geros in Telesite. For the last time, his own right eye tracked five Keepers as they approached. Each bore a black velvet cushion in outstretched hands, on which was placed an heirloom of the Bovyan race.

At Haros' side, the Chief Keeper extended his hand and plucked a ceremonial dagger from one of the cushions. The ancient blade had belonged to their progenitor, Geros, the mortal son of the sun god, Solaris.

Haros took a deep breath. Was it worth losing an eye to become First Consul? He already controlled the Directori and was ruler in fact, if not in name.

Yes.

All his plans were already secretly in motion, carried out by his Nightblades and other units loyal to him, but his peers would only accept the sacrilegious nature of his tactics if he were First Consul.

The tip of the blade touched his right eyeball, which exploded in a flash of searing pain. Squeezing his good eye shut, he gritted his teeth. Unlike many of his predecessors, he didn't so much as grunt.

He opened his left eye and blinked away the tears. Though he couldn't see anything to his right, he knew the Chief Keeper was taking up the Eye of Geros.

Through the pain, Haros' heart pounded. The Eye contained a spark of Solaris' divinity. From the memoirs of previous First Consuls, he'd learned that it helped them perceive combat, and that one of Solaris' angels spoke through it.

Given the separation of powers between the Directori and the Keepers of the Shrine, no previous First Consul understood the angel's Divine language; but as a former acolyte of the Shrine, Haros would. He turned his head to see the cushion bearing the Last Testament of Geros. Written in the language which no one could speak and only a few could read, it held the First Geros' vision for peace and prosperity.

The Chief Keeper seized his chin. "Open your eye."

Was it closed? It was hard to tell through the pain and the lack of sight. Haros did the best he could to open it. The glass pressed into his eye socket. Pain lanced through his head, reaching deep into his brain like a weed's roots.

He fought to maintain consciousness, unwilling to faint like all the previous First Consuls.

It was hopeless. The pain was too intense. His last thoughts, before he passed out, were of the Orc King's promised meeting with the Madurans and Levastyans in Arkos.

* * *

Light from the Blue Moon spilled in through the window at the end of the hall as Myra walked by the mating rooms. The moans and giggles emanating from within were nothing like the horrors she'd heard in lands the Teleri Empire had recently conquered. She shuddered at those memories, and hurried down the corridor toward the bedrooms.

She peeked into a few open doors, where erstwhile prostitutes laughed and chatted with each other. Many looked forward to the boys they would be having, the first expected in the next four months. The lively atmosphere was nothing like the misery endemic to the mating compounds that the Teleri set up in the cities and kingdoms they brought to heel. Using prostitutes to start breeding a local army here had been a stroke of genius.

She sighed. Soon, she would have to return to the front lines, and care for hundreds of girls who had no choice in the matter. Like her mother.

At the end of the hall, she fished out her key and unlocked her door. A light breeze greeted her, and she walked to her desk. She unshuttered her desk lamp, musing for a moment about how the Aksumi Mystics infused and exported thousands of the light baubles. Demon magic, the Bovyans claimed, though the Consul Haros had taken a more pragmatic view. If his plans worked, he'd breed and train a whole army of Bovyan Mystics.

She plopped down on her chair, but then froze. Her window…

"I oiled it for you," the half-elf's voice said from behind.

Myra spun to the source, only to find no one there.

The voice came from her lamp. "You are observant, to have noticed the window was a little more open than you left it."

"Show yourself," Myra said.

The half-elf crawled out from under the desk.

Myra gasped. How could she have not seen the interloper, right by her feet? "What do you want? Are you here to kill me?"

The half-elf shook her head. "Why would I do that?"

Myra shrugged. "If you wanted to, I guess I would already be dead. So what do you want?"

"Where is the Nightblade, Phobos?"

"I heard he was headed to Arkos on one of the Pirate Queen's ships."

The half-elf sucked on her lower lip. It was a cute gesture, though probably hiding malevolent thought processes. "What about the Nightblade I killed?"

Myra frowned. She'd tried to get the half-elf out of the compound without any bloodshed. "His body was sent out to sea, along with the others you killed, as is the Bovyan tradition."

The half-elf made a face, akin to sucking a lemon. "How barbaric."

"All Bovyan combat dead are sent down rivers or out to sea. *All water leads to the sun*, they say."

The half-elf shook her head. "He was Cathayi, and that's not our tradition."

"He was a Bovyan. All Bovyans take on the features of their mother. That's why some have fair skin, and others are bronze." Never before had Myra seen a Bovyan of Aksumi descent, but that would change in the near future.

The half-elf slid the window open and started out. She paused for a moment. "Thanks again for helping me this afternoon. It's reassuring to know not all in the Teleri Empire are evil."

Evil was relative. Not to mention... "Some of the Bovyans aren't bad, either."

"Farewell." The half-elf disappeared.

* * *

Jie took several deep breaths and smoothed out her filthy pink dress as she looked up the broad marble steps to the Regent. Her visit to the Teleri compound had been fruitful, even if she hadn't recovered De Lucca's second knife, nor found any sign of Nightblade Phobos. A visit to his antique shop revealed only records of his people's plunder. Still, she'd learned where he was headed, and also that the Nightblade she'd killed was indeed a Bovyan, and not Cathayi.

Her mission now took her—coincidentally, or perhaps not—in the same direction as Brehane and Sameer, and she had a means of getting them all a little closer to Arkos.

Feigning her best damsel in distress, she staggered up to the landing and paused at a vaulting column.

The two guards, dressed in the blue-and-gold livery of the Regent, side-stepped to block the double glass doors—themselves a marvel.

"You are not welcome here," one said.

Wrist on her forehead, Jie collapsed. The marble felt cold through the dress. "I'm a translator for the Tarkothi. Please alert Prince Aryn."

The guards exchanged glances. Nodding, one hurried inside. Jie pushed herself up onto an elbow, gasping. If there was a place to put on an act, the luxurious landing, framed by columns above the road and the many passersby, was perfect.

A Tarkothi marine appeared in the door with the inn guard. His eyes widened. He exchanged words with the guard, then rushed back in.

The guard came out and beckoned. "You may come in, Miss Jyeh."

As always, her acting skills merited some kind of drama award. She wobbled to her feet and staggered through the doors that the guards held open.

One guided her across the plush red carpet through the spacious foyer to three leather couches, arranged around a low wooden table. She wilted into one, and through half-lidded eyes watched the servants as they scurried every which way.

Aryn appeared at the top of a mezzanine and froze, wide eyes on her. He pattered down the grand stairway, expression at once concerned and relieved. "Jyeh, are you all right?" He loped across the foyer and knelt in front of her. He took her hands in his.

She gave him a tentative nod.

"What happened?" His eyes roved over her, not so much with their typical lust, but more with worry. "I didn't know what to think when we lost you yesterday."

"The crime families," she said, letting his imagination fill in the blanks so she wouldn't have to lie.

"Oh..." His pretty lips formed a local letter O. "They didn't...?"

She shook her head. "Some new friends protected me. By the time the Mafia were ready to do awful things to me, fighting broke out between them and the watch."

He nodded. "My men helped maintain order. How did you escape?"

"Those friends," she said. "A Mystic, a Paladin, and Signore Cassius Larusso."

"Cassius Larusso, the famous Diviner." He whistled.

An unfeigned shudder rattled through her. Back home, whistling at night attracted ghosts; but maybe evil spirits in these lands didn't care. She smiled. "I wish I could do something to repay them."

Aryn's forehead crinkled. "I can pay them a handsome reward."

"You need to reach them soon. They are headed to Arkos."

His expression brightened. "I can offer them passage as far as Elbahia. That's halfway there."

Hook. Line. Sinker.

* * *

Sameer hobbled up the gang plank to the *Indomitable*, his countless wounds burning under their bandages. In the absence of a true Levastyan Akolyte, he'd had to rely on Jie for treatment. Thank the Thousand Gods her hands proved just as good at stitching as they did at picking pockets; and the local healer's salves were now working to make the pain tolerable.

Less tolerable was how Sohini had joined the Golden Scorpions, thereby sacrificing her ideals for him. He would've rather died than have her become what she hated the most. The Paladin way had failed both of them.

Now, without any masters to guide him, he decided to continue on the mission Elder Gitika had been given. If Sohini was headed to Arkos, so was he.

* * *

With her wound washed and stitched by Jie the previous day, Brehane now convalesced in their shared cabin aboard the *Indomitable*. From the way Prince Aryn always gazed at the half-elf, it was doubtful Jie would be spending her nights there. She had the foreign prince wrapped around her finger, using the bat of an eyelash here, a pout of her lips there—the same kind of flirtatious body language one would expect from a man in Aksumi tribal lands.

The relations between men and women were so backward—whether they be from Cathay, the Estomar, the Bovyans, or Tarkothi—that perhaps it was Aksumi culture that was unnatural. Melas and Dawit had thought so.

Were their native customs so onerous that it pushed them both to treason? Brehane thought back to all the young women at the *South Seas* brothel, crying among themselves over their treatment at the hands of the men. Perhaps the Aksumi way was just as bad, only with the roles reversed; and yet, Melas and Dawit didn't even take that into account when they kidnapped and forced themselves on Makeda.

All that didn't matter. Brehane's only way to regain the Biomancer clan honor was to bring Melas back. The fact that he had taken her necklace was added incentive.

She withdrew Kirala's Dragonstones book and flipped through it. In addition to Makeda's Tear and Aralas' Heart, it now showed Tatiana's Eye atop the local pyramid, and...her brows furrowed. Unlike the other entries, De Lucca's orb wasn't named. It was simply referred to as a capstone, and, as they'd experienced, it blocked magic of all sorts...except this book. Maybe—

Cassius' voice carried from the deck. He had true Divining power, and his seed would strengthen her own magic. Wincing as she rose, she went to the door. Once she was better, she'd get him into bed...but play by his rules and expectations. All she had to do was learn how Jie did it.

* * *

Cassius stood on the deck of the *Indomitable*, watching Tokahia as it disappeared in the distance. The Gods' Whispers grew quieter the farther away they sailed from the pyramid's blinking eye. To think, the Gods' Whispers would've quieted altogether had De Lucca succeeded in replacing the Eye with whatever that strange crystal was.

So far, no one could answer that question, and De Lucca's lead box which held it remained locked away in the cellar of his villa.

Brehane now came up beside him, wincing at the pain. Jie had cleaned, cauterized, and stitched the wound De Lucca had dealt her, and the Tarkothi ship doctor had applied an herbal poultice and given her some foul drink to prevent infection. Despite Makeda's betrayal, Brehane still wanted to rescue her.

Cassius suspected she was more concerned about her necklace.

The Mystics had already embarked on one of the Pirate Queen's ships. Though he'd credited the Gods' Whispers, Cassius knew because her agents had informed him. They'd also told him that Prince Dhananad had taken the same ship, with Anish and Sohini as guards.

It didn't take any Divining to know Sameer would insist on joining the chase to Arkos.

Cassius looked from the Paladin, back to Brehane. He didn't know how to describe his feelings for her. Love? He wouldn't know what that felt like. Opportunity? For another chance at wild sex? Or a million drakas?

* * *

Thank you for reading **Masters of Deception**. Jie's adventure with the annoying princess and clueless spy back home is detailed in **Songs of Insurrection**, Book 1 of **The Dragon Songs Saga.** Her next adventure takes place in **Crown of the Sundered Empire**, Book 1 of Heirs to the Sundered Empire, to be released early 2019.

APPENDICES

Celestial Bodies

White Moon: Known as Renyue in Cathay, and represents the God of the Seas. Its orbital period is thirty days.

Iridescent Moon: Known in Cathay as Caiyue, it is the manifestation of the God of Magic. It appeared at the end of the war between elves and orcs. It never moves from its spot in the sky. Its orbital period is one day, and can be used to keep time.

Blue Moon: Known in Cathay as Guanyin's Eye, it is the manifestation of the Goddess of Fertility. Its phases go from wide open to winking.

Tivar's Star: A red star, a manifestation of the God of Conquest. During the Year of the Second Sun, it approached the world, causing the Blue Moon to go dim.

Hunter Kor: A constellation, always in pursuit of the White Stag

Lycea the Betrayer: A star, avatar of the Goddess of Betrayals

White Stag: A constellation, always hiding from Hunter Kor

Fortuna: A constellation of the Goddess of Luck

Time

As measured by the phases of the Iridescent Moon:

Full = Midnight
1st Waning Gibbons = 1:00 AM
2nd Waning Gibbons =2:00 AM
Mid-Waning Gibbons = 3:00 AM
4th Waning Gibbons = 4:00 AM
5th Waning Gibbons = 5:00 AM
Waning Half = 6:00 AM
1st Waning Crescent = 7:00 AM
2nd Waning Crescent = 8:00 AM
Mid-Waning Crescent = 9:00 AM
4th Waning Crescent = 10:00 AM
5th Waning Crescent = 11: 00 AM
New = Noon
1st Waxing Crescent = 1:00 PM
2nd Waxing Crescent = 2:00 PM
Mid-Waxing Crescent = 3:00 PM
4th Waxing Crescent = 4:00 PM
5th Waxing Crescent = 5:00 PM
Waxing Half = 6:00 PM
1st Waxing Gibbons = 7:00 PM
2nd Waxing Gibbons =8:00 PM
Mid-Waxing Gibbons = 9:00 PM
4th Waxing Gibbons = 10:00 PM
5th Waxing Gibbons = 11:00 PM

Human Ethnicities

Aksumi: Dark-skinned with dark eyes and coarse hair. On Earth, they would be considered North Africans. They can use Sorcery.

Ayuri: Bronze-toned skin with dark hair and eyes. On Earth, they would be considered South Asians. They can use Martial Magic.

Arkothi: Olive-skinned with blond to dark hair and light-colored eyes. On Earth, they would be considered Eastern Mediteraneans. They can use weak Mental Magic.

Bovyan: The descendants of the Sun God's begotten son, they are cursed to be all male and live only to thirty-three years of age. They are much taller and larger than the average human. Their other physical characteristics are determined by their mother's race. They have no magical ability.

Cathayi (Hua): Honey-toned skin with dark hair and eyes. High-set cheekbones and almond-shaped eyes. On Earth, they would be considered East Asians. They can use Artistic Magic.

Eldaeri: Olive-skinned with brown hair. With features and small frames, they are shorter in stature than the average human. In a previous age, they fled the orc domination of the continent and mingled with elves. They have no magical ability.

Estomari: Olive-skinned with varying eye and hair color. They are famous for their fine arts. On Earth, they would be considered Western Mediterraneans. They can use Divining Magic.

Kanin: Ruddy-skinned with dark hair. On Earth, they would be considered Native Americans. They can use Shamanic Magic.

Levanthi: Dark-bronze skin and dark hair. On Earth, they would be considered Persians. They can use Divine Magic.

Nothori: fair-skinned and fair-haired. On Earth, they would be considered Northern Europeans. They can use Empathic Magic.

Acknowledgements:

Many thanks to my crit partners JC Nelson, Stacy Lindsay, Kelly Walker, Leanne Yong, and Crystal Trobak for their invaluable input. Thanks to beta readers Sonya Kaspar, Stephanie Ford, Shannon Bryant, and Anne Loshuk.

ABOUT THE AUTHOR

JC Kang's unhealthy obsession with fantasy and sci-fi began at an early age when his brother Romain introduced him to the *Chronicles of Narnia*, *The Hobbit*, *Star Trek*, and *Star Wars*. As an adult, JC combines his geek roots with his professional experiences as a Chinese Medicine doctor, martial arts instructor, and technical writer to pen multicultural epic fantasy stories.

Made in the USA
Columbia, SC
16 August 2024